W9-CIJ-449

SHIVERS VI
This special edition is limited to 750 copies.

SHIVERS VI

edited by Richard Chizmar

SHIVERS VI

edited by Richard Chizmar

CEMETERY DANCE PUBLICATIONS

Baltimore
❖ 2010 ❖

Cemetery Dance Publications 2010
ISBN-10: 1-58767-224-3
ISBN-13: 978-1-58767-224-8

Limited Edition Hardcover:
1-58767-235-9
978-1-58767-235-4

Cover design by Gail Cross
Typesetting and book design by Robert Morrish
Printed in the United States of America

Cemetery Dance Publications
132-B Industry Lane, Unit 7
Forest Hill, MD 21050
Email: info@cemeterydance.com
http://www.cemeterydance.com

10 9 8 7 6 5 4 3 2 1

First Edition

Serial

Blake Crouch & Jack Kilborn

1

The hardest thing about killing a hitchhiker is finding one to pick up.

Donaldson could remember just ten years ago, when interstates boasted a hitcher every ten miles, and a discriminating killer could pick and choose who looked the easiest, the most fun, the juiciest. These days, cops kept the expressways clear of easy marks, and Donaldson was forced to cruise off-ramps, underpasses, and rest areas, prowl back roads, take one hour coffee breaks at oases. Recreational murder was becoming more trouble than it was worth.

He'd found this one standing in a Cracker Barrel parking lot. The kid had been obvious, leaning against the cement ashtray near the entrance, an oversize hiking pack strapped to his back. He was approaching every patron leaving the restaurant, practicing his grin between rejections.

A ripe plum, ready to pluck.

Donaldson didn't even have to initiate contact. He walked in to use the bathroom and strolled out car keys in hand, letting them jingle a bit. The kid solicited him almost immediately.

"Excuse me, sir. Are you heading up north?"

Donaldson stopped, pretending to notice the man for the first time. He was young, maybe mid-twenties. Short, reddish hair, a few freckles on his face, mostly hidden by glasses. His clothing looked worn but of good quality. Donaldson was twice his age, and damn near twice his weight.

Donaldson rubbed his chin, which he knew softened his harsh features.

"In fact I am, son."

The boy's eyes lit up, but he kept a lid on his excitement. Any hitcher worth his salt knew to test the waters before sealing the deal.

"I am, too. If you'd like some company, I can chip in for gas." He hooded his eyes and quickly added, "No funny stuff. I'm just looking for a ride. I was hoping to get to Ogden by midnight. Got family up there. My name's Brett, by the way."

Well played, Donaldson thought. Friendly, a little desperate, making clear this wasn't a sexual hookup and that he had people waiting for him.

As if any of that would keep him safe.

"How do I know you're not some psycho?" Donaldson asked. He knew that was pushing it, but he liked the irony.

"There's a gas station across the street. I can top off the tank, pay with a credit card. All gas stations have cameras these days. Credit card is a paper trail. If anything happens to you, that would link me to your car, and I'd get caught."

Smart kid. But not that smart.

The really smart ones don't hitchhike.

"Won't need gas for a few hundred miles." Donaldson took off his Cubs baseball hat, running a hand over his gray, thinning hair. Another way to disarm the victim. No one feared grandfatherly types. "Until then, if you promise not to sing any show tunes, you got yourself a ride."

Brett smiled, hefted his pack onto his shoulders, and followed his ride into the parking lot. Donaldson unlocked the doors and the kid loaded his pack into the backseat of Donaldson's 2006 black Honda Accord, pausing when he saw the clear plastic covers on the front seats.

"My dog, Neil, usually rides up front with me," Donaldson said, shrugging. "I don't like him messing up the upholstery."

Brett flashed skepticism until he noticed the picture taped to the dash: Donaldson and a furry dachshund.

"Sheds like crazy," Donaldson said. "If you buy a dog, stick with short-haired breeds."

That was apparently reassurance enough, because Brett climbed in.

Donaldson heaved himself into the driver's seat, the car bouncing on its shocks.

"Buckle up for safety." Donaldson resisted the urge to lick his lips, then released the brake, started the car, and pulled onto the highway.

The first ten miles were awkward. Always were. Strangers tended to stay strangers. How often did a person initiate conversation on a plane or while waiting in line? People kept to themselves. It made them feel safe.

Donaldson broke the tension by asking the standard questions. Where'd you go to school? What do you do for a living? Where you headed? When'd you start hitchhiking? Invariably, the conversation turned to him.

"So what's your name?" Brett asked.

"Donaldson." No point in lying. Brett wouldn't be alive long enough to tell anyone.

"What do you do, Donaldson?"

"I'm a courier."

Donaldson sipped from the Big Gulp container in the cup holder, taking a hit of caffeinated sugar water. He offered the cup to Brett, who shook his head. Probably worried about germs. Donaldson smiled. That should have been the least of his worries.

"So you mean you deliver packages?"

"I deliver anything. Sometimes overnight delivery isn't fast enough, and people are willing to pay a premium to get it same day."

"What sort of things?"

"Things people need right away. Legal documents. Car parts for repairs. A diabetic forgets his insulin, guy loses his glasses and can't drive home without them, kid needs his cello for a recital. Or a kidney needs to get to a transplant location on time. That's the run I'm on right now."

Donaldson jerked a thumb over his shoulder, pointing to the backseat floorboard. Brett glanced back, saw a cooler sitting there, a biohazard sticker on the lid.

"No kidding, there's a kidney in there?"

"There will be, once I get it." Donaldson winked at the kid. "By the way, what's your blood type?"

The kid chuckled nervously. Donaldson joined in.

A long stretch of road approaching. No cars in either direction.

"Sounds like an interesting job," Brett said.

"It is. Perfect for a loner like me. That's why it's nice to have company every so often. Gets lonely on the road."

"What about Neil?"

"Neil?"

Brett pointed at the photograph on the dashboard. "Your dog. You said he rode with you sometimes."

"Oh, yeah. Neil. Of course. But it isn't the same as having a human companion. Know what I mean?"

Brett nodded, then glanced at the fuel gauge.

"You're down to a quarter tank," he said.

"Really? I thought I just filled up. Next place we see, I'll take you up on that offer to pay."

It was a bright, sunny late afternoon, clean country air blowing in through the inch of window Donaldson had open. A perfect day for a drive. The road ahead was clear, no one behind them.

"So seriously," Donaldson asked, "What's your blood type?"

Brett's chuckle sounded forced this time, and Donaldson didn't join in. Brett put his hand in his pocket.

Going for a weapon, or holding one for reassurance, Donaldson figured. Not many hitchers traveled without some form of reassurance.

But Donaldson had something better than a knife, or a gun. His weapon weighed thirty-six hundred pounds and was barreling down the road at eighty miles per hour.

Checking once more for traffic, Donaldson gripped the wheel, braced himself, and stood on the brake.

The car screeched toward a skidding halt, Brett's seatbelt popping open exactly the way Donaldson had rigged it to, and the kid launched headfirst into the dashboard. The spongy plastic had, beneath the veneer, been reinforced with unforgiving steel.

The car shuddered to a stop, the stench of scorched rubber in the air. Brett was in bad shape. With no seatbelt and one hand in his pocket, he'd banged his nose up pretty good. Donaldson grasped his hair, rammed his face into the dashboard two more times, then opened the glove compartment. He grabbed a plastic zip tie, checked again for oncoming traffic, and quickly secured the kid's hands behind his back. In Brett's coat pocket, he found a tiny Swiss Army knife. Donaldson barked out a laugh.

If memory served, and it usually did, there was an off ramp less than a mile ahead, and then a remote stretch of farmland. Donaldson pulled back onto the highway and headed for it, whistling as he drove.

The farm stood just where he remembered it. Donaldson pulled off the road into a cornfield and drove through the dead stalks until he could no longer see the road. He killed the engine, set the parking brake—the Accord had transmission issues—then tugged out the keys to ensure it wouldn't roll away.

His passenger whimpered as Donaldson muscled him out of the car and dragged him into the stalks.

He whimpered even more when Donaldson jerked his pants down around his ankles, got him loosened up with an ear of corn, and then forced himself inside.

"Gonna stab me with your little knife?" he whispered in Brett's ear between grunts. "Think that was going to save you?"

When he'd finished, Donaldson sat on the kid's chest and tried out all the attachments on the Swiss Army knife for himself. The tiny scissors worked well on eyelids. The nail file just reached the eardrums. The little two-inch blade was surprisingly sharp and adept at whittling the nose down to the cartilage. And the corkscrew did a fine job on Brett's Adam's apple, popping it out in one piece and leaving a gaping hole that poured blood bright as a young cabernet.

Apple was a misnomer. It tasted more like a peach pit. Sweet and stringy.

He shoved another ear of corn into Brett's neck hole, then stood up to watch.

Donaldson had killed a lot of people in a lot of different ways, but suffocation especially tickled his funny bone. When people bled to death they just got sleepy. It was tough to see their expression when they were on fire, with all the thrashing and flames. Damaging internal organs, depending on the organ, was either too fast, too slow, or too loud.

But a human being deprived of oxygen would panic for several minutes, providing quite a show. This kid lasted almost five, his eyes bulging out, wrenching his neck side to side in futile attempts to remove the cob, and turning all the colors of the rainbow before finally giving up the ghost. It got Donaldson so excited he almost raped him again. But the rest of the condoms were in the car, and befitting a man his age, once he got them and returned to the scene of death, his ardor probably would have waned.

He didn't bother trying to take Brett's kidney, or any of his other parts. What the heck could he do with his organs anyway? Sell them on eBay?

Cleanup was the part Donaldson hated most, but he always followed a strict procedure. First, he bagged everything associated with the crime. The rubber, the zip tie, the Swiss Army knife, and the two corn cobs, which might have his prints on them. Then he took a spray bottle of bleach solution and a roll of paper towels and cleaned out the interior of his car. He used baby wipes on himself, paying special attention to his fingernails. Everything went into the white plastic garbage bag, along with a full can of gasoline and more bleach spray.

He took the money from Brett's wallet—forty lousy bucks—and found nothing of interest in his backpack. These went into the bag as well, and then he soaked that and the body with lighter fluid.

The fire started easily. Donaldson knew from experience that he had about five minutes before the gas can exploded. He drove out of the cornfield at a fast clip, part of him disappointed he couldn't stay to watch the fireworks.

The final result would be a mess for anyone trying to ID the victim, gather evidence, or figure out what exactly had happened. If the body wasn't discovered right away, and the elements and hungry animals added to the chaos, it would be a crime scene investigator's worst nightmare.

Donaldson knew how effective his disposal method was, because he'd used it twenty-six times and hadn't ever been so much as questioned by police.

He wondered if the FBI had a nickname for him, something sexy like *The Roadside Burner.* But he wasn't convinced those jokers had even connected his many crimes. Donaldson's courier route took him across four large, Western states, a land area of over four hundred thousand square miles. He waited at least a year before returning to any particular spot, and he was finding new places to play all the time.

Donaldson knew he would never be caught. He was smart, patient, and never compulsive. He could keep on doing this until he died or his pecker wore out, and they had pills these days to fix that.

⁂

He reached I-15 at rush hour, traffic clogging routes both in and out of Salt Lake, and he was feeling happy and immortal until some jerk in a Winnebago decided to drive ten miles under the speed limit. Irritated motorists tagged along like ducklings, many of them using their horns, and everyone taking their good sweet time getting by in the passing lane.

Seriously, they shouldn't allow some people on the road.

Donaldson was considering passing the whole lot of them on the shoulder, and as he surveyed the route and got ready to gun it, he saw a cute chick in pink shoes standing at the cloverleaf. Short, lugging a guitar case, jutting out a hip and shaking her thumb at everyone who passed.

Two in one day? he thought. Do I have the energy?

He cranked open the window to get rid of the bleach smell, and pulled up next to her under the overpass, feeling his arousal returning.

2

She set the guitar case on the pavement and stuck out her thumb. The minivan shrieked by. She turned her head, watched it go—no brakelights. The disappointment blossomed hot and sharp in her gut, like a shot of iced Stoli. Despite the midmorning brilliance of the rising sun, she could feel the cold gnawing through the tips of her gloved fingers, the earflaps of her black woolen hat.

According to her Internet research, 491 (previously 666) ranked as the third least traveled highway in the Lower-Forty-Eight, with an average of four cars passing a fixed point any given hour. Less of course at night. The downside of hitchhiking these little-known thoroughfares was the waiting, but the upside paid generous dividends in privacy.

She exhaled a steaming breath and looked around. Painfully blue sky. Treeless high desert. Mountains thirty miles east. A further range to the northwest. They stood blanketed in snow, and on some level she understood that others would find them dramatic and beautiful, and she wondered what it felt like to be moved by nature.

Two hours later, she lifted her guitar case and walked up the shoulder toward the idling Subaru Outback, heard the front passenger window humming down. She mustered a faint smile as she reached the door. Two young men in the front seats stared at her. They seemed roughly her age and friendly enough, if a little hungover. Open cans of Bud in the center console drink holders had perfumed the interior with the sour stench of beer—a good omen, she thought. Might make things easier.

"Where you headed?" the driver asked. He had sandy hair and an elaborate goatee. Impressive cords of bicep strained the cotton fibers of his muscle shirt. The passenger looked native—dark hair and eyes, brown skin, a thin, implausible mustache.

"Salt Lake," she said.

"We're going to Tahoe. We could take you at least to I-15."

She surveyed the rear storage compartment—crammed with two snowboards and the requisite boots, parkas, snow pants, goggles, and...she suppressed the jolt of pleasure—helmets. She hadn't thought of that before.

A duffle bag took up the left side of the backseat. A little tight, but then she stood just five feet in her pink crocs. She could manage.

⁂

"Comfortable back there?" the driver asked.

"Yes."

Their eyes met in the rearview mirror.

"What's your name?"

"Lucy."

"Lucy, I'm Matt. This is Kenny. We were just about to have us a morning toke before we picked you up. Would it bother you if we did?"

"Not at all."

"Pack that pipe, bro."

They got high as they crossed into Utah and became talkative and philosophically confident. They offered her some pot, but she declined. It grew hot in the car and she removed her hat and unbuttoned her black trench coat, breathing the fresh air coming in through the crack at the top of the window.

"So where you going?" the Indian asked her.

"Salt Lake."

"I already asked her that, bro."

"No, I mean what for?"

"See some family."

"We're going to Tahoe. Do some snowboarding at Heavenly."

"Already told her that, bro."

The two men broke up into laughter.

"So you play guitar, huh?" Kenny said.

"Yes."

"Wanna strum something for us?"

"Not just yet."

⁂

They stopped at a filling station in Moab. Matt pumped gas and Kenny went inside the convenience store to procure the substantial list of snacks they'd been obsessing on for the last hour. When Matt walked inside to pay, she opened the guitar case and took out the syringe. The smell wafted out—not overpowering by any means, but she wondered if the boys would notice. She hadn't had a chance to properly clean everything in awhile. Lucy reached up between the seats and tested the weight of the two Budweisers in the drink holders: each about half-full. She eyed the entrance to the store—no one coming—and shot a squirt from the syringe into the mouth of each can.

⁂

Kenny cracked a can of Bud and said, "Dude, was that shit laced?"

"What are you talking about?"

They sped through a country of red rock and buttes and waterless arroyos.

"What we smoked."

"I don't think so."

"Man, I don't feel right. Where'd you get it?"

"From Tim. Same as always."

Lucy leaned forward and studied the double yellow line through the windshield. After Matt drifted across for a third time, she said, "Would you pull over please?"

"What's wrong?"

"I'm going to be sick."

"Oh God, don't puke on our shit."

Matt pulled over onto the shoulder and Lucy opened her door and stumbled out. As she worked her way down a gentle embankment making fake retching sounds, she heard Matt saying, “Dude? Dude? Come on, dude! Wake up, dude!”

She waited in the bed of the arroyo for ten minutes and then started back up the hill toward the car. Matt had slumped across the center console into Kenny’s lap. The man probably weighed two hundred pounds, and it took Lucy ten minutes to shove him, millimeter by millimeter, into the passenger seat on top of Kenny. She climbed in behind the wheel and slid the seat all the way forward and cranked the engine.

She turned off of I-70 onto 24. According to her map, this stretch of highway ran forty-four miles to a nothing town called Hanksville. From her experience, it didn’t get much quieter than this barren, lifeless waste of countryside.

Ten miles south, she veered onto a dirt road and followed it the length of several football fields, until the highway was almost lost to sight. She killed the engine, stepped out. Late afternoon. Windless. Soundless. The boys would be waking soon, and she was already starting to glow. She opened the guitar case and retrieved the syringe, gave Kenny and Matt another healthy dose.

By the time she’d wrangled them out of the car into the desert, dusk had fallen and she’d drenched herself in sweat. She rolled the men onto their backs and splayed out their arms and legs so they appeared to be making snow angels in the dirt.

⁂

Lucy removed their shoes and socks. The pair of scissors was the kind used to cut raw chicken, with thick, serrated blades. She trimmed off their shirts and cut away their pants and underwear.

⁂

Kenny and Matt had returned to full, roaring consciousness by 1:15 a.m. Naked. Ankles and wrists tightly bound with deeply scuffed handcuffs, heads helmeted, staring at the small, plain hitchhiker who squatted down facing them at the back of the car, blinding them with a hand held spotlight.

"I didn't think you were ever going to wake up," Lucy said.

"What the hell are you doing?" Matt looked angry.

Kenny said, "These cuffs hurt. Get them off."

She held a locking carabiner attached to a chain that ran underneath the Subaru. She clipped it onto another pair of carabiners. A rope fed through each one, and the ends of the ropes had been tied to the handcuffs on the boys' ankles.

"Oh my God, she's crazy, dude."

"Lucy, please. Don't. We'll give you anything you want. We won't tell anyone."

She smiled. "That's really sweet of you, Matt, but this is what I want. Kind of have my heart set on it."

She stepped over the tangle of chain and rope and moved toward the driver's door as the boys hollered after her.

⁂

She left the hatch open so she could hear them. Kept looking back as she drove slowly, so slowly, along the dirt road. They were still begging her, and occasionally yelling when they dragged over a rock or a cactus, but she got them to the shoulder of Highway 24 with only minor injuries.

The moon was up and nearly full. She could see five miles of the road in either direction, so perfectly empty and black, and she wondered if the way it touched her in this moment felt anything like how the beauty of those mountains she'd seen this morning touched normal people.

Lucy buckled her seatbelt and glanced in the rearview mirror. Matt had climbed to his feet, and he hobbled toward the car.

"Hey, no fair!" she yelled and gave the accelerator a little gas, jerking his feet out from under him. "All right, count of three. We'll start small with half a mile!"

She grasped the steering wheel, heart pumping. She'd done this a half dozen times but never with helmets.

"One! Two! Three!"

She reset the odometer and eased onto the accelerator. Five, ten, fifteen, twenty miles per hour, and the boys already beginning to scream. At four-tenths of a mile, she hit forty, and in the rearview mirror, Kenny's and Matt's pale and naked bodies writhed in full-throated agony, both trying to sit up and grab the rope and failing as they slid across the pavement on their bare backs, dragged by their cuffed ankles, the chains throwing gorgeous yellow sparks against the asphalt.

She eased off the gas and pulled over onto the shoulder. Collected the spray bottle from the guitar case, unbuckled, jumped out, and went to the boys. They lay on their backs, blood pooling beneath them. Kenny must have rolled briefly onto his right elbow, because it had been sanded down to bone.

"Please," Matt croaked. "Please."

"You don't know how beautiful you look," she said, "but I'm gonna make you even prettier." She spritzed them with pure, organic lemon juice, especially their backs, and to the heartwarming depth of their new screams, skipped back to the car and hopped in and stomped the gas, their cries rising into something like the baying of hounds, Lucy howling back. She pushed the Subaru past fifty, to sixty, to seventy-five, and in the illumination of the spotlight, the boys bounced along the pavement, on their backs, their sides, their stomachs, and with every passing second looking more and more lovely, and still making those delicious screams she could almost taste, Lucy driving with no headlights, doing eighty under the moon, and the cold winter wind rushing through the windows like the breath of God.

She made it five miles (no one had ever lasted five miles and she credited those well-made snowboarding helmets) before the skeletons finally went quiet.

⁂

Lucy ditched what was left of the boys and drove all night like she'd done six blasts of coke, arriving in Salt Lake as the sun edged up over the mountains. She checked into a Red Roof Inn and ran a hot bath and cleaned the new blood and the old blood out of the ropes and let the carabiners and the chains and the handcuffs soak in the soapy water.

⁂

In the evening she awoke, that dark weight perched on her chest again. The guitar case items had dried, and she packed them away and dressed and headed out. The motel stood along the interstate, and it came down to Applebee's or Chili's.

She went with the latter, because she loved their Awesome Blossom.

⁂

After dinner, she walked outside and stared at the Subaru in the parking lot, the black rot flooding back inside of her, that restless, awful energy that could never be fully sated, those seconds of release never fully quenching, like water tinged with salt. She turned away from the Subaru and walked along the frontage road until she came to a hole in the fence. Ducked through. Scrambled down to the shoulder of the interstate.

Traffic was moderate, the night cold and starry. A line of cars approached, bottled up behind a Winnebago.

She walked under the bridge, set down her guitar case, and stuck out her thumb.

3

Donaldson pulled over onto the shoulder and lowered the passenger window. The girl was young and tiny, wearing a wool cap despite the relative warmth.

"Where you headed?" He winked before he said it, his smile genuine.

"Missoula," Lucy answered.

"Got a gig up there?" He pointed his chin at her guitar case.

She shrugged.

"Well; I'm going north. If you chip in for gas, and promise not to sing any show tunes, you can hop in."

The girl seemed to consider it, then nodded. She opened the rear door and awkwardly fit the guitar case onto the backseat. Before getting in, she stared at the upholstery on the front seats.

"What's with the plastic?" she asked, indicating Donaldson's clear seat covers.

"Sometimes I travel with my dog."

Lucy squinted at the picture taped to the dashboard—the portly driver holding a long-haired dachshund.

"What's its name?"

"Scamp. Loveable little guy. Hates it when I'm away. But I'm away a lot. I'm a courier. Right now, I'm headed up to Idaho Falls to pick up a donor kidney."

Her eyes flitted to the backseat, to a cooler with a biohazard sign on the lid.

"Don't worry," he said, taking off his hat and rubbing a hand through his thinning gray hair. "It's empty for the time being."

The girl nodded, started to get in, then stopped. "Would you mind if I sat in the back? I don't want to make you feel like a chauffeur, but I get nauseated riding up front unless I'm driving."

Donaldson paused. "Normally I wouldn't mind, Miss, but I don't have any seat belts back there, and I insist my passengers wear one. Safety first, I always say."

"Of course. Can't be too careful. Cars can be dangerous."

"Indeed they can. Indeed."

The front passenger door squeaked open, and the girl hopped in. Donaldson watched her buckle up, and then he accelerated back onto the highway.

Grinning at her, he rubbed his chin and asked, "So what's your name, little lady?"

"I'm Lucy." She looked down at the center console. A Big Gulp sweated in the drink holder. She reached into her pocket and looked at the man and smiled. "I really appreciate you picking me up. I don't think I caught your name."

"Donaldson. Pleased to meet you."

"Is that really your last name, or are you one of those guys who have a last name for a first name?"

"No, that's my first."

They drove in silence for a mile, Donaldson glancing between the girl and the road.

"Highway's packed this time of day. I bet we'd make better time on the county roads. Less traffic. If that's okay with you, of course."

"I was actually just going to suggest that," Lucy said. "Weird."

"Well, I wouldn't want to do anything to make you feel uncomfortable." Donaldson glanced down at Lucy's pocket. "Pretty young thing like yourself might get nervous driving off the main drag. In fact, you don't see many young lady hitchers these days. I think horror movies scared them all away. Everyone's worried about climbing into the car with a maniac."

Donaldson chuckled.

"I love county roads," Lucy said. "Much prettier scenery, don't you think?"

He nodded, taking the next exit, and Lucy leaned over, almost into his lap, and glanced at the gas gauge.

"You're running pretty low there. Your reserve light's on. Why don't we stop at this gas station up ahead. I'll put twenty in the tank. I also need something to drink. This mountain air is making my throat dry."

Donaldson shifted in his seat. "Oh, that light just came on, and I can get fifty miles on reserve. This is a Honda, you know."

"But why push our luck? And I'm really thirsty, Donaldson."

"Here." He lifted his Big Gulp. "It's still half full."

"No offense, but I don't drink after strangers, and I um…this is embarrassing…I have a cold sore in my mouth."

The gas station was coming up fast, and by all accounts it appeared to be the last stop before the county road started its climb into the mountains, into darkness.

"Who am I to say no to a lady?" Donaldson said.

He tapped the brakes and coasted into the station. It had probably been there for forty years, and hadn't updated since then. Donaldson sidled up to an old-school pump—one with a meter where the numbers actually scrolled up, built way back when closed-circuit cameras were something out of a science fiction magazine.

Donaldson peered over Lucy, into the small store. A bored female clerk sat behind the counter, apparently asleep. White trash punching the minimum wage clock, not one to pay much attention.

"The tank's on your side," Donaldson said. "I don't think these old ones take credit cards."

"I can pay cash inside. I buy, you fly."

Donaldson nodded. "Okay. I'm fine with doin' the pumpin'. Twenty, you said?"

"Yeah. You want anything?"

"If they have any gum that isn't older than I am, pick me up a pack. I've got an odd taste in my mouth for some reason."

Lucy got out of the car. Donaldson opened the glove compartment and quickly shoved something into his coat pocket. Then he set the parking brake, pocketed the keys, and followed her out.

⁂

While Donaldson stood pumping gas into the Honda, Lucy walked across the oil-stained pavement and into the store. The clerk didn't acknowledge her entrance, just sat staring at a small black-and-white television airing *Jeopardy,* her chin propped up in her hand and a Marlboro Red with a one-inch ash trailing smoke toward the ceiling.

Lucy walked down the aisle to the back of the store and picked a Red Bull out of the refrigerated case. At the drink fountain, she went with the smallest size—sixteen ounces—and filled the cup with ice to the brim, followed by a little Dr. Pepper, Mountain Dew, Pepsi, and Orange Fanta.

She glanced back toward the entrance and through the windows. Donaldson was still fussing with the pump. She reached into her pocket and withdrew the syringe. Uncapped the needle, shot a super-size squirt of liquid Oxycontin into the bubbling soda.

At the counter, she chose a pack of Juicy Fruit and pushed the items forward.

The clerk tore herself away from a video Daily Double and rang up the purchase.

"$24.52."

Lucy looked up from her wallet. "How much of that is gas?"

"Twenty."

"Shit, I told him just do fifteen. Here." She put a Jackson on the filthy counter. "I'll send him in with the balance, 'cause this is all I've got."

"Don't be trying to steal my gas."

Donaldson was screwing on the gas cap when Lucy walked up. She said, "They still need five bucks. I'm sorry. It came to more than twenty with the drinks and gum. I'm out of cash."

"No ATM?"

"Here? Lucky they have electricity. I'll get you next stop." She flashed a shy grin, sashaying her fingers through the air. "Cross my heart and hope to die."

He just stared at her for a moment, then turned and started toward the store. Lucy opened the front passenger door and traded out Donaldson's Big Gulp for the fresh drink. She tossed the bucket-size cup into a trashcan between the pumps and climbed in.

Donaldson was at the counter. Lucy glanced into the backseat at the cooler with the biohazard sign. She looked into the convenience store, back at the cooler, then spun quickly around in her seat and reached back toward the lid.

Empty. The inside a dull, stained white. She closed it again.

Donaldson's footsteps slapped at the pavement. She settled back into her seat as he opened his door. The chassis bounced when he eased his bulk behind the wheel.

"Sorry about that," Lucy said. "I thought I had another ten. I could swear my snowboarder friend gave me some cash." She stuck out her lower lip, pouting. "I got you some gum. And a new drink."

Donaldson frowned, but he took the Juicy Fruit, ran it under his nose.

"Thank you, kindly. Fresh soda too, huh?"

Lucy cracked open the Red Bull and nodded.

"Cheers. To new friends." She took a sip. A trail of pink liquid dribbled down the corner of her mouth, hugging her chin and neck, dampening her shirt.

Donaldson shifted in his chair and reached for the cup. He sipped on the straw and made a face.

"What flavor is this?"

"I didn't know what you liked," Lucy said. "So I got you a little of everything."

Donaldson chuckled his approval, then turned the key and put the car into gear.

The winding county road ahead was pitch black, like driving through ink. Donaldson sipped his soda. Lucy watched him closely, taking periodic nips at her energy drink. The cool, dry air seemed to crackle with electricity as they climbed into the mountains.

"So is that really a guitar in that case?" Donaldson asked after five miles of silence.

"What do you think?"

"I'll be honest with you, darlin'. You're a bit of a mystery to me. I've been around, but I'm not sure what to make of you."

"How so?"

"You're young. But you've heard of Vietnam, I'm guessing."

"I loved *Platoon*."

Donaldson nodded. "Well then, you were practically there in the rice paddies with me, going toe-to-toe with the Cong."

He drank more soda. Lucy watched.

"Took some shrapnel in my hip in Ca Lu," Donaldson said. "Nicked my sciatic nerve. Biggest nerve in the body. Pain sometimes gets so bad I can chew through a bath towel. Do you understand pain, little girl?"

"More so than you'd think."

"So you should know, then, opiates and I are friends from way back." Donaldson took a big pull off the soda. "So spiking my drink here hasn't done much more than make me a little horny. Actually a lot horny." Donaldson turned to Lucy. "You're about as musical as I am Christian. So you want to tell me what your game is, or do I take you over my knee and spank you right now like the naughty girl you are?"

Lucy said, "It's Oxycontin. Did they have that back in 'Nam, gramps? And you being one fat bastard, I squirted two hundred and fifty milligrams into your drink. I'm not some frat boy trying to roofie up a chunky freshman. I gave you the rhino dose."

She tested the weight of the Styrofoam cup. "Jesus, you've already gone through half of it? I'm actually more concerned you're going to die of a drug overdose instead of the fun I have planned."

She reached across the seat and squeezed his leg. "Look, you will be losing consciousness shortly, so we don't have much time. Pull the car over. I'd like to take you up on that spanking."

Donaldson stared at her, blinked hard twice, and stomped the brake pedal.

Lucy's seatbelt released and she slammed into the metal-reinforced dashboard. Donaldson shook his head, then swiped the zip tie from his pocket. He grabbed a handful of wool cap and the hair beneath it and yanked Lucy up off the floor. She fought hard, but weight and strength won out and he cinched her hands behind her back.

Donaldson glanced through the windshield, then checked the rearview mirror. Darkness.

Lucy laughed through her shattered nose and ran her tongue along her swollen upper lip and gums—two front teeth MIA.

Donaldson blinked and shook his head again. Pulled off the road onto the shoulder.

"We're gonna have some fun, little girl," he said. "And two hundred and fifty milligrams is like candy to me."

He ran a clumsy paw across her breasts, squeezing hard, then turned his attention to the backseat.

The guitar case had two clasps, one on the body, one on the neck.

Donaldson slapped the left side of his face three times and then opened the case.

A waft of foulness seeped out of the velvet-lined guitar lid, although the contents didn't seem to be the source—a length of chain. Four pairs of handcuffs. Three carabiners. Vials of liquid Oxycontin. Cutlery shears. A spotlight. A small spray bottle. Two coils of climbing rope. And a snowboarding helmet.

The front passenger door squeaked open and Donaldson spun around as Lucy fell backward out of the car. He lunged into her seat, but she kicked the door. It slammed into his face, his chin crunching his mouth closed, and as the door recoiled, he saw Lucy struggling onto her feet, her wrists still bound behind her back.

She disappeared into the woods.

Donaldson took a moment, fumbling for the door handle. He found it, but paused.

He adjusted the rearview mirror, grinning to see the blood between his teeth.

"Should we let this one go, sport? Or show the little missus that there are things a lot scarier than a guitar case full of bondage shit?"

Donaldson winked at his reflection, yanked out the keys, yanked up the brake, and shoved his door open. He weaved over to the trunk, a stupid grin on his face, got the right key in on the third try.

Among the bottles of bleach solution, the rolls of paper towels, the gas cans, and the baby wipes, Donaldson grabbed the only weapon an upstanding citizen could legally carry without harassment from law enforcement.

The tire iron clenched in his hand, he bellowed at the woods.

"I'm coming for you, Lucy! And there won't be any drugs to dull *your* pain!"

He stumbled into the forest after her, his erection beginning to blossom.

⁂

She crouched behind a juniper tree, the zip tie digging into her wrists. Absolute darkness in the woods, nothing to see, but everything to hear.

Donaldson yelled, "Don't hide from me, little girl! It'll just make me angry!"

His heavy footsteps crunched in the leaves. Lucy eased down onto her butt and leaned back, legs in the air, then slid her bound wrists up the length of them. Donaldson stumbled past her tree, invisible, less than ten feet away.

"Lucy? Where are you?" His words slurred. "I just wanna talk."

"I'm over here, big boy! Still waiting for that spanking!"

His footsteps abruptly stopped. Dead quiet for thirty seconds, and then the footsteps started up again, heading in her general direction.

"Oh, no, please," she moaned. "Don't hurt me, Donaldson. I'm so afraid you'll hurt me."

He was close now, and she turned and started back toward the road, her hands out in front of her to prevent collision with a tree.

A glint of light up ahead—the Honda's windshield catching a piece of moonlight.

Lucy emerged from the woods, her hands throbbing from circulation loss. She stumbled into the car and turned around to watch the treeline.

"Come on, big boy! I'm right here! You can make it!"

Donaldson staggered out of the woods holding a tire iron, and when the moon struck his eyes, they were already half-closed.

He froze.

He opened his mouth to say something, but fell over instead, dropping like an old, fat tree.

Donaldson opened his eyes and lifted his head. Dawn and freezing cold. He lay in weeds at the edge of the woods, his head resting in a padded helmet. His wrists had been cuffed, hands purple from lack of blood flow, and his ankles were similarly bound. He was naked and glazed with dew, and as the world came into focus, he saw that one of those carabiners from Lucy's guitar case had been clipped to his ankle cuffs. A climbing rope ran from that carabiner to another carabiner, which was clipped to a chain which was wrapped around the trailer hitch of his Honda.

The driver-side door opened and Lucy got out, walked down through the weeds. She came over and sat on his chest, giving him a missing-toothed smile.

"Morning, Donaldson. You of all people will appreciate what's about to happen."

Donaldson yawned, then winked at her. "Aren't you just the prettiest thing to wake up to?"

Lucy batted her eyelashes.

"Thank you. That's sweet. Now, the helmet is so you don't die too fast. Head injuries ruin the fun. We'll go slow in the beginning. Barely walking speed. Then we'll speed up a bit when we get you onto asphalt. The last ones screamed for five miles. They were skeletons when I finally pulled over. But you're so heavy, I think you just might break that record."

"I have some bleach spray in the trunk," Donaldson said. "You might want to spritz me with that first, make it hurt even more."

"I prefer lemon juice, but it's no good until after the first half mile."

Donaldson laughed.

"You think this is a joke?"

He shook his head. "No. But when you have the opportunity to kill, you should kill. Not talk."

Donaldson sat up, quick for a man his size, and rammed his helmet into Lucy's face. As she reeled back, he caught her shirt with his swollen hands and rolled on top of her, his bulk making her gasp.

"The keys," he ordered. "Undo my hands, right now."

Lucy tried to talk, but her lungs were crushed. Donaldson shifted and she gulped in some air.

"In...the...guitar case..."

"That's a shame. That means you die right here. Personally, I think suffocation is the way to go. All that panic and struggle. Dragging some poor sap behind you? Where's the fun in that? Hell, you can't even see it without taking your eyes off the road, and that's a dangerous way to drive, girl."

Lucy's eyes bulged, her face turning scarlet.

"Poc...ket."

"Take your time. I'll wait."

Lucy managed to fish out the handcuff keys. Donaldson shifted again, giving her a fraction more room, and she unlocked a cuff from one of his wrists.

He winced, his face getting mean.

"Now let me tell you about the survival of the fittest, little lady. There's a..."

The chain suddenly jerked, tugging Donaldson across the ground. He clutched Lucy.

"Where are the car keys, you stupid bitch?"

"In the ignition..."

"You didn't set the parking brake! Give me the handcuff key!"

The car crept forward, beginning to pick up speed as it rolled quietly down the road.

The skin of Donaldson's right leg tore against the ground, peeling off, and the girl pounded on him, fighting to get away.

"The key!" he howled, losing his grip on her. He clawed at her waist, her hips, and snagged her foot.

Lucy screamed when the cuff snicked tightly around her ankle.

"No! No no no!" She tried to sit up, to work the key into the lock, but they hit a hole and it bounced from her grasp.

They were dragged off the dirt and onto the road.

Lucy felt the pavement eating through her trench coat, Donaldson in hysterics as it chewed through the fat of his ass, and the car still accelerating down the five-percent grade.

At thirty miles per hour, the fibers of Lucy's trench coat were sanded away, along with her camouflage panties, and just as she tugged a folding knife out of her pocket and began to hack at her ankle, the rough county road began to grind through her coccyx.

She dropped the knife and they screamed together for two of the longest miles of their wretched lives, until the road curved and the Honda didn't, and the car and Lucy and Donaldson all punched together through a guardrail and took the fastest route down the mountain.

The Crate

Stephen King

Dexter Stanley was scared. More; he felt as if that central axle that binds us to the state we call sanity were under a greater strain than it had ever been under before. As he pulled up beside Henry Northrup's house on North Campus Avenue that August night, he felt that if he didn't talk to someone, he really would go crazy.

There was no one to talk to but Henry Northrup. Dex Stanley was the head of the zoology department, and once might have been university president if he had been better at academic politics. His wife had died twenty years before, and they had been childless. What remained of his own family was all west of the Rockies. He was not good at making friends.

Northrup was an exception to that. In some ways, they were two of a kind; both had been disappointed in the mostly meaningless, but always vicious, game of university politics. Three years before, Northrup had made his run at the vacant English department chairmanship. He had lost, and one of the reasons had undoubtedly been his wife, Wilma, an abrasive and unpleasant woman. At the few cocktail parties Dex had attended where English people and zoology people could logically mix, it seemed he could always recall the harsh mule-bray of her voice, telling some new faculty wife to "call me Billie, dear, everyone does!"

Dex made his way across the lawn to Northrup's door at a stumbling run. It was Thursday, and Northrup's unpleasant spouse took two classes on Thursday nights. Consequently, it was Dex and Henry's chess night. The two men had been playing chess together for the last eight years.

Dex rang the bell beside the door of his friend's house; leaned on it. The door opened at last and Northrup was there.

"Dex," he said. "I didn't expect you for another—"

Dex pushed in past him. "Wilma," he said. "Is she here?"

"No, she left fifteen minutes ago. I was just making myself some chow. Dex, you look awful."

They had walked under the hall light, and it illuminated the cheesy pallor of Dex's face and seemed to outline wrinkles as deep and dark as fissures in the earth. Dex was sixty-one, but on that hot August night, he looked more like ninety.

"I ought to." Dex wiped his mouth with the back of his hand.

"Well, what is it?"

"I'm afraid I'm going crazy, Henry. Or that I've already gone."

"You want something to eat? Wilma left cold ham."

"I'd rather have a drink. A big one."

"All right."

"Two men dead, Henry," Dex said abruptly. "And I could be blamed. Yes, I can see how I could be blamed. But it wasn't me. It was the crate. And I don't even know what's *in* there!" He uttered a wild laugh.

"Dead?" Northrup said. "What is this, Dex?"

"A janitor. I don't know his name. And Gereson. A graduate student. He just happened to be there. In the way of...whatever it was."

Henry studied Dex's face for a long moment and then said, "I'll get us both a drink."

He left. Dex wandered into the living room, past the low table where the chess table had already been set up, and stared out the graceful bow window. That thing in his mind, that axle or whatever it was, did not feel so much in danger of snapping now. Thank God for Henry.

Northrup came back with two pony glasses choked with ice. Ice from the fridge's automatic icemaker, Stanley thought randomly. Wilma "just call me Billie, everyone does" Northrup insisted on all the modern conveniences...and when Wilma insisted on a thing, she did so savagely.

Northrup filled both glasses with Cutty Sark. He handed one of them to Stanley, who slopped Scotch over his fingers, stinging a small cut he'd gotten in the lab a couple of days before. He hadn't realized until then that his hands were shaking. He emptied half the glass and the Scotch boomed in his stomach, first hot, then spreading a steadying warmth.

"Sit down, man," Northrup said.

Dex sat, and drank again. Now it was a lot better. He looked at Northrup, who was looking levelly back over the rim of his own glass. Dex looked away, out at the bloody orb of moon sitting over the rim of the horizon, over the university, which was supposed to be the seat of rationality, the forebrain of the body politic. How did that jibe with the matter of the crate? With the screams? With the blood?

"Men are dead?" Northrup said at last. "Are you sure they're dead?"

"Yes. The bodies are gone now. At least, I think they are. Even the bones...the teeth...but the blood... the blood, you know..."

"No, I don't know anything. You've got to start at the beginning."

Stanley took another drink and set his glass down. "Of course I do," he said. "Yes. It begins just where it ends. With the crate. The janitor found the crate..."

*

Dexter Stanley had come into Amberson Hall, sometimes called the Old Zoology Building, that afternoon at three o'clock. It was a blaringly hot day, and the campus looked listless and dead, in spite of the twirling sprinklers in front of the fraternity houses and the Old Front dorms.

The Old Front went back to the turn of the century, but Amberson Hall was much older than that. It was one of the oldest buildings on a university campus that had celebrated its tricentennial two years previous. It was a tall brick building, shackled with ivy that seemed to spring out of the earth like green, clutching hands. Its narrow windows were more like gun slits than real windows, and Amberson seemed to frown at the newer buildings with their glass walls and curvy, unorthodox shapes.

The new zoology building, Cather Hall, had been completed eight months before, and the process of transition would probably go on for another eighteen months. No one was completely sure what would happen to Amberson then. If the bond issue to build the new gym found favor with the voters, it would probably be demolished.

He paused a moment to watch two young men throwing a Frisbee back and forth. A dog ran back and forth between them, glumly chasing the spinning disc. Abruptly the mutt gave up and flopped in the shade of a poplar. A VW with a NO NUKES sticker on the back deck trundled slowly past, heading for the Upper Circle. Nothing else moved. A week before, the final summer session had ended and the campus lay still and fallow, dead ore on summer's anvil.

Dex had a number of files to pick up, part of the seemingly endless process of moving from Amberson to Cather. The old building seemed spectrally empty. His footfalls echoed back dreamily as he walked past closed doors with frosted glass panels, past bulletin boards with their yellowing notices and toward his office at the end of the first-floor corridor. The cloying smell of fresh paint hung in the air.

He was almost to his door, and jingling his keys in his pocket, when the janitor popped out of Room 6, the big lecture hall, startling him.

He grunted, then smiled a little shamefacedly, the way people will when they've gotten a mild zap. "You got me that time," he told the janitor.

The janitor smiled and twiddled the gigantic key ring clipped to his belt. "Sorry, Perfesser Stanley," he said. "I was hopin' it was you. Charlie said you'd be in this afternoon."

"Charlie Gereson is still here?" Dex frowned. Gereson was a grad student who was doing an involved—and possibly very important—paper on negative environmental factors in long-term animal migration. It was a subject that could have a strong impact on area farming practices and pest control. But Gereson was pulling almost fifty hours a week in the gigantic (and antiquated) basement lab. The new lab complex in Cather would have been exponentially better suited to his purposes, but the new labs would not be fully equipped for another two to four months...if then.

"Think he went over the Union for a burger," the janitor said. "I told him myself to quit a while and go get something to eat. He's been here since nine this morning. Told him myself. Said he ought to get some food. A man don't live on love alone."

The janitor smiled, a little tentatively, and Dex smiled back. The janitor was right; Gereson was embarked upon a labor of love. Dex had seen too many squadrons of students just grunting along and making grades not to appreciate that...and not to worry about Charlie Gereson's health and well-being from time to time.

"I would have told *him,* if he hadn't been so busy," the janitor said, and offered his tentative little smile again. "Also, I kinda wanted to show you myself."

"What's that?" Dex asked. He felt a little impatient. It was chess night with Henry; he wanted to get this taken care of and still have time for a leisurely meal at the Hancock House.

"Well, maybe it's nothin," the janitor said. "But... well, this buildin is some old, and we keep turnin things up, don't we?"

Dex knew. It was like moving out of a house that has been lived in for generations. Halley, the bright young assistant professor who had been here for three years now, had found half a dozen antique clips with small brass balls on the ends. She'd had no idea what the clips, which looked a little bit like spring-loaded wishbones, could be. Dex had been able to tell her. Not so many years after the Civil War, those clips had been used to hold the heads of white mice, who were then operated on without anaesthetic. Young Halley, with her Berkeley education and her bright spill of Farrah Fawcett-Majors golden hair, had looked quite revolted. "No anti-vivisectionists in those days," Dex had told her jovially. "At least not around here." And Halley had responded with a blank look that probably disguised disgust or maybe even loathing. Dex had put his foot in it again. He had a positive talent for that, it seemed.

They had found sixty boxes of *The American Zoologist* in a crawlspace, and the attic had been a maze of old equipment and mouldering reports. Some of the impedimenta no one—not even Dexter Stanley—could identify.

In the closet of the old animal pens at the back of the building, Professor Viney had found a complicated gerbil-run with exquisite glass panels. It had been accepted for display at the Museum of Natural Science in Washington.

But the finds had been tapering off this summer, and Dex thought Amberson Hall had given up the last of its secrets. "What have you found?" he asked the janitor.

"A crate. I found it tucked right under the basement stairs. I didn't open it. It's been nailed shut, anyway."

Stanley couldn't believe that anything very interesting could have escaped notice for long, just by being tucked under the stairs. Tens of thousands of people went up and down them every week during the academic year. Most likely the janitor's crate was full of department records dating back twenty-five years. Or even more prosaic, a box of *National Geographics*.

"I hardly think—"

"It's a real crate," the janitor broke in earnestly. "I mean, my father was a carpenter, and this crate is built the way he was buildin 'em back in the twenties. And he learned from *his* father."

"I really doubt if—"

"Also, it's got about four inches of dust on it. I wiped some off and there's a date. Eighteen thirty-four."

That changed things. Stanley looked at his watch and decided he could spare half an hour.

In spite of the humid August heat outside, the smooth tile-faced throat of the stairway was almost cold. Above them, yellow frosted globes cast a dim and thoughtful light. The stair levels had once been red, but in the centers they shaded to a dead black where the feet of years had worn away layer after layer of resurfacing. The silence was smooth and nearly perfect.

The janitor reached the bottom first and pointed under the staircase. "Under here," he said.

Dex joined him in staring into a shadowy, triangular cavity under the wide staircase. He felt a small tremor of disgust as he saw where the janitor had brushed away a gossamer veil of cobwebs. He supposed it was possible that the man had found something a little older than postwar records under there, now that he actually looked at the space. But 1834?

"Just a second," the janitor said, and left momentarily. Left alone, Dex hunkered down and peered in. He could make out nothing but a deeper patch of shadow in there. Then the janitor returned with a hefty four-cell flashlight. "This'll show it up."

"What were you doing under there anyway?" Dex asked.

The janitor grinned. "I was only standin here tryin to decide if I should buff that second-floor hallway first or wash the lab windows. I couldn't make up my mind, so I flipped a quarter. Only I dropped it and it rolled under there." He pointed to the shadowy, triangular cave. "I prob'ly would have let it go, except that was my only quarter for the Coke machine. So I got my flash and knocked down the cobwebs, and when I crawled under to get it, I saw that crate. Here, have a look."

The janitor shone his light into the hole. Motes of disturbed dust preened and swayed lazily in the beam. The light struck the far wall in a spotlight circle, rose to the zigzag undersides of the stairs briefly, picking out an ancient cobweb in which long-dead bugs hung mummified, and then the light dropped and centered on a crate about five feet long and two-and-a-half wide. It was perhaps three feet deep. As the janitor had said, it was no knocked-together affair made out of scrapboards. It was neatly constructed of a smooth, dark heavy wood. *A coffin,* Dexter thought uneasily. *It looks like a child's coffin.*

The dark color of the wood showed only a fan-shaped swipe on the side. The rest of the crate was the uniform dull gray of dust. Something was written on the side—stenciled there.

Dex squinted but couldn't read it. He fumbled his glasses out of his breast pocket and still couldn't. Part of what had been stenciled on was obscured by the dust—not four inches of it, by any means, but an extraordinarily thick coating, all the same.

Not wanting to crawl and dirty his pants, Dex duck-walked under the stairway, stifling a sudden and amazingly strong feeling of claustrophobia. The spit dried in his mouth and was replaced by a dry, woolly taste, like an old mitten. He thought of the generations of students trooping up and down these stairs, all male until 1888, then in coeducational platoons, carrying their books and papers and anatomical drawings, their bright faces and clear eyes, each of them convinced that a useful and exciting future lay ahead...and here, below their feet, the spider spun his eternal snare for the fly and the trundling beetle, and here this crate sat impassively, gathering dust, waiting...

A tendril of spidersilk brushed across his forehead and he swept it away with a small cry of loathing and an uncharacteristic inner cringe.

"Not very nice under there, is it?" the janitor asked sympathetically, holding his light centered on the crate. "God, I hate tight places."

Dex didn't reply. He had reached the crate. He looked at the letters that were stenciled there and then brushed the dust away from them. It rose in a cloud, intensifying that mitten taste, making him cough dryly. The dust hung in the beam of the janitor's light like old magic, and Dex Stanley read what some long-dead chief of lading had stenciled on this crate.

SHIP TO HORLICKS UNIVERSITY, the top line read. VIA JULIA CARPENTER, read the middle line. The third line read simply: ARCTIC EXPEDITION. Below that, someone had written in heavy black charcoal strokes: JUNE 19, 1834. That was the one line the janitor's hand-swipe had completely cleared.

ARCTIC EXPEDITION, Dex read again. His heart began to thump.

"So what do you think?" the janitor's voice floated in.

Dex grabbed one end and lifted it. Heavy. As he let it settle back with a mild thud, something shifted inside—he did not hear it but felt it through the palms of his hands, as if whatever it was had moved of its own volition. Stupid, of course. It had been an almost liquid feel, as if something not quite jelled had moved sluggishly.

ARCTIC EXPEDITION.

Dex felt the excitement of an antiques collector happening upon a neglected armoire with a twenty-five dollar price tag in the back room of some hick-town junk shop...an armoire that just might be a Chippendale. "Help me get it out," he called to the janitor.

Working bent over to keep from slamming their heads on the underside of the stairway, sliding the crate along, they got it out and then picked it up by the bottom. Dex had gotten his pants dirty after all, and there were cobwebs in his hair.

As they carried it into the old-fashioned, train-terminal-sized lab, Dex felt that sensation of shift inside the crate again, and he could see by the expression on the janitor's face that he had felt it as well. They set it on one of the Formica-topped lab tables. The next one over was littered with Charlie Gereson's stuff—notebooks, graph paper, contour maps, a Texas Instruments calculator.

The janitor stood back, wiping his hands on his double-pocket gray shirt, breathing hard. "Some heavy mother," he said. "That bastard must weigh two hunnert pounds. You okay, Perfesser Stanley?"

Dex barely heard him. He was looking at the end of the box, where there was yet another series of stencils: PAELLA/SANTIAGO/SAN FRANCISCO/CHICAGO/NEW YORK/HORLICKS

"Perfesser—"

"Paella," Dex muttered, and then said it again, slightly louder. He was seized with an unbelieving kind of excitement that was held in check only by the thought that it might be some sort of hoax. "Paella!"

❧

"Paella, Dex?" Henry Northrup asked. The moon had risen in the sky, turning silver.

"Paella is a very small island south of Tierra del Fuego," Dex said. "Perhaps the smallest island ever inhabited by the race of man. A number of Easter Island-type monoliths were found there just after World War II. Not very interesting compared to their bigger brothers, but every bit as mysterious. The natives of Paella and Tierra del Fuego were Stone-Age people. Christian missionaries killed them with kindness."

"I beg your pardon?"

"It's extremely cold down there. Summer temperatures rarely range above the mid-forties. The missionaries gave them blankets, partly so they would be warm, mostly to cover their sinful nakedness. The blankets were crawling with fleas, and the natives of both islands were wiped out by European diseases for which they had developed no immunities. Mostly by smallpox."

Dex drank. The Scotch had lent his cheeks some color, but it was hectic and flaring—double spots of flush that sat above his cheekbones like rouge.

"But Tierra del Fuego—and this Paella—that's not the Arctic, Dex. It's the Antarctic."

"It wasn't in 1834," Dex said, setting his glass down, careful in spite of his distraction to put it on the coaster Henry had provided. If Wilma found a ring on one of her end tables, his friend would have hell to pay. "The terms subarctic, Antarctic and Antarctica weren't invented yet. In those days there was only the north arctic and the south arctic."

"Okay."

"Hell, I made the same kind of mistake. I couldn't figure out why Frisco was on the itinerary as a port of call. Then I realized I was figuring on the Panama Canal, which wasn't built for another eighty years or so."

"An Arctic expedition? In 1834?" Henry asked doubtfully.

"I haven't had a chance to check the records yet," Dex said, picking up his drink again. "But I know from my history that there were 'Arctic expeditions' as early as Francis Drake. None of them made it, that was all. They were convinced they'd find gold, silver, jewels, lost civilizations, God knows what else. The Smithsonian Institution outfitted an attempted exploration of the North Pole in, I think it was 1881 or '82. They all died. A bunch of men from the Explorers' Club in London tried for the South Pole in the 1850's. Their ship was sunk by icebergs, but three or four of them survived. They stayed alive by sucking dew out of their clothes and eating the kelp that caught on their boat, until they were picked up. They lost their teeth. And they claimed to have seen sea monsters."

"What happened, Dex?" Henry asked softly.

Stanley looked up. "We opened the crate," he said dully. "God help us, Henry, we opened the crate."

He paused for a long time, it seemed, before beginning to speak again.

❧

"Paella?" the janitor asked. "What's that?"

"An island off the tip of South America," Dex said. "Never mind. Let's get this open." He opened one of the lab drawers and began to rummage through it, looking for something to pry with."

"Never mind that stuff," the janitor said. He looked excited himself now. "I got a hammer and chisel in my closet upstairs. I'll get 'em. Just hang on."

He left. The crate sat on the table's Formica top, squat and mute.

It sits squat and mute, Dex thought, and shivered a little. Where had that thought come from? Some story? The words had a cadenced yet unpleasant sound. He dismissed them. He was good at dismissing the extraneous. He was a scientist.

He looked around the lab just to get his eyes off the crate. Except for Charlie's table, it was unnaturally neat and quiet—like the rest of the university. White-tiled, subway-station walls gleamed freshly under the overhead globes; the globes themselves seemed to be double—caught and submerged in the polished Formica surfaces, like eerie lamps shining from deep quarry water. A huge, old-fashioned slate blackboard dominated the wall opposite the sinks. And cupboards, cupboards everywhere. It was easy enough—too easy, perhaps—to see the antique, sepia-toned ghosts of all those old zoology students, wearing their white coats with the green cuffs, their hair marcelled or pomaded, doing their dissections and writing their reports...

Footfalls clattered on the stairs and Dex shivered, thinking again of the crate sitting there—yes, squat and mute—under the stairs for so many years, long after the men who had pushed it under there had died and gone back to dust.

Paella, he thought, and then the janitor came back in with a hammer and chisel.

"Let me do this for you, perfesser?" he asked, and Dex was about to refuse when he saw the pleading, hopeful look in the man's eyes.

"Of course," he said. After all, it was this man's find.

"Prob'ly nothin in here but a bunch of rocks and plants so old they'll turn to dust when you touch 'em. But it's funny; I'm pretty hot for it."

Dex smiled noncommittally. He had no idea what was in the crate, but he doubted if it was just plant and rock specimens. There was that slightly liquid shifting sensation when they had moved it.

"Here goes," the janitor said, and began to pound the chisel under the board with swift blows of the hammer. The board hiked up a bit, revealing a double row of nails that reminded Dex absurdly of teeth. The janitor levered the handle of his chisel down and the board pulled loose, the nails shrieking out of the wood. He did the same thing at the other end, and the board came free, clattering to the floor. Dex set it aside, noticing that even the nails looked different, somehow—thicker, squarer at the tip, and without that blue-steel sheen that is the mark of a sophisticated alloying process.

The janitor was peering into the crate through the long, narrow strip he had uncovered. "Can't see nothin," he said. "Where'd I leave my light?"

"Never mind," Dex said. "Go on and open it."

"Okay." He took off a second board, then a third. Six or seven had been nailed across the top of the box. He began on the fourth, reaching across the space he had already uncovered to place his chisel under the board, when the crate began to whistle.

It was a sound very much like the sound a teakettle makes when it has reached a rolling boil, Dex told Henry Northrup; no cheerful whistle this, but something like an ugly, hysterical shriek by a tantrumy child. And this suddenly dropped and thickened into a low, hoarse growling sound. It was not loud, but it had a primitive, savage sound that stood Dex Stanley's hair up on the slant. The janitor stared around at him, his eyes widening...and then his arm was seized. Dex did not see what grabbed it; his eyes had gone instinctively to the man's face.

The janitor screamed, and the sound drove a stiletto of panic into Dex's chest. The thought that came unbidden was: *This is the first time in my life that I've heard a grown man scream—what a sheltered life I've led!*

The janitor, a fairly big guy who weighed maybe two hundred pounds, was suddenly yanked powerfully to one side. Toward the crate. *"Help me!"* He screamed. *"Oh help doc it's got me it's biting me it's biting meeeee—"*

Dex told himself to run forward and grab the janitor's free arm, but his feet might as well have been bonded to the floor. The janitor had been pulled into the crate up to his shoulder. That crazed snarling went on and on. The crate slid backwards along the table for a foot or so and then came firmly to rest against a bolted instrument mount. It began to rock back and forth. The janitor screamed and gave a tremendous lunge away from the crate. The end of the box came up off the table and then smacked back down. Part of his arm came out of the crate, and Dex saw to his horror that the gray sleeve of his shirt was chewed and tattered and soaked with blood. Smiling crescent bites were punched into what he could see of the man's skin through the shredded flaps of cloth.

Then something that must have been incredibly strong yanked him back down. The thing in the crate began to snarl and gobble. Every now and then there would be a breathless whistling sound in between.

At last Dex broke free of his paralysis and lunged creakily forward. He grabbed the janitor's free arm. He yanked...with no result at all. It was like trying to pull a man who has been handcuffed to the bumper of a trailer truck.

The janitor screamed again—a long, ululating sound that rolled back and forth between the lab's sparkling, white-tiled walls. Dex could see the gold glimmer of the fillings at the back of the man's mouth. He could see the yellow ghost of nicotine on his tongue.

The janitor's head slammed down against the edge of the board he had been about to remove when the thing had grabbed him. And this time Dex did see something, although it happened with such mortal, savage speed that later he was unable to describe it adequately to Henry. Something as dry and brown and scaly as a desert reptile came out of the crate—something with huge claws. It tore at the janitor's straining, knotted throat and severed his jugular vein. Blood began to pump across the table, pooling on the Formica and jetting onto the white-tiled floor. For a moment, a mist of blood seemed to hang in the air.

Dex dropped the janitor's arm and blundered backward, hands clapped flat to his cheeks, eyes bulging.

The janitor's eyes rolled wildly at the ceiling. His mouth dropped open and then snapped closed. The click of his teeth was audible even below that hungry growling. His feet, clad in heavy black work shoes, did a short and jittery tap dance on the floor.

Then he seemed to lose interest. His eyes grew almost benign as they looked raptly at the overhead light globe, which was also blood-spattered. His feet splayed out in a loose V. His shirt pulled out of his pants, displaying his white and bulging belly.

"He's dead," Dex whispered. "Oh, Jesus."

The pump of the janitor's heart faltered and lost its rhythm. Now the blood that flowed from the deep, irregular gash in his neck lost its urgency and merely flowed down at the command of indifferent gravity. The crate was stained and splashed with blood. The snarling seemed to go on endlessly. The crate rocked back and forth a bit, but it was too well-braced against the instrument mount to go very far. The body of the janitor lolled grotesquely, still grasped firmly by whatever was in there. The small of his back was pressed against the lip of the lab table. His free hand dangled, sparse hair curling on the fingers between the first and second knuckles. His big key ring glimmered chrome in the light.

And now his body began to rock slowly this way and that. His shoes dragged back and forth, not tap dancing now but waltzing obscenely. And then they did not drag. They dangled an inch off the floor…then two inches…then half a foot above the floor. Dex realized that the janitor was being dragged into the crate.

The nape of his neck came to rest against the board fronting the far side of the hole in the top of the crate. He looked like a man resting in some weird Zen position of contemplation. His dead eyes sparkled. And Dex heard, below the savage growling noises, a smacking, rending sound. And the crunch of a bone.

Dex ran.

He blundered his way across the lab and out the door and up the stairs. Halfway up, he fell down, clawed at the risers, got to his feet, and ran again. He gained the first floor hallway and sprinted down it, past the closed doors with their frosted-glass panels, past the bulletin boards. He was chased by his own footfalls. In his ears he could hear that damned whistling.

He ran right into Charlie Gereson's arms and almost knocked him over, and he spilled the milk shake Charlie had been drinking all over both of them.

"Holy hell, what's wrong?" Charlie asked, comic in his extreme surprise. He was short and compact, wearing cotton chinos and a white tee shirt. Thick spectacles sat grimly on his nose, meaning business, proclaiming that they were there for a long haul.

"Charlie," Dex said, panting harshly. "My boy…the janitor…the crate…it whistles…*it whistles when it's hungry and it whistles again when it's full*…my boy… we have to…campus security…we…we…"

"Slow down, Professor Stanley," Charlie said. He looked concerned and a little frightened. You don't expect to be seized by the senior professor in your department when you had nothing more aggressive in mind yourself than charting the continued outmigration of sandflies. "Slow down, I don't know what you're talking about."

Stanley, hardly aware of what he was saying, poured out a garbled version of what had happened to the janitor. Charlie Gereson looked more and more confused and doubtful. As upset as he was, Dex began to realize that Charlie didn't believe a word of it. He thought, with a new kind of horror, that soon Charlie would ask him if he had been working too hard, and that when he did, Stanley would burst into mad cackles of laughter.

But what Charlie said was, "That's pretty far out, Professor Stanley."

"It's true. We've got to get campus security over here. We—"

"No, that's no good. One of them would stick his hand in there, first thing." He saw Dex's stricken look and went on. "If *I'm* having trouble swallowing this, what are *they* going to think?"

"I don't know," Dex said. "I...I never thought..."

"They'd think you just came off a helluva toot and were seeing Tasmanian devils instead of pink elephants," Charlie Gereson said cheerfully, and pushed his glasses up on his pug nose. "Besides, from what you say, the responsibility has belonged with zoology all along...like for a hundred and forty years."

"But..." He swallowed, and there was a click in his throat as he prepared to voice his worst fear. "But it may be out."

"I doubt that," Charlie said, but didn't elaborate. And in that, Dex saw two things: that Charlie didn't believe a word he had said, and that nothing he could say would dissuade Charlie from going back down there.

Henry Northrup glanced at his watch. They had been sitting in the study for a little over an hour; Wilma wouldn't be back for another two. Plenty of time. Unlike Charlie Gereson, he had passed no judgment at all on the factual basis of Dex's story. But he had known Dex for a longer time than young Gereson had, and he didn't believe his friend exhibited the signs of a man who has suddenly developed a psychosis. What he exhibited was a kind of bug-eyed fear, no more or less than you'd expect to see in a man who has had an extremely close call with...well, just an extremely close call.

"He went down, Dex?"

"Yes. He did."

"You went with him?"

"Yes."

Henry shifted position a little. "I can understand why he didn't want to get campus security until he had checked the situation himself. But Dex, you knew you were telling the flat-out truth, even if he didn't. Why didn't *you* call?"

"You believe me?" Dex asked. His voice trembled. "You believe me, don't you, Henry?"

Henry considered briefly. The story was mad, no question about that. The implication that there could be something in that box big enough and lively enough to kill a man after some one hundred and forty years was mad. He didn't believe it. But this was Dex...and he didn't *disbelieve* it either.

"Yes," he said.

"Thank God for that," Dex said. He groped for his drink. "Thank God for that, Henry."

"It doesn't answer the question, though. Why didn't you call the campus cops?"

"I thought...as much as I did think...that it might not want to come out of the crate, into the bright light. It must have lived in the dark for so long...so very long...and...grotesque as this sounds...I thought it might be pot-bound, or something. I thought...well, he'll see it...he'll see the crate...the janitor's body... he'll see the *blood*...and then we'd call security. You see?" Stanley's eyes pleaded with him to see, and Henry did. He thought that, considering the fact that it had been a snap judgment in a pressure situation, that Dex had thought quite clearly. The blood. When the young graduate student saw the blood, he would have been happy to call in the cops.

"But it didn't work out that way."

"No." Dex ran a hand through his thinning hair.

"Why not?"

"Because when we got down there, the body was *gone*."

"It was gone?"

"That's right. And the crate was gone, too."

✠

When Charlie Gereson saw the blood, his round and good-natured face went very pale. His eyes, already magnified by his thick spectacles, grew even huger. Blood was puddled on the lab table. It had run down one of the table legs. It was pooled on the floor, and beads of it clung to the light globe and to the white tile wall. Yes, there was plenty of blood.

But no janitor. No crate.

Dex Stanley's jaw dropped. "What the *fuck!*" Charlie whispered.

Dex saw something then, perhaps the only thing that allowed him to keep his sanity. Already he could feel that central axle trying to pull free. He grabbed Charlie's shoulder and said, "Look at the blood on the table!"

"I've seen enough," Charlie said.

His Adam's apple rose and fell like an express elevator as he struggled to keep his lunch down.

"For God's sake, get hold of yourself," Dex said harshly. "You're a zoology major. You've seen blood before."

It was the voice of authority, for that moment anyway. Charlie did get a hold of himself, and they walked a little closer. The random pools of blood on the table were not as random as they had first appeared. Each had been neatly straight-edged on one side.

"The crate sat there," Dex said. He felt a little better. The fact that the crate really *had* been there steadied him a good deal. "And look there." He pointed at the floor. Here the blood had been smeared into a wide, thin trail. It swept toward where the two of them stood, a few paces inside the double doors. It faded and faded, petering out altogether about halfway between the lab table and the doors. It was crystal clear to Dex Stanley, and the nervous sweat on his skin went cold and clammy.

It had gotten out.

It had gotten out and pushed the crate off the table. And then it had pushed the crate...where? Under the stairs, of course. Back under the stairs. Where it had been safe for so long.

"Where's the...the..." Charlie couldn't finish.

"Under the stairs," Dex said numbly. "It's gone back to where it came from."

"No. The..." He jerked it out finally. "The body."

"I don't know," Dex said. But he thought he did know. His mind would simply not admit the truth.

Charlie turned abruptly and walked back through the doors. "Where are you going?" Dex called shrilly, and ran after him. Charlie stopped opposite the stairs. The triangular black hole beneath them gaped. The janitor's big four-cell flashlight still sat on the floor. And beside it was a bloody scrap of gray cloth, and one of the pens that had been clipped to the man's breast pocket.

"Don't go under there, Charlie! Don't." His heartbeat whammed savagely in his ears, frightening him even more.

"No," Charlie said. "But the body..."

Charlie hunkered down, grabbed the flashlight, and shone it under the stairs. And the crate was there, shoved up against the far wall, just as it had been before, squat and mute. Except that now it was free of dust and three boards had been pried off the top.

The light moved and centered on one of the janitor's big, sensible work shoes. Charlie drew breath in a low, harsh gasp. The thick leather of the shoe had been savagely gnawed and chewed. The laces hung, broken, from the eyelets. "It looks like somebody put it through a hay baler," he said hoarsely.

"Now do you believe me?" Dex asked.

Charlie didn't answer. Holding onto the stairs lightly with one hand, he leaned under the overhang—presumably to get the shoe. Later, sitting in Henry's study, Dex said he could think of only one reason why Charlie would have done that—to measure and perhaps categorize the bite of the thing in the crate. He was, after all, a zoologist, and a damned good one.

"Don't!" Dex screamed, and grabbed the back of Charlie's shirt. Suddenly there were two green gold eyes glaring over the top of the crate. They were almost exactly the color of owls' eyes, but smaller. There was a harsh, chattering growl of anger. Charlie recoiled, startled, and slammed the back of his head on the underside of the stairs. A shadow moved from the crate toward him at projectile speed. Charlie howled. Dex heard the dry purr of his shirt as it ripped open, the click as Charlie's glasses struck the floor and spun away. Once more Charlie tried to back away. The thing began to snarl—then the snarls suddenly stopped. And Charlie Gereson began to scream in agony.

Dex pulled on the back of his white tee shirt with all his might. For a moment Charlie came backwards and he caught a glimpse of a furry, writhing shape spread-eagled on the young man's chest, a shape that appeared to have not four but six legs and the flat bullet head of a young lynx. The front of Charlie Gereson's shirt had been so quickly and completely tattered that it now looked like so many crepe streamers hung around his neck.

Then the thing raised its head and those small green gold eyes stared balefully into Dex's own. He had never seen or dreamed such savagery. His strength failed. His grip on the back of Charlie's shirt loosened momentarily.

A moment was all it took. Charlie Gereson's body was snapped under the stairs with grotesque, cartoonish speed. Silence for a moment. Then the growling, smacking sounds began again.

Charlie screamed once more, a long sound of terror and pain that was abruptly cut off...as if something had been clapped over his mouth.

Or stuffed into it.

⁂

Dex fell silent. The moon was high in the sky. Half of his third drink—an almost unheard-of phenomenon—was gone, and he felt the reaction setting in as sleepiness and extreme lassitude.

"What did you do then?" Henry asked. What he hadn't done, he knew, was to go to campus security; they wouldn't have listened to such a story and then released him so he could go and tell it again to his friend Henry.

"I just walked around, in utter shock, I suppose. I ran up the stairs again, just as I had after...after it took the janitor, only this time there was no Charlie Gereson to run into. I walked...miles, I suppose. I think I was mad. I kept thinking about Ryder's Quarry. You know that place?"

"Yes," Henry said.

"I kept thinking that would be deep enough. If... if there would be a way to get that crate out there. I kept...kept thinking..." He put his hands to his face. "I don't know. I don't know anymore. I think I'm going crazy."

"If the story you just told is true, I can understand that," Henry said quietly. He stood up suddenly. "Come on. I'm taking you home."

"Home?" Dex looked at this friend vacantly. "But—"

"I'll leave a note for Wilma telling her where we've gone and then we'll call...who do you suggest, Dex? Campus security or the state police?"

"You believe me, don't you? You believe me? Just say you do."

"Yes, I believe you," Henry said, and it was the truth. "I don't know what that thing could be or where it came from, but I believe you." Dex Stanley began to weep.

"Finish your drink while I write my wife," Henry said, apparently not noticing the tears. He even grinned a little. "And for Christ's sake, let's get out of here before she gets back."

Dex clutched at Henry's sleeve. "But we won't go anywhere near Amberson Hall, will we? Promise me, Henry! We'll stay away from there, won't we?"

"Does a bear shit in the woods?" Henry Northrup asked. It was a three-mile drive to Dex's house on the outskirts of town, and before they got there, he was half-asleep in the passenger seat.

"The state cops, I think," Henry said. His words seemed to come from a great distance. "I think Charlie Gereson's assessment of the campus cops was pretty accurate. The first one there would happily stick his arm into that box."

"Yes. All right." Through the drifting, lassitudinous aftermath of shock, Dex felt a dim but great gratitude that his friend had taken over with such efficiency.

Yet a deeper part of him believed that Henry could not have done it if he had seen the things he had seen. "Just...the importance of caution..."

"I'll see to that," Henry said grimly, and that was when Dex fell asleep.

⁂

He awoke the next morning with August sunshine making crisp patterns on the sheets of his bed. Just a dream, he thought with indescribable relief. All some crazy dream.

But there was a taste of Scotch in his mouth—Scotch and something else. He sat up, and a lance of pain bolted through his head. Not the sort of pain you got from a hangover, though; not even if you were the type to get a hangover from three Scotches, and he wasn't.

He sat up, and there was Henry, sitting across the room. His first thought was that Henry needed a shave. His second was that there was something in Henry's eyes that he had never seen before—something like chips of ice. A ridiculous thought came to Dex; it passed through his mind and was gone. *Sniper's eyes. Henry Northrup, whose specialty is the earlier English poets, has got sniper's eyes.*

"How are you feeling, Dex?"

"A slight headache," Dex said. "Henry...the police...what happened?"

"The police aren't coming," Northrup said calmly. "As for your head, I'm very sorry. I put one of Wilma's sleeping powders in your third drink. Be assured that it will pass."

"Henry, what are you saying?"

Henry took a sheet of notepaper from his breast pocket. "This is the note I left my wife. It will explain a lot, I think. I got it back after everything was over.

I took a chance that she'd leave it on the table, and I got away with it."

"I don't know what you're—"

He took the note from Henry's fingers and read it, eyes widening.

⁂

Dear Billie,

I've just had a call from Dex Stanley. He's hysterical. Seems to have committed some sort of indiscretion with one of his female grad students. He's at Amberson Hall. So is the girl. For God's sake, come quickly. I'm not sure exactly what the situation is, but a woman's presence may be imperative, and under the circumstances, a nurse from the infirmary just won't do. I know you don't like Dex much, but a scandal like this could ruin his career. Please come.

Henry.

⁂

"What in God's name have you done?" Dex asked hoarsely.

Henry plucked the note from Dex's nerveless fingers, produced his Zippo, and set flame to the corner. When it was burning well, he dropped the charring sheet of paper into an ashtray on the windowsill.

"I've killed Wilma," he said in the same calm voice. "Ding-dong, the wicked bitch is dead." Dex tried to speak and could not. That central axle was trying to tear loose again. The abyss of utter insanity was below. "I've killed my wife, and now I've put myself into your hands."

Now Dex did find his voice. It had a sound that was rusty yet shrill. "The crate," he said. "What have you done with the crate?"

"That's the beauty of it," Henry said. "You put the final piece in the jigsaw yourself. The crate is at the bottom of Ryder's Quarry."

Dex groped at that while he looked into Henry's eyes. The eyes of his friend. Sniper's eyes. You can't knock off your own queen, that's not in anyone's rules of chess, he thought, and restrained an urge to roar out gales of rancid laughter. The quarry, he had said. Ryder's Quarry. It was over four hundred feet deep, some said. It was perhaps twelve miles east of the university. Over the thirty years that Dex had been here, a dozen people had drowned there, and three years ago the town had posted the place.

"I put you to bed," Henry said. "Had to carry you into your room. You were out like a light. Scotch, sleeping powder, shock. But you were breathing normally and well. Strong heart action. I checked those things. Whatever else you believe, never think I had any intention of hurting you, Dex.

"It was fifteen minutes before Wilma's last class ended, and it would take her another fifteen minutes to drive home and another fifteen minutes to get over to Amberson Hall. That gave me forty-five minutes. I got over to Amberson in ten. It was unlocked. That was enough to settle any doubts I had left."

"What do you mean?"

"The key ring on the janitor's belt. It went with the janitor."

Dex shuddered.

"If the door had been locked—forgive me, Dex, but if you're going to play for keeps, you ought to cover every base—there was still time enough to get back home ahead of Wilma and burn that note.

"I went downstairs—and I kept as close to the wall going down those stairs as I could, believe me..."

Henry stepped into the lab and glanced around. It was just as Dex had left it. He slicked his tongue over his dry lips and then wiped his face with his hand. His heart was thudding in his chest. *Get hold of yourself, man. One thing at a time. Don't look ahead.*

The boards the janitor had pried off the crate were still stacked on the lab table. One table over was the scatter of Charlie Gereson's lab notes, never to be completed now. Henry took it all in, and then pulled his own flashlight—the one he always kept in the glovebox of his car for emergencies—from his back pocket. If this didn't qualify as an emergency, nothing did.

He snapped it on and crossed the lab and went out the door. The light bobbed uneasily in the dark for a moment, and then he trained it on the floor. He didn't want to step on anything he shouldn't. Moving slowly and cautiously, Henry moved around to the side of the stairs and shone the light underneath. His breath paused, and then resumed again, more slowly. Suddenly the tension and fear were gone, and he only felt cold. The crate was under there, just as Dex had said it was. And the janitor's ballpoint pen. And his shoes. And Charlie Gereson's glasses.

Henry moved the light from one of these artifacts to the next slowly, spotlighting each. Then he glanced at his watch, snapped the flashlight off and jammed it back in his pocket. He had half an hour. There was no time to waste.

In the janitor's closet upstairs he found buckets, heavy-duty cleaner, rags...and gloves. No prints. He went back downstairs like the sorcerer's apprentice, a heavy plastic bucket full of hot water and foaming cleaner in each hand, rags draped over his shoulder. His footfalls clacked hollowly in the stillness. He thought of Dex saying, *It sits squat and mute.* And still he was cold.

He began to clean up.

⁂

"She came," Henry said. "Oh yes, she came. And she was...excited and happy."

"What?" Dex said.

"Excited," he repeated. "She was whining and carping the way she always did in that high, unpleasant voice, but that was just habit, I think. All those years, Dex, the only part of me she wasn't able to completely control, the only part she could never get completely under her thumb, was my friendship with you. Our two drinks while she was at class. Our chess. Our... companionship."

Dex nodded. Yes, companionship was the right word. A little light in the darkness of loneliness. It hadn't just been the chess or the drinks; it had been Henry's face over the board, Henry's voice recounting how things were in his department, a bit of harmless gossip, a laugh over something.

"So she was whining and bitching in her best 'just call me Billie' style, but I think it was just habit. She was excited and happy, Dex. Because she was finally going to be able to get control over the last...little... bit." He looked at Dex calmly. "I knew she'd come, you see. I knew she'd want to see what kind of mess you'd gotten yourself into, Dex."

⁂

"They're downstairs," Henry told Wilma. Wilma was wearing a bright yellow sleeveless blouse and green pants that were too tight for her. "Right downstairs." And he uttered a sudden, loud laugh.

Wilma's head whipped around and her narrow face darkened with suspicion. "What are you laughing about?" She asked in her loud, buzzing voice. "Your best friend gets in a scrape with a girl and you're laughing?"

No, he shouldn't be laughing. But he couldn't help it. It was sitting under the stairs, sitting there squat and mute, just try telling that thing in the crate to call you Billie, Wilma—and another loud laugh escaped him and went rolling down the dim first-floor hall like a depth charge.

"Well, there is a funny side to it," he said, hardly aware of what he was saying. "Wait'll you see. You'll think—"

Her eyes, always questing, never still, dropped to his front pocket, where he had stuffed the rubber gloves.

"What are those? Are those gloves?"

Henry began to spew words. At the same time he put his arm around Wilma's bony shoulders and led her toward the stairs. "Well, he's passed out, you know. He smells like a distillery. Can't guess how much he drank. Threw up all over everything. I've been cleaning up. Hell of an awful mess, Billie. I persuaded the girl to stay a bit. You'll help me, won't you? This is Dex, after all."

"I don't know," she said, as they began to descend the stairs to the basement lab. Her eyes snapped with dark glee. "I'll have to see what the situation is. You don't know anything, that's obvious. You're hysterical. Exactly what I would have expected."

"That's right," Henry said. They had reached the bottom of the stairs. "Right around here. Just step right around here."

"But the lab's that way—"

"Yes...but the girl..." And he began to laugh again in great, loonlike bursts.

"Henry, what is wrong with you?" And now that acidic contempt was mixed with something else—something that might have been fear.

That made Henry laugh harder. His laughter echoed and rebounded, filling the dark basement with a sound like laughing banshees or demons approving a particularly good jest. “The girl, Billie,” Henry said between bursts of helpless laughter. “That’s what’s so funny, the girl, the girl has crawled under the stairs and won’t come out, that what’s so funny, *ah-heh-heh-hahahahaa—*”

And now the dark kerosene of joy lit in her eyes; her lips curled up like charring paper in what the denizens of hell might call a smile. And Wilma whispered, “What did he *do* to her?”

“You can get her out,” Henry babbled, leading her to the dark, triangular, gaping maw. “I’m sure you can get her out, no trouble, no problem.” He suddenly grabbed Wilma at the nape of the neck and the waist, forcing her down even as he pushed her into the space under the stairs.

“What are you doing?” she screamed querulously. “What are you doing, Henry?”

“What I should have done a long time ago,” Henry said, laughing. “Get under there, Wilma. Just tell it to call you Billie, you bitch.”

She tried to turn, tried to fight him. One hand clawed for his wrist—he saw her spade-shaped nails slice down, but they clawed only air. “Stop it, Henry!” She cried. “Stop it right now! Stop this foolishness! I—I’ll scream!”

“Scream all you want!” he bellowed, still laughing. He raised one foot, planted it in the center of her narrow and joyless backside, and pushed. “I’ll help you, Wilma! Come on out! Wake up, whatever you are! Wake up! Here’s your dinner! Poison meat! Wake up! Wake up!”

Wilma screamed piercingly, an inarticulate sound that was still more rage than fear.

And then Henry heard it.

First a low whistle, the sound a man might make while working alone without even being aware of it. Then it rose in pitch, sliding up the scale to an ear-splitting whine that was barely audible. Then it suddenly descended again and became a growl...and then a hoarse yammering. It was an utterly savage sound. All his married life Henry Northrup had gone in fear of his wife, but the thing in the crate made Wilma sound like a child doing a kindergarten tantrum. Henry had time to think: *Holy God, maybe it really is a Tasmanian devil...it's some kind of devil, anyway.*

Wilma began to scream again, but this time it was a sweeter tune—at least to the ear of Henry Northrup. It was a sound of utter terror. Her yellow blouse flashed in the dark under the stairs, a vague beacon. She lunged at the opening and Henry pushed her back, using all his strength.

"Henry!" She howled. *"Henreeeee!"*

She came again, head first this time, like a charging bull. Henry caught her head in both hands, feeling the tight, wiry cap of her curls squash under his palms. He pushed. And then, over Wilma's shoulder, he saw something that might have been the gold-glinting eyes of a small owl. Eyes that were infinitely cold and hateful. The yammering became louder, reaching a crescendo. And when it struck at Wilma, the vibration running through her body was enough to knock him backwards.

He caught one glimpse of her face, her bulging eyes, and then she was dragged back into the darkness. She screamed once more. Only once.

"Just tell it to call you Billie," he whispered.

⁂

Henry Northrup drew a great, shuddering breath.

"It went on...for quite a while," he said. "After a long time, maybe twenty minutes, the growling and the...the sounds of its feeding...that stopped, too. And it started to whistle. Just like you said, Dex. As if it were a happy teakettle or something. It whistled for maybe five minutes, and then it stopped. I shone my light underneath again. The crate had been pulled out a little way. There was...fresh blood. And Wilma's purse had spilled everywhere. But it got both of her shoes. That was something, wasn't it?"

Dex didn't answer. The room basked in sunshine. Outside, a bird sang.

"I finished cleaning the lab," Henry resumed at last. "It took me another forty minutes, and I almost missed a drop of blood that was on the light globe... saw it just as I was going out. But when I was done, the place was as neat as a pin. Then I went out to my car and drove across campus to the English department. It was getting late, but I didn't feel a bit tired. In fact, Dex, I don't think I ever felt more clear-headed in my life. There was a crate in the basement of the English department. I flashed on that very early in your story. Associating one monster with another, I suppose."

"What do you mean?"

"Last year when Badlinger was in England—you remember Badlinger, don't you?"

Dex nodded. Badlinger was the man who had beaten Henry out for the English department chair...partly because Badlinger's wife was bright, vivacious and sociable, while Henry's wife was a shrew. Had been a shrew.

"He was in England on sabbatical," Henry said. "Had all their things crated and shipped back. One of them was a giant stuffed animal. Nessie, they call it. For his kids. That bastard bought it for his kids. I always wanted children, you know. Wilma didn't. She said kids get in the way.

"Anyway, it came back in this gigantic wooden crate, and Badlinger dragged it down to the English department basement because there was no room in the garage at home, he said, but he didn't want to throw it out because it might come in handy someday. Meantime, our janitors were using it as a gigantic sort of wastebasket. When it was full of trash, they'd dump it into the back of the truck on trash day and then fill it up again.

"I think it was the crate Badlinger's damned stuffed monster came back from England in that put the idea in my head. I began to see how your Tasmanian devil could be gotten rid of. And that started me thinking about something else I wanted to be rid of. That I wanted so badly to be rid of.

"I had my keys, of course. I let myself in and went downstairs. The crate was there. It was a big, unwieldy thing, but the janitors' dolly was down there as well. I dumped out the little bit of trash that was in it and got the crate onto the dolly by standing it on end. I pulled it upstairs and wheeled it straight across the mall and back to Amberson."

"You didn't take your car?"

"No, I left my car in my space in the English department parking lot. I couldn't have gotten the crate in there, anyway."

For Dex, new light began to break. Henry would have been driving his MG, of course—an elderly sports car that Wilma had always called Henry's toy. And if Henry had the MG, then Wilma would have had the Scout—a jeep with a fold-down back seat. Plenty of storage space, as the ads said.

"I didn't meet anyone," Henry said. "At this time of year—and at no other—the campus is quite deserted. The whole thing was almost hellishly perfect. I didn't see so much as a pair of headlights. I got back to Amberson Hall and took Badlinger's crate downstairs. I left it sitting on the dolly with the open end facing under the stairs. Then I went back upstairs to the janitors' closet and got that long pole they use to open and close the windows. They only have those poles in the old buildings now. I went back down and got ready to hook the crate—your Paella crate—out from under the stairs. Then I had a bad moment. I realized the top of Badlinger's crate was gone, you see. I'd noticed it before, but now I *realized* it. In my guts."

"What did you do?"

"Decided to take the chance," Henry said. "I took the window pole and pulled the crate out. I *eased* it out, as if it were full of eggs. No...as if it were full of Mason jars with nitroglycerine in them."

Dex sat up, staring at Henry. "What...what..."

Henry looked back somberly. "It was my first good look at it, remember. It was horrible." He paused deliberately and then said it again: "It was horrible, Dex. It was splattered with blood, some of it seemingly grimed right into the wood. It made me think of...do you remember those joke boxes they used to sell? You'd push a little lever and the box would grind and shake, and then a pale green hand would come out of the top and push the lever back and snap inside again. It made me think of that.

"I pulled it out—oh, so carefully—and I said I wouldn't look down inside, no matter what. But I did, of course. And I saw..." His voice dropped helplessly, seeming to lose all strength. "I saw Wilma's face, Dex. Her *face*."

"Henry, don't—"

"I saw her eyes, looking up at me from that box. Her glazed eyes. I saw something else, too. Something white. A bone, I think. And a black something. Furry. Curled up. Whistling, too. A very low whistle. I think it was sleeping."

"I hooked it out as far as I could, and then I just stood there looking at it, realizing that I couldn't drive knowing that thing could come out at any time...come out and land on the back of my neck. So I started to look around for something—anything—to cover the top of Badlinger's crate.

"I went into the animal husbandry room, and there were a couple of cages big enough to hold the Paella crate, but I couldn't find the goddamned keys. So I went upstairs and I still couldn't find anything. I don't know how long I hunted, but there was this continual feeling of time...slipping away. I was getting a little crazy. Then I happened to poke into that big lecture room at the far end of the hall—"

"Room 6?"

"Yes, I think so. They had been painting the walls. There was a big canvas drop cloth on the floor to catch the splatters. I took it, and then I went back downstairs, and I pushed the Paella crate into Badlinger's crate. Carefully!...you wouldn't believe how carefully I did it, Dex."

When the smaller crate was nested inside the larger, Henry uncinched the straps on the English department dolly and grabbed the end of the drop cloth. It rustled stiffly in the stillness of Amberson Hall's basement. His breathing rustled stiffly as well. And there was that low whistle. He kept waiting for it to pause, to change. It didn't. He had sweated his shirt through; it was plastered to his chest and back.

Moving carefully, refusing to hurry, he wrapped the drop cloth around Badlinger's crate three times, then four, then five. In the dim light shining through from the lab, Badlinger's crate now looked mummified. Holding the seam with one splayed hand, he wrapped first one strap around it, then the other. He cinched them tight and then stood back a moment. He glanced at his watch. It was just past one o'clock. A pulse beat rhythmically at his throat.

Moving forward again, wishing absurdly for a cigarette (he had given them up sixteen years before), he grabbed the dolly, tilted it back, and began pulling it slowly up the stairs.

Outside, the moon watched coldly as he lifted the entire load, dolly and all, into the back of what he had come to think of as Wilma's Jeep—although Wilma had not earned a dime since the day he had married her. It was the biggest lift he had done since he had worked with a moving company in Westbrook as an undergraduate. At the highest point of the lift, a lance of pain seemed to dig into his lower back. And still he slipped it into the back of the Scout as gently as a sleeping baby.

He tried to close the back, but it wouldn't go up; the handle of the dolly stuck out four inches too far. He drove with the tailgate down, and at every bump and pothole, his heart seemed to stutter. His ears felt for the whistle, waiting for it to escalate into a shrill scream and then descend to a guttural howl of fury waiting for the hoarse rip of canvas as teeth and claws pulled their way through it.

And overhead the moon, a mystic silver disc, rode the sky.

"I drove out to Ryder's Quarry," Henry went on. "There was a chain across the head of the road, but I geared the Scout down and got around. I backed right up to the edge of the water. The moon was still up and I could see its reflection way down in the blackness, like a drowned silver dollar. I went around, but it was a long time before I could bring myself to grab the thing. In a very real way, Dex, it was three bodies...the remains of three human beings. And I started wondering...where did they go? I saw Wilma's face, but it looked...God help me, it looked all *flat*, like a Halloween mask. How much of them did it eat, Dex? How much *could* it eat? And I started to understand what you meant about that central axle pulling loose.

"It was still whistling. I could hear it, muffled and faint, through that canvas drop cloth. Then I grabbed it and I *heaved*...I really believe it was do it then or do it never. It came sliding out...and I think maybe it suspected, Dex...because, as the dolly started to tilt down toward the water it started to growl and yammer again...and the canvas started to ripple and bulge... and I yanked it again. I gave it all I had...so much that I almost fell into the damned quarry myself. And it went in. There was a splash...and then it was gone. Except for a few ripples, it was gone. And then the ripples were gone, too."

He fell silent, looking at his hands.

"And you came here," Dex said.

"First I went back to Amberson Hall. Cleaned under the stairs. Picked up all of Wilma's things and put them in her purse again. Picked up the janitor's shoe and his pen and your grad student's glasses. Wilma's purse is still on the seat. I parked the car in our—in my—driveway. On the way there I threw the rest of the stuff in the river."

"And then did what? Walked here?"

"Yes."

"Henry, what if I'd woken up before you got here? Called the police?"

Henry Northrup said simply: "You didn't."

They stared at each other, Dex from his bed, Henry from the chair by the window.

Speaking in tones so soft as to be nearly inaudible, Henry said, "The question is, what happens now? Three people are going to be reported missing soon. There is no one element to connect all three. There are no signs of foul play; I saw to that. Badlinger's crate, the dolly, the painters' drop cloth—those things will be reported missing too, presumably. There will be a search. But the weight of the dolly will carry the crate to the bottom of the quarry, and...there are really no bodies, are there, Dex?"

"No," Dexter Stanley said. "No, I suppose there aren't."

"But what are you going to do, Dex? What are you going to say?"

"Oh, I could tell a tale," Dex said. "And if I told it, I suspect I'd end up in the state mental hospital. Perhaps accused of murdering the janitor and Gereson, if not your wife. No matter how good your cleanup was, a state police forensic unit could find traces of blood on the floor and walls of that laboratory. I believe I'll keep my mouth shut."

"Thank you," Henry said. "Thank you, Dex."

Dex thought of that elusive thing Henry had mentioned—companionship. A little light in the darkness. He thought of playing chess perhaps twice a week instead of once. Perhaps even three times a week...and if the game was not finished by ten, perhaps playing until midnight if neither of them had any early morning classes, instead of having to put the board away (and, as likely as not, Wilma would just "accidentally" knock over the pieces "while dusting," so that the game would have to be started all over again the following Thursday evening). He thought of his friend, at last free of that other species of Tasmanian devil that killed more slowly but just as surely—by heart attack, by stroke, by ulcer, by high blood pressure, yammering and whistling in the ear all the while.

Last of all, he thought of the janitor, casually flicking his quarter, and of the quarter coming down and rolling under the stairs, where a very old horror sat squat and mute, covered with dust and cobwebs, waiting...biding its time...

What had Henry said? The whole thing was almost hellishly perfect.

"No need to thank me, Henry," he said.

Henry stood up. "If you got dressed," he said, "you could run me down to the campus. I could get my MG and go back home and report Wilma missing."

Dex thought about it. Henry was inviting him to cross a nearly invisible line, it seemed, from bystander to accomplice. Did he want to cross that line?

At last he swung his legs out of bed. “All right, Henry.”

“Thank you, Dexter.”

Dex smiled slowly. “That’s all right,” he said. “After all, what are friends for?”

The Last Beautiful Day

Brian James Freeman

Louis Stephenson's work begins with a ringing phone in the middle of the night, but he knows the bad news isn't for him.

This is not the first late night phone call he has received since he put his name on the volunteers list at the hospital. It seemed like a good idea at the time, as morbid as the work sounded, but now he's having serious doubts about his decision.

Louis picks up the phone on the second ring, hoping Melissa wasn't disturbed in the other room. She hasn't been sleeping well these past few months, not since they lost the baby. Insomnia is only one of the symptoms of her emotional instability.

Louis holds the phone but can't open his mouth to answer. His therapist suggested he volunteer for this work. She said it would help him fill the growing void deep inside of him, the emptiness caused by his overwhelming grief, but now Louis thinks maybe the last few months have been the result of God playing a cruel joke on him. First the dead baby inside his wife and now these phone calls.

"Hello," he finally answers. He can hear the sounds of the hospital in the background.

"Mr. Stephenson?" the nurse asks.

"Yes, I'll be there soon," he replies. What else can he say? He has an obligation to fulfill.

Louis slides out of bed and quickly dresses. On his way to the stairs, he opens the door to the nursery, peeks inside.

Melissa is lying on the floor, her head on the tiny pillow her mother made last year. Her hands grip a matching yellow and green blanket that is much too small for her, and she stares back at Louis, unblinking. The Winnie the Pooh nightlight brightens the darkness just enough to keep the plastic moon and stars on the walls glowing.

"I have to go," Louis says. Melissa does not approve of what he is doing and she does not respond. Before he closes the door, he says: "I love you."

Downstairs, Louis retrieves his black briefcase, which is stored in the same place every day, just in case. The first time he received the call, he wasn't properly prepared and he forgot everything he needed in his hurried rush of jumbled nerves, in his fear of where he was headed.

A moment later, he is in the car again and on his way to do what must be done.

Louis parks in a space labeled PHYSICIANS ONLY. He puts a laminated green pass in his front window and then he sits there, his hands on the wheel, his eyes locked on the bushes next to the building but seeing nothing. He is not a doctor, but a nurse gave him the pass when she heard why he was coming to the hospital so often. She cried when she offered the pass to him and he felt he had to accept.

The nurse's name was Linda and she had been with Dr. Green when he brought Louis and Melissa the bad news three months earlier—their baby died in utero, so sorry, better luck next time.

Melissa had remained motionless in the hospital bed while Louis sat in the chair in the corner of the room and stared at the doctor in disbelief, as if everything around him was just a bad dream. Nurse Linda quickly took Melissa's hand when she realized Louis wasn't going to move to comfort his wife.

Then the doctor gave them more bad news: Melissa still needed to deliver their dead baby.

Melissa turned her head toward Dr. Green, the motion slow and deliberate, and quietly said: "Get out."

The doctor did as she asked, but Nurse Linda stayed, saying nothing when there was nothing to be said and answering the few questions they needed to ask.

After the delivery, Melissa remained there on the bed, quiet and distant, staring off into space. When the doctor asked if she'd like to hold the baby just once, she didn't respond. Louis thought this question was horrible, but he later learned it was standard procedure. Everyone reacts differently to discovering they've been harboring a corpse in their womb, his therapist explained, although those were Louis's words, not hers.

In the quiet delivery room, Nurse Linda cleaned the little baby boy, as if he was a real baby and not a dead mass of flesh and tiny bones and miniature, non-working organs. Then the nurse offered him to Melissa again. This time she nodded and Nurse Linda carefully placed the tiny baby into Melissa's arms. For the next half hour, she cried and rocked their little boy while Louis sat in silence, wishing he could do something, anything. Melissa cried, but their baby did not. His name was Kenneth.

Now Louis sits in his car and replays these events like he always does when he arrives at the hospital. The moon is full in the sky to the west, lighting up the world with blue highlights. The city is an empty, lonely place this time of night.

Louis sits behind the wheel, his hand finding the key in the ignition. He could back out of the parking space and leave, driving away before anyone knew he was even here, but what about the woman waiting for him inside the hospital? She needs him to do this thing that disgusts him. He has made a promise.

Louis quickly gets out of the car, slams the door shut, and hurries inside, his black briefcase clutched tightly in his hand. He has to keep moving or he'll lose his nerve.

⁂

The nurse leads Louis by the arm, giving him the little bit of information he'll need. Her name is Heather and they've met before and she thinks why he is here tonight is ghoulish. It's a common reaction. Even Louis agrees.

He cannot get comfortable with the smell of the hospital, no matter how many times he visits. This excessively clean odor is not reassuring. He always forgets exactly how the smell will affect him until he walks in and the emotions strike him in the stomach like a fist. Nothing good has ever come from an encounter with that mix of bleach, disinfectant, peroxide, and floor wax.

Nurse Heather stops short of the patient's room and knocks on the door. Louis isn't surprised to see the room number. He's been here before.

"We're ready," a voice whispers from beyond the threshold.

"Mr. and Mrs. Jones, this is Mr. Stephenson," the nurse says, leading Louis into the room. Although this couple has never met him before, he's become something of a celebrity at the hospital. "He's the gentleman you asked about."

Mrs. Jones is sitting in the bed and cradling her little girl in her arms.

Mr. Jones is sitting in the chair in the corner, his hands held tightly to his face.

"We can take as much time as you need," Louis says, following the script he created with his therapist's help to try to make this easier for everyone, including himself.

He turns and places the briefcase on the table by the door. Nurse Heather stands in the opposite corner of the small room, just in case she is needed. This process doesn't always end well. People often don't know how they'll react to what's about to happen, even though they asked Louis to come to them.

Nurse Heather is not staring at Louis, but he can still feel a coldness radiating from her. She really doesn't approve of what he's doing, but can't she understand he doesn't want to be here? He wouldn't be here if the family didn't ask for him.

Louis opens the briefcase and examines his pristine equipment. He's a professional, after all, no matter how much his emotions might be affecting him.

"What is your little girl's name?" Louis asks while he prepares to do his job.

"Annabelle," the mother replies, wiping her eyes.

Louis stands there, knowing what he has to do, but suddenly unable to move. A cold blade twists in his stomach. Mr. Jones looks up for the first time and Louis can see the anger in the man's bloodshot eyes. Is that rage meant for him? Or maybe for God? Louis has felt a lot of anger toward God this year, so he understands that all too well.

"That's a pretty name," Nurse Heather says to fill the awkward silence. "Mr. Stephenson, would you care to start?"

Louis nods and moves into position next to the bed, raising his camera, taking the first and last family portraits of little Annabelle Jones and her mother.

The dead baby looks like she's merely sleeping, but she is never going to open her eyes or coo or cry or grow-up and run the hundred-meter dash in gym class. Her destination is a tiny coffin the size of a shoebox.

Louis takes the first photo, then the next, and soon he's lost in his work and the coldness drifts away.

Louis is sitting outside the hospital on a bench under a tree, watching the sun peak above the mountains to the east. He sees little dead Annabelle in her mother's arms, so cold and small, and then he leans over and vomits.

Louis wipes his mouth with his sleeve and he sits in the warmth of the sunlight and he wonders what he's doing here. Photographing dead babies makes the void inside him even larger. The process does not make him feel remotely useful or helpful like his therapist suggested it would.

Louis is lost in his thoughts and he doesn't notice Nurse Linda approaching. She spotted him from the parking garage when she arrived to start the day shift.

"I think you're doing a wonderful thing, Mr. Stephenson," she says, stopping just short of where he sits.

Louis looks up, locks his gaze on her soft eyes. He thinks, for just a moment, that it's almost like she was able to read his mind from across the parking lot.

"My wife and some of your coworkers don't agree," he replies. "I'm not sure why I'm even here."

"You're giving these families something special, Mr. Stephenson. They may not realize it today, but in six months, when the worst of the grief is over, they're going to want to thank you. You've given them something more powerful than a stillborn birth certificate. You've given them proof that their love wasn't in vain. Don't you wish you had a photo of Kenneth?"

Louis nods and lowers his gaze, wishing her away. He has found it's easier to agree with people when he doesn't really know what to say. If he agrees, hopefully they'll leave him alone.

"Mr. Stephenson, you should go home and see Melissa. It's going to be a beautiful day."

Nurse Linda pats him on the shoulder and walks inside where she'll be working with all of the living babies today and tomorrow and the day after that.

Louis sits on the bench and watches people come and go. Eventually he heads home to try to comfort his wife and convince her to come outside and sit in the sunlight with him, but as he drives, Louis can't help but wonder what Nurse Linda meant. It may be a beautiful day in the world where she resides, the one where most of the babies survive, but he lives in the world where the babies always die.

It's never going to be a beautiful day for Louis, not as long as the phone keeps ringing in the middle of the night and he keeps traveling to the hospital with his camera. Not as long as little Kenneth keeps dying again and again, every week, every month, for the rest of Louis's life.

Cobwebs

Kealan Patrick Burke

I began to be forgotten on a dawn no different than any other I'd seen during the past few years of my incarceration at Spring Grace Retirement Home. The ever-present burning ache in my bones was no better or worse. The sheets were still too tight, the pillow too lumpy, the room a little too cold. Shadows squatted in the corners where they had no business squatting, but like silent drunks, were too harmless to justify ousting. Pins and needles made hornet-filled trees of my legs. The radiator gave its little metallic *tick-tick-tack,* and belched liquidly. Even the light, splintered by the Venetian blinds to form horizontal bars of cold fire on the puke-green wall, looked the same.

But today something *was* different. When I moved my hand down over my face, over features that had aged badly without my consent and without my noticing, the very ordinary caul of post-slumber confusion clung to the tips of my fingers, and didn't let go as I brought them up for inspection.

Like the memory of old kisses, there was a cobweb stretched across my mouth, violin-string skeins of it stretching out to my fingertips as if waiting for my horrified cry to play them. But I didn't utter a sound, even when I probed the expanse of the web with my tongue and it came away coated in sour-tasting dust. I sat up, not without effort, and beat and pulled and scratched somewhat hysterically at my mouth until all that remained of the cobweb hung in dark brownish clumps from my fingers. *Steady, Al.* My heart was beating fast enough to give me pause, to distract me from the origin of my panic. *Calm down, it's okay, it's all right,* I told myself and waited for the voltage of fear to ebb away. *It's okay.* I looked up at the ceiling. There were cracks in the plaster and cobwebs in the corners, but none on the unremarkable light shade. Of course, there wouldn't be, for it was the obvious suspect, the inanimate villain of the piece, who had shed its cotton candy cobweb skin onto my face as I'd slept.

Grimacing, I got up, every joint and muscle firing off a round of pain, and after a careful inspection of the terrycloth for more invasive gossamer threads, crept into the robe. The smell of disinfectant, nauseatingly familiar, reached me before I opened the door, before I'd cinched the belt on my robe. The smell is meant to hide the odors of age, sickness and death, of hopelessness, but for those of us who call this place a home, it is a constant reminder that we are the creatures from which the terrible stench originates, things better hidden away so the world can be spared the inconvenience of looking at us and seeing its future.

When I got to the lounge after the usual ritual of ignoring the staff's automated cheer, and waiting for mail that wasn't there, I found my friend The Cowboy's chair was empty, and he hadn't made his move. The chess pieces were as we'd left them the evening before. The only other soul in the room was Doris Randle, who had at least been capable of a smile when she'd first been admitted, but now gaped dumbly at me as a string of drool tried to connect the corner of her mouth to her paisley-patterned bosom. Two strokes had made an empty vessel of her. It was my contention another would kill her.

"Morning Doris," I said, one hand absently moving to my mouth to be sure no trace of the cobweb remained, or maybe I feared her drooling was contagious.

She stared without seeing me.

"You know him?" she muttered, and I, mistakenly assuming she was talking about The Cowboy, almost celebrated her words as the most coherent anyone had heard from her in months. But then "The kid?" she continued, and I let out a long low sigh. "The one in the classroom? They let the little bastard loose with his crayons. They asked him to color the heart." Her eyes grew more distant, dropped away from me to the chess set. "He didn't stay inside the lines."

I followed her gaze. Looked at the chair. It shouldn't have been empty. It never was at this time of day. Meeting here for our morning chess and banter was about the only ritual either of us had, and one we had come to depend on to help preserve our wits in a place designed, it seemed, to steal them. Then, as I stared at the cheap plastic-backed chair, envisioning The Cowboy with his small blue eyes, salt-and-pepper hair, and grizzled chin, the light through the room's single window changed, only slightly, but enough to make me think it should have been snowing outside. It was that kind of light. Cold and blue. It diffused the gnarled and sad shadow of the eucalyptus in the planter on the sill, blurring it, making the outthrust limbs look like the desperate arms of one of my fellow inmates, clambering for the sleeve of someone who might care.

I wanted to ask Doris if she had noticed the peculiar change in the room, but knew she wouldn't answer, at least not coherently. So, "You take care now," I told her, and left before she was able to coax her gaze back to where I'd been standing. A man could get lost if he spent too long wading through the overgrowth in her field of vision.

Back in the hall I grabbed the first nurse unfortunate enough to cross my path, and asked her where The Cowboy was. But even before that loathsome look of practiced sympathy crossed Nurse Stanford's taut face, I knew.

"He went peacefully," she said. "In his sleep. You must have been close."

It struck me as odd that she didn't know that. There wasn't enough camaraderie among the withered souls in Spring Grace for our friendship to have gone unnoticed. I thought of the slight chill I'd felt in the lounge, the changing of the light. Now it seemed like an omen. I almost smiled. The Cowboy would have been smugly satisfied to know that his passing had knocked askew some portion of the universe, however briefly.

"Is everything all right, Mr. Ross?"

"Yes, why?"

"No particular reason."

Then why ask? I thought, but said instead, "I'm fine. Thank you." I started to move away, then stopped and looked back. Nurse Stanford hadn't moved. She was still standing there, hands clasped matron-like beneath her bosom.

"Can you please," I said, "if it isn't too much trouble—send someone in to remove the cobwebs from my room?"

She looked momentarily confused by the request. I didn't wait for her answer. Instead I headed back to my room, and was relieved to find the light hadn't changed in my sanctuary.

I sat on the edge of the bed for a while, hands folded in my lap, feeling unpleasantly hollow deep in my chest and alarmingly near tears. Worse, I couldn't tell how much of my burgeoning sorrow was for The Cowboy, and how much was a result of the selfish realization that I was now well and truly alone.

My last remaining friend was gone.

I wondered if he had really gone quietly into the sunset, or if, before they stowed him in the back of that quiet ambulance, they'd had to pause to remove the cobwebs from his lips.

2

Noon brought thoughts of a towheaded kid who'd loved magic. A kid who used to usher his Mom and me into the living room, knowing it would mean he'd get to stay up a little later than usual. He wore a top hat and a cape. He even had the white gloves and the dramatic flourish the costume seemed to instill in whoever wore it. Those gloves cut the air above a red velvet tablecloth he'd spread across a narrow workbench. Props were arranged atop that crimson surface, sleeves shirked back, face impassive but not entirely hiding the look, the barely contained smirk that told us all we were going to be astounded and amazed, whether we believed in him or not.

Beneath the cobwebs Marcia was forever vowing to remove, little Joey called upon his carefully practiced powers of prestidigitation to stun us all, and while many of his tricks were transparent numbers, more often than not, he succeeded.

But the years robbed him of magic and the need to impress. They robbed us all of a lot of things.

He still calls from time to time, but only to assuage his guilt, and to remind himself I'm still there.

Sometimes, I don't wait for his concern to lead him.

After lunch I found myself in the hallway, lamenting my choice of the mushy Salisbury steak and wishing I had some gum, or a mint—anything to rid my palate of the noxious taste. I stepped up to the payphone after patiently listening to Zach Greenburg cursing at his daughter for fifteen minutes.

The earpiece was unpleasantly moist as I listened to the connection worming its way from Ohio to Colorado.

On the third ring, Joey answered.

"Dad? Jesus, how've you been?"

"Not good enough for you to start calling me Jesus."

His laugh was strained, as always. "Nice to hear that place hasn't knocked the wit out of you."

"Not for the want of trying."

"Right."

The stretches of silence grow longer every time we talk, as we both search for something agreeable to say. It has become like trying to find change in a phone booth's coin return. Sometimes you get lucky; more often you don't.

"So how's the weather there?" he asked.

"Sunny." *Aside from a brief change to tell me my friend had died.*

"Nice. It's cold as hell down here."

"I'd still rather be there than here. The idea of stocking up wood excites the hell out of me. Better than sitting in my room waiting for something interesting to happen."

"Yeah." Pause. The rustle of papers in the background. *Multitasking.* "It was Drew's birthday last weekend. Wish you could have been here."

"I didn't know." And in truth, resented the implication in his voice that I should have. "What is he now, nine?"

"Eleven."

I whistled.

"I've been meaning to get up there to see you, you know?"

I didn't know, but as easy—and in truth, pleasurable—as it would have been to say so, I resisted and mumbled affirmation into the phone.

"But it's a long haul, Dad. Especially with Kathy working such long hours. If she takes time off now it'll look bad. She's still in training, did I tell you that?"

"No." Nor did I know what she was in training *for.*

"Yeah. If she took time off, it'd set her back, and she's busted her hump long enough."

"Why not come up here by yourself? Get me out of this dump for a night and tie one on with your old man? Like we did back in—"

"Dad?"

"What?"

"Dad? Yeah. Can you hold on, just a sec? I got a call coming in that I need to take. Seriously. Stay with me OK? I promise...just a sec."

"All r—"

An abrupt click and the phone became a conch shell, whispering to me in the voice of my own blood.

I waited ten minutes, maybe a little less, certainly no more, before I hung up.

He didn't call back, and I knew better than to wait.

3

That Friday, our prison was invaded by a group of high school students, led by a petite raven-haired and bespectacled teacher who seemed convinced she could alter the world and, more specifically, the universes of her charges, with frantic gesticulation and a series of high-pitched yelps. They orbited around her like lazily drifting planets until she meted out their destinations and observed them as they spun off into the hall. While she directed the flow of angst-ridden traffic, we stared with the same kind of fascination a tired dog uses to watch birds eating the crumbs from his bowl.

"Joseph Henner," the teacher wailed. "I know that's not a lighter I just saw in your hand. Make your way to Mr. Ross's room. Number 18; end of the hall. Remember why we're here."

Why we're here. I was still waiting for someone to let *me* in on that little secret. I hurried back to my room.

Henner skulked in a few moments later. He was a scrawny acne-riddled teen dressed in a black trench-coat, scuffed Doc Martens and a T-shirt that displayed a skull-headed man wielding a knife beneath the legend: *We All Gotta Go Sometime. Some of Us Sooner Than Others.*

True enough, I thought.

"What school do you go to?" I asked him, when it became painfully clear he wasn't going to initiate the conversation.

"Crosby High."

A quip about the absence of Stills and Nash from the name rose in my mind like an image in a photographer's developer tray, but I let it pass. Any hope was ludicrous that the sullen mass of baggy clothes and attitude before me would have even the slightest idea what I was referring to.

"I'm Joe," he said.

"Alfred Ross."

"Cool." He didn't look at me. "So, do you, like, stay here all the time?"

"Yes."

"That blows. Doesn't it get boring?"

"Absolutely."

"I'd go nuts."

"Some of us have."

"You got a TV?"

"Sure, in the lounge. And my friend and I play chess." I caught myself too late and felt my polite smile fade. "Used to play chess."

"He die?"

"Yes. Just last night as a matter of fact."

"How?"

Only then, only in that very instant, with the rest home filled with the alien sound of youthful laughter and this morose kid inspecting my room and talking about death like it was an old television show he only vaguely remembered, did I realize I didn't know how The Cowboy had died. *In his sleep,* Nurse Stanford had said, and it had been enough at the time. It wasn't enough now.

Cobwebs got his heart.

"Old age," I said, at last, and knew it wasn't a lie.

"Bummer."

"Yeah. It is. He was a good friend."

"So..." he began as he looked around my room, at the bare picture-less walls and the half-full glass of water sitting on my nightstand, "How long you been here?" It sounded like something he was reading from a cue card, and all the while he avoided looking at me. Maybe he was afraid he'd see a vision of himself in sixty years.

I could have assured him that I'm nobody's future.

"Coming up on six years."

"Long time."

"Feels longer," I said, and that was the God's honest truth. It felt like the tail end of a life sentence.

The kid sighed. His patience wasn't going to hold out much longer, and I couldn't really blame him. At his age humoring old folks would have been way down at the bottom of my priority list too.

At length his gaze settled on the only picture in my room, the grainy, washed-out photograph of Meredith on the windowsill.

"Your wife?"

"Ex."

"Still alive?"

"Yes, and cavorting with the pool boys in Florida, I imagine."

He asked an odd question then, one that, given his demeanor, I'd never have expected to hear from him: "You still love her?" It was also the only question he asked during our short time together that sounded as if the answer mattered to him.

Why, I'd never know.

"Yes. She's my biggest regret. Letting her go, that is."

"Then why did you?"

"I didn't have much of a say in the matter."

He nodded, ran a finger over the cheap faux-gold frame, and I knew I'd lost whatever spark of interest had flared in him. "You have any war stories?"

"No, I never fought in any wars. Do you?"

"Do I what?"

"Have any war stories."

He jammed his hands into his pockets. "Dude...I'm in high school."

"Isn't that a type of battlefield?"

Shrug. "Whatever."

Outcast, I thought. *Probably slouches in the corners at school trying to avoid trouble, rock music blasting in his ears, then goes home and does the same there, avoids life as much as possible. Hides in his shell.*

I felt sorry for him until I realized my life wasn't a whole lot different. Both of us were in cages of different design, but cages all the same.

"How come you've only got one picture?"

"I have more. I keep them under the bed. Would you like to see them?" Only after the words were out of my mouth did I realize how creepy they sounded. I might as well have propositioned the poor kid. *Hey boy, want some candy?* Inwardly, I groaned.

"Nah. Some other time."

"We don't have to talk, y'know," I told him. "You can just tell your teacher we did."

"Suits me," he said without hesitation, and produced from his trench coat pocket a pair of earphones so small I wondered if he'd ever had to reel them out of his inner ear. A small white rectangle with silver buttons followed and he jabbed at it with a nicotine-stained forefinger. The earphones began to hiss.

It felt wrong not to say something else, for the boy looked lost, crumpled up inside himself, desperate perhaps, the true emotion in his eyes obscured by the steam from the anger at the core of him. Maybe I should have been firm instead of grandfatherly. Maybe I should have told him to sit up straight and tell me what his problem was, to have some respect for his elders. Maybe that's what he was missing in his life, someone who looked like they gave enough of a damn to listen to what he had to say. But by the time enlightenment chased away the fog in my brain, Henner had already plugged his ears and thumbed up the volume on his odd-looking player.

"Later, man," he said as he stood up and headed for the door, the angry wasp sound of the music trailing behind him.

"What will happen then?" I murmured as he stepped out into the hall, into the river of students and moved upstream against the current.

I wondered how long it would take for him to erase me and my sad little room with its single picture from his mind.

There was a headcount in the hall sometime later, a chorus of bored responses, and then the roar of a bus engine signaled the departure of youthful laughter from Spring Grace. I trudged to the lounge, took my usual seat at the small Formica table The Cowboy and I always shared. The chess set was still there, but someone had prematurely ended our game and set up the pieces for a new one.

"Ron," I called to a tall thin man in a chenille robe, who was sitting in a worn armchair and grumbling at the television. "Ron!" His shock of white hair rose above the back of the armchair like stuffing.

He looked over his shoulder, his silver stubble scratching against the robe, and gaped fish-like at me through bifocal lenses. "*What* for God's sake?"

"You play chess?"

"What?"

I resisted the urge to scream at him. "Chess. Do you play it?"

"Like checkers, isn't it?"

"No. Not really."

"Then, no," he said, and turned back to his show. "I don't."

No one else present in the lounge did either, and by the time I'd put the question to them all, I didn't feel much like playing anymore. Besides, when The Cowboy and I had played, it hadn't really been about the game.

"He could never do clouds." Doris was sitting by the window, staring out, her eyes like pale gems in the deep pockets of a thief. "They were always dark and crooked, even when the sky was right. Liked to draw the spiders. Made them look like small men crouching in the corners."

"Sounds like a real talented boy," I told her, but knew I was talking to myself. Still, it made me curious, as it always did, to know who it was that had ownership of such a prized lot in her brain that not even her strokes could turn it fallow, or salt the earth of recollection. Whoever it was, whether real or fantasy, living or dead, they would not truly die until she did. And for that, I envied them.

⁂

Summer tired of its sun and dance routine, and moved on. The leaves died and the voice of the wind grew hollow, playing discordant music through the eaves of Spring Grace. The sense of isolation deepened. People stayed in their houses, and we in our rooms. A few more of my neighbors passed away. Some in their sleep; some screaming, while people whispered in the hall. Others were ferried away in the night in the quiet ambulances and never seen again. I told myself they'd escaped, been granted a stay of execution and were enjoying their freedom somewhere warm, but inside I knew better. Nobody ever leaves this place, though we talk about it all the time. *The door's right there,* we'd say, *and no one would even notice if we walked straight outta here.* And yet we never do. In times of excitement, that door looks like the door to Heaven. More often, it looks like the opposite.

We don't know what's out there anymore, you see. At some point none of us can remember, we stepped off the train and it carried on without us. Years have passed, been stolen while we've slept, and beyond our windows the world has changed. The light has changed.

It's safer here, even if it means we have to endure the ghosts of our pasts, the specters of regret, with nary a distraction to keep us sane. It's safer here because the future is guaranteed. There are no surprises left for us within these walls. You pass the time. You smile at kindred spirits in the hall. Maybe one weekend you luck out and end up getting your hands on the remote control before anyone else, maybe get to watch a Western or an old MGM musical. And at night, in bed, you say a small urgent prayer to a God you don't believe in that you'll wake in the morning still in possession of all those things that have made you what you are. That you won't find yourself dazed and drooling in a chair next to Doris Randle, with the needle in your mind stuck in a groove. But most of all, you pray that someone out there still remembers you, still thinks about you every now and then...still loves you, because there isn't a dark memory or shard of guilt inside that terrifies you as much as the idea of being forgotten. *Please,* you whisper, knowing tonight might be the night that quiet ambulance comes for you, its brakes squeaking softly as it pulls up to the curb. *Please...remember me.*

And as sleep comes, you remember *them,* and all the things you did wrong that led you to this place, this desert island forever threatened by the encroaching tide of time and regret. You weep, and in the morning, the cobwebs on your face are larger, denser than before.

⁂

"We did clean your room, Mr. Ross. I sent one of the orderlies in there yesterday while you were having dinner."

"Then they did a sloppy job."

"Are you feeling all right? You look pale. Maybe I should—"

"I'm fine. I need to use the phone. Please have someone go over my room again."

"Of course."

⁂

He didn't mention the last call. I doubted he even remembered it.

"Dad? Great news. I sold a screenplay to Bob Garrison at New Line."

"New Line? What's that, like the fishing channel?"

A chuckle. "It's a Hollywood film company. We're talking *big* time here."

"I see, well congratulations then."

"You don't sound impressed."

My fingers tightened on the phone. I looked over my shoulder and saw Zach Greenburg scowling at me, oxygen mask gripped tightly in one liver-spotted hand. His rheumy eyes radiated impatience. He was no doubt anxious to call his daughter for her bi-weekly lecture. I turned back to the phone.

"It's not that, it's…why haven't you been in touch?"

"I tried a few times. No one answered."

It was a lie, a poor one, and it hollowed me out like a Jack o' Lantern. The phone doesn't ring enough in Spring Grace for it to ever go unanswered. But I accepted it because the alternatives were no better. What did I want to hear? *Dad, I forgot. Sorry.* No, I would take the lie. A starving man can't afford to be choosy about the quality of meat he's given. Unless it's Salisbury steak.

"Okay," I said. "Any plans to come see me?"

"Sure, we'll work something out."

"It's been forever."

"It has. Dad, I'll get up there, I promise. This new deal will mean I'll have to travel to New York now and then. I can stop in to see you on the way back."

"That would be nice. You should bring Kathy and Drew along too."

A sigh. "Maybe. We'll see."

"Is everything all right with you guys?"

"It's fine. You'll see us soon, I promise."

Behind me, Zach shuffled his feet.

"Listen Joey, I have to get going. There's a queue for the phone forming here."

"Okay Dad. Thanks for calling. It's always good to hear from you."

"You too. Stay in touch, will you? Call anytime. It's not like I'm busy around here."

"Will do."

"Give my love to my grandson."

"Bye Dad."

I hung up and as fast as his stiff joints would allow, Zach was in my face, his breath like sour milk, hooked nose inches from mine. "How do you do that?"

I raised my hands, not to placate him, but to remind him there was such a thing as personal space and that he was invading mine. "Do what?"

"Make calls without using money? There a trick to it?"

I looked over my shoulder at the phone, as if the answer to his odd question might be written somewhere there. It was a basic model payphone, silver, with square touchtone buttons. "Collect," I told him after a moment of thought. "Dial zero first, then the number."

He considered this, then nodded sharply. "Wish someone had told me that when I first got here. I've been stealin' nickels for six years." His laugh turned into a coughing fit, then a series of strangled gasps. I waited a moment to be sure he wasn't going to end up dropping dead right there, then left him, red-faced and wheezing, but well enough to complain about the contaminants "those goddamned witches" were putting in his oxygen. After poking my head into my room to ensure the nurse had made good on her vow to have the cobwebs removed (she had), I stared down at my slippers as they traced the same old route back to the lounge.

There could be grass under there, I thought, with a faint smile, *gravel or macadam. I'm the only thing keeping me here. There are plenty of people out there who I can get to know. People who would think of me as a friend, maybe, or a kindly neighbor. People who'd remember me.* And as I passed the glass doors of the main entrance and ignored the pleasant inquiry from the pretty young nurse at the station, my smile grew.

Elm trees lined the long straight path from the door to the street, which in turn led into town. A couple of dozen steps and I could hitch a ride. A couple of steps; a short walk. That was all. Anyone could make it. *I* could make it. Abruptly I was assailed by memories from my youth: of walking barefoot through the grass with my best friend Rusty O' Connor, as oblivious to the mosquitoes as I was to the nurse who spoke to me as if I'd magically reverted to the age represented in the memory. Fishing poles held by our sides, the backs of our necks reddened by the glaring sun, laughing our fool heads off at silly things as we headed for Myers Pond and the promise of catfish we would never catch. The rumble and scrape of trains beyond the pond; the honk of jaybirds warning their brethren of our approach; the low buzz of dragonflies beating us to the shimmering water…

"Mr. Ross?"

A cloud darkened the sun of memory; the color faded, as did the smile it had brought to my face. Out there lay the road, but where did the road lead? To a new life or an overdue death? Rusty had followed a path in his dotage that had erased him from the earth, never to be seen again, nothing but a cryptic message left behind to let his wife know he wouldn't be coming back. Did he choose the wrong road? Did he stand on a similar threshold, lured by the promise of something better? Of a few more years of adventure?

"Mr. Ross? Is everything all right?"

Did he go somewhere he thought he'd be remembered?

"I'm fine," I said curtly, sensing the nurse moving around the desk toward me.

Outside, beyond the glass that might as well have been an iron gate, the elm trees nodded slightly in the breeze. They almost seemed to whisper, *Foolish old man. Remember your place.*

I moved on, watching my feet tread nothing but worn tile, just like yesterday, and a thousand days before it.

Do a trick for me, Joey, I thought, with tears in my throat. *Make me vanish. I'd rather be where you are.*

❖

The man seated at the chess set looked out of place in the lounge. He was dressed like a salesman, from his paisley blazer and yellow shirt, right down to his white socks and worn leather loafers. Beneath a thick head of curly black hair, equally thick eyebrows were knitted in concentration over a pair of silver-rimmed spectacles. His long oddly delicate and perfectly manicured fingers floated above the head of the unsuspecting black queen.

I sat down with an audible sigh, glad to be relieved of my own weight for a while. "Doctor."

He looked up and beamed. "Mr. Ross. How are we this morning?"

"Tired."

As per usual, Ron had commandeered the television and seemed hypnotized by the gymnastic bounce of a female prizewinner's breasts on some game show. I couldn't blame him really. They were far from proportionate, given the woman's slight build.

"Are you still taking your medication?"

I nodded, turning my attention to Doris. She sat in her preferred spot by the window, head tilted as if asleep, but her eyes were still open. She looked more distant than ever. While Ron gaped at his buxom contestant, I found myself watching Doris's chest to be sure she was still breathing.

"She's okay," Doctor Rhodes said.

"Good." I turned to face the board. "Do you play?"

"Not since high school I'm afraid."

"Good enough. It'll still put you leagues above anyone else in here."

He looked at me over the rims of his spectacles. "Except you."

"Except me."

"Wonderful."

I studied the white ranks before me. "The AMA relaxing their dress code?" I nodded pointedly at his atrocious suit.

He smiled and folded his arms. "It's my day off."

"And you're spending it here?"

He shrugged and blew out a breath. "Well, I've been so busy with administrative work lately, I thought it the perfect opportunity to come in and see how people were doing."

I smirked at him and advanced a pawn. "That's very sad, Doc."

"Not at all," he protested. "When was the last chance you and I had a chance to shoot the breeze?"

He copied my move, but I didn't watch it. I was too busy watching him, trying to read his face, but his pleasant expression was an effective shield.

"I hate to disappoint you," I said, moving my bishop into the space the pawn had vacated. "But I very much doubt anything of any consequence has occurred since we last spoke."

Again he copied my move. "Is that so?" He was moving toward a point and his refusal to make it was starting to annoy me, but not nearly as much as the sensation that unseen hands were slowly painting a target on my head.

"I get the feeling you don't agree."

He smiled warmly and flapped a hand at me. "Ah, it's nothing."

"Then why are you here?"

"Well..." He looked around the room, his gaze lingering on Doris longer than it had on any of the other occupants, until finally his eyes met mine. "I can't let even the most innocuous of incidences go unquestioned around here, Alfred, you can understand that. The risk is too high to just pass it off as the vagaries of old age."

My fingers had settled on the bishop. Now they released it, unmoved.

Rhodes seemed to be searching for the right words to say what he'd come to say, and I willed him to spit them out. At length, he did.

"Nurse Stanford mentioned some weeks ago that you were shaken up by what happened to Harold Wayne—The Cowboy—is that right?"

"I was." I frowned at him, saw uncertainty flicker across his face. My unease increased. "Why? Does that make me cause for concern? A special case? He was my friend. One of the few I have...I *had* in here. Naturally losing him would shake me up, just as it would anyone else." I became aware that my voice had risen above conversational level and I was being needlessly defensive. Ron's chair creaked as he finally looked away from the game show and peered at us. Some of the men at a card table in the corner paused to watch. I dismissed them all with a disgusted wave of my hand and glared at Rhodes. "Why? And why are you looking at me like that?"

He clasped his hands together over the chessboard. "I'm worried about you, and I don't think you're telling me the truth about you taking your pills."

"Of course I am. I said I was, didn't I? And what are you worried about me for anyway?"

"I'm worried, Alfred, because The Cowboy died over four years ago."

I stared at him. He stared back, the concern in his eyes maddening. Insulting.

"You *know* that," he said in a low voice as he reached across the table, his sleeve scattering the pieces as he tried to take my hand. I pulled away from him.

"Why would you say that?"

"Because it's the truth. A truth you know, and have known for years. He died in his sleep on Christmas Eve. You were the one who found him, remember? It was snowing like crazy outside. Worst snowstorm we'd had in decades."

Cold blue light, a voice tried to insist but I slammed the door shut on it, just as I intended to slam the door shut on Rhodes and his lies. "Why are you...?" I shook my head. "I won't tolerate this. Not from you, or anyone else. You have no right."

"Alfred, listen..."

"No." I rose and winced as a bolt of pain slammed into my right knee. I braced a hand on the chair to steady myself. "I don't know what it is you're trying to accomplish with this madness, but I won't sit here and listen to it. It's one of the few privileges I have left."

I began to hobble toward the door, heard the sound of chair legs scraping against the floor as Rhodes stood.

Go, Alfred, I told myself, my arms and legs trembling so bad I was afraid I wouldn't make it to the door, *Go before he tells you the rest. Go before he tells you what happened to—*

I froze.

The room itself seemed to send waves of cold air at me, chilling my back through my shirt while heat blossomed in my chest, stealing my breath. Tears welled in my eyes. Unseen fingers squeezed my throat.

I will not hear this. I will not.

The sound of rubber soles slapping against tile and all of a sudden Nurse Stanford was standing in the doorway, blocking my way.

Despite the pain that drilled through me from the top of my skull down into my chest, I almost laughed, though on some distant level I doubted I had the strength. *It's an intervention.*

"You've been using the phone," Rhodes said, and his voice was close, cautious. "Can I ask who you've been calling?"

"My..." My breath burned in my throat. "...Son."

"Alfred...the box beneath your bed..."

"Don't touch it."

"No one has."

"Then...how do you know?"

The cheers from the television were muted. The compassion on Nurse Stanford's face made me want to throttle her, but even if I had the guts to attempt such a thing, my arms refused to move. I felt a tear trickle down my cheek.

"How do I know *what,* Alfred?" He moved to stand in front of me, but his shadow was a second too slow in following.

The fluorescent lights covered my eyes with frost as I felt the strength drain from my limbs. *I'm going to fall and they won't catch me,* I thought, pure terror surging up through me from a bottomless pit in my stomach. *I'll hit my head and die right here in this awful room with all these people here staring at—*

My mind buzzed, chased away the pain, the thought, the awareness. I turned, intending to run, driven by one last automatic impulse to flee from these insane people—

—and fell forward, tried to think my arms into action, but they stayed by my sides. I toppled like the pawns beneath the Doctor's sleeve.

A heart attack, the man in the quiet ambulance told me. *But you'll be fine,* he said.

I know different.

I've lost them all. Their faces only exist now beneath my bed, in the box that has been substituting for memory. Black and white photographs, snapshots, obituaries, and letters from long-silenced voices I have been hearing on the phone.

Doctor Rhodes stopped by in the beginning, to check on me, but as time went by his commitment to the residents at Spring Grace caused his visits to become infrequent. I haven't seen him in almost a month. I have a new doctor now. New nurses, whose faces aren't so sharp or smiles as false. I have a new room.

It has no window.

This frightens me. Because there will come a night when the small men crouching in the corners come out, dancing like lunatics, and maybe one of those small men will be wearing white gloves, and his hands will cut the air above a red velvet tablecloth, and he'll do one last magic trick for me. He'll make endless veils of cobwebs fall from the ceiling and they'll land like muslin on my face. Over and over and over again until my breath stops coming and my heart stops beating. He'll hide me as I have hidden him for so long.

But not yet. I am not done yet.

Not tonight.

There is a sullen high school boy out there who still might remember. There is a sour old man with an oxygen mask back at Spring Grace, who is thankful he no longer has to wait in line. There is a drooling woman who speaks in riddles, who has a golden field in her mind where the people she has known still run.

Maybe I'm there.

Maybe she remembers.

Maybe.

The Old Ways

Norman Prentiss

"Maybe your husband should buy this stuff himself."

Lisa tried not to bristle at the clerk's suggestion. She'd done fine on her own so far, her orange cart already half-filled with cans of wood stain and indoor-outdoor paints, brushes, replacement knobs and handles, screws and nails and tacks and duct tape. Twice already this short, thin teenager had asked if she needed help. He wore a store apron he'd probably wriggled into five minutes after a bell signaled the end of sixth-period social studies.

She held a chip of broken shingle to check it against display samples. "I'm finding what I need, thank you." Lisa didn't add: *I'm more than twice your age.* Or, *This isn't the first hardware store I've stepped foot in, kiddo.*

"Since he'll be doing the work and all," the clerk said, "your husband would know better what supplies to get."

No, Andy was good with words. If you could charm a hundred bucks from a hammer or talk a chisel into a year-long contract, he'd be good with tools, too. More likely, he'd smash his thumb, or twist crooked screws into the wrong hole.

Part of their agreement, when Andy inherited his mother's house, was that Lisa wouldn't find a job right away. Instead, she'd spend days fixing up the place, making the improvements his mother had refused to bother with, as if the woman knew her dilapidated house—mildewed and drafty, paint peeling, shingles sliding off the roof—wouldn't dare fall apart before she did.

His mother's town, Centreville, Maryland, had always seemed behind-the-times to her, an old-fashioned tourist stop with antique stores, a one-room post office, and a drug store with a soda fountain in back. More like a tourist *pause* than a stop, since people raced through Centreville during summer months, frustrated after Bay Bridge slow-downs and anxious to finish the 95 miles remaining before the crowded beaches of Ocean City. Gas and go, with the emphasis on go.

People who stayed in Centreville had stayed forever, like their families had, comfortable with the old ways, like porch-sitting and gossip and minimum wage, and maybe a little prejudice and chauvinism for good measure. Andy had argued the town wouldn't be as backwards as they feared. Television brought modern opinions into the most isolated homes, and the Internet made the world even smaller. What they couldn't find locally, they'd be able to order online: supplies *and* culture, as needed. Hell, Centreville got its own Home Depot last year, and a Blockbuster Video. And really, with the economy the way it was, who could afford to turn down a free house?

Yeah, he'd sold it to her.

So here she stood, her hand on a cardboard carton of roof shingles, the high shelf easily within her reach, and the clerk got all flustered, practically shouted, "Let me get that for you, ma'am." The shelf was too high for *him,* but the little guy brushed her aside, stood on tiptoes and stretched, red faced. The box teetered blind over his head for a perilous moment, then he swung it out and down from the shelf, and nearly heaved it into her cart.

"There you go, ma'am." He smiled like he'd rescued her from a dragon.

Lisa was furious that someone this young held such outdated opinions. She expected such foolishness from her neighbors at Sunrise Apartments, the senior community across the street from their new home. In that generation, gender roles were steadfast, ideas of strong breadwinning men and helpless women etched into their fossil brains. But young people should be more open. She wondered what they were teaching this boy at school.

Lisa had more things on her shopping list, but she decided she'd had enough for the day and headed for the checkout. Against her will, she let the boy load her purchases into her car.

⁂

She used a paint-scraper to chip away at gunk that encrusted the rain gutters around the perimeter of the roof. Lisa fought with the stubborn, sun-dried substance of leaves and dirt and twigs, all baked into a burnt clay. It was a slow process: climbing the ladder, scraping at the layers of grime within reach, then climbing down to reposition the ladder against the house for the next segment.

A calm April wind cooled her forehead as she worked, and music helped relieve the tedium. Her radio was set to 98 ROCK, a Baltimore station—a faint connection to the city they recently abandoned. The music thumped heavy in her headphones, bass rhythm resonating through her body and adding energy to her arm as she chipped at crusted grime. Drum beats seemed to vibrate through the aluminum ladder, like footsteps.

Something tapped her heel. She was so startled, she almost lost her balance.

Lisa turned her head and looked down. An older man with a surprisingly muscular torso had climbed up the ladder beneath her, his eyes monstrous behind thick round spectacles. He held firm to the ladder with one arm, and waved the other wildly.

She screamed, and instinctively clutched her paint-scraper like a weapon. She tensed, ready to scramble up onto the roof to escape him.

The old man clawed at the air with his free arm. He shook his round, gray-bald head; it was close enough for her to kick at it. The man's lips moved, but Lisa couldn't hear him over the radio.

The loud music—that would explain why he'd seemed to sneak up on her. She pulled off her head-phones.

"Get down," the man said. "Get down from there." She heard urgency in his raspy voice, not malice. His words conveyed a warning, and Lisa wondered if there was a problem with the ladder, or if part of the roof was crumbling away.

"You shouldn't be doing this," he said. "Come down, and I'll do it for you."

Lisa couldn't figure out what he was talking about.

"Leave the tool there," he said, like a policeman asking a suspect to drop the handgun. "I'll get it, and finish up for you."

Now Lisa stifled a laugh. This old man had frightened her for a minute there, she had to admit, but only because he'd startled her. She realized now that he was at least seventy years old, and what she'd seen as a muscular torso was an illusion created by an out-of-season, down-filled jacket. He was already out of breath from his short climb and frantic arm waving: he looked like he'd barely make it up the ladder again, let alone have strength to scrape the gutters clean.

"I'm perfectly fine." Because the man was below her, and probably hard of hearing, Lisa shouted. "I know what I'm doing." Then she smiled, doing her best to hide the irritation. Honestly, was he *that* set in his ways? He couldn't imagine a woman doing any kind of physical labor—and so she needed a feeble old man to help her? Ridiculous.

He squinted his magnified eyes, and for a brief instant Lisa got the uneasy feeling he had read her thoughts. Then the old man's mouth twisted into a grimace—an awful, menacing expression. His hand shot up and grabbed her ankle.

His old fingers squeezed tight, and she was afraid he'd pull her to the ground. Lisa held on to the ladder and the roof; she tried to twist her body around, preparing to kick at him with her other leg. He yanked at her ankle.

"Chest," she heard him say. "My heart..."

⁂

Somehow, she'd managed to get him down safely. First she had to break the man's terrified grip, then she had to practically climb over him, finding scant footing on the rungs his body had flattened against in panic. "Come down," she said, "I've got you." She couldn't trust him to hang on by himself, so she guided him, lifting one of his legs at a time and setting it on the next rung, her cheek and shoulder pressed against his back to hold him in place. If she had turned her head, his puffy winter jacket would have suffocated her.

An ambulance was there as soon as they'd reached the ground. But that was why she'd moved him: so she could get to a phone and call 9-1-1. How did the paramedics know...?

She looked across the street, where several windows of the Sunrise Apartments faced an open courtyard—and the front of her house. A few of the curtains fluttered. Some gray-haired ladies emerged from a side door and walked slowly toward the curb. One of them made stuttered steps behind a metal walker, wheels on the back and bright green tennis balls skewered beneath the front legs.

An on-call nurse pushed through the same door. "Ladies, ladies," she said, "step aside, please." She moved fast, dodging the metal walker and stepping past a tight cluster of two stooped women and one rail-thin man in an Orioles cap. The man's wooden cane looked thicker than his leg.

The nurse crossed the street to Lisa's front lawn. An iron-on patch depicting a sunrise adorned the front pocket of her jacket. She held a pair of rubber gloves in one hand, but didn't seem in a hurry to touch anything. Instead, she stood next to the two paramedics and watched as they lifted the man into a stretcher. "How's old Howard doing?" she asked.

"Probably another asthma attack," one of them answered. "We'll know more after we've checked him out."

"He'll be all right, won't he?" Lisa felt concern for this man, even after he'd frightened her. Not responsibility, though. It wasn't her fault "old Howard" had taken it upon himself to climb the ladder.

"Happens all the time," the nurse said. Lisa wasn't sure what she meant. People climb ladders all the time? People have heart attacks all the time?

The paramedics lifted the stretcher into the ambulance, shut the doors, and eventually drove away. They didn't use the siren, however, which made Lisa feel relieved: they must not think the man's condition was too serious.

"Back inside," the nurse yelled at the gathered crowd. "Give Howard his privacy." An odd thing to say, considering Howard wasn't there anymore. The nurse moved toward the seniors, and they turned their attention back to the apartment complex. She urged them inside, on crowd-control duty as they filed slowly through the door.

Except for one woman, who remained behind. She was dressed a little better than the others, with a more confident posture, and Lisa wondered if she weren't the manager for the facility rather than a resident. But as the woman crossed the street toward Lisa, it was as if she aged two years with each step. Her frosted blond hair was a wig; thick makeup over her pinched face couldn't quite disguise the wrinkles. The woman's confident posture seemed more brittle as she got closer, the overcompensation of someone suffering from chronic back pain.

"I'm Miss Teely," she said, extending her hand. Lisa shook it. The woman's fingers remained stiff, making no effort to return Lisa's grasp. "I wish I'd introduced myself earlier, before this...unpleasantness."

"I'm Lisa. Gladys Wittaker was my mother-in-law."

"Sorry for your loss," Miss Teely said. Her head dropped down slightly, as if uncertain what to say, and Lisa got the urge to help her through the awkwardness. She wondered if Miss Teely and Howard were close, and struggled with the right way to ask.

"Is Howard a friend of yours?"

At this, Miss Teely's head shot up, her eyes alight. "Of *course* he's my friend. He's not *much*—but then we haven't *got* much, have we?"

"I'm sorry, I was—"

"Don't flatter yourself. Young as you are, you don't need to be that pretty."

"Now wait a minute!" How did the conversation take *this* turn?

"I'm not trying to insult you. Simply stating facts. You haven't won any beauty contests—not lately, at least. But you got all of us beat, by a long shot."

It was as if the old woman spoke in a different language. Lisa deciphered the emotions behind it—a wounded pride, lashing back in cruelty—but the context was absurd. Here was a woman aware enough to dress herself, apply makeup, adjust a tightly styled wig. She'd lanced an angel pin, perfectly centered, through her lapel; its jade head and gold-wire halo sparkled, wings of frosted glass shaved thin as paper.

The woman's elderly demeanor was precise and composed—but her words were from another realm.

"Younger than us," she continued, "than any of our men would see every day. The nurses don't count. Like harlots, they're paid to smile, put up with toothless flattery."

"Miss Teely, stop," Lisa finally had to say, "stop right there." The implications of "harlot" weren't lost on her, but she couldn't bother to take offense. It was more important to end the woman's misguided jealousy. "I didn't invite Howard over here," Lisa said. "I didn't ask for his help."

"You didn't have to," Miss Teely said. "You put yourself in his way, is what you did. You put yourself in his way."

In Centreville, the rumor mill was faster than cell phone connections. Andy returned her message in-between sales visits, and he'd already heard from a customer about the old man and the ambulance. Lisa told him about her encounter with Miss Teely, too, and by the end of the day he'd collected a handful of anecdotes to share with his wife over fast-food dinner.

"Well, I mean, she's *famous,*" Andy said. "Never was quite right in the head, and being older than dirt hasn't helped her disposition." He waved a french fry, impatient to bite into it, but too involved in his story to stop. "Clatch told me about some doodad ceramic bowl or something at the church rummage sale five years ago, and Miss Teely and his mom reached for it at the same time. Miss Teely *won,* and got the damn thing at a steal price, but she still held a grudge—against Clatch's mom for *daring* to want the same two-dollar bowl, against the woman with the cashbox who didn't settle the dispute fast enough to suit her, and maybe against the church, too, for letting the *wrong people* attend the sale." He bent the fry and stuffed it into his mouth, starting to laugh as he chewed. "Miss Teely didn't talk to his mom for a whole year over that. Some punishment, huh?"

It was Andy's gift, to weave a story that made things better. Here they sat in his mother's kitchen—still *hers* instead of *theirs,* since Lisa hadn't yet replaced the mismatched cabinet doors or added new countertops, hadn't pulled off faded wallpaper that curled away from the wall at the seams. Huge grease stains hovered over the broken stove, sticky with dust: atop the stove sat the single-coil electric burner Andy's mother had used to heat cans of soup in her last years. They'd bought a new microwave, but Lisa dreaded the many evenings of Lean Cuisine or carry-out meals before the kitchen would be ready for actual cooking. After that scare today with the old man, she had wondered—not for the first time—if she'd made a horrible mistake. The house would be a huge amount of work, basement to attic and every room between, the exterior walls a mess and a roof that might collapse with the next rainstorm. And even after months and months of work, they would still be in Centreville, their front door facing apartments full of elderly busybodies. There were some things she'd never be able to fix.

Despite her fears, Andy had made her laugh again. Miss Teely fighting over a beat-up ceramic bowl became Miss Teely fighting over a worn-out man, and maybe *Lisa* would be lucky this time and get the silent treatment over the next year or so. Andy winked at her, said she'd been tempting old men all day while he was at work, and it was funny again, *really* funny, and it was okay to laugh because they'd heard the old man was fine and already back from the hospital:

Oh, God, were you wearing those overalls? with the paint stains and the torn pocket? and that fetching corduroy work shirt from 1980, and your hair bunched up in a scrunchie? Well, no *wonder* old Howard couldn't resist climbing after you!

They laughed, then calmed down, then laughed again. The wax-wrapped burgers tasted greasy, oversalted, and delicious.

⁂

They laughed more that night, in bed together, and he promised not to mention Miss Teely's name while they made love. During the moment of her husband's release, though, Lisa thought of the older man's hand clenched at his chest, his expression twisted in agony, and Andy's face in the half-dark looked twisted, too.

She lay awake long after her husband had rolled over and drifted off. In the late hours, a storm rumbled in—the first big storm in their new house. She stared up at the unfamiliar ceiling and listened to the window frames rattle in the wind, then the gravel patter of rain on loose shingles. Lisa feared she would fall asleep with the house intact, then wake to water staining dark on the ceiling and plaster falling away like wet paper; and downstairs, a new rug soaked and ruined before it's been rolled over the floor, and the wooden coffee table warped and her magazines soggy as sponges; and the television and microwave and computer ready to explode in sparks once she flipped a switch. All the tensions of the move rushed back, banishing sleep.

Sometime in the night, a comforting dream finally answered these tensions. It was based on a fairy tale from childhood, The Shoemaker and the Elves. A beautiful story, as she half-remembered it: a family poised to lose everything, and some last hopeful order arrives for a hundred shoes. The shoemaker stays up late, tapping little nails into little heels, but he's old, and maybe sick, too, and he can't work fast enough to beat the clock. They'll lose everything: the rented house, the medicine his wife needs for her cancer; their son would be sold to the regiment and their lovely virgin daughter married against her will to a wart-faced fifty-year-old banker. If only he could make eighty more shoes before morning and earn the money to pay the landlord, the doctor, the grocer—but it's an hour later, seventy-eight more shoes to go, and he's ruined the leather on the seventy-seventh. His fingers are shaking, but there's no time to rest, he'll never finish anyway but he has to try, he *has* to...Well, that's the worst part of the story, but children know it will turn out okay: exhausted, the man falls asleep, and tiny elves whisper into the shop and go to work. They're gone when the shoemaker awakes at dawn, and—this is the beautiful part—there's one hundred perfect pairs of shoes all lined up on the counter. He thinks, *did I do this all myself?*—but it doesn't matter, because he can sell the shoes in time, and the family's saved.

That's the part she dreamt about: the lovely wish fulfillment at the end. Her house is finished, and dream-Lisa knows it's impossible, but everything's done exactly the way she would have wanted it. She races from room to room, smiling at the handiwork. The tub is refinished in the upstairs bathroom, and light blue tile glistens on the floor. Overnight the kitchen's been remodeled, with a shiny matching stove and fridge; and the living room carpet is in place, plush beneath new furniture, and fresh wallpaper brightens the whole room. Outside, dream-Lisa discovers the house completely painted, replacement shingles nailed expertly into the roof. A wooden railing encloses their front porch; someone has trimmed the unruly trees and bushes in the yard, and a neatly planted vegetable garden has appeared in the back.

The elves had been very busy. And they didn't want anything in return—the smile they imagined (but never saw) on Lisa's face was reward enough.

⁂

The dream was pleasant, but not as relaxing as she'd have preferred. All that running from room to room, around the finished house—and she must have taken mental notes the whole time, getting decorator tips from her subconscious. She woke before Andy's alarm, restless again. She slipped into jeans and a pullover shirt, and headed downstairs to start the coffee.

What if the kitchen really had been finished in the night? (Ha, ha.)

Nope. Everything remained as it was when they'd gone to bed. She looked at the kitchen and what she really saw was a giant "To do" list, with pages and pages of empty check boxes. Every room had its own list.

Well, at least she hadn't discovered any leaks from the rainstorm.

Lisa poured water in the back of the coffee maker, scooped pre-ground Sanka into the filter and flipped the switch. She moved groggily to the front door to see if the newspaper had been delivered.

She turned the front knob and pulled the door toward her, but it didn't budge. Stupid house, she thought—but blamed herself also, because she'd forgotten where she was. In any normal house, the front door opened inward; here, you had to push the wooden door out, over the welcome mat and into the porch—and into anybody standing there, as the postman discovered when she almost knocked him over earlier that week. Yet another reminder of the tough work ahead: shoddy original construction, compounded by half-hearted (if that!) upkeep over the years.

The paper wasn't on the porch, and she didn't see it when she scanned the damp yard, either. Lisa did see something else, however: her ladder, against the front window where she'd been working yesterday.

Except, she'd put it back in the tool shed. After the mess with the old man, she'd decided not to do any more outside work that day. Had someone taken it from the shed...?

Old Howard. Sometime in the night, he'd snuck out here, moved the ladder against the house and climbed feebly up when nobody could see to stop him. He'd tried to finish the job she'd started—maybe even during the blowing rainstorm.

Her paint scraper was still clenched tight in his raised hand. His body curled around the base of the ladder, the jacket shiny from the last bit of rain. The skin of his face was an awful mix of gray and blue, and he stared right at her, not blinking at all.

Lisa ran into the house and grabbed the cordless phone to dial 9-1-1. She shouted upstairs to Andy at the same time, mixing up the conversations, yelling to wake the dispatcher, and whispering to her husband on the second floor, something about "the old man" and "I think he's dead," and maybe she was yelling across the street, too, because when she stepped back outside, the door to Sunrise Apartments had opened and a few gray-haired seniors started to amble out.

"Andy," she yelled, "Andy," praying he would get there before any of the elderly tenants crossed the street to question her. It seemed an eternity before he stepped out onto the porch, hair mussed and a terrycloth robe unfastened over his pajamas. He asked her questions about the ladder (Didn't you put that away?), about the man (Is this the same old guy from yesterday?), and Lisa answered him in a daze. By that point, seven elderly men gathered at the edge of the curb across the street, two of them in wheelchairs. Around them were nearly a dozen women. At different moments, some of the women cast angry, resentful glances at Lisa.

The ambulance arrived eventually. A different nurse in a Sunrise uniform strutted across the street, but she kept her distance from the body.

Miss Teely followed slowly in the nurse's path.

"I'm going to see if there's anything we can do," Andy said, and headed over to the paramedics. Lisa didn't think to stop him.

Miss Teely walked right up to her. She wore a perfectly ironed nightgown, and her eyes were red from crying. "It should have been *your* man up there," Miss Teely said in a harsh whisper. "It should have been *him* doing that work for you."

For Lisa, the rest of the day was awful. Andy had to go in to work—with a new job, he couldn't afford to miss any time. So her husband wasn't there to support her when the police stopped by that afternoon. Just a formality, ma'am, you understand—but still a strange accusation in their eyes, a leading emphasis to some of their questions: You've *no idea* why he would have climbed that ladder, ma'am? and, You've *never* seen Howard Millimet before today, err, yesterday?

While the squad car sat in front of the house, a few Sunrise residents wandered outside and gawked for a minute, then turned forlornly back inside. In the dozen or so facing windows, Lisa thought she noticed several curtains blink aside at different intervals. She wondered which of the units belonged to Miss Teely.

She couldn't work under such scrutiny. Certainly, out of respect for the deceased Mr. Millimet, she'd be expected to forego outdoor work—for how many days: two? three? a week? Among her indoor projects, she decided to prioritize the large bay windows in the living room. Lisa left the house by the side exit, where none of her elderly neighbors could see her, and drove to Wal-Mart for curtains and hanging rods.

Once the new drapes were in place, she tested them, pulling the cord to reveal the clear view of her neighbors, no trees or telephone poles obstructing the facing apartment complex. Then she pulled the cord again, shutting the curtains tight for the rest of the day.

⁂

That evening, Andy was sympathetic, said the right things. The french fry—crinkle cut, this time—waved in the air, and he said nobody could blame her for what happened; word on the street was that Howard was a bit of an odd duck, anyway; and Andy recalled his mother once mentioned the old guy in some pestering context or another. So, there you go.

He tried a bit of humor: "Give it time. I mean, Miss Teely and her cronies may be upset with you *now*, but they're in assisted-living, for Christ's sake. Won't be long before the next one pops off, and they'll have something else to worry about." His words fell flat. They'd had a relationship where they could joke about this kind of morbid thing, but *he* hadn't been home all day, facing months and months of cleaning and repairs in a dark, closed-up house that didn't seem such a bargain any more.

Each time, Lisa's "I'm not sure I can take this" tone was countered with Andy's "Give it time," making it an agree-to-disagree kind of discussion that left her angry and weary by bedtime. The night brought another storm, louder than before, and another fanciful dream:

The friendly elves are setting up to work on the house again, but this time she's determined to catch them before they start. She will thank them, grateful for the thought, then will graciously decline.

I'm not helpless. I can do my own work here.

I'm not even sure I want this house anymore.

Dream-Lisa tiptoes down the stairs, a child on Christmas morning hoping to steal a glimpse of Santa. There's a noise from the kitchen, a bustle and clank and clap of wood, and a stretched rectangle of light spills from the doorway. Her bare feet pad closer, and she peers around the door frame and sees…

Dozens of them, tiny as dolls or garden gnomes, moving in a cheerful blur. The kitchen has become a miniature city under construction. The elves have their own tools: bent sewing needles and fishing line, used to grapple themselves to the uppermost cabinets; a system of winches and pulleys to lift cans of paint and wood stain to the countertop. They have hammers as tall as they are, metal nails the length of their arms, and they loop the tools through thick twine and scramble up after them. They've made a painter's scaffold out of cardboard, and two elves in white overalls raise themselves to the air vent over the stove.

On the counter, two other elves balance a hammer across an overturned soup can, its claw-end positioned under a rotted cabinet door, and then their chubby friend jumps on the handle-end. The hammer pivots up, and the claw tears the door off its hinges. It's delightful how they've made things work!

Which makes it a shame she has to stop them. Lisa clears her throat, says "Excuse me" in a gentle girl's voice.

And they freeze, startled. One elf, in the act of guiding the broken-away door to the countertop, loses his grip. The cabinet door falls at an unpredicted angle, and another elf tries to dodge out of the way. His face is like Mr. Millimet, Lisa notices, and he wears a tiny puffy coat that isn't enough to cushion him as he trips to the side and falls from the counter, high as a cliff for him, and his round bald head breaks heavy against newly installed linoleum tile. In shock, some other elves rush to the edge, and some on the floor crowd around the tiny Mr. Millimet, and none of them attend to the hammer, which flips off the soup can in a new arc, the metal edge sailing like an anvil through the air to crack another tiny skull. The soup can starts to roll across the counter, heavy as an oil drum, and it flattens one of the elves. Another elf dodges out of the way, but slips over the edge; instead of falling all the way to the ground, he gets entangled in the rope and pulley system, the twine catching on his neck and strangling him.

"Stop it," Lisa yells in her dream. "Stop it. This is never what I wanted."

The elves—the ones who are still alive, at least—turn toward her. Several of them line up at the edge of the counter, level with her waist, and stare longingly at her. "We can't stop," one of them says. "We have to help you." His voice is ridiculous, like he's breathed helium.

It occurs to her now that they're all men. Tiny old men with gray beards, lacking the carpenter energy and elf-like, work-whistling spirit they'd exhibited seconds earlier. A few of them scrape across the floor in rickety, toy-sized wheelchairs.

She's so horrified that all she wants to do is get away. A group of them crowds around her, gathering under her feet like hungry kittens, and Lisa almost trips. Then her foot presses into something soft and warm that crackles and collapses beneath her bare heel, and oh God, where was Andy, where was Andy when she needed him...?

Where *was* Andy?

Her husband's side of the bed was empty when she woke. Lisa tried to shake the strange dream out of her head. It was after seven, early light breaking through the upstairs shades. The sunlight must mean the storm was over, if there'd been a storm at all. Perhaps the commotion was all part of her dream.

She heard something outside. Crying.

Miss Teely's voice rose above the somber silence of the morning. "Your husband should have done the work," she said. Her voice shook with sobs and age and anger.

Lisa pulled a robe hastily over her night clothes and rushed into the hallway. On the stairs, she again heard Miss Teely's accusing voice from outside. "We've no one left now. It's not right."

No one? There were twenty-five units in the apartment complex across the street. Lisa had counted at least seven men in yesterday's crowd of elderly spectators.

Before she got to the front door, she needed to maneuver through the boxes and supplies spread out through the living room. In the bay window, the risen sun illuminated the closed curtains she'd installed yesterday. The light hatched through the shadow rungs of a ladder.

No, two ladders. Three. At least three, and one against the side window as well.

She heard the sound of sirens in the distance, getting closer. Red strobe mixed with the colors of sunrise.

Lisa grabbed the handle and tried to open the front door, but it was stuck. That's right, she had to *push* instead of pull. Stupid house. Stupid—

But she *was* pushing. Something was blocking the door on the other side. Something heavy, like a rolled up carpet.

Outside, Miss Teely continued to cry.

Waiting For Darkness

Brian Keene

Trying not to cry, Artie waited.

His older sister, Betty, had buried him up to his head in the sand. He'd been reluctant, but Artie feared her disapproval more than being buried. Betty liked to tease him sometimes.

The sand had been warm, at first. Now it was cold. His skin felt hot. His lips were cracked. Blistered. His throat was sore. When he tried to call for help, all that came out was a weak, sputtering sigh. Not that anyone would come, even if he could shout. It was the off season, and the private beach had been deserted all day. Just him and Betty.

And the men.

They'd appeared while Artie pleaded with Betty to free him. Their shadows were long. Betty's laughter died. The men didn't speak. Didn't smile. Just walked right up and punched Betty in the face. Again and again, until she bled.

Then they carried her away.

Artie licked the film of snot coating his upper lip. Gnats flitted around his face. A small crab scuttled near his ear, waving its claws in agitation.

The sun disappeared beneath the ocean. The waves grew dark.

Artie watched the darkness creep closer.

It was very loud.

Like Lick 'Em Sticks, Like Tina Fey

Glen Hirshberg

⌘

"Under the heat there's a coldness, and even the coldness can't be pinned down...His fleeting pleasures and undeniable pain aren't so much depthless as unfathomable."

—Robert Christgau on George Jones
in *Growing Up All Wrong*

⌘

"Take the goddamn gun out of your mouth and give me a Juicy Fruit."

Sophie leans back her head with the barrel on her tongue and the sea wind whipping through the trees, through the car-window into her bobbing blonde hair. The road rolls on before them through the Georgia pines, and the headlights play across it like stones they're skipping.

"You can still taste that?" she says. "You like that taste?"

"Take the goddamn gun out of your mouth," says Natalie, and puts a hand to her own windblown hair.

It looks blacker in this light, Sophie thinks. Or it is blacker. She lowers the gun from her lips. "Better?"

"Juicy Fruit," says Natalie.

Sophie pads her hand around the glove-box until she finds the last stick of gum, shriveled into its foil wrapper like a dead caterpillar. She hands it to Natalie.

"Ugh. Even touching it gives me the wallies. How can you eat that?"

"This from the woman last seen sucking a gun barrel."

Natalie glances down to unwrap the gum, and the car swerves onto the gravel shoulder before she catches the wheel with her knees and jerks it back toward the road.

"Watch your driving," Sophie says.

"So I can see the nothing when I hit it?"

"Seriously," says Sophie. "You're going to wreck us."

Wrenching the wheel to the right, Natalie spins the car onto a dirt trail, and they bump along it until the pines clear and they're idling in front of three sand dunes that have humped up out of the ground, side by side, like whales surfacing. The moonlight burns their sand-skin white. Natalie shuts off the car.

"You know," Sophie says, "a gun is just like a Lick Em Stick someone stuck a trigger on."

"What?"

"A gun is just like—"

"And there you have it. The single dumbest thing I have ever heard. And I've been driving around with you all night, every night, for almost a month."

"And sharing Moon Pies and tent-sleepovers and *Gilmore Girls* and at least two boyfriends for a good twenty years before that."

"I'm trying to block all that out."

"And yet, a gun is like a Lick Em Stick someone—"

"A gun is nothing like a Lick Em Stick anyone stuck anything on. A gun couldn't be less like a Lick Em Stick if it were a...Guns aren't even straight. And even if they were. Saying something's like something else because they have sort of the same shape—or not at all the same shape, in this case—is just stupid. It's like saying a brain is just like a sponge-blob someone stuck a thought in."

"Now, see, that's just cynical, that's what that is. It's worse. It's nihilistic."

"*Nihil.* Rhymes with *bile.*"

"Oh. I thought it was nil. Rhymes with kill."

Natalie's slap rocks Sophie's head off the seat-rest into the door. "Shit," she says, "I'm sorry."

"Didn't hurt." Sophie sits up. Natalie puts her cold hand on her friend's cold cheek.

"Sorry," she says.

"For what?"

"Three weeks," Natalie murmurs.

"As of tonight," says Sophie. "I know."

"I'm hungry."

"Me, too."

They watch the dunes, waiting for them to sink, but they don't. Unconsciously, Natalie fishes in the pocket of her denim skirt and draws a cigarette from the crumpled pack. The second the cigarette touches her lips, before she has even thought of lighting it, she gags, spits it out the window into the sand.

"Well, hell," she says. "I'm cured."

"One good thing, anyway," Sophie says. "Hey, maybe we could open a business. Let them pick us, instead of our picking them."

"Shut up, Sophie."

"Guaranteed to work. They get their lungs, we get—"

"Shut *up.*"

Reedy sand-grass nuzzles against the sides of the car, and the stars dangle like a mobile. Somewhere not too far, an alligator bellows.

"Nat?" Sophie half-whispers. "Let's just go see them. We could just look in the window. Please, let's—"

"Sophie, I swear to God, don't—"

"Just to see. Just once more. Those little faces. Little feet."

Natalie starts the car, grinds into reverse, wrenches the wheel around and sends it bumping back down the trail. When they reach the asphalt, she fishtails onto it, her wheels kicking up a spray of dirt like a Jet-ski throwing wake. They hurtle down the rolling road between the pines.

"You hit some nothing," Sophie says, lifting the gun off the seat and sticking the barrel back between her teeth.

"Baby," says Natalie.

⁂

Sometime just after midnight, Natalie surprises Sophie by pulling into the parking lot of a Waffle House. The building is low and brick. Teenagers crowd around two booths near the front, and a couple of solitary truckers sip coffee in the back. Through the grime and the flittering moths on the windows, all of them look yellow.

"Where are we?" Sophie says, and fabricates a yawn. Yawning, of all things, turns out to be something she genuinely misses.

"Waffle House," says Natalie.

Sophie smiles. "Thanks, Sparky. Waffle House where?"

"Waffle House is its own where." Again, Natalie reaches into her pocket for a cigarette. But this time she doesn't even glance at her hands, just tosses the whole pack out the window. "No," she says. "Waffle House is nowhere. Always." And she looks at Sophie.

"Oh, shit," says Sophie, and her tongue sneaks onto her lips. "Here? Now? It's time?"

Natalie puts a hand to her own chin. The hand doesn't shake, but she wants it to. Wishes it would. "I don't know. How do we know? The bastard didn't say. I don't know, I don't know, I don't know."

"I'm going to call them," Sophie says, catching Natalie off-guard, and before she can grab an arm and stop her, she's out of the car, walking fast into the shadows of the pines.

Natalie considers giving chase, opens the door to do just that. Then she just sits with her legs swung onto the pavement, feeling the sticky night air rush up her skirt. So warm. How did they stand it all those years? From this distance, all she can see is her friend's silhouette. The stocky, bouncy frame—like a gym-bag full of volleyballs, Sophie's fiancé Willie used to say happily, stroking her thigh—the blond head bobbing. Phone against her ear.

Against her ear. With her baby boy's voice filling it.

Unless she's talking to Natalie's baby boy.

At the last second, Sophie senses her coming, whirls around as her friend swoops out of the light and rips at the phone. "They're not home," she squeals, but Natalie's long nails are raking the inside of her wrist and the phone has flown from her hands. "Ow," she says.

"What do you mean they're not home?" Natalie drops to her knees, padding around in the shadows for the phone. "It's after midnight, where would they be?"

"Maybe your mom did what you said. Maybe she took them. Maybe they're gone, and we won't ever—"

Silencing her with a growl, Natalie stands with the phone in her hand, staring like it's a heart she's ripped out. Then she slams it to the pavement and stomps it to pieces.

When she looks up a few seconds later, meaning to apologize, wanting to clutch her oldest friend to her and scream, Sophie is gazing over her shoulder. Natalie turns slowly and sees the trucker.

Just a boy, really. Long, lanky southern boy, skin like a slicked summer peach and an alligator smile he hasn't mastered and doesn't mean.

"Well, damn," he says, and then his smile goes slack, and Natalie feels a twinge, a real one. *You're not so far over your head,* she wants to tell him. *Don't stop now.*

Or else, *Stop right now. Turn around. Run.*

"Thelma and Louise," Sophie whispers, and Natalie jerks back to herself.

"What?"

"Thelma and Louise. Taking back the night. Look at him. He's perfect."

"Sophie..."

"Who'd miss him?"

I would, Natalie thinks, knows that makes no sense and probably isn't true, and steps into the light. Even from ten feet away, she can feel him vibrate like a string she's struck.

"Well, damn," the boy says again, swaying in place. He takes a woozy step forward.

"Don't," Natalie murmurs, and he takes another step. Still five feet between them, but she can already taste his breath, bubble-gummed and maple syrupped and hot with him. It's as though she's developed a new shark-sensitivity to every twitching, fumbling, ridiculous movement living things make.

"Don't," she says again, and he steps closer still.

"But I really want to," he murmurs. So close, now. His mouth so near. His cheeks no longer yellow but sweetly tan and red.

"So do I," she says.

"Thelma and Louise," chants Sophie. "Thelma and Louise."

Grabbing her wrist, Natalie yanks her past the kid toward the Waffle House. She really has to pull because Sophie is jamming her feet down like anchors, and from her mouth comes a brand-new, mewing sound. The kid shudders, desire unfurling from him like a sail. *They weren't home,* Natalie thinks. *They're gone. Oh, Mom. Thank you.* She practically has to hurl Sophie into the restaurant while holding the door with her hip.

For a second, she thinks Sophie's going to turn on her, that they're going to have it out once and for all. But there's something instantly soothing in here, familiar in a way almost nothing else has been these past few weeks. The fluorescents are bright, the music on the radio is Buck Owens, and the dead-eyed, red-haired counterwoman halfway smiles as she nods them toward a booth. All they have to do is…act naturally.

But there's a mother and daughter at the counter. The mother is wrapped in bright-colored scarves, and the daughter, who can't be more than twelve, is feeding her French fries. Maps lay spread in front of them between the ketchup bottles. The woman tucks a stray strand of hair behind her daughter's ear and laughs. Natalie's mouth has formed an O. Her heart isn't really hammering, she knows.

"Well, hi, y'all," Sophie says to the teens in the front booth.

They're staring, of course. The girls, too, though the too-thin redhead in the back is forcing her eyes down to the table, playing pitifully with her napkin. She looks like a French fry dipped in ketchup, barely noticeable even when she's right in front of you, and she knows it. God, Natalie remembers that sensation. Remembers whole Saturdays traipsing around the Goodwills with her mother, trying to find clothes to bring out the blue in her eyes. The only feature she was sure she could do anything with. Once, not more than a year ago, when they were sitting half-drunk on the lawn chairs in the dirt, Natalie's mother had told her, "It's so sad, really. One more proof of just how much God hates women. You only really start to radiate sexuality—the confident kind, the kind that's you and that you really intend—long after you have any use for it. Also long after it's probably healthy for you to have it."

A wise woman, Natalie's mother. Wise today, anyway, now that she's a grandmother at 37 with a double-wide and two new babies to look after, only one of them blood-related, neither of them hers. *Is she that wise, though? Has she really gone?* Natalie doesn't think so. And even if she has gone, she's left a trail. In the hopes that Natalie will come one day and find her.

Veering away from the booth, she tugs Sophie to the counter and orders a double patty melt to go.

"Hey," Sophie says. "That sounds so good." She orders one, too. Behind them, the teenagers return uneasily to themselves.

"Be just a minute," the counterwoman says.

Natalie fumbles in her pockets for the cigarette pack. Patsy comes on the radio, "Walking After Midnight," and Sophie makes clip-clops to the beat with the salt and pepper shakers.

"You know," she says, in the chirping-bird voice Natalie has loved since they were kindergarteners. "A patty melt's just like a dead thing someone slapped cheese and onions on."

Smiling, grateful, Natalie turns. "That doesn't work at all."

"Why not?"

"It's not a metaphor. It's not even a comparison. It's just what it is."

"Well, that there's the difference between you and me, Nat. I call things what they are."

"I think I'll go throw up, now."

"Got to eat something first," Sophie says, grinning, and Natalie feels sick but starts to smile back anyway, and then the woman in the scarves touches her hand.

"Oh, honey," says the woman. "You're just like me."

Stunned, Natalie almost collapses right there. She turns shakily, but all she can see is black and gray hair sneaking from under the scarves on top of the woman's head.

"What do you mean?" Natalie whispers.

"Cold all the time," the woman says. "Bad circulation. I can't ever get warm. Want your fortune read?"

"What?"

"Come on, she needs the practice," says the woman's daughter. "No paying customers for a week. I'm going to the bathroom, Mom." Hopping off the stool, the girl wanders away.

The counterwoman returns with the burgers in a bag, and Natalie turns to go, but Sophie pushes her down onto the stool.

"Give her good news," Sophie says to the woman. "She could use some." She keeps her hands on Natalie's shoulders while the woman produces a deck of cards and shuffles them. Natalie's mother was better at shuffling. Bad at winning, though.

Humming a melody Natalie assumes is meant to be gypsy but sounds like Patsy out of tune, the woman shuffles again, then fans the cards on top of the map.

"Touch two," she says, and Natalie does.

The woman sets aside Natalie's choices, reshuffles the deck, fans it open again.

"And two more."

Natalie touches two more. The woman smiles. Her teeth are grainy and brown, but her black eyes are bright.

"Good. Let's see what we can know." The woman turns over a card. A black ace, Natalie thinks, from the brief glimpse she gets, then a second one. The woman's hands slow, and her smile twitches.

"That's not funny," says Natalie, her voice a bobcat-murmur, her whole body tensing. "You have no idea how not funny—"

"I'm sorry," the woman says. "I did this wrong. Out of practice, as my daughter told you. I'll just reshuffle, and we'll..." Suddenly, her smile vanishes completely, and she looks up. "Oh," she says. "Oh, I'm so sorry. Goddamn it."

From the direction of the bathroom comes a giggle which explodes abruptly into full-blown laughter. The daughter is still laughing as she hurtles past the stools, past the teenagers in the front booths, and out of the restaurant.

Staring after her, the woman in the scarves stands and begins to collect her things and fold the maps. She flips over the deck so Natalie and Sophie can see it. Every single card is a black ace.

"She thinks she's hilarious," the woman says. "Thinks she's Tina fucking Fey. I'm sorry. I hope I didn't scare you." On impulse, she reaches into her purse and lays down an extra ten dollars on top of her check. "For your patty melts." She leaves.

A few moments later, after Sophie has slathered her burger in ketchup, she and Natalie follow. Back in the car, Natalie switches on the radio and dials through the stations until she finds the one from the Waffle House. It's Loretta, this time, sending 'em all to Fist City.

"This is the best DJ on earth," she says, tears streaming down her face. Real tears. How did those get there?

"Wow," Sophie says.

"Shut up," says Natalie, and pulls them out of the lot into the dark.

⌘

"You know," Sophie says, after they've driven another long while, the pines far behind them and in their place peach trees squatting in rows on their stubby trunks like old women under hair-dryers at the beauty salon, "she's got it all wrong."

George Jones on the radio this time, the static sewn into his voice like a smoker's rasp. Singing flat and sad, no drama at all. "Just a Girl I Used to Know."

"Who?" Natalie murmurs.

"Tina Fey."

"Has got it wrong?"

Sophie swats her on the arm. But carefully. Or at least softly. Not like Natalie swats, these days.

"Tina Fey wouldn't be the daughter loading the deck. She'd be the customer getting mistakenly told she was going to die."

"You think so?"

"Complications would ensue."

"Complications."

"Hello? Ground control to Natalie Robot? Switch brain back to on position. Over."

"We have to get rid of these burgers," Natalie says, and Sophie looses an explosive sigh.

"My God, yes, even the smell is giving me the wallies."

"The willies, goddamnit."

"I know."

"Well, what's wrong with the willies?"

"I liked my Willy," Sophie says.

Natalie almost rockets them off the road. One good kick to the pedal, a quick swerve, and they'd be launched through the peach trees. Maybe if they got going fast enough, they'd just fizz away into the dark like an Alka Seltzer tablet. Which is a Sophie comparison if ever there was one.

She glances toward her friend. Sophie's the one crying, now. The sight makes Natalie furious, but she has no idea at what.

"Nat, I'm so hungry," Sophie says. "We have to choose."

"I know," says Natalie.

"Anyone you want, Nat. Any way you want to do it. Anything you think is fair. We can't shirk it. We can't pretend we can avoid it. It's just—"

"What do you suggest, Sophie?" Natalie doesn't mean to start shouting, barely notices that she is. "Next breakdown victim? Next guy in bad pants? Oh,

I know, how about next black dude, you always had a thing for black dudes."

"That's just mean."

"Damn right."

"Natalie, I'm serious. It's killing me."

"Maybe we should let it kill us."

"You know it won't work. You know what he said. It'll be like trying to kill yourself holding your breath. In the end, instinct will take over. Then we'll just act. We won't have any choice. That's what he said. Is that what you want?"

"He said a lot of things. Maybe we're stronger than he is."

"Maybe you are, Nat."

Natalie can't even remember his face. Can't remember whether it hurt. Can't even remember how she and Sophie wound up with him that night. But she can see him straightening over her, mouth already dripping with her. The pull of him overwhelming, sucking up every little passing ball of magically cohering, animated dust like a black hole. She'd wanted him to kiss her some more.

No. She'd wanted to feed herself to him.

What will it be like? she'd asked, not really caring.

And he'd actually paused for a second, as though between courses, or maybe he was thinking about it for the first time. Eventually, he shrugged.

Like coming loose. Like letting go of all those stupid, prickling, hurtful sensations you were always told are what matters. Like a slow slipping away. Same thing that happens to everyone before they die. Only it won't be slow. And you won't die.

As he'd finished her, Natalie had thought of her mother. And now, she thought of her mother's resigned, almost dispassionate reaction later that same night when Natalie banged on the door, handed her grandson and also Sophie's son, and told her she should disappear. Leave no trace. And never come back.

He'd been right, of course. What's happening isn't slow. Just not quite fast enough.

"Natalie," Sophie whimpers.

"Shush." Natalie leans her head back, closes her eyes, feels them roaring into the blankness. Watch out, nothing. Bad moon rising.

"Natalie, what if we went home?"

"Shut the fuck up."

She opens her eyes just in time to see the deer's flank as they slam into it. The animal's head snaps sideways and the antlers bang down on the hood so hard that the back wheels come off the asphalt momentarily, and when Natalie jams on the brake, the thing doesn't fly off, it stays stuck a second and then just slides down the grille, the bones booming as they splinter underneath like 4th of July firecrackers. Even as they skid to a stop, Natalie knows there's part of it still trapped in the rear tires, its weight like a trailer pull dragging them back.

"Oh my God," Sophie whines. "Oh my God."

Natalie is gripping the wheel so hard, her knuckles are threatening to explode through her skin. With a grunt, she makes herself let go, draws her hands into her lap.

"You hit it," Sophie says.

"You think?"

"Is it dead?"

Opening her mouth to give that the response it deserves, Natalie freezes. Then she turns. Sophie shrinks back. It takes an absurdly, almost endearingly long time before understanding dawns.

Neither of them has any idea whose throat is making that sound as they spin to their doors, wrench them open, and leap from the car. The animal is a splayed, shredded ruin locked to the bumper, its head bent up under the rear axle and its antlers shattered all over the road. Natalie and Sophie dive together into the pumping gore in its crumpled ribs like little kids diving for candy in a burst piñata. Blood saturates Natalie's skirt, pools around her thighs when she kneels atop a rib and snaps it as she plunges her face down, almost banging her forehead against Sophie's. The sound Sophie is making might be laughter. Natalie reaches out as she buries her lips in the foam, spitting aside the hairy skin, and strokes her friend's hair.

Sophie is the first to straighten, moments later. Natalie follows, settling back on her haunches, her fingers still twisted in Sophie's hair. Gently, she disentangles them and lets go. Sophie's face has twisted up, and she's spitting over and over, trying to clear the taste from her teeth and her lips. Natalie just wipes a disgusted hand repeatedly across her own mouth. Still kneeling in the mangled deer, they stare at one another.

"So..." Sophie finally murmurs, glancing down one more time at the animal, then back at Natalie. "We're vegetarians?"

Natalie closes her eyes, shudders just once, opens her eyes.

"Humanitarians?" Sophie says.

They stand together, their arms around each other, bits of cartilage clinging to their skin, their legs and skirts dripping. Natalie is about to return to the car when Sophie's hands tighten on her arms.

"Nat," she says. "I'm going home."

"What?"

"Just listen, okay? Stop looking at me like that and pretending you're better and be my friend and listen."

"Okay," Natalie whispers. Merle on the radio, sweeping gently out the open driver's side door. "Mama Tried."

"I've been thinking about this. A lot. And what I've been thinking is—seriously, now, just wait, just hear me out—what better gift could a mother give her children?"

"Sophie..."

"Think about it, Nat. I am. I can't stop. He's all I think about. His little feet. God, his little feet. We could be back there in three hours. We could be with our children three hours from now, and never have to leave them again."

"Sophie, please, you've got to—"

"What did you hope for when Eddie was born, Nat? What did you think you could do for him? What did you want for him? How about no worries, ever? How about no pain? Ever."

"Sophie, you need to—"

"How about living forever?"

It was like a cobra strike, Natalie thinks seconds later, her teeth still buried in the softness under her best friend's chin, Sophie's dead, twitchless body flat beneath her. Like a goddamn bolt of lightning, Natalie thinks as she gulps and drinks. The only concern she'd had at the instant she'd acted was that it wouldn't taste good. Would make her retch and gag like the deer had.

And it was cold, alright. A little sour, not quite right. But it tastes fine. She's still lapping away, burying her face deeper in Sophie's throat, hips rocking side to side to Merle's rhythm. It tastes fine.

Ghost Writer in My Eye

Wayne Allen Sallee

How the hell can you commit suicide in purgatory? I was thinking this as I crossed the parking lot of the Big Lots towards my apartment. The parking area is stark and grey and wet from the August rain, and I miss the sweet smell that used to come from the Panera Bread store next to the dollar store. The walk from Cicero Avenue can be long or short, depending on what he is thinking, and the one thing that matters most is that he took the bread store away. There's nothing in its place, it's as if the strip mall simply squeezed tighter together, fitting the dollar store to Value City. I don't know why he would've chosen that particular business to leave my world, after all he left me with the memory of the buttered rolls in the darkened windows. Now there are garbage cans next to shampoo and home pregnancy tests past their expiration date in boxes next to tricycles and suitcases that all cost much more than a single dollar.

The only reason I can think of for him taking Panera Bread away, but leaving the memory of it to me, and me alone, just as in real life one can recall the Santa Fe Speedway and the Arthur Audy Home, their remnants now salt quarries or gated communities, is that he is punishing me.

And he knows that I cannot commit suicide as long as he pulls the strings. I had hoped for so long that I was simply in purgatory, serving out time for sins committed over almost half a century of living, the stolen comics from Archer Heights Comix, the conveniently misplaced jumpsuit from when I worked with the Elvis band, the lies I told to my editors when I missed a deadline or to my employers when I was doing my work badly because I was hearing the voices in my head again.

I now know that there were no voices, no Elvis band, not even a writing career.

This is not purgatory. This is me living the life that another person has created, and at times he is working on a short deadline or simply doesn't have his heart and soul divested into the storyline.

You see, when I was real and lived in the three-dimensional world and could get nose bleeds and stomach aches and an occasional kiss from a beautiful woman, I would always end up dying in a heroic manner after a predetermined length of time. Saving someone from being hit by a car at 55th and Fairfield. Trying to free someone's foot before the onslaught of a Metra commuter train. Well, except for that story involving strychnine enemas. Besides, there were vampires in that story, and we all know that the only monsters in the world are werewolves, American Dreams, and the Crawling Abattoir.

Now, I simply careen or meander through insubstantial situations, some lacking the details that had made my past so happy in meager ways.

All because Marty Mundt starts a story and then discards it.

After the rains earlier, as the skies cleared, I could see his distorted, blurred face, a wrinkled blob of Play-Doh with glasses, erasing the clouds with his big, giant Ticonderoga #2 pencil, then pointing the pencil nub accusingly at me.

Not smiling, simply with a look of dire concentration. Changing the scene.

Marty Mundt always reads his stories in Bughouse Square every Saturday afternoon. The place is really Washington Square Park, but the nickname came from the borderline futurists of a century ago, standing on soap boxes to rave about the world to come. Now, writers both published and unpublished will share a story or two to anybody wandering the shady paths. I worked weekends for twenty years and was able to see him read often, and I also read, back when I thought it was my own past that I was reading from. Then I lost my job and had a long line of temporary jobs, and once, I couldn't make Marty's reading because I had to babysit and accidentally stuck the kid's head in a revolving fan. Damn baby. Damn temp agency.

Damn Marty.

My current psychosis started just prior to 9/11, when Marty asked permission of me to use one of my so-called real life experiences in a story. I told him that he could, just put me in the story, not realizing the joke of that request.

He then wrote a story about a man named Mr. Heaven who was standing over my grave at Graceland Cemetery.

I understood the implications, regardless of how melancholy Marty wanted the story to play out. *He had to be above me.*

Now I am in my apartment, just like that. I guess Marty wanted to hear Huey Lewis and The News because they are on some late night talk show. My roommate's favorite show. My roommate's name changes from time to time. He is a rodeo clown or an astronaut or Jerry Lewis, if he didn't use a stunt double in his films and really took all those pratfalls himself.

I look to my open palm, not truly expecting to see my keys, and sure enough, there's a prescription bottle of anti-seizure medicine in my palsied grasp. Marty always seems to give himself an out. My roommate is now bouncing ideas off the wall while a commercial for erectile dysfunction plays out on the television.

I was a writer, a living, breathing, balding writer for almost twenty years, and then Marty Mundt put me in a grave and these planes went into those towers and the doctor gave me this medicine and when I look at the ceiling I can see him, scratching out words, making more cracks so that water drips down and my pills get wet, my roommate's clown face melts in his astronaut helmet, making him look like some kind of ice cream treat, and the ideas...well, the ideas stop bouncing. They just hit the sopping floor with a dull splat. It sounds like the word Mundt.

Mundt.

Mundt.

I used to start my stories only after I had the ending line, like the scene with the strychnine enemas in "From Hunger" or the approaching train in "Don's Last Minute."

But now...now I'm stuck starting over and over.

The babysitting job might as well have been a dream. Because Marty stops writing and scratches it out and starts over. Maybe it is his incessant scratching that has been causing my seizures. For God's Sake, he had me prancing around calling myself the Scarlet Corgi as I fought the Crawling Abattoir to a standstill back in 1956. But even I know that I was born in 1995, *1959,* that is.

He created TessLass and Willy Sid, and all my other friends. I was in love with TessLass, back when I thought I'd leave Chicago forever and move to Denver, where it wasn't just the mountains that hypnotized a man.

And now, now I'm working at B. Fanning Printing and Cathode Ray Design in a suburb I have never heard of. His face looks up at me from the scanner, from the fax machine, from the mirror near the eye wash area. He has created a supervisor named Casey Mann who is a drunken cretin. In office terminology, he has no people skills. In Marty's story, he is an asshole. And my seizures start again, flickering in my brain like a cathode ray in the back of an old television set.

⁂

The two cops looked over the entire apartment on Capitol Hill. It had been a hot summer in Denver and even with the windows open you could smell black marker ink in every corner of each room. The dead man had written a rambling and mostly incoherent suicide note with the black marker on every possible surface. The backs of manila envelopes. Bathroom tiles and mirror. The ceiling above the shower had several arrows pointing to cracks where water dripped as if to illustrate some point. Nothing was dated, so the words were disjointed and out of order.

"Why does this guy write Bughouse Square instead of Neal Cassady Square," one cop asked the other. "Remember when we caught that drug buy in Washington Park, over by the statue?" Good point, I thought. I had written about the correct place—with the plaque dedicated to the real star of Keroauc's ON THE ROAD—when I wrote about Rachel in my novella "For You, The Living." How could I have gotten *that* wrong?

Words were written in very tiny print on the screen of his computer. One cop scratched his head, wondering why he just didn't type all this shit out. The other cop said he never owned a computer.

The John Doe lay in a chair, his eyes gouged out. He had taken an ink cartridge from his computer printer and jammed it deep into his left eye. He had chosen a blue gel pen to poke and ultimately scoop his remaining eye out, where it dangled like a giant red snot on his cheek.

He had written his final words with the blue gel pen on a piece of typing paper. The words made as much sense as the rest of the scrawlings. *I saw something else in the sky tonight. Marty still changes my life. But someone is writing about Marty, as well.*

"Crazy guy, huh?" The cop who didn't own a computer said.

"Yea," his partner replied. "Make a great story, though."

Palisado

Alan Peter Ryan

The wind slammed the cabin hard, again, and slipped in through numerous unknown cracks, or perhaps cracks newly clawed open, and guttered the flame of the candle. The howling outside varied in pitch but had not let up for hours. Trask sat hunched before the flickering candle, his left hand in its heavy canvas glove awkwardly holding the book open flat on the table. His right, hidden away, clutched a blanket tight around his shoulders. He sat sideways at the table, getting the light and the thin warmth from the fire on his right side but doing little for his left. He had another and heavier blanket, a Hudson's Bay that had not been cheap, and he could wrap that around his head and body too, over the other, but two blankets would only serve as a barrier to the heat from the fire. Or he could get into the bunk with the two blankets around him but then he'd be farther away from the feeble heat of the hearth. It was not snowing outside now but the wind snatched up handfuls, armfuls of snow from the laden trees and the drifts on the ground and flung it fiercely about and from time to time it rattled against the cabin walls and clattered at the shutters on the windows like an animal scratching to get inside or a soul pleading for rescue.

He had no watch but he figured it was about one in the morning. Many hours of darkness remained.

His feet were starting to freeze and he stomped them hard a few times on the plank floor, his boots making a racket in the one-room cabin. The movement gave relief to his stiff knees and legs and he realized he'd been sitting not only sideways but with his body tensed at the table. He stretched upright and twisted his torso left and right to ease the aching muscles in his back. Strange how a man could sit on a horse all day long but a few hours of stillness at a table made him sore all over. But it wasn't the table or the chair that had done it. It was the storm. It was the wind. It was the unrelenting intensity of the wind that was making his muscles bunch and knot.

He'd been a fool, a damned fool, he told himself, and not for the first time. Not for the first time being a fool, and not for the first time telling himself that he'd been a fool. He should have known better. He'd seen the storm coming but he had underestimated it, most often a fatal mistake out here in these mountains. Oh, it was going to be a good one, he'd known that when it started, and that was the trick in it. He'd wanted to see it. He wanted to see everything, see and grasp and make his own everything the land could offer, everything it could throw against him. He liked to see the snow piling up in the clefts and crevices, the mountainsides turning white, the skeletal trees trimmed in white, the snow swirling madly, the smooth drifts shaping up and then shifting elsewhere, the trackless untouched land with its details muffled, its sharpness blurred, and its ferocious grandeur proclaimed. But he couldn't do that down on the flat, down in the valley, down at the ranch, so he'd taken out Ulysses and ridden up to the line cabin, alone and breathing hard in the thin cold air with the wind stealing his breath away, and by the time he was two thirds of the way up there, past the point of turning back, the storm came in roaring with fury and he was caught. And not even oil for the lamp at the cabin. Have to rely on candles with a fierce wind blowing. If one of his own riders had done that, made that mistake, and for such a damned fool reason, he would have spoken harsh words to him for putting his life at risk that way. And now here he was himself, trapped.

And now here he sat, sleepless, half frozen, muscles tensed and aching, the breath streaming in vapor from his mouth in the chill air of the room, the candle flickering in the cutting drafts from the walls and the window so wildly that half the time his page was in darkness, the night not yet halfway finished, and the storm still raging outside.

He had made some soup earlier from a piece of beef, some potatoes and carrots, salt and pepper, and eaten it with some hard bread soaked in it, as much as he could manage as a bulwark against the cold. Coffee, too, and he'd taken plenty of that but then regretted it. Coffee made him pee and after a while he'd had to go outside for that and nearly froze his fingers working the buttons on his pants and his sad limp instrument shriveled up in the process.

He looked over at the pot. The soup was frozen now. He stood up and stepped over to the fire and added a log and then moved the pot into place to boil up the soup again. As long as he was up, he boiled water for coffee too. He'd just have to pay the consequences for it later.

While he was at the fire, the wind got in again and banged around the room. The fire itself fluttered for life, the candle flickered, died, flamed up again, jerking like a body being burned at the stake. The wind caught the pages of his book and riffled them loudly, making the sound of a bird desperately rattling its wings, trying helplessly to escape the noose that holds its leg.

Trask crouched before the fire, waiting for the soup and the coffee to boil. He resettled the blanket around his shoulders, holding it out wide and open to trap the heat against his body. He told himself he felt a little warmer. He shifted and knelt like a votary before the leaping flames. He had taken the glove from his left hand and he flexed the fingers in the heat. The restored flow of blood made his fingers tingle. He bethought himself of the dried and ground Mexican pepper he had and he stood and got the little sack from the food shelf and sprinkled it liberally into the pot and stirred it around with the ladle.

When the soup was ready, he filled his bowl and spooned it up slowly to get as much of it into him as he could. The Mexican peppers quickly went to work on his mouth and then on the tips of his ears and the back of his neck and the top of his head. It wasn't heat exactly but it helped and he felt a little less like a shapeless heap of frozen clay and a little more like a living human being. When he was done with the soup, he filled his mug with coffee three times and drank it down, still steaming. Then he set a fresh pot of water to heat at the fire.

He didn't feel the urge to pee yet but it would come more quickly with movement. He left the bowl and the spoon and mug on the table and walked up and down a few times to stretch his legs, the few steps the small space allowed. Then he pulled the blanket over his head, took up the eating implements, and went to the door. He left the gloves behind.

When he unlatched the door and pulled it open, the wind, as if waiting to pounce, punched him in the face and lungs and snatched his breath away. He gasped and doubled over against it and rushed outside, pulling the door closed with some effort behind him. Snow swirled like icy gravel and bit sharply at his face and eyes, blinding him for a moment. He ducked his head lower. The snow was drifted into a high bank at the corner of the cabin to his left. He stepped over there quickly and thrust first the bowl and then the mug through the icy crust of the drift, filled them with snow, used his red and stinging fingers to wipe them out quickly, then thrust them again into the drift, stepped back to the doorway, and set them on the ground to await his return. He turned away at once, again to his left, twisting his head and shoulders away from the worst impact of the wind, and hurried doubled-over to the stable. Snow crunched beneath his boots but he could feel it more than hear it, so loud was the wind in his ears.

Ulysses snorted and stamped by way of greeting as he came inside. Trask went directly to the big black horse and stroked his face and talked softly to him and cleared some of the crystallized vapor from his nose and muzzle. The wind moaned and called outside and the horse shifted in his narrow space. He had two heavy blankets. The one that came up high on his neck had slid down a little and Trask carefully arranged it back in place. Then he hefted the heavy grain sack from the floor and dumped more feed into Ulysses's bin. The horse pushed his nose in at once. Trask patted him on the neck and talked to him some more. Then he hurried out of the stable and back to the cabin. At the door he picked up the bowl and the mug and carried them inside. He had a hard time again with the door because the wind kept pushing its way in. Moving quickly, he took up the pot from the fire and hurried out again and back to the stable. There he murmured to Ulysses as he poured the hot water into the bucket of ice that hung from the wall beside the grain bin. It would melt the ice in the bucket and quickly get cool enough for the animal to drink when he finished eating.

The cold was sinking deep into him now and it was hard to keep the blanket in place with all this moving around. He closed the stable door and stepped quickly away to the side of the cabin. His fingers were red and aching as he fumbled at his buttons but the call was on him and as soon as his pants were open he relieved himself, the hot stream making a brief cloud of vapor. He tucked himself away inside and closed two buttons and left the rest to do up inside. He stepped over to the corner of the cabin and was about to turn it and go to the door when the wind came around the corner and buffeted him hard and made him stagger for a moment. He grunted in surprise and got his footing again and lifted his head and that was when he saw the snowman standing near the trees.

The wind had not let up its roaring and moaning and the snow-heavy trees groaned before it. The air was a blur of wind-driven snow. It rushed upward and down in clouds, the clouds dissolved and shifted into visible currents and rushed right to left, left to right, swirled close to the ground and swept up more and then spun upward again to the branches of the trees and around the skeletal trunks and then back down to the ground again. There were no shapes that stood still, no forms that were solid, all was in white movement. All this Trask could see, if he was seeing it at all, in the dim silvery light that seemed to emanate from the snow itself in the otherwise dark of night. It was an endless whirl of icy snow, swooping and diving and sweeping along the white ground and wrapping itself around the white-edged trees and rushing apart and rushing together again in a terrible clash.

But Trask was certain he had seen a snowman.

It was off to his left, right over there by the trees at the edge of the clearing. Trask snapped his face back toward it to see it again but the flying icy snow stung his eyes and made him blink. Where? There. Yes. It was a snowman.

Trask's mouth fell open and the bitter cold made his teeth hurt.

He stood where he was, with the snow rushing past his face, but he could see it clearly now, its shape dim but distinct in an otherwise unruly and undefined world.

He had built just such a snowman as a boy. It was made of three great balls of snow, a large one at the base on the ground, a middling sized one for the upper body, and a smaller one for the head. There was no mistake about it. He knew what he was looking at.

The face had no features, no black-painted walnuts or lumps of charcoal for eyes, no carrot for a nose, but now Trask could see two extensions of snow at the sides to serve for arms. And though it had no facial features, Trask knew for a certainty that it was looking at him.

The cold was getting to him, it was freezing his brain, he wasn't thinking clearly, he was imagining things.

He jumped to the door of the cabin, pushed it in, rushed inside, and slammed the door shut behind him.

He passed a long time warming himself at the fire.

By now it must have been getting on for two o'clock. In less than four hours there would be a little pale daylight, if he and Ulysses didn't freeze to death before then.

He made another pot of coffee, warming himself as he crouched before the fire. He poured it out once and drank that and left the rest.

He brushed a hand over the front of his body and his clothes felt slightly warm to the touch, but his fingers were so cold it was hard to tell. He took off the blanket and then wrapped it around himself anew and crouched again at the fire to warm both it and himself. Then he pulled on his gloves, both pairs, first the thin ones of dark blue wool and then the heavy canvas ones he used on the range for roping. Then he went to the door, jerked it open, stepped outside, and pulled it closed behind him.

Now there were five snowmen and they were no more than a dozen feet away from the cabin and from him where he halted in front of the door. They were huge, tall, taller than him, as tall as bears standing upright. They stood side by side, ranged in a ragged line, immobile, but looking as if—Trask did not know what made him think this—they had been suddenly arrested in some silent and furtive movement. The snow had not ceased its mad whirling and howling across the clearing and now it raced in the roaring wind and whirled and swept around the snowmen who stood so perfectly still in the night.

Trask stared at them. The wind struck his eyes and made them water and blurred his vision. He blinked. But there they were.

The gigantic balls of snow of which they were made were perfectly round and each figure was identical to the others. Trask scanned over the five of them, looking at each, and then back in the other direction. No, they were not identical. The balls of snow were all round, in their three sizes, lower body, upper body, head, but they were not all exactly the same. Upon being studied, one revealed a slightly greater width than the others, one appeared to have slightly greater height in the lower body, another in the upper body, and the heads, he could see, while all more or less the same shape and size, were all slightly different too. So too with the blunt appendages of snow affixed to the sides of the figures to serve as arms. They were all the same, too, yes, except for the very minor ways in which they differed, one with arms a trifle thinner than the others, one with arms a trifle heavier, fuller, than the others, one with ever so slightly longer arms, one with slightly shorter.

Trask scanned them again from left to right and back from right to left and it struck him suddenly that if they'd had faces, eyes and mouths and noses and ears, the truth would have been instantly clear. They were individuals. Trask, as mesmerized as frightened, marveled at this individuality as much as at their very presence here, their very existence. Their presence here, yes, that was a question that needed answering. He looked at the ground around them, the ground behind them, trackless and covered evenly with snow except where it drifted and blew into ridges and ripples across the clearing. Of course there would not be footprints. Of course not. Snowmen do not walk on legs and leave tracks in the snow. Snowmen do not move at all.

Even so, barely half an hour ago, there had been one of them over there at the other side of the clearing, over there by the trees, and now that one was no longer there but there were five of them here, near the cabin, right in front of him.

Not for a moment did the wind reduce its speed and its erratic hammering of cabin and trees, not for a breath did it cease its moaning and howling, not for a moment did it desist from snatching up the snow and flinging it about in twisting sheets of white. Now the wind and snow flung themselves around the five towering white figures and the snow was already beginning to drift up against the huge balls on which they rested. Already the roundness at the very bottom was being a little obscured.

Trask, hunched forward, the blanket held tight over his head and clutched close together at his neck with only his face peering out through the narrow aperture remaining, studied and contemplated the impossible scene before him. He shook his hooded head for a moment, then backed up to the door, reached behind him and opened it, took a last quick look at the five snowmen, and then backed into the house and closed the door tight.

He stood there breathing hard for a minute, for two minutes, then moved to the wooden chair and sat down at the table near the fire. He pushed back the blanket to let the warmth reach his body.

He had built a snowman once, as a boy. He was eleven and his pa had helped him. He remembered the cold weather, the feel of it on his face, stinging his cheeks, and the big fat snowflakes that fell straight down from the gray sky and landed on his brown woolen mittens and stayed there for a few seconds before melting. You said you want to build a snowman, didn't you? said his pa. And I told you we'd do it as soon as there come a day with the right kind of snow. Well, it looks right today, so let's go do it. And his ma had bundled up the two of them in their warmest clothes and tied scarves around their necks so tight that they thought they were going to choke and could hardly move in the heavy layers of clothing but out they went and they did it, laughing and throwing snowballs at each other and impeding their own work but getting it done nonetheless. It took two hours, scooping up the snow and packing it and pressing it into the rounded balls, first for the base and then the harder work of forming the second ball on top of the first and keeping both of them round, or nearly so, and then adding the smaller ball, though still a good size, for the head, and then still having to shape the arms at the sides, and all the while the snow falling and they were covered in snow themselves and their hands were red and raw and stinging and their eyes watering and their noses running. And then, with the body and head finished, his pa went over by the house to where ma grew her flowers in the spring and summer and came back with a handful of black stones he had stored there for the purpose and with the stones they formed the eyes and a curving line for a smiling mouth. He needs a nose, pa, he'd said, and his pa grinned and brought forth from a pocket of his coat a fat woody carrot and they had to poke a hole in the middle of the face to plant it there and it was hard work because the snow was beginning to freeze and the carrot fell out three times before they got it to stick out just right and when they did they fell back in the snow and just laughed and laughed and laughed.

And then at last it was done and they went to the door and ma stood there with them in her coat and admired the snowman no end and then she got them inside and no dawdling, you two, she said, and pulled off their heavy clothes and dried their hair with a thick towel and then she sat them down at the table and fed them porridge to take off the chill and she put big dabs of butter to melt in the middle of each bowl, porridge in the middle of the afternoon, and never in his life before or since had Trask tasted porridge so hot and thick and good.

He warmed up the last pot of coffee and poured it out and drank it slowly.

The candle had blown out that last time the door was opened and now he took it and bent over and got it going again at the fire. When he set it back on the table he was glad of the little extra light it gave in the cabin.

He drank the coffee and poured another cup and tasted it. He watched the steam curling up from it, dispersed this way and that by the rushing drafts that found their way inside the cabin. He pulled out his pouch and built a cigarette and lighted it at the candle and smoked it, blowing out the smoke together with the vapor from his breath, and then tossed the butt end into the fire.

He knew what he was going to find the next time he went out there, or something, at least, of what he would find. But why? It was the why of it that puzzled him.

He built and smoked another cigarette and finished the second cup of coffee and then sighed and flexed his fingers a few times and then arranged his blanket to go outside again.

And there they were. He stood in the bristling wind and the cutting snow before the door and there they were in front of him. They were not five this time. He could not tell how many there were, for the line of them stretched left and right before him and curved around the corners of the cabin. He counted quickly. He could see twelve maybe, no, fourteen of them, and they stood in a neat row, like soldiers, arms length apart, though their white arms of snow remained fixed at their sides.

The two that were farthest away, facing the corners, stood at an angle to the others so that maybe the line stretched down along the ends of the cabin. And they were bigger than before, thicker, bulkier, and taller even than they had been, these giant snowmen, their round white featureless faces well above his own so that he had to turn his head upward to look at them. To build them with human hands would have needed ladders, even scaffolds, to set those heads in place so high and there was not a human hand other than his own in that night, in that clearing, in the midst of that killing storm on that mountain.

When after a minute or two he went back inside, he meant to spend an hour in the cabin this time but he could not wait that long. He drank coffee and smoked cigarettes and built up the fire and huddled in his blanket in front of it and thought he felt a trifle warmer than he had before. But there was something strange in the cabin and for a minute he could not think what it was. The candle flame was not fluttering but welling up with a steady yellow light. He built another cigarette and smoked it and watched the candle. He could even read by it now comfortably if he chose, but it was burning down and he would have to get another to see him through the rest of the night.

He stood up and rubbed his hands together rapidly and settled his blanket. Time to go outside again.

This time, though the wind still roared with a fury, it did not sting his face or try to pluck the blanket away. Above his head snow still swirled madly through the air but little of it touched him. The snowmen were bigger than before, much bigger, big enough and tall enough to tower above him, to tower above the cabin. He had to throw his head back to look up at what would have been the face of the one directly in front of the door where he stood. And they were close together now. Now they stood shoulder to shoulder, lacking shoulders as such though they did, close enough together to seem pushed against each other, crowded together in a tight immoveable line, an impenetrable line, around the cabin. He knew it went all the way around the cabin and probably the stable too. He looked them up and down and they, in their vaguely human shape, made him feel short, a strange sensation for a big man to feel.

They had left a narrow pathway, maybe three feet in width, between their own bodies and the wall of the cabin. Above his head the wind roared but it did not touch him here in this narrow space. Trask turned to his left and made his way through the alley to the corner and there he saw that the line of snowmen encircled the stable too. He went to the door of the stable, his boots squeaking on the snow, and pulled it open a little and even in the darkness he could see the horse toss his head in affirmation. Trask closed the door quickly and leaned against the wall of the stable in the space between that and the cabin and pulled quickly at his buttons, his fingers less frozen than formerly, and peed and closed his pants and went back to the front door, hurrying through the narrow passageway against the wall. The air was cold still, as cold as before, he thought, but it was hard to be sure of a thing like that because the line of snowmen blocked the wind with their backs and kept it away from here and away from the walls of the cabin. He swung his gaze left and right again and craned his head upward to look at the sturdy white palisado that stood up between the rage of the wind on one side and him and the horse and the little cabin on the other.

It was definitely the wind that had frightened him, that had made him stay awake all night for fear of losing himself in sleep, and he could not feel that wind now and so the cold itself felt less. The wind might still touch the roof of the cabin and it might blow an odd breath at the walls but the cabin was behind the palisado now and it was safe.

Inside again with the door closed, Trask fetched a new candle and lit it from the stub and replaced the stub and then sat at the table and studied the flame. It did not flicker, only burned bright and steady and unmoved. A good light to read by. A good light to live with, untouched by harsh winds. He dropped the blanket from his shoulders and sat up straight. He concentrated his attention and waited. He could hear the wind howling outside but he felt nothing moving against his hands or his face or his neck, no icy drafts at all creeping in from outside. The candle continued to burn as peaceably as a candle in a church recalling a departed soul.

Satisfied, Trask built up the fire once more, then went to the bunk. He unfolded the big Hudson's Bay blanket and shook it out and spread it over the bunk and then folded it down to the bottom half. Then he sat down with the other blanket still around him. He opened the gun belt at his waist and hung it on the nail and slid out the gun and laid it on the floor within reach. Then he tugged off his boots and lay down and pulled up the big blanket until it touched his chin and in a matter of seconds he was asleep.

Four days later, with the snow stopped and the wind abated, as Ulysses was picking his careful way down the icy trail, Trask met Beauchamp slowly making his way up on the red mare.

When they came up together and reined in the horses, Beauchamp looked hard at Trask.

"Well, I thought you froze to death up there," he said. "It's four days. All the boys thought you were done for."

"Nearly was, I reckon," said Trask.

"Worst storm I ever recall seeing," said Beauchamp. "That wind took part of the roof off the horse barn. Took two of the window shutters off the bunkhouse too. Looked fit to take the roof off the house. Sounded like it wanted to get inside there and tear something apart."

"Men alright? Livestock?" Trask asked.

Beauchamp nodded and pounded his gloved hands together a couple of times to warm them up.

"Must have been bad up at the cabin," he said. "Colder up there, and the wind is worse too. Much worse. It's the wind that gets you."

"Wind was pretty bad," Trask said.

"No damage?" Beauchamp asked.

"No," Trask said.

Beauchamp nodded but did not take his eyes from Trask's face.

Trask leaned forward and patted Ulysses on the neck. The big horse was tossing his head, eager to get on home.

Beauchamp laid the reins over the mare's neck and she turned around and came alongside the back. The two horses and the two men remained still a moment, facing down the trail with the mountain behind them.

"What happened up there?" Beauchamp said. From the way he said it, it hardly even sounded like a question.

Trask turned his face away briefly, then looked back and directly at Beauchamp.

"You ever make a snowman?" he said.

Beauchamp was surprised. "Sure," he said. "When I was a kid. Couple of times with other boys. First time with my pa. Recollect it like yesterday. That was the best, that time with my pa."

Trask nodded. "To be sure," he said.

He nudged Ulysses and they started together down the trail to the ranch.

After a while Trask said again, "To be sure," and after that they rode in easy silence the rest of the way home.

Stillness

Richard Thomas

Darkness spilled over the land. Ten locks were fastened, turned, and keyed as fast as his ruddy hands could move. If you fell asleep with the pale sunshine drifting down on your face, you could wake up in a room full of strange men with a gun in your mouth. He shook the door handle several times, satisfied that it was indeed locked.

Out of breath, his chest heaved, brow coated with sweat. Michael flicked off the lights and squatted in the corner. A lone red dot flashed across the room, his only link to the outside world. Another night of cold corned beef hash right out of the can. Unprepared, again. It would be his demise.

He crawled to the one open window, floor to ceiling, a towering presence. He had to move as if a ghost. He had to close the thick metal shutters without drawing any attention. He eased up to them and with all the patience he could muster, pushed them closed, meeting with a familiar clink. Silence.

"So how was your day, honey?" he asked the tiny, dim apartment.

"Great Michael, and yours?"

"Same old same old. Spent four hours remote gassing the vehicles. Posted to my blog. Had a can of Minestrone soup. Lite, because I'm watching my cholesterol. And then I fell asleep on the mattress covered in a blanket of dust, bed bugs, and an odd stain or two."

"I'm sorry baby. Do you miss me?"

"Every day, Missy. Every goddamn day."

Michael buried his face in shaking hands while his body was wracked with grief. Two years. Not a single solitary voice or face in two years. But his role was essential. Leave, and the swarms would come. The masses would flock. The herds would migrate, and all would be lost.

He crawled over to the ancient computer monitor that sat on the floor, its beacon a dull bleed from this scab of a life. It was time. He punched the enter button, and out the tiny slots in the metal shutters he saw flames shoot high into the sky. Brilliant yellow masked with velvet and rust. The screeches came next, crackling and bellowing, as the frames fell from the sky, the musculature tipping over with a dull thud. He shoved his fingers in his ears while he rocked back and forth, empty inside, with little reason to care.

Shirtless, his thin frame toned and tan, Michael shoveled the dead creatures into the fire pit. He glanced up and down the wall, as he did every morning, watching it extend as far as his eyes could track. To the horizon in every direction. Nothing new today, but he had to look. It was his only television. This one opening, the one gap, was his to maintain. It was his trap to set, and it worked like a charm. In the pit, the long thin bones of the airborne creatures mingled with the massive limbs of their masters. And others.

Leaning the massive shovel against the stone wall, he limped to the far side of the courtyard to wrestle the chicken fat over. Giant tubs of oil, grease, fat and other waste. Tubs, cans, buckets, whatever he could find. It still remained, scattered all over the city. Leftovers from every abandoned McDonald's, Burger King, and Kentucky Fried Chicken. Especially the KFC. He grabbed an old milk carton, twisted off the top, and poured it over the towering pile of bone and sinew. Around and around the pit he walked, dousing it in the rotting liquid. When he was done, he tossed the carton on the pile and stood back. Let it sink in before lighting it on fire.

Decisions today. Into town, or stay here. Canned food, or a nap. The heavy gun at his hip said nap, but his boredom and hope said town. As he strolled past the rotting pile, a crimson claw shot out of it, clasping down on his thigh.

The pistol was out of its sheath before the claw could sever his limb, and he shattered the exoskeleton into a thousand pieces with a single shot. Sometimes they didn't go down easy. Eyeing the opening to the vast desert that lay before him, he blinked several times, and then gently placed his hands on the tear in his leg. The faded Levis had been no match, and the parting of his flesh oozed fresh blood over the fabric.

"OK, staying here today. Time to play medic."

Ambling back inside, now limping with both legs, Michael pulled a pack of matches out of his pocket and bent one back. Striking it across the cover it burst into flame and ignited the rest of the pack. He tossed it onto the scrap heap and went inside. A dull *whoomp* ran around the base of the bones and up the pyramid of flesh. The smell made his stomach growl, against all will and hope.

⁂

There was only so much automation could accomplish. He had to be here. But why the journey across the valley of death couldn't be made, he didn't know. So little communication, and what he got was difficult to decipher. His family was long gone. Missy, and his son, Mike Jr. Mikey. Mikey Mouse. Junior. The little man. He didn't let himself revisit those days very often. His son, not at all. It was too much. So he held his station, and did his job. His service had been up three months ago, but nothing had come across the transom. He wouldn't know where to go if he did take off. What direction, how far it would be, where they were. He'd been in the dark since the beginning.

Michael lay on the same rotting mattress as yesterday. The door was locked. The shutters were closed. He sat up and reached across to the computer to push the button.

Enter.

Shrieks. Bellows.

He lay back in the dark, and contemplated his options. He gazed over at the medication on the floor, the pile of empty plastic containers. No more.

The days passed as they always did. Piles of bones, and the endless beatdown of the hot summer sun. Nights were filled with nothing but the pulsing of his heart, and the crackling of bodies burning down into a pile of ashes.

Until they came.

He thought they were coming to save him.

A loud chopping noise outside his apartment jolted Michael out of his sleep. Running to the window, he pressed his eye up against the slot, and was rewarded with a glimpse of a low flying helicopter. Sections of light panned across the courtyard, voices in the night, lost in the whir of blades slicing the air.

They were here. Finally. He could leave.

Running to the door, he clicked open the lone lock. A phone in the kitchen rang, a startling jingle out of the void. Rushing out into the hallway he left behind several things. A pile of mail pushed to one side of the door, almost three feet high. An overflowing garbage can in the living room, filled with empty Chinese take-out, fast food bags, and pizza boxes. A fully furnished apartment, complete with brown leather sectional, four-post king size bed, and plasma TV bolted to the wall. And a small wooden table covered with prescriptions, some empty, some spilling onto the table. But the ones with the most recent dates were full and unopened.

Down the stairs he flew, as voices and radios crackled all around. Boots crushed in the front door, the thin frame splintering as he ran out the back.

"They're here. I can go home," he said, lips moving in a barely audible mumble.

Into the courtyard of the apartment building he flew. A row of bushes almost ten feet high ran to both sides, with a gap in the middle, chain link fence wide open. Three Weber grills sat next to each other, covered in gasoline, charcoal and greasy black soot. To one side a circle of rocks formed a makeshift fire pit, filled with bones of all sizes. Tiny bones the size of cats and dogs. Larger bones, a femur, a foot, the size of a small child. And even bigger still, the skulls of adults, tibias and jawbones. Bits of fabric, denim and leather mixed with the melted down stubs of shoes, boots, and purses.

He stared at the mess, the stench of burnt flesh overwhelming. Sweet and meaty, the sour tang of rotting underneath. Side to side he glanced as the light poured back and forth over him. A garbled mess of squawking and rotor blades as the wind whipped around him. Bits of cement and ash swirled, striking him in the face and arms. Looking down he was only clad in a dingy pair of what had once been white underwear, his arms and legs covered in scrapes. He looked up to the gap between the hedges as the storm troopers poured through, guns raised, masks and helmets tight.

They were on him like a swarm. A herd of beasts.

In the Raw

Brian Hodge

As a kid I used to daydream about being executed. Even then I must've guessed where the road more than likely had to end. All that was left was what I'd say at the loser's finish line, after the walk from Death Row. It would have to be something good. Memorable.

Uncle Thurman once laughed about a guy he'd heard of, looking at everybody on the other side of the glass who'd come to watch him die. Told them, "Good people are always so sure they're right."

I figured at least one of them must have come right back at him: "And bad people don't care when they're wrong."

Stalemate.

Right or wrong, though, good or bad, the convict was still the dead one.

Might as well start thinking of something quick, I told myself. *My luck, I'll be needing it sooner rather than later.*

What else was I going to talk to myself about while washing my hands at a basement sink that still smelled like wet dog? It had been like that for a few days, ever since Misty gave the mutt the bath of his life after he'd rolled in something dead.

I knew that smell too. Knew the smell of dead better than I knew the scent of my wife.

Two nights earlier I'd stood on the other side of the basement. At the vise bolted to the workbench and a shotgun in the vise. Enough Old Milwaukee down me to not mind the back-and-forth drudgery of the hacksaw.

Years ago, when we were both in lockup, Hector told me you could meditate on anything. He was right.

I got lost in the high, grating rasp of metal through metal, until there was no such thing as time or guilt or consequences. Didn't snap out of it until those last cold inches of barrel I wouldn't need went clanging to the concrete.

Six times I'd washed my hands so far but they never seemed to get any better. I figured I could lather through the whole bar of Lava soap, let the pumice strip my raw hands down to tendon and bone, and I still wouldn't be any better off than when I first cranked the water hot and scalding.

I could barely notice wet dog any more.

There were worse smells to worry about.

Things like that never have a true beginning. Every time you think you can pin it down, you remember something earlier that made a difference, opened a door, pushed a button, cleared a path.

Try the week before, though, on a catwalk at the plant, getting an overview of the job that waited for me down on the main floor. And Hector, a day shift manager in our lives as free men, coming up to relay the mix for the morning, the proportions for the pit. He gave me a glance and got that look in his eyes, like he just *knew* what was going on behind mine. He'd been doing this for years, and whenever he didn't like what he saw, he had just one thing to say: "Where's your feet?"

The thing is, when Hector puts that to you he's not really asking about your soles and ankles and ten stanky toes. It took a moment before I knew how to answer this time, even if he would've known anything other than the truth to be a lie.

"My uncle's been coming around lately," I said. "Keeps hinting that"—how to put it in Hector's terms?—"that he's got some new shoes for me."

"Is he the only one doing the talking?" Hector asked.

"Yeah." *So far.* Me, acting like just listening was an accomplishment to be proud of.

And Hector knew it. "Even when you got your own voice to tell him to keep his ass clear of you, if that's all he's got to talk about. You can't even say that much?"

"He's family. About all the family I got left."

"Except for the family you *made,"* Hector said. "Family like your uncle, those are the people begging the most for a boot in the ass."

Figured if I tried that with Uncle Thurman, he'd only laugh. I was no Hector. Hector just *looked* like a guy you couldn't move without a case of dynamite and a wrecking ball. One of those Mexican guys that looked like a bull, and he'd gotten to an age where the skin of his face seemed as thick and tough as a bull's hide, especially in the crinkled brown folds at the corners of his eyes.

Underneath his shirt he was as gaudy and contradictory as the guys he'd grown up with, and who had his back in the pen. Most of them had an overlay of tattoos from two different worlds, the edges of their cheeks running with black-ink teardrops, every one of which meant a dead man, and below the neck were crosses and the Sacred Heart of Jesus. Hector had no teardrops but his contradictions were weirder still. Jesus and Mary and the cross shared skin with Buddha and a wolf and a raven and cryptic Asian figures and a lotus flower and a Star of David and a star in a circle and things Hector never got around to explaining.

Just this, to whoever didn't understand and acted like they expected a holy war to break out on his skin: *"If you're going down on a sinking ship,"* he'd say, *"you gonna care all that much what name it says on the lifeboat?"*

"Let me ask you something," I said. "You know who my uncle is. You know what he does and where he does it. A few times you've even known when he's gonna do it, when I've known enough to tell you. So how come you never made a phone call? One anonymous phone call."

Hector looked amused and a little insulted. "What good would that do?"

"Get him sent away, for one thing."

"That why you tell me so much about him? Hoping that's what I'll do?"

I couldn't say it hadn't crossed my mind.

"If you been wanting somebody to make that phone call, why didn't *you?* They got no payphones around where you live?"

Nailed. Nailed to the wall.

Hector shook his head. "Your uncle's a problem, yeah. But not the *real* problem. You *listening* to him... you thinking maybe you'd like to follow to the only place he's got to lead...you creeping up on that border between straight time and whatever you think looks easier...that's the real problem. And it ain't going away, even if your uncle does. Cause if it ain't him tempting you, then it's gonna be someone else. Even if it's only that little voice in your head whispering for you to cross over."

I knew that voice, all right. Except most of the time it didn't whisper so much as it seemed to stand on the other side of the line and shout.

"You wanna walk the straight and narrow, then walk it. That's what I'm here to help with. That's why I am still alive on God's earth. But I ain't here to clear the weeds for you. You gotta find it in yourself to take care of that."

I looked down on the floor. All those sad carcasses waiting for me and my scoop.

"Besides," Hector said. "I ain't nobody's fucking snitch."

You've seen my house before.

Maybe you took a wrong turn and were suddenly glad you didn't live nearby, and your foot got heavier until you liked the scenery better. Or maybe you meant to come, because your idea of charity was dropping off a holiday turkey at the house next door. Or you saw the place on the news—a meth lab bust, or someone here won the lottery and you hated them on sight and knew they'd blow it all within five years and what's worse you were probably right.

You've seen my house more times than you can count. The kind of house that, even if it was painted a nice cheery yellow, that would just make it sadder, because it fools no one and changes nothing.

Sometimes I find myself dreading the day my kids get old enough to look at it and feel ashamed, and ask why we don't live someplace better. They'll get there, and sooner rather than later if they spend enough time in front of the TV. For now, they're old enough to wrinkle their noses when I come home from work and tell me that I stink.

Keep yourselves out of trouble, then, or else the only jobs they'll give you are the kind that leave you smelling this way, I want to tell them. Colm, at least. It's always boys that need it most. Serena I worry less about, because girls usually seem to me to have more sense, and Serena likes books, but maybe I'm just being naïve. Keep hearing that the fastest growing part of prison population these days is women.

So maybe I should hug them both close whenever they complain about the smell of the plant on me. Keep their little faces pressed into my clothes until they can't hold their breath anymore. *Take a good whiff and remember this smell, so you can think about it whenever your feet start to take you someplace they shouldn't.*

Not exactly father-of-the-year material, but you work with what you've got.

It might even work, but I can't see it going over well with Misty. She preferred to treat that part of my life like it never existed. Which is good, because she never throws prison in my face like an insult, but I guess with a thing like that, and what put me there, you can pretend it away only so far. Because there come times I'll see it cross her soft, oval face just as surely as a set of bars slammed between us, without having given her any reason for it. Just lying on the floor with my legs in the air, say, a kid balanced on the soles of my feet, giving airplane rides to Colm and Serena, and you'd think being domestic couldn't get any more blissful, except Misty's got this look in her eyes like part of her senses it's not enough for me.

Dear God, how is it that women see these things, no matter how deep we think we've buried our secrets, how seldom we let them see the light of day?

As second chances go, you got yourself a pretty sweet one, she seems to beam into my head when she thinks I don't notice. *And if you blow it after all this time, the years I've put in with you, I just might have to cut your balls off before they take you away.*

But sometimes it goes the other way, too. When it's plain that my years in lockup are on her mind, even if she hadn't known me then, and she doesn't say a thing because she doesn't have to, yet instead of judgment, there's an air of understanding coming off her, as if she knows from the inside-out how tough a thing it is to live down. Because no matter how hard we may work to keep from mentioning the past, we can't erase it.

Perfect example: when she told me about the note that Serena had brought home from her teacher.

"Next week, in her class...one of us should probably be there." Misty sounded like she'd rather tell me the car had blown its fuel pump. "They're having Career Days."

"Are you kidding me?" Career Days. "She's in first grade, for God's sake."

"I can go, if you want," Misty said. "Where else are they going to learn about the finer points of putting a salad bar together, if not from me?"

Had to love her for that. I kissed her and told her no, it would be all right, that I'd come up with something. But the hell of it was, what kid wouldn't be spellbound by a father who came to school telling tales of armed robbery?

She kissed me back and moved her hand on my shoulder like she was trying to rub out a stubborn stain.

If this were a made-up story instead of the truth, right about now would be the part where the lucky guy asks the good woman why she ever married him, what she ever saw in him.

Not this time. I knew better than to ask. The last thing I wanted to do was give her a reason to think it over and come up empty.

The first time Hector asked me *"Where's your feet?"* I didn't have a clue what he meant. But he liked to catch a man by surprise that way, to make him stop and really *think* about that straight and narrow path he was supposed to be on after getting out.

It did the trick, and it needed to. Because I get crooked feet sometimes. They start to point in different directions...although, as Hector noted, it could be worse. They can only do that when you're standing still. It's when you start moving that you have to pick one direction.

Hector only had to explain himself the first time, but it was a crucial time, the day I'd showed up for my second shift at the job where he'd put in a solid for me before my parole officer sent me over.

That second day is a big deal. Because your first day at a rendering plant puts all kinds of thoughts in your head. Doesn't matter how hard you've promised yourself you won't go back to the old life. *Jesus God,* you tell yourself that first day working your grotesque new career, *there's gotta be an easier way to turn a few dollars than this.*

You already know there is. It's what got you locked up in the first place.

Hector knows all about that. Recognizes the look in a man's eyes when he wants to cross the line again. Understands the itch that lodges beneath a man's skin and soul, won't let him go, won't let him have peace, and keeps coming back and back and back again to remind him there's an easier way. He can see it even when all the face you try to show the world is just one more clock-puncher putting in his hours.

Rendering: It's a shit job on the best of days, and when you're a new hire, you see the very worst of it right off the bat. They gave me a facemask with an elastic band and enough training on a Bobcat mini-dozer to be dangerous. Then they steered me toward the plant floor, just inside the receiving doors, and turned me loose on the piles that are constantly being renewed. What everybody calls *the raw.*

All those cats and dogs that get put down because nobody wants them? Nobody ever thinks much about where they go next. Or roadkill scraped off the black-top. Or the livestock that turns up dead and bloated in the farmer's field. Or the heads and hooves cut from the ones that lived long enough to be more useful. Or the meat that sits past its supermarket sell-by date.

All the world's lost pets that never find their way home again...I'm the last guy to see them, in what is truly Hell's own kitchen.

Working the levers and pedals inside the mini-dozer's cage, I square off against the raw, and the mask is no protection against the reek. Most of the year, except when it's cold and the flies aren't on the wing, the dump zone appears to shimmer and stir before the scoop touches so much as one hair. Because the maggots always get there first. For their industrious nature they share the same fate, as I push and hoist and dump that devil's stewmeat into a pit so deep that one man standing on another's shoulders would barely be able to see above the stainless steel rim.

This is assuming the man on the bottom isn't having the legs sliced off him.

Down bottom are the grinders and augers. I could poke holes in my eardrums today and fifty years from now still hear the crunch of bones and the tearing squelch of the rest.

You wouldn't think there's a craft to it, but there is. The man we call the chef sends down orders for more of this or that, to keep a prime balance between livestock and house pets, poultry waste and butcher spoilage.

Shred it up, cook it down, skim the fat and squeeze what's left until it's dry enough to grind into powder. Sift out the hair and collar buckles and nametags and the last stubborn bits of skeleton, and that's how meal and bone meal are made.

Then back out into the food chain it goes.

Read a label sometime.

This is existence, after prison.

I'm still not sure I'd call it living.

⁂

The night before I took the hacksaw to the barrel of the shotgun, my uncle and I sat at my kitchen table watching the empty cans mount up between us.

"I heard another good one," Uncle Thurman told me. "More last words before they fried the guy."

I looked to see if Colm or Serena were within earshot. Didn't want them picking up anything I'd rather they not repeat, especially in front of their mother, and double especially if it was something they'd picked up while Misty had left me in charge of them while she was at work.

"Are they clean?" I asked.

"Clean enough. This guy back in the thirties." Thurman put on a defiant face, but over-the-top, like something from an old black-and-white gangster movie. "'You sons a bitches. Give my love to Mother.'"

We laughed. And who knows, maybe guys back then really were like that right up to the very end, down to the cartoon snarl and jutted jaw.

Uncle Thurman didn't look like all that hard a man unless he wanted to, but when he did, it was real enough. The rest of the time he kept it inside, behind a pair of eyes so flat you'd swear the life had drained out of him years ago. It was his disguise. He was as alive as any snake waiting to strike from tall grass.

I went to the fridge for two more cans.

Our routine, whenever Uncle Thurman visited, was almost always the same. We'd drink awhile and talk awhile, and exchange whatever memories of my dad were closest to the surface, and we'd have a few laughs, and pretty soon Thurman would ask if I was doing okay for money. I'd tell him that I was.

"You sure?" he would ask, something resembling concern on his face, and he'd shift in his chair like a man about to reach for his wallet.

"Yeah. We're fine." Always the same answer, even when we weren't.

Thurman nodded in his usual way, seeming satisfied, and then not, as though something had suddenly eroded my credibility. He went for his wallet anyway and slid three or four fifties across the tabletop, with its faded map of old coffee and Kool-Aid stains.

"I couldn't take that, Uncle Thurman. Really, I couldn't. Go on and take it back."

"Now, Renny, let's not lose sight of priorities here." On cue, he pretended to look aggrieved until my hand relented and swept the bills on the rest of their journey. "That's it," he coaxed. "You don't want it for yourself, put it toward something for the kids. A man with two kids the ages of yours, he's not got much room to be too proud."

"Says the man who never had any of his own."

He shrugged it off. "You know me. I'm the type to get more joy out of helping the families of others."

"I'll tell you what I could use next week for them, and that's another job." I told him about the career day plans for Serena's class. "Where do I even begin to explain to a roomful of first-graders what I do?"

"Tell 'em..." He paused, looking thoughtful. He had the head for it, with a bristly hairline that started halfway back on his crown, and three days' worth of a beard that had turned white before he was fifty. "Tell 'em you work in the pet care field."

It was all the invitation Uncle Thurman would need, and I suppose I knew all along that it was, and that I just wanted to hear him ask again without having to come right out and say so. Better if it looked like his idea.

"You could come to work for me," he said. "Not that you wouldn't still have to make up something to tell the kiddies, but at least you'd smell better."

I slid my can around the tabletop, something to look at instead of Uncle Thurman's eyes. "You got a start date in mind?"

"I could use somebody I trust this weekend." Now it was his turn to check for my kids, if they'd wandered too close. But we were okay. In the next room, the TV was still too loud and one of them, Colm probably, was banging on a table. "We're going to jack a trailer transport on its way to a Honda dealership. I could use another man. Be glad to have you."

Uncle Thurman worked stolen cars out of a self-storage facility he owned. The larger bays were wide enough to drive into, and each one made a perfect place to keep a car out of sight before sending it out again whole, or while chopping it up for parts.

"Hijacking, that's kind of a heavy operation for you, isn't it?" I said.

Whatever familial warmth his eyes were capable of, they lost it, and took on that flat sheen. "You don't think this is the first time, do you?"

"Is the driver in on it?"

He shook his head. "I bought the intell from a mechanic at the dealership."

"What *about* the driver, then?"

"Restrain and detain. What did you think?" When I didn't say anything, he went on. "Are you armed these days?"

"With two kids? Christ, no."

One corner of his mouth gave a tic of a smile, as if he'd pictured Misty and me in a discussion about guns. "Better *get* armed, then."

"Is that necessary? What about the rest of you? Won't you already...?"

"Think of it as a deterrent. The more guns there are, the less likely anybody has to use one."

"You got no loaners, something I could borrow?"

He snorted a laugh through his nose. "If you were a plumber, would you show up at a house call asking if they've got a pipe wrench?"

I sat for a few moments, listening to the sounds from the living room. Loud Disney music, louder laughter. A few yaps from the dog. Tippy—that's the kind of name your dog ends up with when you get him when your daughter's four. And sometimes I had to ask myself why I ever let Uncle Thurman through the door.

"If you don't know anybody to buy from these days," he said, "I could point you toward a guy."

I shook my head, too quickly, a sure sign of a pin-prick to my pride. "Don't worry about that, it shouldn't be a problem."

He checked the time on the oven clock, double-checked it on his watch. *Yeah,* I wanted to tell him, *it works. You don't have to make a show of how you're not sure.*

"I should be getting on my way," he said. We both knew why. "I wouldn't want to pass her going the opposite way down the street and spoil her night." He laughed. "Or her mine. That woman you married, she could burn a hole through titanium with that look she gives me."

Misty tolerated my uncle's visits, but just barely, and only because he was all the family I had left. She felt some sympathy for me over this that overcame her natural aversion to him, which she harbored for reasons she'd never been able or willing to clarify, although they seemed plain enough to me: She didn't trust him. Even though Misty didn't know half as much about him as I did, she sensed enough to fill in some gaps.

She tolerated him best when she wasn't around, so Thurman tried to keep his drop-bys confined to when she was at work. Like I was cheating on her, in a way, only without the sex and anticipation. And my uncle was the one who left behind fifty-dollar bills.

He drained his last can and I saw him to the door, and he said goodbye to the kids along the way. He had this way of ruffling their hair that sometimes made me feel like shampooing it after he was gone. But they liked him. Genuinely liked him. They were too young to put on an act.

"Call me in a couple days," he said on the stoop. "Call first, then swing by. We can go over the details."

I watched until he was nothing but a pair of shrunken taillights shining through the frosty gloom. Gulping the chilly air and telling myself it was the cold, and nothing but the cold, that made me feel so awake, like I might not need to sleep for a week.

When you're on the inside, doing your time and trying to figure out how to make it pass faster, all you've got is routine. It keeps you stable even as it drives you toward numbing madness. Then you come out and trade it all for a new set of routines. You tell yourself they're better, and if you're lucky they are, and for a while that's enough. But eventually you realize it doesn't matter where you are—either way, you're still locked in.

I hated getting caught, years ago. But always loved the feeling when I didn't know whether I'd be getting away with it or not.

⁂

"Working rendering's a good job for an ex-con," Hector told me in the early days. "These pits, this is where we take what's rotten and turn it into something useful. Makes you puke first time you see it happening, but if you look at it right, it's the best lesson you're ever gonna get. Cause you and me, we come out of lockup and we ain't no better than the raw. But one day you'll walk out this place and you won't be anything like the man you are now."

True. Except I wonder if he ever allowed that it could make a man worse.

Years after I heard this spiel the first time, I heard him give it word-for-word to a kid barely out of juvie.

"How long's this transformation supposed to take?" I had to ask him. "I mean, Jesus, Hector, *you're* still here."

He had no answer for that, at least not one that I could believe, and it was the only time I ever saw him wear a look of shame, like everything he said and promised and believed he stood for was just so much bullshit, and in that moment he knew it.

Sights, sounds, smells...a man with enough reasons can put up with anything.

The next step, when he loses himself, is forgetting there was ever anything else.

❖

The day after Uncle Thurman's visit, once my shift was over, I didn't go straight home. What little sun the day had seen was about played out, and the shadows didn't so much lengthen as pool up like tar in the spaces between the brick buildings and fences and cars.

He went by the name Chill, and if I'd really been sincere about keeping on the straight side of the line, I never would've known who he was all this time. Always told myself I made it a point to know for safety's sake. To defend my family, if the worst kind of need ever came up.

Shrugged deep inside a stadium jacket, Chill seemed not to feel the cold, maybe because he spent all day outside, acclimating to the seasons one dawn and dusk at a time. He chatted me up awhile, maybe making sure he didn't catch a whiff of cop, but when I mentioned that he just laughed, and so did his friends.

"Man, I'm four feet downwind of you," he said. "You smell more like a morgue attendant than popo."

They all laughed again, half a dozen of them crowded around a fire barrel and sipping from styro cups filled with a drink the color of a grape popsicle. Around them, the ground was littered with empty bottles of Sierra Mist and Prometh cough syrup.

"Come on," Chill said. "Showroom's this way today."

We fell into step together. He produced a yellow walkie-talkie the size and shape of his palm and gave somebody a heads-up. Halfway down the block we cut between a couple of houses that made me feel better about my own, and crunched on back to something that once might've been a respectable garage. The door scraped open from the inside, then shut again, and the boy he'd radioed popped the trunk lid of a big boat of a sedan.

They were loose, on blankets and in inch-deep boxes, like the kind holding cans of green beans at the supermarket: revolvers, semi-auto pistols, and on up from there in size and firepower. I rummaged around, trying different pieces for their fit and feel in my hand.

"Looking for anything in particular?" Chill asked.

"Something that makes enough of an impression upfront that I won't have to use it," I said. "And cheap. Cheap's good."

"Narrows the field some." He leaned in, reaching into the shadows at the back of the trunk, and tugged out a shotgun, or what was left of one. "If that's your priorities, how 'bout this? This one ain't been going nowhere for a while now. Got no bling factor to it."

No, it most definitely did not. The metal was dull and the wood was scuffed, and its days as a hunting gun were long over. The barrel was still full length, but someone had sawed away the stock to leave a makeshift pistol grip.

"But if it's impression you're after, it's hard to beat that pump action, know what I'm saying? Won't matter what comes outta your mouth—that puts the exclamation point behind it."

I hefted it, held it, racked the slide. It seemed sound. Chill gave me a price of one-seventy-five, and I held up the last four fifties that Uncle Thurman had slid across the kitchen table. It was hard not to believe he was thinking of them as an investment all along, knowing how they'd be spent if he kept it up long enough.

Chill looked at the bills before plucking them away. "This ain't Wal-Mart. I don't do change."

"How about shells? We can make up the difference in shells."

He tipped his chin to the kid who'd opened the garage door. "Give the man some twelve-gauge, then."

They came in a baggie. I dropped them in a pocket on one side of my coat and slipped the shotgun beneath the other side, wedging it in place with my arm. Glad it was over and done with, feeling a hollowness in my stomach—committed now, and this had been so easy it made me wonder what I'd been afraid of all these years.

I turned for the door, and an instant later Chill's hand was on my shoulder and his voice in my ear: "Hold up a sec."

It all went through me in a fraction of that—which one I should try taking out first, using the shotgun as a club, or if I could get lucky enough to handle both of them without getting shot, or if I'd stand a better chance dropping one and then using the car for cover while I loaded. Except the shells wouldn't be any good, would they, because nobody's going to give you good shells before trying to rob you of more than you'd paid already, and the joke was on them because I didn't have it anyway, and win or lose here, live or die, at least I wasn't chewing myself out for walking into a trap, because it was all about survival now—

An instant later there was Chill's voice again, into the yellow handset: "Coming out in five. We're cool."

So what did it say about me that I wasn't as relieved as I should be that things were concluding on a peaceful note after all? No way could I have walked out of the garage in one piece, if at all, but sometimes you get to a place where in one piece is two stops from the last thing that matters. A part of you *wants* it to go south, and maybe you're too smart to throw the first punch or fire the first shot, and too bad for you, because smart doesn't change the fact that there's some kind of pressure building on the bad side of a weakening valve, and you've got to let it out any way you can, even though it's sure to mean blood.

The door creaked open on a gasoline breeze and the last of the day's gray light.

"Don't mind the red dot on your chest none if you notice it," Chill said. "Ain't nothing personal. Just can't be too careful's all."

"Yeah you can," I told him, in some other guy's voice. "I got seven goddamn years of stink on me that says so."

⁂

That night, with Misty at work, I sneaked the shotgun into the house and took most of the barrel off. I let the TV babysit while I did it, and the kids knew better than to bother me while I was in the corner of the basement I optimistically called the workshop. But Colm already knew something was up. He had seen, poking out from beneath my coat, the paper I'd wrapped around the shotgun on the way home, and the bulk of something tucked under my arm.

"Is that a surprise for me, Daddy?" he asked. Full of the kind of hope that, once it gets squeezed out of you, never comes back. Which I wanted to keep from happening to him as long as I could.

"Not this time, partner. But maybe there'll be a surprise for real before long."

"When?"

"Then it wouldn't be a surprise, would it?"

He mulled this over and decided it made sense, even if he didn't like it. Oh, we learn a hundred ways to deceive and stall our kids. Sometimes they even combine.

"But you have to promise not to say anything about that to Mommy," I told him. "Or Serena either. Okay? It'll be our secret. Just between men."

Colm gave me his word, and it spooked me to see how solemn he turned when he did it. Like he was swearing a vow on life itself. *Cross my heart and hope to die, stick a needle in my eye.*

When Misty came home that night I was cracking another beer, and assured her it was my first. While she played with the kids and the dog before bedtime, I stepped out on the porch with the can and breathed the night into me. Felt the frozen boards give and creak underfoot. A tiny thing, as porches go, and I hadn't noticed it in such terms before, but it seemed only about as big as the stained wooden pallets that were delivered to the plant, brimming over with spoilage waiting to be rendered.

And about half the size of my old prison cell.

No wonder I felt so comfortable out here.

I listened through the door as they roughhoused and tickled, and could picture it in my head as they laughed and shrieked, and Tippy barked, and in spite of everything I hadn't given them, they sounded happy.

Why isn't that enough? I asked myself. *By all rights, it should be.*

I'd been telling myself that I'd finally taken my uncle up on his offer for their sake, so I could provide more and better. To be the husband and the dad who showed up with the fun surprises.

It's easier to call bullshit when you're alone in the cold. Money was only the half of it, and maybe less. Even if I *made* enough at the plant, or any other straight job, made what I considered a decent wage, I don't know that it would ever *be* enough.

I stood in front of the door like its guardian until the cold seeped into every pore, and still couldn't bring myself to turn and reach for the knob. Listening to the sound of some other fellow's family and wondering how they could love him, when they didn't even know who he was.

Two nights running I reached for the past and tried to remember if I ever lost sleep before a job, back in the day. I couldn't recall it if I had. Couldn't recall staring at the darkened ceiling until it seemed that this was all the night would let me do.

Misty woke up beside me at some point, even though I knew I'd been lying still enough, as still as dead meat, so I could only imagine she'd been jolted out of sleep by that scary female radar of hers, that it worked even through the deepest reservoir of her dreams.

Her hand crabbed across the mattress and touched my hip. "What's wrong?"

"Nothing. You just woke me up is all. Go back to sleep, babe."

I could hear her swallow, a soft smack of her lips. Waking-up sounds. We-need-to-talk-even-though-it's-the-middle-of-the-night sounds. "Is that Career Days thing next week still bugging you?"

"Yeah," I said. "It weighs. Yeah."

I counted one breath, two, thought I could listen to her breathe all night, three, thought I might even have to, four, and when she said, *"Look at me,"* something inside felt like it got a sudden coating of frost. I turned onto my side, up on one elbow, and made out what I could of her face, but in the dimness her eyes were too shadowed to read.

"You've got nothing to be ashamed of," she said. "You'll do great."

I gave no sign of how alert I was for what she said and how she said it.

"Bring in a picture of a mini-dozer, why don't you. Just tell them you drive one of those. The boys'll love it, for sure. Probably some of the girls too, the tom-boys...and as for the rest of them, *you're Serena's dad*. That counts for something. So remember that."

It was a good idea, actually. "They'll ask me what I move with it. Some smart kid'll think to ask."

"The earth. Tell them you move the earth," Misty said, then giggled. "You move it for me. So it's not a lie. Remember that, too."

I promised her that I would, adding it to all the other promises, like to love and honor and till death do us part. We scooted closer under the covers and I held her until she drifted off to sleep again. And I wondered how she knew something was going on and how much she suspected. It wasn't just me. It *couldn't* be just me. It really had been there in the tone of her voice.

You've got nothing to be ashamed of, she'd said, only saying it like she knew I'd be forced to think of the closest thing there was. To let me know that her eye was on me. Might as well have asked, *"Where's your feet?"*

I slipped my arm from around her and my shoulder from underneath. Tiptoed out for a piss and then ended up in the kids' room. Nobody would be waking up in here, both of them sleeping as soundly as two kids could. I looked at the dark sunburst shapes of school ribbons on the wall on Serena's half of the room. Perfect attendance? Spelling? I should've been able to remember what they were for.

She'd be needing her own room in a few more years. It wouldn't do, sharing a room with a brother while she was...changing. She'd want her privacy. And Colm would need his, too, soon after. There were too many changes coming, so many that I wished I could open the doors, the windows, let the early winter winds swirl through and freeze us all into place. In that perfect world, morning would never come and the moon never drop from the sky, so we could all stay like we were right now and the secrets could remain hidden in the dark, and I'd never have to make a tough decision again, right or wrong.

My babies...

They lay in their beds, skinny little Serena on the bottom bunk, Colm on top, my monkey boy who loved to climb, and their breath puffed soft and high.

I'd named them myself. Came up with each name and was lucky enough that Misty liked both, and so that was that, with no need for compromise. Such a burden I'd put on them, though, from the time they were newborns, and no one had ever known the truth of it but me.

Serena. Colm.

Serene. Calm.

I'd made them into reminders of the qualities it would take to keep me on the right side of the line. Every time I spoke one's name would force me to remember what I needed to be, to keep myself living the straight life until I was too old to remember I'd lived any other way.

A part of me wanted to wake them up.

You didn't do your jobs, I could tell them, and they wouldn't understand, but they'd know by the sound of it that something was far from what it was supposed to be. *So whatever happens next, it's on your little heads almost as much as mine. Because we're a family. And if she leaves me, you'll be all the family I have left.*

I'd been coming in while they slept ever since they'd been born. To look at them, to breathe the air they sweetened, to remind myself of the old vows.

Never once, though, had I imagined what it would feel like if I knew I was coming in for the last time, or close to it—a day or two left, depending on what I'd done and how it had gone and the chance of it catching up with me.

And dear God, however faint it may have been, I could feel an understanding coming on that I never wanted to have. Most every prison has one or two: a man with distant eyes, calm and serene, who's there because he got up one day and decided this was the day he would wipe out his entire family, maybe burn down the house around them while he was at it. He usually hasn't been cruel about it, only efficient. He bore no malice, just crumbled under the pressure of trying to be something he wasn't, and the rest of them lost.

I always hated those men to the bone.

Still did.

And never considered it was possible that I might be living with one.

When I called my uncle's cell, I did it from a gas station payphone a mile from the plant, and he said he was glad to hear from me, and it felt good to hear him say it. Then he gave this curt little laugh he'd bark out whenever someone disappointed him or whenever they hadn't but it had come as a surprise, and told me he'd only half been expecting me to call.

"Why wouldn't I?" I said. "You told me we had some plans to go over before the weekend."

"So I did. So we do." He told me where I'd be able to find him once I got there.

It was starting to sleet, needles of ice shooting from a sky the color of oily water and peppering at the windshield as if trying to chip through. The wipers scraped the buildup toward the sides, and every so often I felt the tires shimmy as they hit a slick patch. I took it slow and made a wager of fate: If I lost control in any way, even if I were to steer out of it, that would be a sign I was supposed to forget about it all and go home.

The closer I got, the more the car rolled straight and true.

Uncle Thurman had picked the ugliest part of town to set up shop, that last mile or two before commerce and industry petered out into nothingness. Everywhere you looked you got an eyeful of empty parking lots and chain link fencing and off-ramps. Weeds sprouted in whatever cracks they could find, hanging on until the life was choked from them too, and the only color came from billboards hawking everything I didn't want or didn't need or couldn't afford if I did. The ice seemed right at home.

The storage lot was enclosed within its own fence, row after row of low buildings that looked like bunkers, gray cinderblock shells subdivided into bays with corrugated metal doors that scrolled up out of the way. It was the wrong time of day for most anyone to be hauling something in or out, and the wrong weather too. At any rate, he didn't rent many of them to paying customers—just enough to give the place a veneer of legitimacy. Several of the other bays were reserved for hot cars. Some were outfitted to chop the cars for parts, and in others incoming vehicles were left to cool down before they went somewhere else. A lot of units sat empty and always would. Uncle Thurman used a ledger full of false rental records to launder the cash.

He'd been looking at it as a family business for years, I suppose, even though I was all the family he had left. He'd started in on me a couple years after I made parole. Probably waiting to see if I was inclined toward a swift fuckup that would send me back again before he took a chance.

As I drove in along the rows, I couldn't believe I'd held out this long. He'd been just persistent enough to ask, then go silent awhile, so I would wonder when he was going to ask again. Making me wait for it, think about it when he didn't mention anything. He'd been the trickle of water that wore down the rock.

Bay 514—I parked and stepped into the stinging rain of ice, hunched inside my coat while knuckling the metal door and calling out to let Uncle Thurman know who it was. The door curled upward enough for me to stoop inside, then he shoved it down again and kicked the deadbolts along the bottom back into place.

And everything was dry and warm and quiet again.

He used it as an office, his *real* office. A space heater, a couple of battery-operated lights, a footlocker for a file cabinet, a trestle table and a chair or three... what more could you need?

"Anybody else coming?" I asked.

He shook his bristly head. "They know the drill already. You're the virgin. We just need to make sure you don't act like one."

He pointed at a map unfolded on the table and began tracing the transport trailer's expected route into town, and where the spotter would be stationed to pick up its trail, then cue everyone else it was on the way.

"I want that to be you," he said.

"Me? Why me, my first time out?"

"You don't think you'll recognize a trailer full of Hondas when you see it?" He snorted and cuffed me on the back of the head. "You'll do fine."

As I'd done a million times before, I tried to recognize some small piece of my father in him, and had no more success this time than all the others. He was harder than my father would've been, if he'd lived, and Thurman's face wasn't even close, with a rounded, subtly crooked jaw that seemed to slew toward his right shoulder even when he was looking straight ahead.

For once, for a change, I was relieved not to see my father.

Uncle Thurman turned serious on me. "I told you the other night: I can use somebody I trust. Couple weeks ago I heard one of my crew on a call, and I'm not even sure what I heard, but...there are ways to get these things sorted out."

I used to be like my son once, too: pure and unspoiled, ignorant of everything that's worst in people, squashing ants to see what would happen and then unspeakably sad when they didn't move again. What changes? What in God's name changes?

My uncle narrowed one eye. "What the hell's wrong with you?"

I took a couple steps back and then the shotgun was between us, and if he went blurry for an instant, surely that was the runoff from the ice melting in my hair. Except I couldn't pull the trigger right away, so we stood looking at each other, as if neither one of us could believe what was happening.

"Why couldn't you just take no for an answer?" I whispered. "Ever?"

For a man who got plenty of laughs out of other men's last words, he didn't seem to have prepared much of anything for himself. "You coward piece of shit," was all he could manage, right before I found enough balls to pull the trigger.

The first shell didn't kill him, so I made sure with the next that he didn't suffer.

Then it was back out into the sleet, with the pair of Pacific Locks that he used to secure the bay from the outside. It seemed colder now, cutting through the coat and down to the bone, and left me shaking so much I could barely roll the door down again. I felt the sting of ice, but could no longer hear it pecking at the car and every other hard, frozen thing around. The sound of two shots slapping off block walls had left my ears feeling thickened and numb.

I dumped the shotgun on the way home.

Took my time getting there, though, because the later it got, the less likely it would be that I'd have to look anyone in the face.

You lose one sense, they say, and the others will compensate.

Maybe that was why, no matter how fiercely I scrubbed and lathered my hands in the basement sink, I couldn't seem to rid them of that firecracker smell of gunpowder. I gave up and went for the shower next, as I always did when I got home from the plant, and stayed under until there was no more hot water in the house.

She woke up when I came to bed and turned on the light. I had to watch her when she spoke, to be sure of what she said, because while my hearing was returning, the high end was still shaved off, and everything sounded like it was coming through a plaster wall.

"Those time-and-a-half shifts are going to be the death of you, Renny," she said.

"Can't be helped sometimes," I told her. "How do I smell?"

She smiled. "You'll do."

I asked if she knew where they had the most flowers in the world, plentiful and fragrant, as far as the eye could see and the nose could smell. Misty said she wasn't sure, but that she'd heard Hawaii had plenty, and that sounded good to me.

"Tell me what it's like there," I said, and sank beneath the covers as if they were waves.

"I've never been. How should I know?"

"Tell me anyway."

So she made it up as she went, and I floated along for the ride, as much as my ears could make out, and let imagination fill in the rest.

Maybe if I could've heard every word, it would've been enough to keep me from thinking about the shotgun, and the part of me that wished I hadn't dumped it.

Second hardest thing I'd ever had to do.

Couldn't be helped.

But my feet, I feared, would know the way back.

I Found a Little Hole

Nate Southard

MAY 21
I found a little hole today.

I was playing with my Army Guys, and I nearly set my bazooka soldier on top of it. It wasn't very big around, maybe the size of my thumb, but something about it looked cool. Maybe it was the way its smooth edges curved in like the top of a whirlpool. Maybe it was how the grass didn't grow around it. There was just wet dirt surrounding the hole for a few inches, followed by grass that had turned yellow. The yard didn't become green again for almost a foot in each direction. I thought that was neat, like all the color had been sucked down the hole I'd found.

I wondered what could have dug it. It looked too big to be from a worm and too small for a snake. I couldn't think of anything else that lived underground except gophers, and the hole was *way* too small for one of those.

So I leaned forward, squeezed one of my eyes shut, and peered into it. Maybe what I did was stupid. There could have been wasps inside, or spiders.

But instead there was an eye.

I gasped, and Mom asked if everything was okay. I jumped a little and said everything was fine. I pretended to play with my Army Guys, having a bunch of G.I.'s shoot at a group of terrorists. She shrugged and went back to hanging laundry. That was good, because I didn't really care about the Army Guys anymore.

As soon as I could, I looked in the hole again. The eye was still there, looking back at me. It was blue, bright and clear even though it was surrounded by dirt. I blinked hard, thinking maybe I was imagining things or it was really just a marble—something like that. Nope. It was an eye, all right. I could tell because it winked at me. Or blinked. I couldn't tell because I could only see the one eye.

I smiled at it. I waved. It winked (or blinked) back at me a bunch of times, like it was waving hello. I chuckled a little, and that got Mom's attention again. I pretended to make an Army Guy explode. Mom said she was heading back inside, so I told her I wasn't done playing yet. She said something about supper and left.

I wondered how there could be an eye in the bottom of the hole. Was there somebody buried alive in the backyard? That sounds crazy, but it's possible. How long could a person survive like that? Days, maybe? A week or a month? I'm pretty sure I would have noticed if the backyard had been dug up recently. No, there's something special about the eye, something that makes it fit in the hole. I'm sure of it.

After twenty minutes of smiling down at the eye, Mom called me in for supper. I waved goodbye, then gathered up all my Army Guys and ran inside. I wanted to go back outside after dinner, but Mom told me I had homework to do. Man, I hate homework!

I wish I knew who the eye belonged to. I think it might be another boy, like me. I don't know why. I guess it just feels right.

I'm going to call him Tommy.

MAY 22

School felt like it took forever today, but that was just because I couldn't stop thinking about Tommy. I wanted to get home and see if he was still there. Once I got off the bus, it took everything I had to keep from running straight to the backyard. I couldn't do that, or else Mom would think something was up. Instead, I ate a few cookies and drank a glass of milk while Mom asked me how school went. Her questions nearly drove me crazy, but after a half-hour or so she said I could go outside to play.

Tommy was still there. He winked (blinked) a few times when I waved hi. I told him the name I'd given him, and he seemed to like it. He didn't shake his head or anything, so I guess he's okay with it.

I asked him a bunch of questions, but he couldn't answer, so eventually I just started telling him about myself. I can't tell if he liked listening to me talk so much, but I think he did. I told him that I think caves and stuff are cool, and I asked him if he lived in a cave under our yard. His eye shook a little bit, and I think he was telling me, "No."

I like Tommy. He's cool. I don't know anybody else who lives in the ground. I wish I could live in a cave or something like that. That would be so awesome.

I better go now. Mom is telling me it's time for bed.

MAY 23

Guess what? I saw Tommy's finger today! When I went out back after school (and Mom's daily questioning), it was poking through the ground. I ran over and touched it. It disappeared down the hole like I'd scared it or something, and when I looked into the hole Tommy's eye appeared. I waved, and he stuck his finger through again.

It was big, kind of like how I remember my dad's fingers being. Dirt covered it, but I cleaned all that off with my shirt. It wiggled like a snake, and that made me laugh. I reached out to grab it, and it disappeared. Then, it peeked out of the hole like it was afraid. It stood up straight, then bent and did a little dance like Egyptian guys do when they walk in those old movies

Mom watches sometimes. I couldn't help but laugh my butt off. Tommy's real funny.

I reached out and touched his finger again, and it closed real slow around mine. It was like we were holding hands. Suddenly, I felt real safe, like when Mom kisses me goodnight. I liked it.

I stayed that way for a long time, just holding Tommy's hand.

I've decided I'm going to dig him out tomorrow.

MAY 24

Tommy didn't like my idea. I told him what I was going to do, and I showed him the shovel. When I looked back in the hole, his eye was moving back and forth, and I could tell he was shaking his head. I asked him why, but I knew he couldn't answer that question.

I got mad, then. I told him if he didn't want to be my friend, then that was just fine. I didn't need him around, anyway, and I have plenty of friends. He doesn't know how many friends I really have, so he couldn't tell I was lying. I stomped away and sat on the back porch. I watched the hole for a long time.

After a few minutes, Tommy stuck his finger through. It sounds stupid, but it looked sad. I felt real bad then. I was already crying, but I think that's because I was so mad. I ran over and grabbed Tommy's finger with mine, holding hands like we did yesterday. I told him I was sorry, and he squeezed my finger real hard. Not so hard it hurt, but hard like he really meant it. Hard like a good hug.

I think I love Tommy. Not in a weird way, but how I loved my Dad. I still love my Dad, but I can't tell him that now.

I don't want to talk about this anymore.

I can't wait until tomorrow. I like spending time with Tommy. I want to see him so bad I can't sleep. I wonder what he looks like?

MAY 25

Tommy's gone!

I went out to play with him, and his eye wasn't there. I called, but he didn't show up. I called again and again, and I even cupped my hands to the hole and yelled down it.

Tommy didn't come. Instead, I heard a noise like a dog growling. It sounded like the Nelsons' bulldog, but a lot bigger. It sounded meaner, too.

I leaned away from the hole. I felt scared. I smelled something like old garbage, and I think it was coming from the hole. I saw blood, too. There wasn't much, but there was enough that I could tell it was there, spattered around the hole like old paint. The wind picked up, and I felt real cold. It's May, though. It's not supposed to be cold anymore.

I heard that growl again, and I got up and ran inside. I must have been more scared than I thought, because Mom nearly screamed when she saw me. I don't want to tell you why, but she made me change my pants and underwear. She asked me if everything was okay, and I lied. I couldn't tell her the truth. She thought it might be the kids at school picking on me again. I wish!

She gave me a kiss and asked me what I wanted for supper. She said I could have anything I wanted, so I asked her to order pizza with pepperoni and bacon. I wasn't hungry, but I didn't want her to worry. It smelled great, but I couldn't taste it. I still ate three pieces, though. I didn't want Mom to worry. She does that too much. After supper I took a bath. I told Mom

I was tired, so I was going to bed early. I think she bought it.

I miss Tommy. I don't think he's coming back. I think the growling thing got him. Maybe he knew about the growling thing. Maybe that's why he didn't want me digging him up.

Tomorrow, I'm going to fill in the hole. I'm not sure what I'm going to use, but I don't think regular dirt will do the trick. That growling thing's down there. It killed my friend, and now it knows I'm up here.

I think it's going to try to dig free.

Fallow

Scott Nicholson

Denyse Hammen eyed the bent stretch of fence and sized it up for sturdiness.

The withered plot of dirt on the other side promised a slightly slower death than that afforded by starvation. The shriveled, gray rags poking from the ground suggested a deformed row of turnips. Sickly corn stalks leaned, tassels too dry and corrupt to attract pollinating critters. A crucified tomato plant hung with knobby green balls dangling, blossom-end rot painting them half black.

"My kingdom for a horse," Denyse said to herself. "Because I'd eat the son of a bitch."

She wracked the top strand of barbed wire, putting her foot on the bottom strand and leveraging a gap. Ducking inside, she tangled her hair and a few strands came out at the roots. Compared to the sick, bald people she'd seen streaming out of the city, she didn't mind losing a little of herself. Besides, malnutrition might do what the bombs or the fallout hadn't accomplished: human extinction.

They were all getting to the end, some faster than others. Denyse planned on being among the last. She'd suffered some lingering nausea, her kidneys didn't work too well, and the sores on her arms failed to heal despite the salve she'd picked up from looted stores. Her feet hurt, despite the top-of-the-line Northface hiking boots she'd copped from a corpse in Wilkesboro.

But she could rest here and scrounge up a meal in the bargain. The garden had been tended, and someone had obviously set up a temporary home here. Since the bombs, all homes were temporary. But those who claimed a piece of ground in the timid new world were wont to protect it with firearms.

Once on the other side of the fence, Denyse edged around the tilled earth. On the road, she'd heard of booby-trapped stores and houses, and figured a source of fresh nutrition was more valuable than real estate now, given the population decline.

Thing about bombs, they blow a free economy all to hell. So much for the farm welfare system.

Even if she had money, nobody would take it. Especially here in the Southern Appalachian Mountains, which were rumored to be the outpost of the paranoid and strange. She understood the appeal of high ground—it was easier to see your enemies coming. And it also offered the tactical advantage of being far removed from the population centers.

The mountains were where you came for a slow death, and if you were already living here when the bombs fell, then you had even more reason to distrust outsiders. And she was a flatlander through and through.

Denyse, a sales rep for a medical supply company, had been doling out samples at a Piedmont hospital when the news came. She'd abandoned her car to the streets, realizing the highways would remain as clogged as the arteries of a Dixie fast-food cook. The daycare center was only a few blocks over, and by the time she arrived, the radio was blaring the destruction of New York and Washington, D.C.

Los Angeles and Chicago hung in there until she reached the outskirts of town, and the Research Triangle Park, home of many of the firms most likely to come up with new treatments for radiation poisoning, was a smoking hole before sundown. Little Randolph wailed as she trudged mile after mile, scarcely resting, sensing the poisonous and invisible wave that would soon be settling over the sky.

She shaded her eyes now against the sinking sun, early September painting the leaves in gold and burgundy. The Appalachian slopes, the oldest in the world, had somehow resisted the worst of the decay, as if being forged in the furnace of the world's creation had tempered the peaks against any future calamity. Once one of the world's most biologically diverse regions, it was now stunted with the bleached bones of trees. The fauna was dying, the ridges taking on the harsh aspect of desert terrain.

A tractor with flat tires and a rusty hay rake clawing out from its rear was parked in the weeds along the fence. A shed, constructed of locust poles and covered with tin roofing, stood at the far end of the garden, which was about the size of a baseball infield. A frayed dress hung on a pole, a mockery of a scarecrow made all the more obscene because birds had been among the first casualties of the fallout. A dried, orange winter squash was speared on the pole to suggest a head, though the impromptu jack-o-lantern had remained featureless.

Denyse, who had a .38 revolver tucked in the back of her waistband, decided to try a neighborly approach. "Anybody here?" she called.

The wind answered, and the draped dress twitched.

She approached the shed, peering between the rough-hewn boards. Since the collapse of virtually every system that required cooperation and mutual incentive, fuel was limited to fire and whatever petroleum product could be bartered, stolen, or seized. The larger, more organized groups had formed around urban centers, where warlords held sway until their lieutenants decided to make their own brief play for the throne. For women like Denyse, the barter system had become as simple as it had been in the cave-dwelling days—meat for meat.

She'd endured a couple of months as a time-share in the world's oldest profession. The warlords had dominion over the retail sectors and therefore the canned goods and provisions, and Denyse figured little Randolph still deserved the best opportunity she could give him. If that meant taking off her clothes and closing her eyes while some stinking stranger grunted away on top of her, she figured it was just part of the new order. As Randolph's lips lost enthusiasm for her nipples and he became thin and pale, Denyse increased her protein intake and did whatever it took to get vitamins and vegetables.

Once Randolph died, she buried him, secured the revolver, and made her way west, where the red sunset made the mountains appear backlit by a lake of fire, a lake long promised by Baptist ministers who now weren't so eager to go around claiming "I told you so." Smart-alecks and sages had no place in God's precious new Gomorrah.

Denyse circumvented the shed, careful to watch the edge of the forest. There was no thread of smoke to indicate a campfire or chimney. She couldn't imagine anyone leaving a garden unattended, and a pitchfork and hoe leaned against the warped walls of the shed as if they had been rested only minutes before. The shed itself contained nothing more than a pile of rotted burlap sacks and a few horseshoes nailed to the wall. She was about to help herself to some of the produce when the wind aroused a fluttering in the eaves. A tiny, curled figure fell from a gap under the tin. Denyse retrieved it, wondering which era it was from: Before or Since.

It was a corn husk doll. A dried, shrunken apple was stitched to the "dress" with a piece of fishing line. The apple's flesh had been gouged, making eyes, a nose, and mouth that had twisted into eerie deformities as the fruit dried. The simple doll made her think of Randolph, and her eyes misted before she flung the doll to the ground, the apple popping free and rolling across the dirt.

"Screw the children," she said. "Only a sadist would make a child walk through this hell."

She collected one of the more integrated sacks and went to the garden. She used the hoe to clear away some stringy potato vines and pulled a few wrinkled tubers from the soil. The dirt was black and had a soft texture, obviously tended with care. With the sudden decline of the gasoline era, acquiring fertilizer wasn't as simple as a drive down to the local feed store. Someone had not only tended the plants but invested time in preparing the garden across the seasons.

The cabbages were small, the size of infants' heads, and she collected two of them. She didn't want to be greedy but she also couldn't count on finding an abandoned store or canning shed later. And she didn't think she could knock down a squirrel with the .38, even if she were willing to risk wasting the last of her four bullets. She plucked a fistful of turnip greens and stuffed them inside her frayed canvas satchel. Denyse was reaching for the beets when the sickly moan came from the forest.

Sick child.

She'd heard plenty such cries, misery and pain and disease and anger and sadness rolled into a chorus that swept across the tainted land. Randolph had gone from four-alarm shrieks of distress to a soft gurgling whimper as the last breaths faded.

The moan came again and she slipped the bag closed, securing the revolver. Sick children posed no threat, but sick adults became desperate. She negotiated the fence again, on the other side this time, and entered under the hushed canopy of forest. The sun filtered through in a jewelry box of sparkles, and a creek ran with a merry laugh that seemed a mockery of the poison it carried.

The moan shifted, went higher in tone, running in musical counterpoint to the flowing water. Denyse, who had played the clarinet as a high schooler back in

Before, no longer cared for melody and harmony. The song had changed into a funeral dirge and every coda ended with the gasp of a contaminated lung.

"Who's there?" she said, stooping inside a thicket of scrub and rhododendron whose browned flowers cast the musk of dead rot.

The moan became a bleat and she entered a clearing of flattened grass. A slick newborn goat wobbled on its forelegs, trying to lift itself. A larger goat, no doubt its mother judging by the gruesome trail of bloody placenta strung across the weeds, lay on her side, ribs rising and falling slightly. The momma goat's eyes were glazed and focused on an unseen horizon, a look Denyse had come to know well: the thousand-yard-stare of death.

The little kid bleated and rose, back legs trembling, the matted stump of tail wiggling back and forth. It staggered toward its mother and collapsed at the swollen udder, latching its dark-red lips onto a nipple. Unsatisfied with the supply, it backed off and bumped the bag of milk a few times with its forehead, then settled in for a suck. The momma goat appeared to give one last contented sigh and expired. The oblivious kid drew sustenance, not knowing the warm fount would soon be dry.

"Damn, little goat," Denyse said. "Starving is no way to die."

Yet, compared to what she'd witnessed since the fallout festival, maybe starving was as good a way to go as any. Beat slow homicide, leukemia, gang rape, intestinal cancer, an erratic thyroid gland, or food poisoning. Besides, the kid didn't have to die a meaningless death.

She drew the six-inch blade from her satchel. The momma goat's meat was no doubt tainted, but the kid might be fairly clean, if the mother's liver had provided a sponge to absorb the nastier poisons. Then again, radiation was insidious, and it was probable that Denyse's roentgen count was higher than the kid's.

"Hey, little guy," she said, hunching and tiptoeing across the grass. The kid kept on with its suckling, a contented burring coming from its throat. One stroke across the throat. Painless. Then she could use one of her last few matches to build a fire and—

As she knelt by the animal, it twitched, finally aware that a large moving shape loomed over it. Instinct caused it to freeze but it didn't have the muscle control to flee. Besides, its role model was doing the bottle fly belly flop and in no condition to teach its new charge the proper way to run like hell.

Denyse gripped the kid's neck with her left hand, feeling the animal's pulse race as she drew the knife close.

Blood ran like poison in this new world. People were made of meat.

The kid bleated, and again the sound elicited a memory of Randolph's final days. She rammed the knife into the dirt.

"Damn you and your cute eyes," she said. "You're costing me a full belly."

The kid blinked and stared as if to say, "What are you talking about? You have all those stolen vegetables."

"They aren't stolen," she said, "merely reappropriated. If you were off the tit, I'd share them with you."

A metallic click sounded to her left. She looked away from the goat into the barrel of a rifle. It was pointed by a bearded man in a collapsed and dusty fedora, the brim notched and a crow feather stuck in the band. His wool shirt and pants were too hot for the balmy weather and sweat ringed his eyes. He was maybe fifty, maybe twenty going on fifty; radiation poisoning had solved any problems of ageism that had existed back in the old days.

"You making a sacrifice?" the man said, his hillbilly twang carrying a trace of the city.

"A sacrifice to my appetite," she said. "What's it to you?"

"That's my goat."

"I don't see any property boundaries. And all the 'No trespassing' signs must have been knocked down by the thermal pulse."

"Property is property," he said, "and this gun makes the law around here."

"I didn't know anybody was up here." She risked death by challenging him, but she figured death was fifty-fifty anyway, and a bullet at least got the job done a lot faster than cancer.

"Put down the knife."

"There's enough for two." She licked her lips, leaving it up to him any innuendo he cared to take from it. The barter system played as well in the sticks as it did in the concrete forest. And at least it would take the gun out of his hands.

"I got other mouths to feed."

As if on cue, a boy stepped out of concealment from the other side of the clearing. His face was dirty and his overalls ragged, bony knees showing through the frayed fabric. He had the gaunt cheeks of a late-stage cancer victim. "Minnie's dead, Poppa," he said, his tone flat, as if such declarations were all too common in his life.

"The kid come out fine," his poppa said. "The wheel o' life still turns."

Denyse thought the homespun philosophy was a bitter joke, but the man's dark eyes stayed serious. The rifle didn't blink, either. She tossed the knife toward the man's scuffed boots.

"It ain't got no momma now," the boy said. He appeared to be about ten, and whatever schooling he'd had must have dimmed from lack of use.

"We'll raise it up ourselves." Poppa's voice was as steady as the gun he held. "Nurse it through the winter."

Denyse wondered if they had a herd somewhere. Obviously the mother goat had been bred, and though she wasn't sure of a goat's gestation period, she figured it was probably a half a year or more, given the size of the offspring. But goats, like all ruminants, were herd animals by nature. Even sporting horns and thick skulls, they found safety in numbers, or at least better odds of not being the one hauled down by pack predators.

Denyse released the kid and it turned its moist nose back to the udder. Perhaps sensing the fading of the milk's heat, it emitted a bleat of unease.

The rifle barrel dipped at last. "Get up and let's see what you stole."

The boy rummaged through her sack, pulling out the vegetables she'd collected. As Poppa leaned in to look, Denyse thought of going for her .38, but it wasn't a quick-draw situation and she'd never shot a person before. The man appeared much handier with a gun that she did, and it didn't seem the time to try new tricks. Since the revolver was hidden by her long blouse, she figured that option would remain open.

"She took a big bite," Poppa said. "Take the kid to the house."

Poppa threw the sack over his shoulder while the boy gathered the kid in his arms. The boy headed up a path Denyse hadn't noticed before, a black strand of dirt that wound between tall yellow poplars and led up the ridge. Poppa's rifle pointed her to follow, and they walked in silence a few hundred feet, passing between chunks of granite that jutted from the ground like the prehistoric teeth of giants. The "house" turned out to be a structure built into the side of the mountain, rotted wood walls giving way to moist dirt and stone. The cave smelled of old sweat, mold, and wood smoke.

A metal cook stove was tucked into one corner, and desiccated onions hung by a thread from the ceiling. A lantern burned in one corner, fueled by noisome oil and casting jagged shadows across the cramped space.

The room had one bed in the corner, the mattress sodden. A cradle sat beside it, made of hand-hewn wood. The lone window was covered with a sheet of tarpaper and only a crack of sunlight appeared. She wondered if this were the hillbilly version of a fallout shelter or if it had been constructed after the war. The clammy air suggested a constant temperature, which meant it was probably easy to heat in the rough mountain winters.

The boy set the goat down and it teetered a moment before collapsing near a crooked chair. The boy laid some kindling in the belly of the rusty stove and lit some gray newspaper.

"May as well earn your keep," Poppa said, pointing to the stove.

"I'm just trying to survive, same as you."

"Skillet's in the cabinet there. Might as well fry some taters and cabbage since you took them out of the ground."

The skillet had half an inch of congealed grease in the bottom. She didn't ask. As the stove heated, the grease turned from ash-colored to yellow. Poppa gave her knife back and watched as she sliced the vegetables and spread them in the pan. Soon the rancid stench of cabbage filled the cave.

The little goat, which had been drowsing, woke up and gave its prating cry.

"The baby's hungry," the boy said.

"We'll take care of it," Poppa said. "We always do."

Denyse busied herself with preparing the meal, such as it was. She scraped her knife along the bottom of the skillet, figuring when bedtime came and

Poppa showed his intentions the same as any man, she'd have to go for the revolver.

The boy set out plates and they ate in silence, Poppa taking the knife from her again before sitting on the bed with his food. The boy sat cross-legged by the goat, trying to interest it in a strand of cabbage. The goat sniffed but wasn't going for it. Denyse relished the meal despite the rancid grease, taking comfort in the probably erroneous notion that the fallout was less severe in the mountains. She'd also heard crops acted as natural filters for the worst poisons, though some of those strontiums lingered for centuries. After all, Poppa didn't show any signs of sickness or weakness, though the boy moved slowly and expressed little appetite.

"Got to keep your strength up," Poppa said, belching and expelling a scrap from his mouth. "Got mouths to feed."

She imagined Poppa planned to keep her around, turn her into a wife and mother. She had no destination, no real plan, and at least he was a provider. She could die here as easily as anywhere else.

"Can we keep this one, Poppa?" the boy said, rubbing the goat though he was staring at Denyse.

"Depends," Poppa said. "Such things are out of our hands and in the hands of the Almighty."

The boy put away the plates. It had grown dark outside, or at least the sunlight no longer snuck through the tarpaper. In a world without electric lights, true darkness once again held sway in its domain, even if the nocturnal creatures that once prowled it had taken their measure of poison.

"You any good with a hoe?" Poppa asked her.

"I can work."

"You're an extra mouth."

She debated licking her lips, but coyness no longer seemed necessary, The job was hers, whether she wanted it or not. "I can…earn my keep."

The boy slipped out in silence, probably to relieve himself in the woods. Denyse wondered whether he suffered the runs or if blood clouded his urine. In the deep night, perhaps it didn't matter.

"The boy's not been right since he lost his momma," Poppa said.

Denyse nodded, staring at the stove, whose door was now open and casting suffused amber light. The pile of embers throbbed like the laughter of hell. "We've all come to know loss," she said, allowing a bit of his twang to enter her accent.

"And plenty more awaitin' ahead," he said.

"There will come trials, for sure." She wondered if she should bake up some bit of scripture for him, but none of the few verses she remembered seemed appropriate.

"This family's been split, but it still got needs."

"We all have...we all got needs." She wondered where she could hide the revolver. She wouldn't need it tonight, and probably not next week, but a trial and judgment would come eventually.

"The ground will lay fallow," he said. "But we got six weeks of harvest left."

She wanted to say the harvest had commenced the moment the red buttons had been pressed, but she doubted this bearded mountain mystic would make the leap with her. She'd best keep things down to earth. "Your garden's green, considering."

"It's all in the soil and how you tend it."

"I can help raise things. I lost my child."

"Maybe you'll find something else."

The boy returned, face paler than before. Or maybe the fire had fanned into flames and brightened the room.

"Get your brother," Poppa said to him.

The boy went to the cradle, his bare feet slapping the dirt floor. The kid goat looked up at its master, no longer bleating. The boy bent over the cradle and emerged with a small bundle of filthy blankets. He carried his offering to Denyse.

"He sure sleeps sound," she said, reaching out, wondering if the breasts that still leaked from her feeding of Randolph would lactate enough to nurse the child. "I heard nary a—"

The blankets fell away, revealing the mummified face of the dead infant. She screamed and almost dropped the corpse. Its face resembled the shriveled apple head of the corn-husk doll she'd found near the garden.

Poppa had the rifle pointed at her. "Got mouths to feed."

She wondered at what point the man's mind had cracked: during the nuclear annihilation, when his wife had died, or when his infant son had died. Or maybe she was the mad one, because the boy sat cross-legged at her feet, holding the new kid as if awaiting a messianic miracle.

Denyse closed her eyes and undid the top two buttons of her blouse, fishing around and bringing out a bare breast. She worked and squeezed it until she pinched a drop of milk to the nipple. She was moving the long-dead infant to her breast when Poppa's shout caused her to blink.

"You crazy or something?"

Weeping silently, Denyse let the cold bundle rest in her lap. She looked down and saw it was only blankets. Not Randolph.

"Give her the kid," Poppa said.

The boy brought the newborn goat close, and she could feel its warm breath on her nipple, causing the point of red flesh to involuntarily harden.

Maybe if her breasts offered enough yield, they would keep her. Maybe if she fed all the mouths they required, she could last through the fallow season. Maybe her trial was not far off.

Or only as far as the .38 in her waistband.

As the kid's lips and tongue began working with an unwholesome greed, she settled in for winter.

Last

Al Sarrantonio

In
the
night:

A wash of blue light blinded Mathis. The car passed, then directly behind came another with its brights on. Mathis shielded his eyes with his forearm, squinting, trying to see through the windshield. The car slowed, curbed next to him.

"Shields?" Mathis asked, still blinded, bending to look close into the tinted glass on the driver's side.

The window lowered. The twin cold metal eyes of a shotgun barrel slid out to focus in Mathis's returning vision.

The shotgun went off.

In
the
day:

More light. Mathis tried to move his eyes away from it, found he could not. He tried to close them. Again, nothing. He couldn't move his head; tried to signal his hands, arms, legs, feet to move and nothing happened. He felt suspended, two eyeballs frozen in space surrounded by bright light.

The light softened: a long band of bulbs rheostated down, giving him a view of the mirrored ceiling, a hint of mirrored wall.

He saw himself in the mirror on the ceiling.

He was two eyeballs frozen in space.

⁂

In
the
screaming place:

They were talking to him over and over. After five days, he had figured out that they had done it deliberately, into a recording, and let it run over and over. For the first four days he had screamed, not hearing any of it. Then, on the fifth day, he had figured out what they had done and the words had begun to penetrate the screams. Soon he had stopped screaming and listened.

"You are alive," the recording said, again and again. "You are alive, and whole."

He had listened for a little while, then he had begun to scream again.

⁂

In
the
quiet place:

"This is what happened to you," the man with the gray lab coat said. The man's back was to Mathis; he had yet to turn around and Mathis didn't think he would. "You were hit just under the jaw with shot from one barrel of a 12-guage shotgun at a range of less than a foot. Your head was nearly blown from off your body. If we hadn't gotten to you when we did you would be dead now."

"Are you sure I'm not?"

The man in the gray lab coat hesitated, then went on. "What was left of your brain, which was most of it, was brought here and digitally copied. The rest of you was almost useless. By analyzing tissue, we were able to reconstruct your features to a reasonable degree. There wasn't enough time to be fancy; there are little things, such as eye color, that do not match your original."

Mathis looked at the mirrored ceiling. His eyes had been brown, and now they were blue.

"You will find that you are stronger than you were. Your senses are sharper. You can run very fast now, Mr. Mathis. You can lift a weight of four hundred pounds; you can crush a heavy gauge metal can with one hand. You are not a superman...but you are a better-made human than you were before. You're the best we could make you."

The man in the gray lab coat paused again. Still he had not turned around to face Mathis.

"We...want you to find Shields."

"And kill him," Mathis said.

The pause. "Yes. It's been programmed into you. We felt it was the only way you would do it. We've programmed certain things into your brain, removed other things, memories and such, we didn't think were... useful."

"You realize that I was trying to help him when he shot me. I can't figure out why."

"That doesn't matter now. We...thought you might still be able to get close to Shields. No one else can. He is much like you, only without some of the...enhancements we made in your case."

"So Shields is a freak, too. Did he start as just two eyeballs hanging in space?"

"As a matter of fact, yes."

"What happens to me after I kill him?"

The pause again, longer. "We'll cross that bridge when we come to it."

"I wish I could hate you."

"You can't. We programmed that into your brain also."

"I'll see what I can do about changing the program."

In
the
night:

Mathis smoked a cigarette. He lay back on his bed with his arm behind his head, staring at the Venetian blind-slatted glow of blue light from outside on the ceiling. His mind was sharper than it had been. They must have washed out his brainpan, cleaned the synapses, while they were in there. The cigarette burned his fingers; idly, he ground the remaining bits of rolled tobacco into the ashtray on the nightstand and lit another. He drew deep, letting the smoke fill his new lungs, then blew it out slowly, trying to make the ceiling go away, obscuring it with clouds of his own making.

They're going to kill you when you've done the job.

This much he knew. They must have programmed him to take the inevitability of it evenly, with no passion. And that was what he felt—no passion.

The fact that Mathis had been able to find Shields would, in their minds, only justify what they had done to him. The larger problem of morality might plague them momentarily, as they had obviously plagued his faceless, lab-coated programmer, but the larger picture was more important and would supersede all matter of Mathis's personal rights.

In short, since they had made him, he had no rights.

Just like Shields had no rights.

And they could kill him when and how they liked.

Mathis felt the burn of his last cigarette reaching his fingers; he let the flaming tobacco continue its course until the pain reached from his flesh into his head and made him want to cry out. He smiled.

The pain was exquisite; it told him he was alive.

Between his singed fingers, the tobacco finally spent itself; idly, Mathis reached over for another cigarette and lit it, drawing deep.

He lifted the heavy hand weapon they had given him, aimed at the wall and pulled the trigger.

There was a loud sound and part of the wall exploded.

He lay the weapon carefully down on the nightstand.

He meant to stay alive.

⁂

In
the
lab:

"I see no reason to stop Mathis now. He seems to be making progress."

The man in the gray lab coat hit the table with his fist. "I'm telling you it's wrong! What we've done to him is wrong! This isn't the way we started this experiment!"

"We should never have started it to begin with. And now we're going to end it, once and for all."

The man in the gray lab coat's hand was shaking.

"It's *wrong*. And I won't be a part of it anymore."

His companion said, "I think perhaps you need a rest. We'll find someone else to take your place."

The man in the gray lab coat was helped out of the room, slumped between two burly guards, and his companion idly stroked his chin, and stared dispassionately after him.

⁂

In
the
night:

Mathis knew he was close. He could almost smell Shields. After weeks of searching, he had found himself on the same stretch of street where he had confronted the car that shot at him; now he was less than four blocks away, standing before a door.

He knew Shields was inside.

He reached for the doorknob and hesitated. Something roiled within him. He felt a touch of dread, a tiny sharp remembrance of the whitely mirrored room and opening his eyes to see nothing but his own eyes and the discorporealation of his own body. For a moment he felt nauseous; dislocated; and a suppressed memory almost came back, fleeting, sending a chill down his back. Then, like a ghost, it was gone.

He closed his eyes and the nausea left him.

He kicked open the door and drew his weapon.

⁂

In

the

room:

Shields was there, sitting at a table lit by a single overhead bulb, smoking. She was thin, her clothes hanging loose on her emaciated frame. Her eyes were black sunken pools under thinning hair.

"You're a woman," Mathis said.

Her hand trembled when she lifted her cigarette to her lips. "They programmed that out of you, too?"

"Yes."

"I've been waiting for you, Mathis," she said, and for a moment she looked at him with a wan smile, though her eyes were still deep unreadable pools. "After all, it was inevitable that you'd find me. You were plenty clever the first time around."

Mathis advanced to the table and looked down at the woman sitting in the chair.

Shields looked up, and now Mathis could see her eyes: deep blue. A tear stained one corner, and traveled down her rough cheek.

"You really don't remember, do you?" Shields asked. "They really washed it out of you, didn't they?"

"Remember what?" Mathis said. Though he wanted to sound hard and matter-of-fact, his voice, almost on its own, had softened.

Again that terrible trace of memory nudged at the edge of his consciousness, then floated away like a wisp of fog.

"You and I. We used to be the same. They made us at the same time, you know."

"They told me that."

"Did they? Did they tell you *what* we are?"

Mathis noted that Shields' cigarette was burning down toward her own flesh, and that the woman was ignoring it.

"You mean simulacrums? Androids?" Mathis asked.

Somewhere outside in the alley there was a sound, but Mathis ignored it.

Shields laughed, then coughed. The cigarette dropped from her fingers to the table and gave off its last hint of smoke before extinguishing.

"Tell me," Mathis demanded.

Shields shook her head, and again smiled. It was a sad gesture. She turned her hands over and looked at them. "These were pretty hands, until I had to hide. As I said, they made the two of us. Just to see if they could. Then, when they got scared, they changed you from what you were, and charged you with finding me, so they could end the experiment."

"But I won't let them," Mathis said. "When I'm done with you I'll get away from them."

"Will you? They really did bleed you dry of memories, didn't they? Have you tried that gun they gave you lately?"

Mathis aimed at the wall over Shields' head, pulled the trigger. Nothing happened.

Shields laughed, drily, then coughed.

Out in the alley, the sound was closer. Mathis turned his head quickly to look out through the open door.

"It's too late, Mathis," Shields said quietly. "They did their job too well. And now they've found both of us."

"What do you mean!" Mathis demanded, as dark shapes, their eyes glowing redly, filled the room and surrounded the two figures.

Shields reached for another cigarette, but her trembling hand dropped to the table instead and lay there. She looked up at Mathis.

"They made us," Shields said, her voice almost inaudible "The robots, the metal men, made us. It was just an experiment, to see, after a thousand years of extinction, if they could resurrect flesh and blood humans. And they succeeded, and you and I got away from them and were much more clever than they thought we would be." She looked down at her belly, which, Mathis now saw, was slightly swollen, before looking up at Mathis again. The wan smile returned. "I even became pregnant. And they got scared, because you were much too smart to lead them to me. So they set a trap for you and blew you to bits and then put you back together. Only they altered the original unpredictable blueprint. And here we are."

A circle of shotguns appeared, aiming in at the two humans. Red eyes flared in the darkness, and metal fingers tightened against metal triggers.

"And," Shields said, "we're the last mistake they'll ever make."

Mole

Jay Bonansinga

1.

The last person you would expect to see brushing past the beaded doorway of the Jean-Baptiste de la Salle transient hotel on the corner of Bourbon and Dumaine is Father William Slavatore Buonaserra. Compact, dark, and brush-cut, with an Ivy League air about him, the priest wears the standard collar of the clergy under his London Fog, but he enters the squalid lobby with an almost military purpose, a purpose that speaks more of a highly specialized Jesuit than your average neighborhood pastor. He pauses for a moment in front of the deserted desk with his shiny black attaché at his side and his two good wing-tip shoes gleaming in the dim light, quickly scanning the dilapidated room for any sign of life. The place is vintage French Quarter, its Louis XIV settees and padded chaise lounges now shopworn and weary from years of panhandling and prostitution. The air hangs heavy with must. A ceiling fan squeaks. Father Bill reaches out and rings the bell on the counter, rings it hard, several times.

"Hold ya horses," croaks a voice within the depths of a cluttered inner office. An ancient black man in a threadbare terrycloth robe shuffles out of the darkness. He holds a small video game in his gnarled, pecan-colored hands. "Help ya with somethin', Suh?"

"Blake please."

"What was that?"

The priest sighs and enunciates the words with tense formality. "Here to see a Miss Blake. Cornelia Blake. Understand she's a resident?"

The old man finally figures out what the priest is saying and looks up the name in a dog-eared register and then mumbles something about that nutty bitch needing a head-shrinker more than a priest.

Father Bill follows the clerk through a battered metal security door and down a narrow reeking hallway bordered with more battered doors missing letters and slathered with faded graffiti. They reach the last door on the left and the geezer pounds on the scarred steel. "Cornelia! Man of the cloth here to save ya soul!"

A mumbled reply from the depths of the room. "Let 'im in Chauncy."

The old man fishes on his key chain, finds the skeleton, unlatches the door, and walks away without another word. Father Bill goes in.

The room—a long narrow studio—is a disaster area redolent of urine and burnt tar. The sparse furniture is painted black, the walls festooned with voodoo paraphernalia, inverted crosses, and Satanic bric-a-brac. There are peculiar details that strike the priest's awareness—seen and unseen—that he will remember later: a light bulb painted Rustoleum black, a broken trombone, something that was once alive floating in a fluid-filled jar on the bureau, an umbrella sprung inside-out in the corner like the corpse of a giant starfish, a sense of decay in the seams of the cabbage rose wallpaper. The single occupant lounges in the corner on a broken-down chaise, an emaciated, tattooed woman in black. She bites down on a small rubber hose, clenched in her stained incisors, and she mumbles as she gets the last drops of a fix into her skinny needle-tracked arm. "You got the scratch with ya?"

Father Bill closes the door, walks over to the unmade bed, and drops an envelope on the blankets. "How long is this going to take?"

"Never can tell," she purrs as she loosens the makeshift tourniquet, the hose uncoiling with a snap.

"You mind if we get on with it?" He sets the attaché down in the center of the room and crosses his arms across his chest and waits. This is a first for him, and he's not too crazy about the prospects. Over the years, in the commission of his myriad duties for the church, he has presided over a grand total of twenty-seven exorcisms, some of them more successful than others, some of them obvious visitations by entities known to him, lower demons with patterns and signatures as recognizable as bank robbers, but he has yet to actually *summon* a specific entity by name. It has taken him months to find a back channel, a denizen of the dark foolhardy enough to serve as a vessel, a liaison.

He watches the junkie as she languidly prepares for the black mass. She stashes the money in a drawer, finds a Mason jar of blood under the bed, and then drips a pentagram pattern across the floor in front of her chair. She positions black candles here and there with ritualistic care, and she sprinkles herbs, and she breaks the neck of a dead sparrow, and she burns human hair, and she does a lot of hooey that Father Bill finds ridiculous and pathetic. Why do demons need to torment the innocent when there are so many imbeciles in the world who welcome the attention? The junkie gets comfortable and starts summoning the entity that goes by the name of Malefar.

2.

"Buonassserra I presume."

The priest hops out of his chair, the newspaper tented over his midsection fluttering to the floor. It has taken over an hour to bring forth the unclean spirit—the girl sitting cross-legged on the floor in her circle of black candles—and now her head lolls forward, her black, stringy hair dangling across her features as the room is filled with the reek of rotting meat and an alien voice coming out of her. The priest raises the crucifix half-heartedly, a splinter of rage mixing with the repulsion. He knows he's breaking a sacred rule here—priests are not to address a lower demon directly under any circumstances—but this is not exactly "any" circumstance. "Let me guess. Malefar right?"

"We got a winnerrrrrr," the thing inside the drug-addict replies with relish. Then it says: *"Okeeeee-dokeeee then..."*

The priest stares. "Okay so...all these messages you've been sending, the hemography, the child in Arkansas with the letters scourging his body. You got my attention. Now what the hell do you want?"

The girl's head snaps up as though on a puppeteer's string. Her eyes are gone. Her lips curl back into a horrible twitching rictus, as the drone of pipe organ comes out of her: *"This is important, Padre, I will not regale you with this more than once."*

"So regale me already so that I can get the hell out of this place."

The girl's head lolls again for a moment. *"What I am about to tell you...I want you to know I'm putting my immortal soul at risk."*

Father Bill rolls his eyes. Another first—an unclean spirit coming clean. "I'll be honest with you, Malefar, I don't give two whits about your immortal soul."

"AAAAAAAAAAHHHHHHHHHHHHHHHHHHHHHHHHHHHHH—!!" The force of the howling noise makes the junkie's neck bulge and contort with such alarming force it looks positively amphibious, the swelling of an over-inflated inner-tube, her body shuddering furiously. *"You don't seem to understand what I'm offering, Holy Man—I'm offering you information! You need to know what those letters mean."*

The priest feels like giving him the raspberries. "How thoughtful. Information you're offering now. One problem though: I don't give a shit."

A slow, hissing noise resembling laughter: *"You will soon give more than a shit, Holy Man."*

"Stop wasting my time. There's nothing you could possibly offer me in the way of information—other than the fact that you're a miserable liar and I should take everything you say with a busload of salt. But that's just me."

The demon inside the girl is silent for a moment, the girl's head lolling again. The voice that comes out of her then is softer, more contrite: *"You have noticed the signs, the little boy in Arkansas, the apparition of Mary in the morgue, the statistics in your files, those spread-sheets that you keep in your ssssssssssssecret files, they don't lie. Do they? The numbers don't lie."*

Father Bill gives the demon a shrug. "Are you going to get to the point tonight or should I send out for beignets?"

"I can help you...give you inside information...what they are planning in hell, it's all contained in the code. I can be your informant, Father. A simple bargain, a deal—"

"No deals you pathetic foul-smelling—!" Father Bill catches himself, swallowing his emotion, tamping down his anger. Is this a dream? Is he dreaming? Hallucinating? He stares at the twitching, cadaverous shell of a girl on the floor, looking past her black-button eyes, looking into her empty soul at the shapeless thing lurking there. At last the priest adds in a softer voice: "Let me get this straight, what you're telling me is, you want to turn snitch."

"In a manner of speaking yes."

"You want to rat out the devil."

A black smile creases the girl's reanimated face. *"A somewhat imprecise way of putting it, diluted by the Catholic penchant for mixing metaphors, but yes, indeed, that is the case."*

The priest thinks it over, and thinks it over some more. After a long, long pause, a pause that brings to mind geological eras passing, glaciers forming and reforming, the priest tells the demon, "I'm going to have to get back to you on this."

The girl collapses, and the odor goes away, and the room is filled with the sounds of a ticking clock and the girl snoring, and it's obvious the demon is gone.

3.

Over the next few weeks, the incident at the Jean-Baptiste de la Salle transient hotel fades in Father Bill's memory. The only trace of that evening that lingers—at least in the priest's mind, gnawing at him even now—is the proposition that a man of the cloth would consider an alliance with an unclean spirit. For nearly a month, the very idea of it lies in the pit of Father Bill's midbrain like a cyst, keeping him up at night, making even more aware of the shadow-spaces in the corners of every anonymous alley, every boarded storefront, every dark window. And for someone in Father's Bill's line of work, this added layer of cognitive dissonance is an unwelcome distraction. He lives a monastic life—the life of a ghost—moving from assignment to assignment in his battered mobile home, with its nicotine-yellowed cabinets, dusty old Philco record changer, particle board bookcases crowded with occult tomes and theological apocrypha, and peach crates stuffed with Stan Kenton albums. He has no regular friends, no living family, no dependents or responsibilities other than to serve the *Sanctum Instrumentum.*

A secret unit of the Catholic church known only to a handful of functionaries at the Vatican, the S.I. (or Holy Instrument) is the sum total of Father Bill's entire *rasion d'être.* Other than a few harmless vices—a taste for unfiltered cigarettes, old whiskey, and bebop jazz (especially Thelonious Monk, in whose music Father Bill believes God resides)—the priest lives and breathes solely for the unit, an arcane group whose purpose stems from a long and convoluted history. For years the Church has employed a group of clerics and specialists to investigate alleged miracles around the world—from weeping Madonna statues to the face of Christ manifesting itself in grilled cheese sandwiches—with varying degrees of success. Even the most rigorous of these investigators can fall prey to either the power of suggestion or mass hypnosis. And like a venerable old insurance company, the Church is obliged to conduct due diligence on all claims. This is where the *Sanctum Instrumentum* comes in. Agents of the shadowy S.I.—and there are only six in the world, Father Bill being the only one based in the U.S.—are charged with investigating the *investigators.*

Which is precisely what Father Bill is doing—weeks after the events at the Jean-Baptiste de la Salle—when he begins to believe he's being followed.

The realization hits him in stages, a little more each day, as he goes about his business. In Natchitoches, Louisiana, Father Bill is in a backwater settlement of tin shanties and kudzu-covered cabins, lurking in the cool blue shadows of the neighboring cypress grove, making notes in a his log book, keeping tabs on the visiting emissaries in their black frocks and wide-brimmed hats, as they poke and prod a ghostly reflection of Satan on the oily surface of rain-water caught in an upturned satellite dish, when a twig snaps in the darkness behind the priest. Footsteps, furtive footsteps, in the woods, thirty yards away, making Father Bill start, then whirl. There's nothing there, but Father Bill feels the presence shadowing him. He's been feeling it for days.

Less than a week later, he's standing on a viaduct over Highway 127 just north of Harrodsburg, Kentucky, in a hard spring rain, his London Fog drenched and sticking to his back, when he hears a whisper—right next to him—so close, in fact, it seems to emanate from *within his skull,* as he peers through binoculars at a group of clerics in the gray distance, about a quarter mile away, gathered around a lightning-struck telephone pole, the timbers contorted into the shape of an inverted cross. The invisible whisperer seems to *think* at him more than speak the words: THEY'RE COMING FOR YOU...DO YOU KNOW WHY?

With greater and greater frequency, the strange disembodied warnings accompany his investigations. As the months pass, he begins to see more and more signs of anonymous pursuers, more and more shadowy figures skulking just on the edges of his vision, in the peripheral blur of his travels, as he zigzags across the country in his ramshackle trailer, investigating the investigators, his intake of Bushmills and Camel Straights increasing.

Even his dreams become stuck like a needle on a defective record album, haunted by the incessant advances of the demon Malefar.

4.

"Your time is running out." In the lurid cinema of Father Bill's dreams, the demon always appears black on black, the antithesis of a human figure, an anti-figure without face or features—a vacuum within a vacuum. *"They're planning something over here...and it concerns you in the most personal manner."*

"Where's 'over here'?"

"The place without God."

"Hell is an actual place?"

"What is it with you Catholics? Always with the literal interpretations. Do you or do you not want to know what the letters mean?"

"I'm not signing anything."

"It's a simple proposal, Father, a bargain—your trust is all I require."

"Sorry no."

"A one-time only deal."

"All due respect, I'd rather die."

"Then you will. You will. Every last one of you. In the worst possible way."

5.

As the weeks pass, Father Bill begins having second-thoughts about the demon known as Malefar. During World War II, Pope Pius XII tried to work with Nazi liaisons. The foundation of the modern world has been shifting subtly yet *tectonically* beneath Father Bill's feet. Even the alleged "miracles" themselves—the once banal flirtations with the supernatural, more suited to the pages of tabloids than to theological studies—are becoming more and more foreboding. Salamanders falling from the sky in Memphis. Tributaries of the Amazon changing direction and hue, running as red as ox blood. A woman in a New York morgue reanimating for five and a half minutes, long enough to say three Hail Mary's and tear the flesh from her face. Something is shifting in the netherworld. The people who pay attention to this sort of thing are noticing changes. The agents of Hell seem to be marshaling forces, perhaps to make another play for power in the earthly dominion, as they attempted in 1902 in Martinique with their invasion of snakes, or in 1883 when they set off Krakatoa, or way back in 1346, in Crimea, when they unleashed the Black Plague. Father Bill keeps updating a stack of Excel spreadsheets locked in his files, most of which reflect this ascension: Demonic possessions over the last ten years have increased 37% over the previous decade. Phenomena have started to center around certain areas of the world for unknown reasons. Never-before-seen instances of dual and multiple possessions have increased—with unprecedented combinations of lower demons, entities who were previously antagonistic toward each other. Perhaps all of this is why Father Bill is not only paranoid—hearing footsteps behind every blind corner—but why he's not altogether surprised when they finally come for him.

They come on a warm June evening, a few minutes before the stroke of midnight. Father Bill is alone at that point, striding down a narrow footpath along the east boundary of Resurrection Cemetery, just outside Hammond, Indiana, playing his flashlight across the base of a two-hundred-year-old elm that has allegedly formed stigmata-like sores in its bark, when he hears two things that raise the hackles on the back of his neck.

The first is the distant noise of footsteps—or perhaps three or four pairs, muffled by the thick grass of graves—coming toward him from the heart of the cemetery. It's too dark to see who it is, but the *sound* of it, the inertia in those steps—the solemn *vigor* of the sound, like the muffled march of brown shirts—tells Father Bill this is no girl-scout troop coming to sell him cookies.

The second thing that makes his flesh crawl—and it takes a *lot* to make the flesh of a man like Father Bill crawl—is the faint sound of a voice. It comes from above him, and it's a tinny, papery whisper, like the voice of a doll triggered by a pull-string.

"Too late, Padre, you're surrounded," the voice informs him. The footsteps are closing in on all sides. Are they apparitions of the dead? Are they figments of Father Bill's whiskey-ravaged brain cells? He looks up and sees an enormous crow perched on the elm branch above him—a bird the size of an anvil—glowering down at him through black ball-bearing eyes. The raven shivers, its oily wings convulsing as though molting from the force of the spirit possessing it, its tiny beak contorting as it speaks. *"Only chance you've got is to try and flee to the north."*

Father Bill does not pause more than a nano-second to make all the connections, to allow the situation to sink in: *the blackbird has the demon Malefar inside it, and the footsteps are approaching fast.* He wheels around and runs as fast as he can—his duffel bag and flashlight flying out of his hands—toward the distant gravel lane to the north.

The crow takes wing in a flurry of black slimy feathers, soaring after the priest, as the hunters converge on the tree line from all corners of the cemetery. The bird swoops down and lights on the fleeing Father Bill's shoulder with the force of a grappling hook digging into his frock. It makes the priest stumble and nearly fall. *"They're the* Segreto Polizia," the bird warns in its plastic toy-voice. *"They investigate the investigators of the investigators."*

"Why...should I...trust...*you?"* The priest gasps for breath as he keeps sprinting for the row of gaslights bordering the property. Father Bill can see, in his peripheral vision, the men gaining on either side, a brigade of dark cloaked figures, their duster-tails billowing behind them, as they charge closer and closer.

The raven's voice in his ear: *"Ironically I'm the only friend you have left."*

Running, lungs heaving: "Evil spirits...are...congenital liars."

"I'm giving it up for Lent. Besides...you're about to learn just how alone you really are."

Father Bill is about to form a reply when the hood comes out of nowhere, plunging down over his face, taking away the moonlight and making him stumble.

He falls in a puddle and feels the weight of two men pressing down on him, a heavily-accented voice bringing this phase of his life to an end: "Eet ees best for you, *Signore,* if you do not struggle."

6.

For most of the journey, they keep a black muslin hood over Father Bill that has that candlewick and cardamom odor of the church. In fact everything has the smell of the Church with a capital 'C'—the shiny new SUV in which the thugs whisk Father Bill off to the nearest international airport, the sterile atmosphere of the private jet in which they spirit him across the Atlantic—all of it screams Vatican. But Father Bill also knows that the alphabet soup of Holy See intelligence agencies can be so convoluted it is nearly impossible to keep the factions straight. One thing he knows for sure: these six burly *fascinonorosi* who have, in effect, kidnapped him, are as far removed from the Church as the caged wolves are from the zookeeper.

By mid-morning, the plane has reached the Bay of Biscay, descending through lightning storms over the Pyrenees, then bumping over the Mediterranean. Father Bill, blind and wheezing for air in the hood, grips the arm-rests and picks up little clues: the hushed radio chatter in Italian, the g-forces pushing up through the cabin as the plane begins its descent into Roman air space. Less than an hour later, the plane is on the ground at Leonardo da Vinci International, and Father Bill Buonaserra is being ushered, as helpless and sightless as a troglodyte, through noisy jet-ways and corridors. Another three sweaty hours in the hood, and the priest realizes he's descending into the earth. He can smell the musky stench of loam, as the vehicle bangs over steel thresholds, and the odor of defunct olive groves and withered lemon trees give way to the tarry black chill of the underground. The engine echoes, and the tires whine for what seems an eternity.

Rome was established twenty-seven centuries ago, but the catacombs, which perforate the earth for miles around the *Viate Vaticano,* worming their way under the Basilicas and outlying ruins, are endless and virtually uncharted. And it is within these labyrinthine worm-holes, at some nameless terminal point miles outside of the sacred city, that they finally disembark and lock Father Bill in a crumbling, fetid, windowless cell—keeping him there for days without charge or explanation, feeding him prison fare and questioning him in the manner of an enemy counter-intelligence officer.

At last, on the eleventh day, a guard comes and escorts Father Bill deeper into the warren of stone tunnels.

Moving through pools of dim, incandescent light, they pass the various and sundry offices of the *Segreto Polizia*—the secret vigilante organization that has long ago splintered away from the Holy See—the rooms clicking with keyboard chatter and buzzing with muttered prayers. A rag-tag assemblage of the defrocked and the demoted, dedicated to eradicating the influence of the netherworld, the *Polizia* is the theological analogue of 1960s militant groups such as the Weathermen, the PLO, and the Brigate Rosse. And as Father Bill passes the last doorway on the left, he notices something that he had always disparaged as urban legend: the padded, electrified armchairs of the remote viewers, mounted to the floor in the stark, gloomy room, awaiting the next team to plug in and perform their uncanny reconnaissance. Father Bill remembers hearing rumors about the "viewers" in the early 1970s. Allegedly recruited out of the Defense Intelligence Agency, this select group of gifted psychics can remotely "see" through the eyes of enemy operatives, and gather intelligence for military purposes. But only the *Segreto Polizia* would think of targeting their vision downward—or perhaps *inward* is more precise—into the circles of hell.

Finally they usher Father Bill into a Spartan, desolate interrogation room, where a high-ranking cleric in the *Polizia* is sitting behind a steel desk. They sit the American priest down across from the clergyman. "One last time I will ask you, Father," the cleric says in a low monotone, without emotion. The interrogator is an old man in a threadbare silk vestment with a thick manila file in front of him. He may or may not have once been an archbishop. The deep wrinkles around his sunken eyes are magnified by half-moon reading-glasses. "What exactly is the meaning of the sequence?"

The old man pushes a forensic photograph across the steel table.

In spite of his malnourishment and exhaustion, Father Bill recognizes the close-up of welts on the body of a comatose boy from Little Rock, possessed by the demon Malefar for twenty-three days, the sores appearing as strings of crow's feet raised on the tender flesh of the child, forming the letters: AAAGTCTGAC AGAATTACCT TAATAACAT. The series—which had come to be known as Undetermined Sequence 'A' in Father Bill's notes—is the reason Father Bill is here, the reason he is being broken, softened up. "I wish to see a *consigliare,"* Father Bill says for the umpteenth time.

"YOU ARE NOT IN AMERICA!" the old man shrieks at the top of his lungs, making the guard—a burly man draped in a monastic robe, standing behind the cleric—jerk with a start. "You have consorted with the unclean," the old man goes on with veins bulging. "You have addressed lower demons by name. The hemographic wounds—what do they mean? We have studied them for months, and have found nothing. You will tell me now. What. They. Mean!"

Something shifts in the earth beneath the room, the joists creaking.

"I wish to see a *consigliare,* a *procuratore,* and that is the last word I will utter on the subject until I do," Buonaserra declares in a hoarse murmur, despite the fact that he has no earthly clue what the letters mean. He has consulted his own experts, cryptologists at the University of Chicago, theologians, and nobody can make any sense of the sequence. The only thing Father Bill knows for sure is that the sequence is a message—either a riddle, a codex, or a trick—proffered by the demon Malefar.

"Take him back!" The old man barks the words in Italian to his beefy functionary, slamming a gnarled fist on the file. "And withhold his rations until he decides to loosen his filthy tongue!"

Father Bill goes peacefully, but cannot help but notice two things as he is roughly ushered out of the room and into the festering tunnel. A tiny droplet of blood, as shiny as a ruby, has formed in the corner of the old renegade cleric's sagging left eye, and the inky mildew along the seams of the back wall of the interrogation chamber, has started, as though unbound by the laws of physics, to drip *upward.*

7.

Hell breaks its bonds at precisely midnight that evening. Alone in his cell of leprous limestone walls and bare-steel cot, Father Bill senses the malodorous presence rising all around him, flooding the labyrinth. Like a ship in a sudden, unexpected riptide, the tendons of that vast maze begin to creak.

At 12:01:59, Central European Standard Time, the iron-barred door to Father Bill's cell suddenly, abruptly, spontaneously swings open.

The bars bang into the opposing wall with the clang of a clarion bell—a church bell—and Father Bill has no choice. He slips into the corridor, and he discovers that the length of the moldering stone tunnel, as far as he can see in either direction, is silent and still. Fifty feet away, a single hooded lamp begins swinging as if on invisible currents, the flashing, sweeping dances of yellow light illuminating the body of the archbishop sprawled on the floor, its neck wrenched at an alarming angle. The color of the cleric's face is wormy gray with death, his eyes frosted with early rigor mortis.

Father Bill starts to back away when the body begins twitching.

This is neither the neuromuscular twitch of a corpse, nor the spasm of the living. Something has highjacked the archbishop's corpse, and now the flaccid, enrobed body jerks up to its knees, as though yanked into a praying position by the unseen puppeteer. *"You should have listened,"* the voice of the lesser demon hisses out of the slack mouth, the eyes of the archbishop as black as pitch. *"You should have struck the bargain."*

"What's happening, Malefar?" Father Bill is still backing away, until his lower back strikes the intersecting tunnels behind him.

"Something I neglected to mention," the demon's voice announces, and starts to explain, but is cut off summarily as a higher demon takes control of the lower.

Father Bill is momentarily paralyzed, as he watches the transformation, about which he has only heard folk tales and rumors among the *Instrumentum's* demonologists. In the dim light, Malefar is possessed in stages, the ragged, animated corpse of the archbishop convulsing, then flopping down on all fours, its tendons buckling, its thighs and hocks bowing outward like the haunches of a dog. The wattled neck contorts and bends upward, and the cleric's head elongates with a sickening wet crunch, until its dripping, oozing nasal cavity has bulged into a simulacrum of a large canine with pointed incisors, and inside these very teeth there appears a *second* set of teeth, like the embryonic bicuspids of a prehistoric fish. *"THE INFERIOR SPIRIT...IS NO LONGER...AVAILABLE,"* a new voice rumbles, a voice born of oily subterranean channels and primeval pistons firing deep within antediluvian cylinders.

Father Bill finds his legs, and whirls toward the sole egress available to him.

The tributary running under the Tiber River, connecting the outskirts with the *Piazza di Ottaviano.*

8.

For nearly a mile, stumbling through absolute darkness, Father Bill manages to keep moving, banging off the walls, feeling for a way out, the sound of the abomination close behind him, its deformed feet padding on the stone floor, the wet guttural engine of its voice repeating ancient Sumerian incantations that echo maddeningly through the passageways, and certainly, at this point, a lesser man would lose the moorings of his sanity, but Father Bill is not a lesser man, Father Bill is a fighter, Father Bill is the last *good* man, and he somehow fixes his sights on the ambient light ahead of him, growing like a pink bruise under the roots and stalactites of the ancient river, and as he draws nearer and nearer, he realizes it's a ladder protruding down from a manhole shaft—an oxidized remnant of World War II era civil defense—and without pause, as he approaches the ladder, he leaps up to the lowest rung, just as the monstrous desecration of flesh behind him catches up with him and pounces up at his dangling legs and sinks its jagged mutant teeth into the exposed meat of Father's Bill's left calf, and the pain shrieks up his tendons as he pulls himself up with every last shred of strength, crying out—"SAINT MICHAEL PROTECT US!"—and somehow, somehow, somehow, Father Bill manages to scurry up the rest of the moldy iron treads, shimmying up a narrow channel too small for the beast, climbing and climbing for what seems like an eternity but is only a few moments of white hot agony, the blood making Father Bill's foothold slip every few rungs, until finally, finally, the American bursts through a rotting enclosure, and all at once he gasps and tastes the delicious cool nectar of the night.

9.

The last few kilometers of Father William Buonaserra's frantic flight across the outskirts of Rome, across the scorched patchwork of industrial parks and boarded marketplaces stretching in cinder-strewn sediments over ancient viaducts, is a hallucinatory coda, a final act, a summing-up of his life in service to some higher purpose that he has never fully understood. A rabid dog chases him. The animal hisses at him in a voice as cold and brittle as tensile steel: *"The letters are more than letters. You should have seen that—they hold the future in them."*

"WHAT DIFFERENCE DOES IT MAKE?!" His voice in shreds, his wounded leg throbbing, the gashes in his flesh leaving a leech trail of blood like ribbons of India ink in the moonlit darkness, his brain swimming with terror, his system already shutting down from blood-loss and shock and trauma, he fights the impulse to lie down and die. He keeps going, and in rhythm with his wounded strides, he utters sacred words from very old texts: "Accursed spirits...we enjoin you under God's penalty...cease to deceive human beings...cease to offer them the poison of eternal perdition...go spirit...give way to Christ!"

A moment later, Father Bill hurls past a beggar lying in the shadows near the *Via Urbano* bridge. The slumbering derelict addresses the priest as a sleepwalker might address someone in a fragmented dream: *"The rituals are useless, Padre—the battle lines have vanished—the symbols on the boy are the future now—the new dominion."*

"MORE LIES!—ALL OF IT!" Father Bill stumbles on broken glass and tumbles down the littered bank of the Tiber, landing on the fossilized promenade of oily cracked stone, near the water, where the boots of Centurions once pounded. Tears well in his eyes.

Then he sees through his bleary vision the Devil's secret revealed in a puddle—a tiny oil slick forming on a shelf of slate—the cuneiform *AAAGTCTGAC AGAATTACCT TAATAACAT* appearing in blood and scum on the rock, the letters metamorphosing, melting and reshaping themselves, as the immense shadowy presence looms in the darkness behind the fallen priest.

"Our Father who art—who—who art in—" Father Bill freezes up when he sees the beast, visible now in the watery reflection on the rock—a ghastly giant in the form of a human-hybrid bat, with massive leathery wings, and a face carved out of mortified flesh—swooping down upon the priest like a black wave breaking. The priest weeps then, a single tear tracking down his face in that last instant of lucidity. He cries not for the imminent loss of his own soul. Nor does he sob for the impending doom awaiting the earthly realm. On the contrary, Father Bill weeps for the end of a great and long era—an era marked by many battles between Church and kingdom of darkness—which has now died with a whimper of homogeneity. Good and evil are no longer opposite poles. Love, hate, truth, lies... all gray areas now...the devil's plan all along.

And at the precise moment the monstrous avatar lands on the priest, with talons protracted, giant black thorns penetrating the American's soul, Father Bill sees in his last conscious moment the letters on the rock twisting into a Möbius strip of chemical symbols for proteins, nucleotides, adenine, guanine, thymine, cytosine, which Father Bill, in his fading consciousness, remembers from his undergraduate biology classes at Loyola. The letters represent a very special variant of the human genome—a delicate strand of DNA from Hell—which flows into the priest, and seeds his soul, and almost instantly, silently, a dark flower blooming in it unholy amniocentesis, the new combination of proteins begin to form a new hybrid being. And the darkness plumes and grows and radiates upward and outward until it covers the moon.

10.

Most of Rome is quiet at 4:00 in the morning, save for the red light district, way out on the *Ostia,* where the *puttana* sit on lawn chairs in front of torch-lit sheds, and the night breezes waft fishy musk across the tops of swaying olive trees, and an anonymous American priest appears out of the shadows on the edge of the tree line, licking his lips, eager to spread his new gospel to the first willing vessel.

The Shoes

Melanie Tem

"Cool shoes," Nicole said to the gorgeous man with the ulcer on his penis. Gently she checked the cysts on his arms and neck to be sure none had popped yet. The shoes, red with white mesh and lifts on the heels for running, not a name brand, made bright spots of color on the gray tile floor beside the bed.

"Thanks, darling. Cool's important when you're dying, don't you think?" Not knowing how to react, Nicole glanced at the nurse, but he was busy preparing the syringe.

The serious narcotics didn't help much because the patient had had so many drugs in his system for so long. The veins in his neck were always distended and he flinched and grimaced constantly, even when he was bragging about his sexual conquests and flirting with every man from doctors to cleaning crew. Soaking his hand in the Betadine solution did seem to soothe him, but she hated to think of the pain she'd cause him when she dressed the bone-deep infected lesion. Could you really shoot up in your thumb? Even Adam, with all his terrible wounds, hadn't had anything like this, not from the first day she'd been assigned to take care of him in the nursing home until the day he died alone in their apartment and struggling to get the oxygen canula back in his nose (unless he'd pulled it out on purpose).

Adam.

For her patient's sake and her own, Nicole kept talking about the shoes while she prepared the gauze bandage. "Do you run?"

"Oh, honey, I run all the time." He grinned in that God's-gift-to-women way she knew all too well, except that he was obviously at least bi if not totally gay. In fact, right now he was flirting with the nurse, who had a wife and three kids.

This nurse was the best she'd ever trained with. Carefully withdrawing the patient's hand from the basin, Nicole observed how he did the education part of the job. His voice was calm, kind, and professional, without a hint of judgment. She didn't know if she could do that. "You're aware that you have AIDS, right, Eric?"

"I sort of guessed."

Nicole patted the thumb dry as lightly as she could, but still Eric groaned and she whispered an apology.

"And you understand that unprotected sex puts you at risk of contracting another form of the virus?"

Eric actually laughed. "That doesn't really worry me all that much, sweetheart."

"And you know that if you have unprotected sex you can pass the virus to your partners?"

Eric gasped as Nicole draped gauze over his thumb. She had to hold it in place while she wrapped tape lightly around the base, and knowing she was hurting him made her hands shake. When he could, he said, "Nobody seems to mind." With his good hand he patted the nurse's arm. "I can still get men."

Nicole finished her work hastily as Eric launched into graphic tales of his sexual exploits, several just last night before he'd checked himself into the hospital. Exchanging a quick look with the nurse, she hurried out of the room and hid in the bathroom for a few minutes to calm down before she went on to her next patient.

This guy had open, draining sores, one of them covering half his penis. He was knowingly, even purposely exposing who knew how many people to a terrible disease, and his partners had to know. Dizzy and nauseated, she leaned against the cool tile wall.

He was really attractive, though. Something about his face and body and attitude was really sexy. Shuddering, she allowed herself a few minutes of mourning Adam *from the very first moment taking care of him he smelled of illness and desire.*

Nicole had learned how to stop the crying before it got totally out of control. She couldn't make herself stop thinking about Adam *leaning from his wheelchair to stroke and pat, always a sweet little shock* and she didn't ever want to stop thinking about him, but by now she was able to set it aside for a while. She washed her hands thoroughly, splashed cold water on her face, and hurried back to the floor.

It was pouring rain when she got off, and she had to stop at the store on her way home. The kids would be back from Keith's tomorrow and it was one thing for her to get by on crackers and peanut butter but they needed real food, fruits and vegetables. She and her grocery sacks got soaked. She set the dripping bags on the floor, pulled off her wet jacket, turned around and stumbled over a shoe.

Damn kids. She kicked the shoe out of the way, then saw it was red and off-brand with white mesh and heel shocks for running, and adult-size, men's size. The mate was in the corner under the coat rack. They must be Keith's, though why he'd leave his shoes in her entryway she couldn't imagine. She hated him coming into her place when she wasn't there, but the kids had to have keys.

She gathered her spilled groceries and carried them into the kitchen, kicking savagely at the shoes again but missing. Putting the milk away and leaving everything else on the counter, she went to bed and fell into exhausted, nervous sleep.

Her first waking thoughts were always of Adam. *Adam. Singing, whispering, "I love you." Making new kinds of love with mouth and hands and penis split from the gunshot wound and all the surgeries that had more or less saved his life, making love like nobody else.* It scared her when she didn't dream about him. She couldn't lose him. She lay in bed and cried for a little while, dozed off and still didn't dream about him, then got up late and put the coffee on while she rushed around looking for clean scrubs and chips for her lunch.

The charge nurse today was younger than Nicole and already an RN who seemed to think they were buds and always wanted to chat about clubbing and shopping and how she should have become a flight attendant or a model because, really, sick people made her sick, especially people who'd done it to themselves. Eric's room was close enough for him to overhear, and the nurse talked loudly and rolled her eyes in his direction.

Nicole shut the door when she went in to dress his wound. "Well, if it's not my favorite little nurse-in-training and dominatrix."

"What does that mean?" She set about preparing the soak for his hand.

"You don't know what a dominatrix is? Oh, honey."

"I know what the word means. I don't know why you call me that." This conversation was probably unprofessional. Nicole set the basin down and began unwrapping the gauze from his thumb, careful that her annoyance didn't make her rough.

He threw his head back and squeezed his eyes shut. "Shit!" he whispered. "Where'd you learn to give such good pain?"

Nicole didn't know how to tell a man dying of AIDS to back off, and she didn't like how he was making her feel. Good thing she didn't have to take care of the wound on his penis. Preparing the clean dressing for his thumb, she looked for some way to change the subject and her gaze fell on the red running shoes tucked neatly under the bed. She almost said, "My ex has shoes like that," but decided against giving Eric any personal information. "Where'd you get those cool shoes?"

It took him a moment to answer. "This snazzy little shop in Amsterdam. They're custom-made. A gift from a lover. I forget his name. He's dead now."

"Custom-made, huh?"

"Surely you don't think I'd buy shoes off the rack."

When she took his good hand and raised his arm to check the cysts, a sudden wave of tenderness swept over her. *Adam's beautiful artist's fingers always shaking, sometimes holding on until it hurt. That last afternoon, his stiff hand half-curled on the floor and lit by a shaft of cold sunshine.* As she forced herself to complete the exam, Eric said, "You should see the babe I'm going out with tonight. Mmm-mmmm, is he hot."

"You're having a date in the hospital."

He tilted his head helpfully as she checked the cyst on his neck, somehow making the motions seem sexy. "My dear, this is good-bye. I am outta here."

At first she thought he meant he was going to die. *Of course he's going to die. What did you expect?* Then another explanation occurred to her. "They're discharging you?" She couldn't keep the incredulity out of her voice.

"My doctor says I'm stable." He laughed shrilly. "I don't think anybody's ever called me that before."

"There's nothing more we can do for him. Just take him home and make him comfortable."

"Just love me, Nicole. That's all I ask."

She had the urge to take his face in her hands and kiss him—gently, not to hurt him. At the door she said over her shoulder, "Good luck to you, Eric," and then realized he'd probably think she was wishing him luck picking up men. He was singing, "Back in the Saddle Again" as she left the room.

"Is Eric Rossi really being discharged today?"

The nurse didn't look up from her charting. "Who?"

"The guy with AIDS? In 324?"

The nurse finished what she was writing, closed that chart, opened Eric's, and pointed. "Yep, there's the order." Wondering grimly how the woman could keep her nails so nice, Nicole balled her fists.

"But his wounds—his thumb, and his penis—"

"Outpatient, I guess."

"But he's sexually active. Very. He's spreading AIDS."

The nurse snorted. "Just like a little plague-infested rat, only smarter. High h.i., I'd say."

Nicole was pleased to know what that meant from her psych class last semester. "H.i., not s.i.?"

"Oh, please. There's not a suicidal ideation in his pretty little head. But he's sure doing his best to be a serial killer."

"Then he ought to be on a hold. For his own protection, too."

The phone rang and the nurse answered it briskly, then practically purred and Nicole, not wanting to listen to another conversation with the boyfriend, went off to answer a call bell from the other end of the hall.

The rest of the shift was busy, which kept her from thinking too much about Eric, *Adam calling, "Nicole," whispering, "Nicole!"* By the end of it she was tense and exhausted. But on her way to the elevator she ducked into Eric's room.

"Well, if it isn't," he said. "Come to kiss me goodbye?"

Her throat hurt but she managed to retort, "Nah, you're not my type." Lightly she scanned his arms and neck with her fingertips one last time. A real nurse would check his penis, too. She was glad she wasn't a real nurse yet.

"Truly," he said, looking straight at her, "you've been great, Nicole." It was the first time he'd said her name.

"For all the good it did."

He caught her hand in a surprisingly strong grasp. "It did," he told her. "Good."

Pulling her hand free, she blurted, "I'm so sorry," and fled.

After work she had to go to Target for school supplies and get gas and stop by her school for an A&P handout and pay her phone bill in person before they cut off service, and she barely made it home before Keith dropped the kids off. She meant to complain about him being in her apartment and give him back his red shoes, but she couldn't find them now, and he didn't come to the door.

The kids were terrible, the way they almost always were when they came back from Keith's or got ready to go there. Knowing it was her fault for not having stayed with their dad, Nicole tried hard to be patient, but the evening ended up with all of them in tears and in bed early. Tired as she was, tired as she knew she'd be at 5:00 in the morning, she couldn't fall asleep for a long time and then kept waking up because she thought she heard weird noises or the house was too quiet—half-dreaming that Adam was dying again and again she wasn't there to save him.

Thirty-seven minutes before the alarm was set to go off, she woke up gasping from a dream of making love with a gigantic bifurcated penis with holes in it, hurting her and bringing her to multiple orgasms. Trying to go back to sleep now was pointless, and she didn't want to risk falling into that dream again and over-sleeping and making everybody late. So she went to check on her children, standing very still in their doorway to be sure they were breathing and no kidnappers were bending over their beds.

On her way into the kitchen in the pre-dawn half-light, she stumbled over something. *Damn kids,* she thought fondly, and without looking squatted to pick up whatever it was.

Shoes. Big man's shoes, side by side in the kitchen doorway, one tipped over now. Mesh, heel shocks. Off-brand and red, she saw when she turned on the light.

Adam's here. But she'd never seen Adam wear shoes like that.

Adam's dead.

Nicole crouched there and tried to think how Eric Rossi's shoes could be in her apartment. Could he have found out where she lived? Could he have been here last night? Why would he have come here, and why in the world would he have left his shoes?

Eric wasn't the only one in the world who had shoes like that, no matter how he bragged about custom-made and his dead lover in Amsterdam. Pulling her robe tighter, Nicole sank back onto the cold floor and cast about wildly for some other explanation. Maybe the management company had sent somebody to fix the leaky shower. But why would they leave their shoes?

Steeling herself, she reached for the shoes, then went to get latex gloves. Protected, she picked them up gingerly by the shoestrings and carried them out to the dumpster behind the building. Then she hurried back inside to strip off the gloves and wash her hands for long minutes with lots of soap under water as hot as she could stand.

The morning chaos started before she'd even finished her first cup of coffee, and it was worse today than usual, with lost homework, fights over the bathroom, phantom stomach aches, sudden dislike of the cereal they'd been having for breakfast for months. Everybody was in a foul mood by the time they all got out the door, and Nicole sped to her eight-o'clock class thinking more about how she was a terrible mother than about the shoes.

But the shoes were in her apartment again when she got home from school, toes poking neatly out from under the couch. Nicole swept them onto a dustpan like dead mice and took them out to the dumpster again, then emptied all the trash cans into a bag and dumped it on top of the shoes. When the kids got home she was lugging old newspapers and magazines and empty boxes out, and she got them to help by making a game of it. By dinner time they'd actually cleaned out some of the junk in their room and the dumpster was almost full. Tomorrow was trash day.

Adam's stuff pitiful in three black plastic trash bags, ragged clothes and beautiful sketches and years worth of frantic letters from his mother who he'd said hated him and he didn't know where she was, medical records from the first surgery stating the gunshot wound had been sustained in a drug deal gone bad and not in a random mugging or a fight with his father as he'd said at one time or another, pictures of an unidentified baby and three old pairs of shoes none of them red and bottles and bottles of meds. "Take care of me, Nicole. Love me, Nicole. Promise me you'll love me forever."

I'm sorry, Adam. I'm so sorry.

The kids had a long weekend but she didn't. When she called Keith's to check on them Wednesday after school, there was no answer. They were probably just out somewhere, but her throat ached with worry. She didn't really feel like going out, but she hated being alone in the apartment, so she found somebody to go to a movie with. Standing in the hallway among odors of other people's dinners, she checked the door lock twice, came back into the building from the parking lot and up the elevator to check it again.

When she got home the red shoes were on the kitchen counter, among the cans of soup and Spaghetti-Os she still hadn't put away. She stood there and stared and shouted, "What?" Then, not knowing what else to do, she just went to bed.

In the morning the shoes were in front of the shower stall. She stepped over them getting in and out, feeling stupid that she kept a towel wrapped snugly around her but shuddering at the idea of being naked in front of the shoes. As she left for the library to study, the shoes were perched on the kitchen counter again, and she just gave up and left them there.

On a page in the middle of her notebook was one of Adam's drawings she'd never seen before, left for her as a surprise, a human figure with holes in it everywhere and a rose for a penis, signed "Love always. Remember me. Adam." Gazing at his name and the many layered petals of the rose, Nicole could hardly breathe for missing him.

His cold blue flesh. The awful stillness of him, no pulse in his wrist or behind his ear, no heartbeat, no breath in and out of his nose and mouth. No way to save him, no way to love him enough.

The good nurse was on and Nicole resisted the temptation to mention the shoes to him. He showed her how to find the pressure point between the thumb and forefinger that could help ease pain, demonstrating on her and having her practice on him; her headache did subside, but it roared back the instant he stopped touching her. He taught her how to turn the huge heavy woman with the terrible decubs without throwing out her own back. They showed each other pictures of their children.

Casually Nicole asked if he'd heard anything about Eric Rossi. He looked at her over the med tray they were setting up. "He was discharged. That's all I know."

"I was just wondering." She met his steady, compassionate gaze. "He kind of got to me."

The nurse nodded. "This was a hard one."

"I know he's not a very nice person and I know we're not supposed to get attached to our patients. I wasn't really attached—"

"The day we don't care about our patients is the day we should find something else to do. But you have to set boundaries, Nicole. That's what lets you care"

That night, she eased open her door and crept inside in the dark like an intruder in her own place. Tripping over and bumping into things, she found the light switch, gathered her courage and flipped it on as if ambushing something.

Canned goods were still on the counter along with dirty dishes, school papers, hair ties, opened and unopened bills. But the red shoes were gone. Sickened by relief and fear and loss, Nicole leaned over the sink but couldn't quite throw up. *Adam choking, aspirating, turning blue, finger down his throat in a desperate French kiss, the soft intimate quivering mucusy membranes, choking, choking on him.*

The nausea and headache subsided enough that Nicole was able to study for a while before bed. She called the kids at Kevin's to say good-night, as she always did, but there was no answer, so she left a message that she wasn't sure he'd give them and that sounded so forlorn she wished she could re-record or erase it.

The shoes were way down at the foot of her bed between the sheets like the heated bricks people used to use to warm their feet. She didn't discover them until she was almost asleep, but she knew right away what they were and it wasn't even a surprise. The mesh rubbed her soles pleasantly. Her toes pressed against the heels, squishy from the shocks. She could feel the shoestrings and the tread, and was dangerously comforted.

Then she jerked awake, cried out, and leaped from the bed. To get to the shoes she had to yank all the blankets and sheets onto the floor, and still they were buried. She could see and feel the lumps they made in the tangle of bedclothes, and she could hear them squirming. She threw herself on top of them, but they slithered out from under her and every time she grabbed for them they were just out of reach.

"Hey, Nicole."

Eric Rossi was naked on his back on her stripped bed. She recognized him by his penis—huge, erect, decimated, glistening, the lesion gleaming red from base to tip. "Eric?"

"Who'd you think it was? Adam?"

"What are you doing in my house?"

"I need a place to stay."

"You're not serious." Shaking and dizzy, she couldn't quite stand, but she straightened up on her knees. Now she could just see his face, contorted in pain but still with that cocky God's-gift grin. "Eric, this is crazy. I have children—"

"You did it for Adam."

"I didn't! I didn't do it right! He's dead!"

"So." His tone was sly. "Here's your chance."

She could do it. She knew how to take care of him. "No," she said, and hated herself.

"Love me."

What she felt for him could be called love, she supposed, a kind of love. "I could never do that to Adam."

"Adam's dead."

She reached for him and he was gone. "I'm sorry."

When she'd finally worn herself out sobbing into the bedclothes on the floor and could get to her feet, Nicole left a message on the management company's emergency number demanding that the lock on her door be changed. Chances were slim to none that anything would happen on a weekend.

Gratified by how strong she was from all that lifting and turning of patients, she pulled the couch in front of the door and bookcases in front of the windows in the living room and the kids' room. She set stuff on her window sill so at least she'd hear if anybody tried to get in, and put a kitchen knife under her pillow.

Adam was with her all night, in dreams and half-dreams and when she thought she was wide awake. Adam singing to her. Adam wounded and exposed under her hands. Adam wanting to live and wanting to die and begging her to help him. Adam split inside her. One of the many times during the night when she was drifting off to sleep or startling awake, it occurred to her to wonder how Eric knew about Adam.

When the alarm went off and she stumbled to the kitchen, the red shoes were propped up against the coffee pot. When she hurried to the bathroom to get ready for her 8:00 midterm, the shoes were in the shower. She stood over them and let the soapy water fill them like little red-and-white sinking boats.

When she dragged the chair away from the front door, the shoes came with it, toes peeking from under the edge like evil little animals with beady eyes. Not daring to risk being late, she just left them there.

The midterm was easy. She knew she aced it, and allowed herself a little bit of pride, though it scared her.

Waiting at Starbuck's for her friends to finish the test and meet her for a celebratory mocha latte, she tried to think about Eric and the shoes and Adam, but everything was too mixed up and she was too tired. She called the kids on her cell, but they were getting ready to go someplace with their dad and didn't have time to talk.

She found excuses to stay away from the apartment all day, and would have spent the night somewhere else but the one girlfriend from school she could have asked to stay with was sick. A couple of guys hit on her at the club but she couldn't do that to Adam.

It wasn't very late when she got home, and the building was noisy, mariachi and rap and oldies music blaring from various apartments, parties going on here and there, loud laughter in the parking lot and elevator. Nicole stood outside her door for a few minutes until strange looks from people passing in the hallway forced her to either go in or leave before somebody asked her what was wrong, and she couldn't think of anywhere else to go.

Her key worked so the lock hadn't been changed, which was a good thing. She eased the door open. *The smell of Adam, waiting, dead.* Nothing blocked her way, no shoes. She was afraid to turn on the light. *Adam in his chair, holding out his hands, slumped forward into the seat belt.* Shadows made the place look even more a mess than she'd remembered leaving it, bookcase in front of the street windows, chair in the middle of the room, kids' stuff everywhere.

She crouched, then lay on the carpet (which badly needed vacuuming but her vacuum cleaner was broken) to search for the shoes. They weren't there. She was alone. *Adam.*

Adam. The outside noise made her place seem weirdly quiet as she crept from room to room. Illumination from streetlights and security lights seeped around the blinds and the furniture blocking the windows, creating distortions and unfamiliar shadows. Eric wasn't here. Adam wasn't here. There were no red shoes with white mesh and heel shocks anywhere in the apartment. *Oh, Adam.* She started to breathe more easily, and she started to cry.

"Nicole."

She froze.

"Nicole." *Nicole Nicole Nicole*

Nicole "Adam?" She didn't see him but she knew he was here.

"No, sweetheart, it's me. Adam's dead, remember?"

Eric Rossi lay in the jumble of bedclothes on the floor. She stumbled over him, cried out, jumped back. A shaft of pinkish light bathed the length of his body: mouth in a grin like a rictus but still cocksure, cysts on his neck and arms now burst and oozing, a huge open sore where his penis should be, red shoes glowing.

"How'd you get in here?"

"Why, darling, you let me in."

"Liar!"

"Now, now, don't be crude."

"What do you want from me?" That was closer to what she needed to know.

"Love me. Love me, Nicole."

Her heart started to open to him. Her wound-care supplies were in the bathroom cabinet right around the corner, and she knew what to do. Probably he wouldn't live much longer anyway; she could love him until he died, and afterward. She could do that. Maybe, if she loved him enough and took care of him well enough, she could even save him. It wasn't impossible.

Nicole, don't.

"You died!" she screamed at him. then she lowered her voice to a whisper so Eric wouldn't hear. "You lied to me all along, and then you died! I wasn't good enough."

You loved me fine. And I loved you. That's enough, Nicole. Let it go now.

"Adam, I don't want to be alone for the rest of my life."

But he didn't answer, and he never would. A terrible understanding came to her: she knew how to let him go. She gathered herself and said to Eric Rossi, "You have to leave."

When he re-positioned himself to kick off the shoes, Nicole saw that the hole in his groin went all the way through his body, her blue-flowered quilt visible underneath. The left shoe slid off easily and burrowed into the tangled sheets, hiding itself. The right shoe at first wouldn't budge, then came sailing at her, laces flying. She tried to catch it but missed. The shoe hit her in the stomach and thumped at her feet.

"Get out of my house!"

"You don't mean that," Eric told her smugly.

She picked up the shoe and threw it at him. It passed through his body and she heard it hit the floor. "Get out!"

"You're just upset. You know you need me."

"No. I don't." Nicole started to back out of the room, then instead advanced. It was her room, after all, her house.

Holding out his bleeding arms to her, Eric didn't move from his nest. Obviously he had no intention of leaving. Obviously, he expected her to come to him.

She lunged, grabbing for an arm or a leg to drag him out of her house if she had to, out of her life, bleeding or not, dying or not, needing her or not. She was strong enough.

In the split second it took to get to him, he vanished, leaving nothing but the blankets and sheets that still smelled faintly of Adam even though she'd finally been able to wash them. She wrapped up in them, ran through a mental checklist to be sure her children weren't there and she didn't have to go to work or study for anything, and gave herself over to wild tears.

Adam

Adam

Adam

She must have slept. When she woke the outside noise had subsided a little and the apartment was as dark as it ever got. She heard footsteps.

She lay very still and held her breath. Footsteps, irregular and not very loud, something wrong with the sound of them, the direction shifting: by the front door, from the kids' room, up near the ceiling, circling her, getting closer, getting closer, feinting, teasing, not quite reaching her but any minute, any minute.

Then she saw the shoes, glowing red and white, twinkling as if they had lights in the heels, bouncing dancing, skipping. Coming for her. Pretending to play, pretending to love her, maybe honestly loving her, but if she let them they would destroy her life and, suddenly, she wasn't going to let that happen.

When she held out her bare hands to them, they came right to her. She flinched at the first touch of their smooth fleshy soles, mesh like crisscrossed combed hair, uppers dry as skin. She picked them up, one and then the other, and cradled them in one arm while she opened her shirt with the other hand. At first the shoes were cold against her belly, but quickly they absorbed her body heat.

Now what? She could cut them up with the kitchen shears, but the thick soles and heel shocks were probably too tough. She could find somebody to give them to—they were nice shoes, and expensive, maybe even custom-made—but then she'd be like Eric, spreading contagion. She could just stick them in the back of her closet, but she didn't think they'd stay there and maybe her children would be in danger.

"What am I going to do with you?" she whispered. The shoes wriggled cozily against her.

Prying off the ugly sensible shoes she was wearing, she managed to reach her socks and pull them off. Bare, her feet itched.

She set the red shoes in front of her, and stepped into them. They were much too big, and no matter how tightly she laced them their slipping against her toes and heels would cause blisters. The spring and lift created by the heel shocks threw her off balance as she walked around the apartment. *Adam,* she thought deliberately, and then said his name aloud. "Adam." But he was gone.

Nicole made up her bed with clean sheets and blankets and slept through the night with the red shoes on. Her dreams were quiet and pastel. In the morning she shuffled around in the shoes while she had her coffee.

When it was time, she stepped out of the shoes and wrapped them in a pillow case that smelled of Adam. With the warm moving bundle on her lap, she drove to work a little early and detoured into the dirty linen room. She dropped the bundle down the trash chute where it would be taken away with the hospital waste to be incinerated. She let herself cry for a while until housekeeping came with their carts and looked at her funny.

Then she found the nurse, told him she was sick, and went home to make herself a good breakfast and clean up the apartment. The kids wouldn't be home until evening. She had the whole day to herself.

Bits and Pieces

Lisa Tuttle

On the morning after Ralph left her Fay found a foot in her bed.

It was Ralph's foot, but how could he have left it behind? What did it mean? She sat on the edge of the bed holding it in her hand, examining it. It was a long, pale, narrow, rather elegant foot. At the top, where you would expect it to grow into an ankle, the foot ended in a slight, skin-covered concavity. There was no sign of blood or severed flesh or bone or scar tissue, nor were there any corns or bunions, over-long nails or dirt. Ralph was a man who looked after his feet.

Lying there in her hand it felt as alive as a motionless foot ever feels; impossible as it seemed, she believed it was real. Ralph wasn't a practical joker, and yet—a foot wasn't something you left behind without noticing. She wondered how he was managing to get around on just one foot. Was it a message? Some obscure consolation for her feeling that, losing him, she had lost a piece of herself?

He had made it clear he no longer wanted to be involved with her. His goodbye had sounded final. But maybe he would get in touch when he realized she still had something of his. Although she knew she ought to be trying to forget him, she felt oddly grateful for this unexpected gift. She wrapped the foot in a silk scarf and put it in the dresser's bottom drawer, to keep for him.

Two days later, tidying the bedroom, she found his other foot under the bed. She had to check the drawer to make sure it wasn't the same one, gone wandering. But it was still there, one right foot, and she was holding the left one. She wrapped the two of them together in the white silk scarf and put them away.

Time passed and Ralph did not get in touch. Fay knew from friends that he was still around, and as she never heard any suggestion that he was now crippled, she began to wonder if the feet had been some sort of hallucination. She kept meaning to look in the bottom drawer, but somehow she kept forgetting.

The relationship with Ralph, while it lasted, had been a serious, deeply meaningful one for them both, she thought; she knew from the start there was no hope of that with Freddy. Fay was a responsible person who believed the act of sex should be accompanied by love and a certain degree of commitment; she detested the very idea of "casual sex"—but she'd been six months without a man in her bed, and Freddy was irresistible.

He was warm and cuddly and friendly, the perfect teddy bear. Within minutes of meeting him she was thinking about sleeping with him—although it was the comfort and coziness of bed he brought to mind rather than passion. As passive as a teddy bear, he would let himself be pursued. She met him with friends in a pub, and he offered to walk her home. Outside her door he hugged her. There was no kissing or groping; he just wrapped her in a warm, friendly embrace, where she clung to him longer and tighter than friendship required.

"Mmmm," he said, appreciatively, smiling down at her, his eyes button-bright, "I could do this all night."

"What a good idea," she said.

After they had made love she decided he was less a teddy bear than a cat. Like a cat in the sensual way he moved and rubbed his body against hers and responded to her touch: she could almost hear him purr. Other cat-like qualities, apparent after she had known him a little longer, were less appealing. Like a cat he was self-centered, basically lazy, and although she continued to enjoy him in bed, she did wish sometimes he would pay more attention to her pleasure instead of assuming that his was enough for them both. He seemed to expect her to be pleased no matter what time he turned up for dinner, even if he fell asleep in front of the fire immediately after. And, like many cats, he had more than one home.

Finding out about his other home—hearing that other woman's tear-clogged voice down the phone—decided her to end it. It wasn't—or so she told him—that she wanted to have him all to herself. But she wouldn't be responsible for another woman's sorrow.

He understood her feelings. He was wrong, and she was right. He was remorseful, apologetic, and quite incapable of changing. But he would miss her very much. He gave her a friendly hug before they parted, but once they started hugging it was hard to stop, and they tumbled into bed again.

That had to be the last time. She knew she could be firmer with him on the phone than in person, so she told him he was not to visit unless she first invited him. Sadly, he agreed.

And that was that. Going back into the bedroom she saw the duvet rucked up as if there was someone still in the bed. It made her shiver. If she hadn't just seen him out the door, and closed it behind him she might have thought...Determined to put an end to such mournful nonsense she flung the duvet aside, and there he was.

Well, part of him.

Lying on the bed was a headless, neckless, armless, legless torso. Or at least the backside of one. As with Ralph's feet there was nothing unpleasant about it, no blood or gaping wounds. If you could ignore the sheer impossibility of it, there was nothing wrong with Freddy's back at all. It looked just like the body she had been embracing a few minutes before, and felt...

Tentatively, she reached out and touched it. It was warm and smooth, with the firm, elastic give of live flesh. She could not resist stroking it the way she knew he liked, teasing with her nails to make the skin prickle into goose bumps, running her fingers all the way from the top of the spine to the base, and over the curve of the buttocks where the body ended.

She drew her hand back, shocked. What was this? It seemed so much like Freddy, but how could it be when she had seen him, minutes before, walking out the door, fully equipped with all his body parts? Was it possible that there was nothing, now, but air filling out his jumper and jeans?

She sat down, took hold of the torso where the shoulders ended in smooth, fleshy hollows, and heaved it over. The chest was as she remembered, babyishly pink nipples peeking out of a scumble of ginger hair, but below the flat stomach only more flatness. His genitals were missing, as utterly and completely gone as if they had never been thought of. Her stomach twisted with shock and horror although, a moment later, she had to ask herself why that particular lack should matter so much more than the absence of his head—which she had accepted remarkably calmly. After all, this wasn't the real Freddy, only some sort of partial memory of his body inexplicably made flesh.

She went over to the dresser and crouched before the bottom drawer. Yes, they were still there. They didn't appear to have decayed or faded or changed in any way. Letting the silk scarf fall away she gazed at the naked feet and realized that she felt differently about Ralph. She had been unhappy when he left, but she had also been, without admitting it even to herself, furiously angry with him. And the anger had passed. The bitterness was gone, and she felt only affection now as she caressed his feet and remembered the good times. Eventually, with a sigh that mingled fondness and regret, she wrapped them up and put them away. Then she returned to her current problem: what to do with the part Freddy had left behind.

For a moment she thought of leaving it in the bed. He'd always been *so* nice to sleep with...But no. She had to finish what she had begun; she couldn't continue sleeping with part of Freddy all the time when all of Freddy part of the time had not been enough for her. She would never be able to get on with her life, she would never dare bring anyone new home with her.

It would have to go in the wardrobe. The only other option was the hall closet, which was cold and smelled slightly damp. So, wrapping it in her best silken dressing gown, securing it with a tie around the waist, she stored Freddy's torso in the wardrobe behind her clothes.

Freddy phoned the next week. He didn't mention missing anything but her, and she almost told him about finding his torso in her bed. But how could she? If she told him, he'd insist on coming over to see it, and if he came over she'd be back to having an affair with him. That wasn't what she was after, was it? She hesitated, and then asked if he was still living with Matilda.

"Oh, more or less," he said. "Yes."

So she didn't tell him. She tried to forget him, and hoped to meet someone else, someone who would occupy the man-sized empty space in her life.

Meanwhile, Freddy continued to phone her once a week—friendly calls, because he wanted to stay friends. After a while she realized, from comments he let drop, that he was seeing another woman; that once again he had two homes. As always, she resisted the temptation she felt to invite him over, but she felt wretchedly lonely that evening.

For the first time since she had stored it away, she took out his body. Trembling a little, ashamed of herself, she took it to bed. She so wanted someone to hold. The body felt just like Freddy, warm and solid and smooth in the same way; it even smelled like him, although now with a faint overlay of her own perfume from her clothes. She held it for a while, but the lack of arms and head was too peculiar. She found that if she lay with her back against his and tucked her legs up so she couldn't feel his missing legs, it was almost like being in bed with Freddy.

She slept well that night, better than she had for weeks. "My teddy bear," she murmured as she packed him away again in the morning. It was like having a secret weapon. The comfort of a warm body in bed with her at night relaxed her, and made her more self-confident. She no longer felt any need to invite Freddy over, and when he called it was easy to talk to him without getting more involved, as if they'd always been just friends. And now that she wasn't looking, there seemed to be more men around.

One of them, Paul, who worked for the same company in a different department, asked her out. Lately she had kept running into him, and he seemed to have a lot of business that took him to her part of the building, but it didn't register on her that this was no coincidence until he asked if she was doing anything that Saturday night. After that, his interest in her seemed so obvious that she couldn't imagine why she hadn't noticed earlier.

The most likely reason she hadn't noticed was that she didn't care. She felt instinctively that he wasn't her type; they had little in common. But his unexpected interest flattered her, and made him seem more attractive, and so she agreed to go out with him.

It was a mistake, she thought, uneasily, when Saturday night came around and Paul took her to a very expensive restaurant. He was not unintelligent, certainly not bad-looking, but there was something a little too glossy and humorless about him. He was interested in money, and cars, and computers—and her. He dressed well, and he knew the right things to say, but she imagined he had learned them out of a book. He was awfully single-minded, and seemed intent on seduction, which made her nervous, and she spent too much of the evening trying to think of some way of getting out of inviting him in for coffee when he took her home. It was no good; when the time came, he invited himself in.

She knew it wasn't fair to make comparisons, but Paul was the complete opposite of Freddy. Where Freddy sat back and waited calmly to be stroked, Paul kept edging closer, trying to crawl into her lap. And his hands were everywhere. From the very start of the evening he had stood and walked too close to her, and she didn't like the way he had of touching her, as if casually making a point, staking a physical claim to her.

For the next hour she fended him off. It was a wordless battle that neither of them would admit to. When he left, she lacked the energy to refuse a return match, the following weekend.

They went to the theater, and afterward to his place—he said he wanted to show her his computer. She expected another battle, but he was a perfect gentleman. Feeling safer, she agreed to a third date, and then drank too much; the drink loosened her inhibitions, she was too tired to resist his persistent pressure, and finally took him into her bed.

The sex was not entirely a success—for her, anyway—but it would doubtlessly get better as they got to know each other, she thought, and she was just allowing herself a few modest fantasies about the future, concentrating on the things she thought she liked about him, when he said he had to go.

The man who had been hotly all over her was suddenly distant and cool, almost rude in his haste to leave. She tried to find excuses for him, but when he had gone, and she discovered his hands were still in her bed, she knew he did not mean to return.

The hands were nestling beneath a pillow like a couple of soft-shelled crabs. She shuddered at the sight of them; shouted and threw her shoes at them. The left hand twitched when struck, but otherwise they didn't move.

How dare he leave his hands! She didn't want anything to remember him by! She certainly hadn't been in love with him.

Fay looked around for something else to throw, and then felt ashamed of herself. Paul was a creep, but it wasn't fair to take it out on his hands. They hadn't hurt her; they had done their best to give her pleasure—they might have succeeded if she'd liked their owner more.

But she didn't like their owner—she had to admit she wasn't really sorry he wouldn't be back—so why was she stuck with his hands? She could hardly give them back. She could already guess how he would avoid her at work, and she wasn't about to add to his inflated ego by pursuing him. But it didn't seem possible to throw them out, either.

She found a shoebox to put them in—she didn't bother about wrapping them—and then put the box away out of sight on the highest shelf of the kitchen cupboard, among the cracked plates, odd saucers, and empty jars which she'd kept because they might someday be useful.

The hands made her think a little differently about what had happened. She had been in love with Ralph and also, for all her attempts to rationalize her feelings, with Freddy—she hadn't wanted either of them to go. It made a kind of sense for her to fantasize that they'd left bits of themselves behind, but that didn't apply to her feelings for Paul. She absolutely refused to believe that her subconscious was responsible for the hands in the kitchen cupboard.

So, if not her subconscious, then what? Was it the bed? She stood in the bedroom and looked at it, trying to perceive some sorcery in the brand-name mattress or the pine frame. She had bought the bed for Ralph, really; he had complained so about the futon she had when they met, declaring that it was not only too short, but also bad for his back. He had told her that pine beds were good and also cheap, and although she didn't agree with his assessment of the price, she had bought one. It was the most expensive thing she owned. Was it also haunted?

She could test it; invite friends to stay...Would any man who made love in this bed leave a part of himself behind, or only those who made love to her? Only for the last time? But how did it know? How could it, before she herself knew a relationship was over? What if she lured Paul back—would some other body part appear when he left? Or would the hands disappear?

Once she had thought of this, she knew she had to find out. She tried to forget the idea but could not. Days passed, and Paul did not get in touch—he avoided her at work, as she had guessed he would—and she told herself to let him go. Good riddance. To pursue him would be humiliating. It wasn't even as if she were in love with him, after all.

She told herself not to be a fool, but chance and business kept taking her to his part of the building. When forced to acknowledge her, his voice was polite and he did not stand too close; he spoke as if they'd never met outside working hours; as if he'd never really noticed her as a woman. She saw him, an hour later, leaning confidentially over one of the newer secretaries, his hand touching her hip.

She felt a stab of jealous frustration. No wonder she couldn't attract his attention; he had already moved on to fresh prey.

Another week went by, but she would not accept defeat. She phoned him up and invited him to dinner. He said his weekends were awfully busy just now. She suggested a weeknight. He hesitated—surprised by her persistence? Contemptuous? Flattered?—and then said he was involved with someone, actually. Despising herself, Fay said lightly that of course she understood. She said that in fact, she herself was involved in a long-standing relationship, but her fellow had been abroad for the past few months, and she got bored and lonely in the evenings. She'd enjoyed herself so much with Paul that she had hoped they'd be able to get together again sometime; that was all.

That changed the temperature. He said he was afraid he couldn't manage dinner, but if she liked, he could drop by later one evening—maybe tomorrow, around ten?

He was on her as soon as he was through the door. She tried to fend him off with offers of drink, but he didn't seem to hear. His hands were everywhere, grabbing, fondling, probing, as undeniably real as they'd ever been.

"Wait, wait," she said, laughing but not amused. "Can't we...talk?"

He paused, holding her around the waist, and looked down at her. He was bigger than she remembered. "We could have talked on the phone."

"I know, but..."

"Is there something we need to talk about?"

"Well, no, nothing specific, but..."

"Did you invite me over here to talk? Did I misunderstand?"

"No."

"All right." His mouth came down, wet and devouring, on hers, and she gave in.

But not on the couch, she thought, a few minutes later. "Bed," she gasped, breaking away. "In the bedroom."

"Good idea."

But it no longer seemed like a good idea to her. As she watched him strip off his clothes she thought this was probably the worst idea she'd ever had. She didn't want him in her bed again; she didn't want sex with him. How could she have thought, for even a minute, that she could have sex for such a cold-blooded, ulterior motive?

"I thought you were in a hurry," he said. "Get your clothes off." Naked, he reached for her.

She backed away. "I'm sorry, I shouldn't have called you, I'm sorry—"

"Don't apologize. It's very sexy when a woman knows what she wants and asks for it." He'd unbuttoned her blouse and unhooked her bra earlier, and now tried to remove them. She tried to stop him, and he pinioned her wrists.

"This is a mistake, I don't want this, you have to go."

"Like hell."

"I'm sorry, Paul, but I mean it."

He smiled humorlessly. "You mean you want me to force you."

"No!"

He pushed her down on the bed, got her skirt off despite her struggles, then ripped her tights.

"Stop it!"

"I wouldn't have thought you liked this sort of thing," he mused.

"I don't, I'm telling the truth, I don't want to have sex, I want you to leave." Her voice wobbled all over the place. "Look, I'm sorry, I'm really sorry, but I can't, not now." Tears leaked out of her eyes. "Please. You don't understand. This isn't a game." She was completely naked now and he was naked on top of her.

"This *is* a game," he said calmly. "And I do understand. You've been chasing me for weeks. I know what you want. A minute ago, you were begging me to take you to bed. Now you're embarrassed. You want me to force you. I don't want to force you, but if I have to, I will."

"No."

"It's up to you," he said. "You can give, or I can take. That simple."

She had never thought rape could be that simple. She bit one of the arms that held her down. He slapped her hard.

"I told you," he said. "You can give, or I can take. It's that simple. It's your choice."

Frightened by his strength, seeing no choice at all, she gave in.

Afterward, she was not surprised when she discovered what he had left in her bed. What else should it be? It was just what she deserved.

It was ugly, yet there was something oddly appealing in the sight of it nestling in a fold of the duvet; she was reminded of her teenage passion for collecting bean bag creatures. She used to line them up across her bed. This could have been one of them: maybe a squashy elephant's head with a fat nose. She went on staring at it for a long time, lying on her side on the bed, emotionally numbed and physically exhausted, unable either to get up or to go to sleep. She told herself she should get rid of it, that she could take her aggressions out on it, cut it up, at least throw it, and the pair of hands, out with the rest of her unwanted garbage. But it was hard to connect this bean bag creature with Paul and what he had done to her. She realized she had scarcely more than glimpsed his genitals; no wonder she couldn't believe this floppy creature could have had anything to do with her rape. The longer she looked at it, the less she could believe it was that horrible man's. It, too, had been abused by him. And it wasn't his now, it was hers. OK, Paul had been the catalyst, somehow, but this set of genitalia had been born from the bed and her own desire; it was an entirely new thing.

Eventually she fell asleep, still gazing at it. When she opened her eyes in the morning it was like seeing an old friend. She wouldn't get rid of it. She put it in a pillowcase and stashed the parcel among the scarves, shawls and sweaters on the shelf at the top of the wardrobe.

She decided to put the past behind her. She didn't think about Paul or Ralph or even Freddy. Although most nights she slept with Freddy's body, that was a decision made on the same basis, and with no more emotion, as whether she slept with the duvet or the electric blanket. Freddy's body wasn't Freddy's any-more; it was hers.

The only men in her life now were friends. She wasn't looking for romance, and she seldom thought about sex. If she wanted male companionship there was Christopher, a platonic friend from school, or Marcus, her next-door neighbor, or Freddy. They still talked on the phone frequently, and very occasionally met in town for a drink or a meal, but she had never invited him over since their break-up, so it was a shock one evening to answer the door and discover him standing outside.

He looked sheepish. "I'm sorry," he said. "I know I should have called first, but I couldn't find a working phone, and...I hope you don't mind. I need somebody to talk to. Matilda's thrown me out."

And not only Matilda, but also the latest other woman. He poured out his woes, and she made dinner, and they drank wine and talked for hours.

"Do you have somewhere to stay?" she asked at last.

"I could go to my sister's. I stay there a lot anyway. She's got a spare room—I've even got my own key. But—" He gave her his old look, desirous but undemanding. "Actually, Fay, I was hoping I could stay with you tonight."

She discovered he was still irresistible.

Her last thought before she fell asleep was how strange it was to sleep with someone who had arms and legs.

In the morning she woke enough to feel him kiss her, but she didn't realize it was a kiss goodbye, for she could still feel his legs entwined with her own.

But the rest of him was gone, and probably for good this time, she discovered when she woke up completely. For a man with such a smooth-skinned body he had extremely hairy legs, she thought, sitting on the bed and staring at the unattached limbs. And for a woman who had just been used and left again, she felt awfully cheerful.

She got Ralph's feet out of the drawer—thinking how much thinner and more elegant they were than Freddy's—and, giggling to herself, pressed the right foot to the bottom of the right leg, just to see how it looked.

It looked as if it was growing there and always had been. When she tried to pull it away, it wouldn't come. She couldn't even see a join. Anyone else might have thought it was perfectly natural; it probably only looked odd to her because she knew it wasn't. When she did the same thing with the left foot and left leg, the same thing happened.

So then, feeling daring, she took Freddy's torso out of the wardrobe and laid it down on the bed just above the legs. She pushed the legs up close, so they looked as if they were growing out of the torso—and then they were. She sat it up, finding that it was as flexible and responsive as a real, live person, not at all a dead weight, and she sat on the edge of the bed beside it and looked down at its empty lap.

"Don't go away; I have just the thing for Sir," she said.

The genitals were really the wrong size and skin-tone for Freddy's long, pale body, but they nestled gratefully into his crotch, obviously happy in their new home.

The body was happy, too. There was new life in it—not Freddy's, not Paul's, not Ralph's, but a new being created out of their old parts. She wasn't imagining it. Not propped up, it was sitting beside her, holding itself up, alert and waiting. When she leaned closer she could feel a heart beating within the chest, sending the blood coursing through a network of veins and arteries. She reached out to stroke the little elephant-head slumbering between the legs, and as she touched it, it stirred and sat up.

She was sexually excited, too, and, at the same time, horrified. There had to be something wrong with her to want to have sex with this incomplete collection of body parts. All right, it wasn't dead, so at least what she felt wasn't necrophilia, but what was it? A man without arms was merely disabled, but was a man without a head a man at all? Whatever had happened to her belief in the importance of relationships? They couldn't even communicate, except by touch, and then only at her initiative. All he could do was respond to her will. She thought of Paul's hands, how she had been groped, forced, slapped, and held down by them, and was just as glad they remained unattached, safely removed to the kitchen cupboard. Safe sex, she thought, and giggled. In response to the vibration, the body listed a little in her direction.

She got off the bed and moved away, then stood and watched it swaying indecisively. She felt a little sorry for it, being so utterly dependent on her, and that cooled her ardor. It wasn't right, she couldn't use it as a kind of live sex-aid—not as it was. She was going to have to find it a head, or forget about it.

She wrapped the body in a sheet to keep the dust off and stored it under the bed. She couldn't sleep with it anymore. In its headless state it was too disturbing. "Don't worry," she said, although it couldn't hear her. "This isn't forever."

She started her headhunt. She knew it might take some time, but she was going to be careful; she didn't want another bad experience. It wouldn't be worth it.

Something good had come out of the Paul experience, but heads—or faces, anyway—were so much harder to depersonalize. If it looked like Freddy or Paul in the face, she knew she would respond to it as Freddy or Paul, and what was the point of that? She wanted to find someone new, someone she didn't know, but also someone she liked; someone she could find attractive, go to bed with, and be parted from without the traumas of love or hate.

She hoped it wasn't an impossible paradox.

She asked friends for introductions, she signed up for classes, joined clubs, went to parties, talked to men in supermarkets and on buses, answered personal ads. And then Marcus dropped by one evening, and asked if she wanted to go to a movie with him.

They had seen a lot of movies and shared a fair number of pizzas over the past two years, but although she liked him, she knew very little about him. She didn't even know for sure that he was heterosexual. She occasionally saw him with other women, but the relationships seemed to be platonic. Because he was younger than she was, delicate-looking and with a penchant for what she thought of as "arty" clothes, because he didn't talk about sex and had never touched her, the idea of having sex with him had never crossed her mind. Now, seeing his clean-shaven, rather pretty face as if for the first time, it did.

"What a good idea," she said.

After the movie, after the pizza and a lot of wine, after he'd said he probably should be going, Fay put her hand on his leg and suggested he stay. He seemed keen enough—if surprised—but after she got him into bed he quickly lost his erection and nothing either of them did made any difference.

"It's not your fault," he said anxiously. It had not occurred to her that it could be. "Oh, God, this is awful," he went on. "If you only knew how I've dreamed of this...Only I never thought, never dared to hope, that you could want me too, and now...you're so wonderful, and kind, and beautiful, and you deserve so much, and you must think I'm completely useless."

"I think it's probably the wine," she said. "We both had too much to drink. Maybe you should go on home...I think we'd both sleep better in our own beds, alone."

"Oh, God, you don't hate me, do you? You will give me another chance, won't you, Fay? Please?"

"Don't worry about it. Yes, Marcus, yes, of course I will. Now, good night."

She found nothing in her bed afterward; she hadn't expected to. But neither did she expect the flowers that arrived the next day, and the day after that.

He took her out to dinner on Friday night—not pizza this time—and afterward, in her house, in her bed, they did what they had come together to do. She fell asleep, supremely satisfied, in his arms. In the morning he was eager to make love again, and Fay might have been interested—he had proved himself to be a very tender and skilful lover—but she was too impatient. She had only wanted him for one thing, and the sooner he left her, the sooner she would get it.

"I think you'd better go, Marcus. Let's not drag this out," she said.

"What do you mean?"

"I mean this was a mistake, we shouldn't have made love, we're really just friends who had too much to drink, so..."

He looked pale, even against the pale linen. "But I love you."

There was a time when such a statement, in such circumstances, would have made her happy, but the Fay who had loved, and expected to be loved in return, by the men she took to bed, seemed like another person now.

"But I don't love you."

"Then why did you—"

"Look, I don't want to argue. I don't want to say something that might hurt you. I want us to be friends, that's all, the way we used to be." She got up, since he still hadn't moved, and put on her robe.

"Are you saying you never want to see me again?"

She looked down at him. He really did have a nice face, and the pain that was on it now—that she had put there—made her look away hastily in shame. "Of course I do. You've been a good neighbor and a good friend. I hope we can go on being that. Only..." She tried to remember what someone had said to her once, was it Ralph? "Only I can't be what you want me to be. I still care about you, of course. But I don't love you in that way. So we'd better part. You'll see it's for the best, in time. You'll find someone else."

"You mean you will."

Startled, she looked back at him. Wasn't that what she had said to Ralph? She couldn't think how to answer him. But Marcus was out of bed, getting dressed, and didn't seem to expect an answer.

"I'll go," he said. "Because you ask me to. But I meant what I said. I love you. You know where I live. If you want me...if you change your mind..."

"Yes, of course. Goodbye, Marcus, I'm sorry."

She walked him to the door, saw him out, and locked the door behind him. Now! She scurried back to the bedroom, but halted in the doorway as she had a sudden, nasty thought. What if it hadn't worked? What if, instead of a pretty face, she found, say, another pair of feet in her bed?

Then I'll do it again, she decided, and again and again until I get my man.

She stepped forward, grasped the edge of the duvet, and threw it aside with a conjurer's flourish.

There was nothing on the bare expanse of pale blue sheet; nothing but a few stray pubic hairs.

She picked up the pillows, each in turn, and shook them. She shook out the duvet, unfastening the cover to make sure there was nothing inside. She peered beneath the bed and poked around the sheet-wrapped body, even pulled the bed away from the wall, in case something had caught behind the headboard. Finally she crawled across the bed on her belly, nose to the sheet, examining every inch.

Nothing. He had left nothing.

But why? How?

They left parts because they weren't willing to give all. The bed preserved bits and pieces of men who wanted only pieces of her time, pieces of her body, for which they could pay only with pieces of their own.

Marcus wanted more than that. He wanted, and offered, everything. But she had refused him, so now she had nothing.

No, not nothing. She crouched down and pulled the sheet-wrapped form from beneath the bed, unwrapped it and reassured herself that the headless, armless body was still warm, still alive, still male, still hers. She felt the comforting stir of sexual desire in her own body as she aroused it in his, and she vowed she would not be defeated.

It would take thought and careful planning, but surely she could make one more lover leave her?

She spent the morning making preparations, and at about lunchtime she phoned Marcus and asked him to come over that evening.

"Did you really mean it when you said you loved me?"

"Yes."

"Because I want to ask you to do something for me, and I don't think you will."

"Fay, anything, what is it?"

"I'll have to tell you in person."

"I'll come over now."

She fell into his arms when he came in, and kissed him passionately. She felt his body respond, and when she looked at his face she saw the hurt had gone and a wondering joy replaced it.

"Let's go in the bedroom," she said. "I'm going to tell you everything; I'm going to tell you the truth about what I want, and you won't like it, I know."

"How can you know? How can you possibly know?" He stroked her back, smiling at her.

"Because it's not normal. It's a sexual thing."

"Try me."

They were in the bedroom now. She drew a deep breath. "Can I tie you to the bed?"

"Well." He laughed a little. "I've never done that before, but I don't see anything wrong with it. If it makes you happy."

"Can I do it?"

"Yes, why not."

"Now, I mean." Shielding the bedside cabinet with her body, she pulled out the ropes she had put there earlier. "Lie down."

He did as she said. "You don't want me to undress first?"

She shook her head, busily tying him to the bedposts.

"And what do I do now?" He strained upwards against the ropes, demonstrating how little he was capable of doing.

"Now you give me your head."

"What?"

"Other men have given me other parts; I want your head."

It was obvious he didn't know what she meant. She tried to remember how she had planned to explain; what, exactly, she wanted him to do. Should she show him the body under the bed? Would he understand then?

"Your head," she said again, and then she remembered the words. "It's simple. You can give it to me, or I can take it. It's your choice."

He still stared at her as if it wasn't simple at all. She got the knife out of the bedside cabinet, and held it so he could see. "You give, or I take. It's your choice."

Trouble Follows

David B. Silva

1.

I've been an old woman for a good long time, and death has been no stranger to my life. I lost my husband of four years after he fell six stories down an empty elevator shaft while working a construction job in Chicago. My sister Abigail died in '81 from complications brought on by her diabetes. To this day I still miss her something terrible. My father, who worked his entire life for Southern Pacific before retiring in '67, died five years later, after his second heart attack. Mamma managed to hang on well past her seventy-seventh birthday, which I'll be approaching next year, but she was never quite the same after Dad died. And don't get me started on all the friends I've lost over the years.

I knew what death looked like.

And it never scared me nearly as much as Noel Robinson's dark side.

2.

The Robinsons moved into the neighborhood last June, a couple weeks before the big Fourth of July weekend. Three houses down, on the same side of the street. Connie, her husband Kurt, and their boy, Noel, who was eleven. It was my understanding—this from the real estate agent, who was the nephew of a friend—they had lived up north, in a suburb of Redding, until Kurt recently lost his job to the recession. Supposedly, there had been a bit of a drinking problem as well, though you don't soil a man's name based on rumors unless you want your own name soiled right along with it, so I kept that blemish to myself.

The afternoon they moved in, I took them a warm, homemade cherry cobbler. In my day that was what you did when a new family moved into the neighborhood. You introduced yourself and you welcomed them. I suppose I should have waited a day or two longer; it was rude of me to pop in while they were still unpacking. Mamma always said I was too impulsive for my own good. "You'd run out the door for the school bus without your dress on if I didn't keep an eye on you," she'd say.

"Just ignore the clutter," Connie said, as she led the way to the kitchen past a living room stacked higher than a church organ with boxes. She brewed a pot of coffee, served up the cobbler on a set of dessert plates that had originally belonged to her grandmother, and we sat at the dinette table.

I apologized for intruding.

"Don't give it a second thought," she said. "There's only so much unpacking you can do before you need a break. Kurt's off with Noel, getting a haircut. So this is the perfect time."

I liked her immediately.

She was a petite little thing with reddish-brown hair and a warm, friendly smile. Her high cheekbones gave her a thin face and drew you into her dark, festive eyes, which in my humble opinion have always been the lure of a pretty woman. If I had to describe her in a single word, I would say Connie was *sweet.*

We talked about what it was like living up north and what it was like here, and before I realized it, half an hour had passed. A short time later, Kurt and Noel returned from the barbershop. Connie introduced me, raved about the cherry cobbler, and cut them each a slice.

Kurt was a pleasant man, cordial and polite, and like all men, antsy to get out of the crossfire of two chatty women as fast as he could. "Nice to meet you," he said at the first opportunity. Then he excused himself and carried the plate of cobbler out into the garage with him.

Noel had his father's blond hair, which was thin and fell perfectly into place. When he smiled, he revealed wide, little-boy dimples that surely melted the hearts of little girls. His curse—if you cared to think of it as such—was that he had one ice blue eye and one eye as black as night. It was the strangest thing I think I'd ever seen.

He didn't say much, but he hung around until we finished our cobbler and the conversation began to lose its freshness. By that time, I knew I had overstayed my welcome and offered a polite goodbye. They were eager to get back to unpacking, I imagined. I knew I would have been.

3.

Kurt found a job within a month. I don't believe it was in the same field. Connie had said something about him working in Redding as the advertising manager for a small FM station. This new position was in a printing shop, working behind the counter. She said he seemed surprisingly happy in his new environment, though, and I imagined that was all that mattered.

In late August, Noel started classes at Piedmont Elementary. He was in the sixth grade. I saw him a few times, standing off by himself as the kids waited for the morning school bus. In my day, I worked summers in the orchards with my sister, and attended a one-room schoolhouse in the winter. Everyone knew everyone else back then. It was easy to make friends. Times had changed, though. People were always on the move and making friends wasn't nearly as easy.

I felt sorry for the boy.

That was...until a couple weeks later when we had our first run in.

It was at night, shortly after eleven, which was why I found it so disturbing. I usually read awhile in bed because it helps me sleep. My mother used to leave the television on to help her sleep. And my sister, Abigail, she usually drank a glass of warm milk with a little whiskey. But for me, reading always did the trick.

I had just crawled under the covers, turned on the reading lamp next to the bed, and opened *Silent Night* by Mary Higgins Clark—you can't do better than a good mystery—when I caught a movement out the corner of my eye. I peered over the rim of my glasses at the bedroom window, and there—peering back at me—was Noel.

He leaned back slightly, deeper into the shadows but he was still visible, and he didn't appear the least bit rattled that I had caught him.

"What in *tarnation* do you think you're doing, young man?" I yelled, putting aside my book.

He stepped deeper into the shadows.

I climbed out of bed, unlatched the window and threw it open. "Noel? You know better than to be out here this time of night."

But by then, the shadows had swallowed him whole and he was gone.

4.

I called Connie the next day. I think I caught her on her way out the door. There was a certain curtness in her voice that you hear when a person is hurried and doesn't appreciate the interruption.

"I'm not really sure how to tell you this, Connie. So I'm going to just spit it out and trust you'll accept it in the spirit it's offered."

"What is it?"

"I caught Noel peeking in my bedroom window last night."

She paused a moment, and then without a hint of emotion in her voice, she said, “Are you sure it was Noel?”

“I am.”

There was another short pause, and when she spoke this time her voice was just above a whisper. “I’m very sorry, Eleanor. I promise it won’t happen again. I’ll have a talk with him as soon as school lets out.”

I thanked her for that, mildly surprised, and admittedly a bit ashamed at my surprise. I had feared she would be one of those mothers who thought her child was the second coming and could do no wrong—we’ve all met them—but thankfully I was mistaken. Connie Robinson made no excuses for her son. She simply accepted responsibility and promised to correct the misbehavior.

I thought that was quite admirable in this day and age.

And in my mind, that had been the end of it.

But apparently, it hadn’t.

5.

The following morning when I went out to get the paper, I couldn’t believe my eyes.

Someone had painted filthy words all over my car. Goodness gracious, I couldn’t believe the foul language. Words that belonged on the bathroom walls of dirty service stations. There they were, in white paint, scrawled across the hood and down both sides of my precious Volvo for all the neighbors to see.

I nearly broke down crying.

I couldn’t imagine why on Earth anyone would ever do such a thing.

6.

I never did pick up the newspaper that morning. I went back into the house and changed into my gardening clothes. Then I gathered up a plastic water pail, some old rags, a bottle of dish detergent, and took them all outside.

The paint smelled like cleaning solvent and I wasn't having much success getting it off when Noel arrived on his bicycle. He rode up the driveway a bit, slammed on the brakes and left a black scuffmark on the concrete. "What happened?"

"Do you know anything about this, Noel?" Of course, he did. He was angry because I called his mother about him peeking in my bedroom window and this was his way of getting even.

"No, ma'am." He climbed off the bike, and came up to stand beside me. He was a few inches short for his age, wearing a blue T-shirt under a black-and-white plaid shirt with the long sleeves rolled up to his elbows. He pushed the baseball cap—with an old Yankees emblem on the front—back on his head and sighed.

"I don't think it's going to come out," I said. "It may have to be repainted."

"It'll come out," Noel said. "At least I think it will. I read something on the Internet about using acetone to get paint off."

"Acetone?"

"Yeah. You have any?"

"I don't believe so," I said. "What is it?"

"It's like paint thinner. I think we have some. I'll go get it."

He went running off down the street with energy that God grants us all when we're children and then slowly takes back as we get older. I watched him disappear through the front door of his house, and found myself trying to understand what sort of a game he was playing. I knew he was the one who had sprayed those horrible words all over my car. So why was he pretending to be helpful?

Within a minute or two, Noel came bounding out of his house again, slamming the door loud enough to send an echo down the empty street. He had a rectangular metal can in one hand and a white rag in the other as he plopped down on the driveway in front of the back tire.

"You have to be careful with this stuff," he said, unscrewing the cap and dipping the rag into the liquid. "It's not supposed to, but sometimes it can take off some of the other paint—you know, the stuff you don't want to take off. So you have to try it in a little corner where no one'll notice if it messes things up."

"I don't want to make it worse."

"I know. I'll be careful." He dabbed the liquid over a small area where some of the paint had run down the side of the Volvo and off the edge. "It wasn't me. I know you think it was, but it wasn't me who looked in your window."

"I saw you, Noel." I dipped my rag into the soapy water in the pail and returned to scrubbing an area of the driver's door. The white lettering expanded, blurring the borders, and a very thin layer washed away.

"It wasn't me."

"Who was it then?"

Noel stopped. He looked up at me with his dark eye squinting against the early morning sun, and shrugged. "I don't know. All I know is it wasn't me."

The paint where he had dabbed the acetone had completely washed away.

"It's working," I said, pointing it out. I didn't know why he would paint graffiti all over my car then help me clean it up, but I was thrilled that the neighbors wouldn't have to be subjected to all those filthy words.

Noel pulled the hand away, blew his warm breath over the area, and then rubbed it down with a dry section of the rag. "Didn't mess up the shine, either."

Letter by letter we washed the words off, one thin layer at a time, before moving on, much as we had moved on from the discussion of him looking into my bedroom window.

It took nearly two hours.

Noel stayed to the end. He said he was sorry about what had happened to the car, and then excused himself because he was late getting home. I thanked him, and told him to have his mother call me if he got into trouble.

Maybe he hadn't been the one who had peeked into my bedroom window after all?

Maybe he hadn't been the one who had painted those filthy words on my car?

Suddenly, nothing about the eleven-year-old boy seemed certain.

7.

Connie stopped by with a coffee cake the next afternoon. I invited her in and we sat on the Davenport in the living room, each with a slice of cake and a cup of tea. She said she was still unpacking boxes and couldn't believe how much *stuff* they'd accumulated over the years.

"But we're beginning to settle in," she said, sounding tired.

"It takes time before a new place feels like home," I said.

She nodded, and then took a sip of her tea, peering over the lip of the cup at me as if she were trying to read my state of mind. "I wanted to apologize for the other day when you called about Noel. I was on my way out the door and I'm afraid I might have been a little curt with you."

"Not at all," I said.

"I wanted you to know that I did sit down and have a talk with Noel when he got home from school. He admitted he snuck out that night and stood outside your bedroom window."

I didn't know what to say to that. He had told me it hadn't been him outside my window.

"Noel can be a handful at times, but in his heart, he's a good boy."

"I'm sure he is," I said, having my doubts. I didn't tell her about the incident with my Volvo, nor did I tell her about the two hours Noel spent helping me wash the paint off. What would be the point? It seemed she didn't understand her boy any better than I did.

Connie smiled weakly—and a little *sadly,* I thought—and her hands began to tremble. "He got suspended from school today. Three days. For slashing the principal's tires."

"Oh, Connie, I'm so sorry," I said.

"And we didn't leave Redding because Kurt couldn't find work," she added, tears collecting in her eyes now. "We left because Noel killed one of the neighbor's cats."

In one of the rare moments in my life, I found myself speechless. It was one thing to be caught peering in a neighbor's window, another to be slashing tires and painting filthy words on your neighbor's car, but killing a cat...killing a cat was despicable. What kind of a sick mind could do such a thing?

"I don't know what to do about him anymore."

I put down my cup of tea, moved to sit next to her on the sofa, and put my arm around her shoulders for comfort. "He's lucky he has you as his mother," I said, though later, after Connie had left, I worried for her.

I couldn't imagine it was easy being a parent. Before my husband died, we had put off having children until we were financially stable. So I never experienced motherhood for myself. But I'd been privy to the goings on in enough families to know that even a good child could turn your hair gray.

Connie might not have even known it, but she was raising a monster.

8.

It was overcast the next morning. Nothing ominous in the way of rain, but maybe a warning of other things to come.

I went through my usual morning routine—believe me, it gets entrenched at my age—and ended up in the kitchen filling the coffee pot with water when I glanced out the window and saw Noel standing on the sidewalk. He was slightly hunched forward, his arms limp at his sides. He appeared fixed on the car or the corner of the house, I wasn't sure which, but somewhere in that general area.

I watched him a moment, curious—and yes, more than a bit rattled. Then I gradually moved down the kitchen counter until I could clearly see the Volvo in the driveway. By all outward appearances, it seemed no worse than yesterday's wear. Thank goodness, I thought. I certainly didn't want to go through that nightmare again.

I turned my attention back to Noel, who had remained motionless. He didn't fidget the way little boys do when they're forced to stand still longer than a few seconds. He didn't shift his weight from foot to foot. He didn't even shade his eyes against the morning sun that was just above the line of the roof now and chasing the shadows from his face. It appeared as if time had stopped for him and he was waiting for it to start up again.

How odd, I thought.

Then two things happened, one right after the other.

A figure came running down the driveway from somewhere up by the corner of the house. It could have been Noel's twin. It was dressed in the same clothes, had Noel's thin blond hair, and even ran with

Noel's awkward gait, which included an occasional double step.

I'm not sure how to describe what happened next without sounding like a foolish old antique, but God's honest truth, cross my heart and hope to die...when that figure arrived at the edge of the lawn, it stopped, turned until it was facing the same direction as Noel, and then took a step back, entering the boy's body.

Noel shuddered, as if he was going into a fit or some such thing, and then time suddenly seemed to start up for him again. He raised his head, shaded his eyes, and...

That was when the second thing happened.

It was a puff of smoke, off to my left. I imagined that figure—Noel's dark side, as I came to think of it—had somehow managed to get inside the garage and set a fire. I had no idea how serious it was; all I knew for certain was that something was burning, and there was an angry gray-black cloud forming in my front yard.

9.

The fire had not originated inside the garage after all. Noel's little helper had crumpled up some newspapers, stuffed them into an opening under the corner of the door and set them on fire. When I emerged from the house, having already called 911, Noel had the garden hose unrolled and was doing his best to minimize the damage.

Minutes later the first fire truck arrived. By that time, there were no visible flames left and the smoke had turned milky-gray.

I sat on the front porch steps as they put out the last of the smoldering embers. The garage door was charred up and down one side and would need to be replaced, I was told, but otherwise there was no structural damage and surprisingly little smoke damage.

"It could have been much worse," a fireman by the name of Lewis told me.

I nodded and thanked him as I watched Noel roll up the garden hose.

"You do know, ma'am, that someone did this on purpose?" Lewis said.

I glanced up at him, feeling strangely hollow inside. "I'm sorry?"

"It wasn't an accident, ma'am. It was arson. Someone started this fire on purpose. You have any idea who would want to burn down your house?"

Noel placed the hose behind the shrubs under the living room window where it belonged and came up to stand next to the fireman. His eyes were downcast. There was a black smudge across his forehead. Smoke had dulled the white letters that formed the word MESSENGER on the front of his dark green T-shirt. He shoved his hands into the front pockets of his jeans.

"Ma'am?"

"No," I said. "I can't think of anyone who would want to do such a thing."

While the crew finished up, Noel sat down with me on the porch steps. "I'm sorry," he said.

"Do your parents know about...about your *accomplice?*"

"I tried to tell them when I was little, but they thought I was making it up. They thought he was like an imaginary friend or something. Just make believe."

"Has he always been with you?" I asked.

"As long as I can remember."

"You afraid of him?"

"I'm afraid of what he might do."

"Me, too," I said.

You don't live as long as me without running into some strange things along the way. When we were living in Chicago we had a neighbor in the apartment building that used to go into a trance and speak fluent

Russian even though she'd never been to Russia and had never studied the language. Years later, I met a woman at a library book sale who could read an entire book upside down just by shuffling through the pages. Pick any line on any page and she could recite it back to you verbatim.

The human mind is a mysterious universe.

And Noel was a mysterious boy.

I gave him a playful nudge, doing my best to break the tension. "Ever try to ditch him?"

"No-o-o," Noel said with a grin that brought out his dimples. It was the first time I'd seen a smile cross his face. He briefly glanced up at me, his eyes bright—even the dark one—then looked away again.

"I don't think I know how to help you," I said.

"I don't think anyone can."

The firemen finished putting away the last of their gear and climbed into the truck. From the passenger side window, Lewis waved and the truck pulled away from the curb. Noel and I watched until it disappeared from sight, and then sat in silence for a while.

"Does he come and go as he pleases?" I eventually asked.

Noel nodded, and began to fiddle with his shoelaces.

"Can you force him out?"

"Never tried. When he's inside me I can keep him from doing the bad things."

"Really? What if he can't get back?" I asked.

"I don't know," Noel said with a shrug. "He always comes back."

I fell silent again, thinking back over my life and all the things I'd grown to regret. I had brought frivolous lawsuits against people I didn't like. I'd lied to my husband about money I'd misspent. I once watched a man die in the street after being struck by a pickup without ever making an effort to help him. There were worse regrets. Too many to count, I supposed. I had always done my best to separate myself from *that* person, that *dark side* of me. But I'd never completely escaped it.

"Trust me?" I asked.

"I guess."

"Good. Let's see if we can get rid of your friend."

"He's *not* my friend."

I extended my hand, Noel took it, and we walked down the porch steps.

"What are we going to do?"

"I thought you were going to trust me?" I said, leading him across the yard to the Volvo. I opened the rear passenger door. "Hop in."

"Why?"

"No arguing with your elders. Just trust me."

Noel sighed the sigh of all eleven-year-old boys who don't like being told what to do, and scooted across the seat to the far side to express his displeasure. "Okay. Now what?"

I closed the door. "Now, we wait."

People will tell you that old antiques like myself, we don't have much patience left. In my case, that was true long before my so-called golden years. I'd always been full of piss and vinegar, and a bit impulsive to boot. But I'd *never* been as impulsive or as impatient as an eleven-year-old boy. Just try to get him to sit still for longer than it takes to swat a fly.

Noel slumped into the seat, a scowl on his face. "How long do I have to sit here?"

"As long as it takes."

"As long as *what* takes?"

"For your little friend to come out."

"I told you, he's not my friend." Noel glared at me, his ice-blue eye turning nearly as dark as the other one, and then he kicked the back of the seat, and crossed his arms defiantly.

"Drives you crazy, doesn't it? Having to sit still?"

"No."

"Yes, it does, you little snot."

And that was all it took.

An animal-like growl erupted from his throat, and a moment later, Noel's counterpart followed. It flew across the seat, slamming into the passenger window, its palms pressed against the glass, exposing two-inch nails.

Startled, I pulled back.

It bore its yellow fangs and slammed its forehead into the glass, creating a web of cracks down the middle of the window. A trickle of blood ran down its face. It growled again, the noise as harsh and disagreeable as anything I'd ever heard.

I stepped back into the door, blocking it with the weight of my body, buying as much time as I could. It was going to break out—I was going to *let it* break out—but first I needed to catch my breath and summon what little courage I still had left to me.

After a short prayer, I opened the door and Noel's *dark side* came bursting out like an eighty mile an hour gust of wind.

The door swung wide, slamming me against the car and pinning me there until the momentum gradually took the door in the other direction. The latch caught, I was sure I heard it, but it didn't close.

Noel's counterpart caught its balance and turned back in my direction.

I pounded the back of my fist against the car. "Noel! Close the door, Noel! Close the door and lock all the locks."

Then his dark side pounced.

I turned to protect myself, and it took the opening to sink its teeth into my right shoulder. I whimpered, then a scream slipped out of me that I wished I had been able to control. Pain radiated down my arm and across my back. I closed my eyes.

My knees buckled, and I went to the ground.

It took another bite, this one out of my exposed left shoulder.

And for some reason, this time the pain felt dull and faraway. I felt a strange calmness fall over me. *This is the way you're doing to die, you old antique. Not so terrible after all. Even a bit silly if you think about it. It's been a good life. A long life.*

From somewhere behind me, I heard the latch on the car door finally click into place. A moment later, I heard the dull double *thump* of the locks.

Atta boy, I thought dreamily. *Atta boy.*

The pressure on my shoulder eased a bit, and I realized Noel's dark side had released its grip. I glanced up at it, mildly amused to find it peering into the car window, both bewildered and enraged at being separated from its host.

It slammed its forehead into the glass again, adding a new web of cracks to the mosaic.

Another growl came up from its throat—this one not inhuman, but pained and mournful—and it staggered backward, dazed.

Then the Dark Ones came.

Shock had set in by this time, and I was on the verge of passing out. I drifted through a dark landscape and a midday sky with thousands of black stars. And I saw them climb out of the earth, the Dark Ones. They came in hoards, small dark creatures that amassed around Noel's counterpart, embracing it, and dragging it screaming back into the earth with them.

Then everything turned black.

10.

I spent two days in the hospital. The doctors were skeptical when I told them the bites were from a wild dog, but for nearly a week county animal control had the residents in the area on alert.

Connie came by to visit while I was there, and later at home until I was feeling better. Noel came by on his own several weeks after that. The first thing I noticed about him was his eyes—the dark one had turned ice-blue. He thanked me, and said his counterpart hadn't returned.

I didn't imagine it would, though I wouldn't be willing to bet one way or the other.

We rarely saw each other after that. The paths of old ladies and little boys don't often cross. I was all right with that.

I don't know if the Dark Ones were real or I had imagined them in my moment of shock, but I do know that we all have a dark side and that sometimes it can overwhelm us. Noel was one of the lucky ones. He was able to break free.

I guess I've been lucky as well.

For the most part, I've learned to control mine.

Keeping It in the Family

Robert Morrish

My sister moved in with me toward the end of the year. We'd never liked each other all that much, and we liked each other even less when we were living under the same roof, but what choice did I have? Her MS was getting worse, almost by the day, inching towards the point where she couldn't function any more on her own.

We may not have been a storybook example of loving siblings, but I couldn't just sit back and watch her fall apart, or let her wind up abandoned in some low-rate group home. I may be a bastard but I have my principles.

The fact that there was nowhere else for her to go made the decision a lot simpler. Our parents had died in a car accident two summers previously, and our brother Colin had long since slunk out of state, like a good black sheep should. No one in the family had heard from him for years. He hadn't bothered to show for our parents' funeral, if he even knew about it.

And so Gretchen moved in with me on a gray December morning as slush clumped on the sidewalks like melting wax. A lifelong gypsy suddenly running on empty, she brought few possessions with her.

"This feels like failure," she said that morning, after trundling a box up the stairs and collapsing in a garage-sale chair that couldn't take many more collapses. "I don't like it."

"Come on, Gretchen—"

"I appreciate your doing this and all, but..."

"Since when does accepting a little help from family qualify as failure? Besides, this is only temporary until you can get back on your feet again. Hell, one of those new medications you mentioned will probably—"

"Just stop, Geoffrey. Please. It's likely none of the meds will help. You know that." She liked to call me Geoffrey, when she lectured me, which was fairly often. "Chances are, I'm only going to get worse."

She was right. Six months later, she was dead.

⁂

Before she died, I learned some interesting things about my sister. And some not very attractive things about myself.

I learned, for instance, that Gretchen had some friends who'd taken up residency on the fringe, or beyond. And I learned that I wasn't especially tolerant.

Winston was the first of her cohorts to show up, and one of the last to leave. One of the few who came to her funeral. I never did figure out if Winston was his first name, last name, or a nickname (he chain-smoked his namesake).

He showed up early in January with matted beard, skull-capped and shaven head, and distracting tremors. Thinking him to be a wayward homeless guy, I tried to turn him away from our door until he mentioned Gretchen's name. She hobbled up behind me while I was still trying to figure things out.

"Winston," came her voice over my shoulder. "You found me." Her voice seemed to tremble, expressing surprise or disappointment, or maybe some odd mixture of both.

"Had to. Couldn't just let you go. You're too important to the rest of us."

"I'm dying, Winston. How important can I be?"

"Could be real important. You know that. We could learn something before you go." He was still standing in my doorway, talking in riddles.

"So you want me to be your guinea pig instead of theirs. That's a real win."

"You know better."

She might have, but I didn't. That first conversation, like most of the others that I was later privy to, left me twisting in the wind, groping for meanings that were forever just beyond my reach.

Once Winston had tracked my sister down, she seemed to readily welcome him, and his brethren, back into her life. It was as if she hadn't really wanted to desert them, just test the depths of their allegiance.

Before too long—but after hearing many ominous references to *them* and *they*—I came to the conclusion that my sister and Winston and the others caught in the whirlpool of their inner circle were all suffering from paranoid delusions. There were six or seven of them that I met, plus a couple others who were never more than mumbled names. All of them had served together in the Army, where Gretchen had been a communications specialist. More importantly, they'd all served together in Afghanistan.

They were convinced, one and all, that they had been exposed to something over there. Something gradual, insidious. And eventually lethal. The specifics were unclear to me, and maybe to them, but the consensus seemed to rest on some newly-engineered and hitherto-unknown virus.

I was confused. I'd heard about soldiers from the first Gulf War who were supposedly infected by some unknown substance, but nothing similar about Afghanistan vets.

I tried to understand what they were talking about. I really did. I learned that they had all served in the Army's 10th Mountain Division, and that they believed the exposure had occurred in Kandahar province in early September, 2006. They were part of a unit nearest a cave mouth when apparently some kind of portable lab was destroyed within, sending plumes of smoke billowing out.

They had all since been discharged from the service, their individual circumstances ranging from honorable to medical to dishonorable. And they had since sought each other out, banding together to share their obsession and their misery.

The symptoms they were experiencing included chronic fatigue, skin rashes, hair loss, and terrible headaches. There were apparently other symptoms as well, but they wouldn't discuss them in front of me.

My sister eventually admitted that she believed it was the effects of the virus she was experiencing, not a reemergence of her MS. I tried reasoning with her, citing medical examinations and confirmed diagnoses, but logic held no sway. She knew what she knew, and that was that.

It's not that I didn't have any sympathy for their claims. By that time, I'd read enough about Gulf War Syndrome to readily believe that some type of so-far unpublicized problems could have similarly resulted from serving in the war in Afghanistan. That part seemed plausible.

It was their claims about activities subsequent to the war—vague notions that their movements were being tracked, their symptoms monitored—that I had a problem with. Who, I wondered, would be watching them? The government? Some private organization, seeking to gauge the virus's effects? Neither made any sense. Regardless, I never heard Gretchen's clan give a name to their observers. Whenever I sought such details, their eyes would narrow and their mouths would close.

"We've tried to tell people before," Gretchen said to me once. "We've seen how they react. We know better than to waste time trying now."

"Trust me, Gretch," I said. "I'm on your side."

"You really want to hear this, hmm? You think you can lend a sympathetic ear?" She gave me a challenging look. I waited.

"Try this," she said finally. "What if a virus was intelligent? What if it was capable of communicating, coordinating its efforts, not just within one organism, but across many?"

I tried to play along, see what else she had to say, but I think some aspect—the tone of my voice perhaps, or a subconscious hint of a smirk—betrayed the fact that it sounded like a bad *X-Files* episode to me. Whatever it was, Gretchen picked up on it and refused to talk about it anymore. I shouldn't have been surprised. Condescending and patronizing were two of my last girlfriend's favorite descriptors for me.

After that, the group held fewer and fewer of their meetings at my apartment. And so, with increasing frequency, Gretchen would totter out in the evenings, sometimes to the bus stop, sometimes to a waiting car, always refusing my offer of a ride, no matter how insistent I might be.

She was slipping away, before my eyes and behind my back, growing weaker by the day. Helpless, I found myself wondering what my parents would do if they were still alive.

One thing was clear. Gretchen was right. It did feel a lot like failure.

⁂

That feeling had intensified into one of outright defeat by the time we buried her in June. The day of the funeral dawned gray and wet, not that different in its way from the day that she'd moved back into my life those few months earlier. Looking back, I couldn't believe it had been as long as it had. The end of her life had streaked past like a tracer, casting just enough illumination to make the shadows seem even deeper with her passing.

The funeral was held at a small cemetery near where we grew up; only about 20 miles from my current residence. Although Gretchen had spent her years since high school on a global trek, first on her own and then in the military, I had never strayed far from my hometown. I knew she wouldn't have traded her life, even given its short duration, for mine. Would I have traded mine for hers? Sometimes I wondered.

The drizzle was constant, lightly coating the headstones like a sheen of sweat. There was a decent-sized crowd, larger than her small circle of acquaintances would've led me to expect. The weather caused people to huddle together, seeking warmth both literal and figurative. Gazing around at the pale, drawn faces, I was struck by how few I really recognized. Winston was there, and a couple others from the Afghanistan group; some cousins and former neighbors; and a few faces I dimly recognized from high school.

The service was mercifully short, the minister's brevity perhaps influenced by the weather. When he finished, the crowd separated and began to drift away, each carried by their own wind and most never to converge again.

More condolences were offered to me from beneath passing umbrellas, and I was invited to join a gathering at a nearby bar (hosting a wake was something I could neither endure nor afford). I absently murmured noncommittal responses as I made my way from the grave.

"It's a shame, Mr. Timmerman. Your sister would have made an excellent vector."

It took a few seconds for the words to sink in. My brain felt as numb as my fingers. When the comment finally registered, I stopped and spun around, searching for the speaker.

"What? What was that?" I asked, to no one in particular. Two women, nearest to me, looked at me warily and veered past. "Who said that?" I persisted.

I was drawing attention, turning into the sort of morbid attraction that most people find themselves unable to look away from. The stares, together with those strange words still dripping in my head, finally made me shiver and turn away.

When I got back to my apartment, I grabbed a bottle of bourbon, sagged into the creaky garage-sale chair, still in my wet clothes, and proceeded to drink myself into a stupor as the afternoon settled down around me. I stopped counting how many times the phone rang. Mercifully, my answering machine was broken. Someone obviously wanted to talk to me, but the feeling wasn't mutual.

By the time darkness was seeping in through the windows, my hands were shaking so bad I could barely get the glass to my lips. I tried to tell myself it was exhaustion, reinforced by the liquor, but I'd tried to tell myself a lot of things lately, and for the most part, I wasn't buying.

The tremors had actually started a few weeks earlier, about the same time that numbness in my feet and hands and an occasional loss of balance had emerged. The fact that these symptoms mirrored some of what my sister had been experiencing was not lost on me.

I hadn't known what to make of it. I'd at least understood that it was highly unusual for someone my age to suddenly develop MS. And I didn't believe I'd caught anything communicable from her. I couldn't let myself even consider that notion.

I'd ignored the symptoms for a bit, but when they didn't go away, I felt like I had no choice but to see a doctor. Precautionary tests were taken—including the pleasure of a spinal tap—which confirmed that MS was not at the root of my problems. More tests ruled out other possible causes. The doctor wanted to order even more tests, but—saddled with a mediocre insurance plan that left me holding the bag for a not insignificant portion of the costs—I declined.

The doctor closed by gently asking if I'd considered that my symptoms could be "sympathetic," a psychosomatic reaction to my sister's condition. I mumbled that I'd considered that thought, thanked him for his efforts, and got out of there as quickly as I could. That was two weeks ago.

And I really *did* contemplate what he suggested. It was possible, I supposed. Stranger things had happened. But Gretchen had now been dead five days, and here I was, still shaking.

I pushed myself up out of the chair to fetch some ice. I lingered at the front window, watching a pickup truck splash past in the twilight. My gaze was drawn to the sidewalk, where a man stood, staring up at my window. He was tall, gaunt, completely bald, pale to the point of transparency. A black trenchcoat and completely out-of-place sunglasses completed the picture. I found myself staring at him, drinking in his bizarre appearance, unable to look away, even as he gazed back at me, until finally his brazen behavior began to irritate me. Emboldened by the liquor, I made my way to the front door, forcing my trembling fingers to focus on the chain and deadbolt.

By the time I made my way outside onto the concrete walkway and around the corner to where I could see the street again, he was gone. It seemed as though there was a hole, an empty void, where he'd stood. The drizzle had stopped, but dampness clung to the air, and floating upon it I could still see his image, like a stain left by the rain. I realized suddenly that I'd seen him before. Although he'd been effectively disguised at the time, wearing a hat and lurking beneath an umbrella, I was sure he'd been at my sister's funeral.

It was a couple of days before I sobered up enough to return to work. Not that anyone had really missed me. When you're 38 and assistant manager of a camera store, you've long since learned that the world doesn't revolve around you. The prize-winning and gallery-exhibiting dreams of my youth had been extinguished beneath a flood of cheap-wedding jobs and freelance assignments for bare-bones magazines and newspapers. I hadn't even set foot in my makeshift darkroom in over two months. I'd briefly thought about taking some shots at Gretchen's funeral, but couldn't for the life of me figure out why I'd want a record of that event.

I gradually settled back into my routine, such as it was. I kept the drinking to a manageable level, showed up for work most of the time, and was able to keep my symptoms–of what, I still didn't know—under control. They didn't lessen or cease as Gretchen's death faded, but neither did they grow worse. Vague worries about my health came and went, but I didn't want and couldn't afford to submit myself to more tests, so there was nothing to be done. Life, in general, returned to what passed for normal.

Except for one thing – the man on the sidewalk.

Two days after that first occasion, I saw him again, across the street, as I was pulling into my parking lot. By the time I'd parked and come back out to the street, he was nowhere to be seen. A few days later, I looked out the window at work and saw him staring in at me. I stuttered in the midst of answering a customer's question about how many megapixels were enough. It took me several moments to extricate myself from the aborted sales-pitch and, yet again, when I stepped outside, my watcher had departed. I can't honestly say whether I had the nerve while sober to directly confront the man, strange and menacing as he appeared, but I wanted to at least get a better look at him. That time outside the store, he'd looked a little different—shorter, perhaps, with more of a rounded face, and mottled skin. It had almost seemed like it was a different man, but with all the same strange characteristics and unusual attire.

The next time I saw one of them, my suspicions were confirmed. It was a woman that time, a waif with skin like sculpted ice and just a hint of hair, like frozen filament. She almost seemed to smile as I drove past. I felt myself shiver, and the shiver became a tremor and soon I had to pull over because I couldn't stop shaking.

I saw more of them in the days and weeks that followed, more frequently and with enough variation to allow me to distinguish between four or five of them. I began to wonder just how many of them there were. Not to mention what they wanted with me, and a host of other items—including the simple question of whether I was losing my mind.

At least the experience prompted me to get my cameras out of mothballs. I started carrying one with me most everywhere, and started to become obsessed with getting a picture of one of *them*. I realized, not without a sense of irony, that I'd begun to sound like my sister.

I told myself I only wanted pictures so I could study them, their appearance. But I think I wanted photographs just to prove to myself that my watchers were real. But if they didn't show up on film, did that mean they weren't real? Or merely that they didn't show up on film? My mind had taken to playing lots of little games like that, asking questions that would've seemed ridiculous to me a few weeks prior.

I figured I could start to answer those questions once I'd actually snapped a picture with one of the watchers directly in my crosshairs. But I never got the chance.

I got home on a Friday night, stressed from the Labor-Day-sale crowd as well as the general anxiety that had come to be my constant companion. I parked in the lot and stepped out into the kind of humidity that painted your clothes to your body within seconds. I was obviously dazed, or else it wouldn't have taken me so long to see him, sitting in a car not twenty feet from me.

Once I did see him, I froze, unsure what to do. I'd seldom been this close to one of them, and never with a clear path between us. Finally, I remembered that my camera was in my backpack. I pulled the pack off my shoulder and began wrestling with the zipper, before I was struck by the absurdity of what I was doing. I stopped fumbling with the bag and walked over toward the car. His eyes were unreadable behind the dark lenses, but he was clearly unperturbed by my approach. I faltered when I got close, stopping a few feet from his door.

"Who are you?" I shouted, not caring how crazy I might sound to anyone nearby. "What the hell do you want?"

He smiled then, and if I thought I'd had an idea of how unpleasant that sight could be, having seen the woman's brief smirk from a distance, the truth was I had no idea.

His lips quivered apart like dying earthworms, revealing a mouthful of crumbling yellow teeth, as uneven as the battlements of an ancient castle. His tongue roamed sluggishly beyond, caressing the decay.

The worms twitched as he breathed a single word: *"Soon."*

I staggered back as if I'd been pushed.

He'd been sitting there with his engine idling, facing out, and after he spoke, he gunned the engine, nearly leaving rubber as the nondescript vehicle—an old Chrysler, maybe—flashed past me.

I stood there for a long time, unsure what to do. I don't know if I was really, seriously considering leaving everything I had and just running as far away as I could, but it sure felt like it. In the end, though, I couldn't take such a drastic step, no matter how much a part of me wanted to. Instead, I made my way slowly up the stairs, eyeing every movement, every shadow, with suspicion.

Then I did the only thing I could think of: I called Winston. I'd been weighing the idea for a while, and I'd run out of reasons not to do so.

I was about to hang up the phone when he finally answered on the eighth ring.

"Yeah?" His voice was guarded but defiant.

"Winston? It's Geoff, Gretchen's brother."

"Yeah?" He'd always been a man of few words.

"Listen, this is going to sound strange, but...I know I was always pretty, umm, skeptical when you would talk about, you know, not your illness, but...about somebody following you. Watching you."

I waited, but he didn't say anything.

"Well, I'm not so skeptical anymore," I tried.

"Why's that?"

"I've...seen them."

"They following you?"

"Yes."

"Then God help you if they get too close. Stay clear of them, and you might have a few months left."

He hung up.

I tried calling back, but there was no answer, I finally gave up, cradled my head in my hands. Whatever I'd hoped to achieve by calling Winston, it hadn't been achieved. I felt completely alone, adrift in a Sargasso Sea of absurdity and mystery.

I went out that night, to a nearby bar. I wanted to be with people.

But it was no better than being alone. There was no way I could talk to anyone there about the thoughts running through my head. Eventually, I gave up and went home, sticking to the pools of streetlight as though they were islands in a stream where something deadly lurked just beneath the surface.

When I got back to my apartment, the phone was ringing. Hoping it might be Winston, having a change of heart, I hurried to pick it up. But the voice on the other end of the line was not Winston's.

"Brace yourself, Geoff. It's me. Colin."

⁂

We met in an all-night diner, coming up on midnight. I'd started to tell him to come to my apartment, but a furtive voice in my head whispered that might be a bad idea. My brother had been bad news before he disappeared. Who knew what kind of trouble he might be up to now?

I got there quickly, and was still nervously eyeing passing faces when my second double espresso arrived. None of the faces beyond the window looked familiar; all seemed in a hurry to get somewhere and eager to avoid eye contact. It hadn't rained much for a while, but it would be wrong to say the skies had cleared. Dark clouds blotted out the moon, casting a gray pall over the street like a layer of ash that stubbornly refused to blow away.

I was getting jumpy, starting to question what the hell I was doing there, when he finally arrived. It's a cliché, but the truth is I almost didn't recognize him at first. He'd shaved his moustache, and his hair was close-cropped and hidden beneath a baseball cap. He seemed hunched, shorter, as if his past, or whatever pursued him—for something surely did—had caught up with him and was squatting on his shoulders.

By the time it registered who I was looking at, he was standing over me. I stumbled to my feet, reached out awkwardly to shake his hand, but he was already crouching to sit while simultaneously looking around for a waitress. It occurred to me that he seemed in at least as much of a hurry as the people I'd been observing on the street. And that he was just as much of a stranger to me.

"It's been a long time, Colin," I said carefully. "It's good to see you."

He looked at me for a few seconds, taking stock. "You sure about that? The 'good to see you' part?"

I started to object, but he held up a hand to ward me off. "Tell you what. You listen to what I have to say, then you decide if you're still glad to see me. Sound fair?"

"Fair enough." I nodded. "But you've got to tell me where you've been all these years, what you've been up to—"

"No. There's no time for that. Not now. I'm just here to tell you about Gretchen. What she was up against, and why she killed herself."

He snapped his fingers and an annoyed-looking waitress sidled over, taking his order of a black coffee with an ill-concealed roll of her eyes. I did my best to wait patiently. I sensed that pressuring him the wrong way could send him careening back outside, on a course that might not ever veer my way again.

And maybe I was also moved to silence by Colin's blunt statement about Gretchen. Her suicide had become my dirty little secret, discussed with no one and barely acknowledged even to myself. There were several people who knew how she'd died—choking on her vomit after taking a handful of pills—but for the ones who didn't know the specifics, I certainly didn't volunteer any information. Thinking about how I'd kept her death cloaked in secrecy made me realize the obvious question.

"How did you know she killed herself? How do you know anything about her? You've been gone for nearly ten years..."

"I know plenty about her," he said, turning towards me suddenly. "She wrote, she called, she stayed with me a few times. Even lived with me for a couple months after she got out of the service."

Stunned, I leaned back and stared at my brother. "She talked to you?" I finally managed. "She *lived* with you? She never told me. How could she not tell me something like that? We..." I trailed off, unsure what else to say. "For all the rest of us knew, you could've been dead."

He looked out the window, watching a withered dog sniff for crumbs on the sidewalk. "I think at first she was afraid to tell you. You can be pretty judgmental, you know. She said you got worse after mom and dad died. Anyway—" He waved a hand, dismissing the tangent before I could latch onto it. "—I think that's why she didn't say anything. I know it was the reason that *I* didn't get in touch with you. I didn't need to hear about what a fuck-up you thought I was. And as time went on, it just seemed like it would be more and more difficult to explain why we'd left you out. Difficult, like it feels right now." He paused as the waitress deposited a cup in front of him.

"I still can't believe—" I started.

"Get over it. There are more important things to talk about than how hurt your feelings are."

That hit a little too close to home. *"Fine.* What's so goddamned important to bring you out of hiding?"

"Look, I know they're following you," he said suddenly. "You look like you haven't slept in days. How close have they—"

"How do you know about *them?"* I said, slamming my fist down, sloshing coffee on the table. "Tell me what you know, dammit. Right from the beginning."

"I don't know the beginning," he said. He laid down some napkins to sop up the mess. "Besides, it's the ending that you should be worried about."

I sighed in exasperation.

"Look," he said. "I know how you feel. They've been following me, too. Why do you think I'm here?"

"I've been wondering that."

"I'm here because Winston told me you'd called." He kept on, before I could interject. "Yeah, I know Winston. I met all of them, through Gretchen."

By that point, all I could muster was, "And...?"

"And all I really know is what they told me. And a lot of it is pretty hard to believe."

"Try me. I think I'm past the denial stage."

Colin frowned. "What do you know about the people that've been watching you?"

"Almost nothing. I first saw one of them after Gretchen's funeral. They've been following me ever since. Getting closer. I have to figure they're the ones Gretchen and her pals were always talking about. Although I have a helluva hard time believing that they're government agents, or foreign agents, or whatever Gretchen thought they were."

"They're the ones Gretchen was talking about." He nodded. "But they don't work for anybody. Unless they work for the virus."

"What is that supposed to mean? It doesn't even make any sense."

"The virus...it crosses the blood-brain barrier. Affects your thoughts. But it takes a long time to really...insinuate itself. There's an incubation period."

I looked into my cup, seeking something that would help me understand what Colin was saying, wondering if he knew how he sounded. "Ok, Ok. So, let's just pretend for a second that I believe all this. Why are you bothering to tell me? After all these years where you couldn't be bothered to even speak to me, why go out of your way to tell me all this?"

"Oh fuck." Colin was staring out the window.

I turned my head slowly, not wanting to see what was there.

They were out there, beyond the glass. Not just one, or even two, but three of them, looking in at us with a malevolence that seemed to burn right through their dark glasses.

I heard a crash and looked to see Colin's chair on the floor, and him headed for the rear exit.

"Colin, wait! Don't—"

But he was already gone. The handful of other customers were eyeing me strangely. When I looked outside again, the three watchers were gone.

I went home because I didn't know where else to go. Talking to the police would get me nowhere fast. Running away seemed pointless.

I paced the small confines of my apartment for hours, checking the windows and doors every few minutes until I finally collapsed on the couch and fell into a thorny sleep.

I tossed and turned, drifting in and out of consciousness. I didn't have air conditioning, and the day's mugginess had never dissipated. It settled down on me like a thick blanket.

When I awoke again, sweating, it was still dark. The room felt as black and claustrophobic as a coalmine. In need of water, I pushed myself up on one elbow, blinking away sleep.

Two hands rifled down out of the darkness, pinning me to the couch. A face followed, descending slowly towards me. I squirmed, unable to pull free from the cold, iron grip. The watcher's face stopped mere inches from mine.

Up close, his skin was like parchment, blood crawling through spiderwebbed veins just beneath the surface. Uncovered, his yellowed eyes bulged pregnantly from deep black sockets. His misshapen mouth yawned open, exhaling something unspeakably putrid into my face.

"Now," he said.

Screaming, I thrashed wildly, pulling free, falling to the floor.

Waking up.

There was no one in the room.

I wanted to believe that there'd never been anyone there. But the vile smell from my dream lingered, clinging to me like a caul. And the front door was ajar.

I slept no more that night.

I tried to get in touch with Colin the next morning, but he wasn't at his hotel. He never returned to retrieve his luggage.

Yesterday, my hair began to fall out in tufts. And the light now burns my eyes.

Worst of all, my thoughts sometimes do not seem to be my own.

An incubation period, my brother said.

It Is the Tale

Bev Vincent

Mike and Al point their flashlights straight down at the ground to minimize the chance of being seen. When they reach the cabin, they separate. Al creeps to the front to get in position for the second phase of their plan. Mike remains at the back, where there are no windows.

The cabin is only a few feet from the edge of the forest. Stepping carefully to avoid anything that might betray his presence, Mike sweeps his light back and forth. He's looking for something to brush against the back wall. They expect that the strange sounds will make the girls inside stop their gossiping and giggling to listen. Once they're quiet, Mike will pound on the boards and yell like a madman.

If all goes according to plan, the girls will scream and bolt out the front door, where Al is waiting to roar at them—and then burst out laughing once they realize what happened. Mike hopes he can make it around front in time to see them, dressed in their skimpy nightclothes, yelling at Al for playing such a mean trick on them. He intends to act as if he had nothing to do with the prank and join them in their outrage. Al will probably get bent out of shape once he figures out what Mike's doing, but that's life. He'll be the girls' hero. It's a perfect plan.

His light reveals an aspen branch that's exactly what he's looking for. He steps forward to pick it up but stops when he hears something behind him. A footstep, perhaps. For a second he wonders if Al might be double-crossing him. Nah, Al wouldn't give up a golden opportunity to scare the girls. A raccoon? He shrugs and redirects the flashlight beam at the dead branch.

Something enormous lumbers out of the forest two feet away. It's big enough to block out the moon and the stars. A bear, Mike thinks as the creature looms over him, but deep inside he doesn't believe it. It's massive, like a dinosaur or a mastodon.

He takes a step backward, trips, falls to the ground. His flashlight goes out. He can't see anything, but he still feels the creature's presence. He senses its size and proximity, and hears a dull thud as it steps toward him. He scrambles to his feet, back pedals a few steps, then turns and runs. Something that big probably can't move very fast, he tells himself. Branches whip and scratch at his face. He can no longer hear the creature. Is it still following?

A growl emanates from the darkness, but it sounds like it's in front of him, not behind. Has it passed him, or is there more than one? The ground shakes as something approaches—it's definitely ahead of him. If he keeps going straight, it will intercept him, whatever it is.

In the moonlight, Mike sees a gap in the woods. He's near the opening to the path where they often go on hikes. It runs about three miles into the woods, ending at a bend in the river where they swim. Maybe he can lose whatever it is by taking the narrow path.

He runs as fast as he can in the near darkness. Several minutes later, a stitch burns in his side and he pauses to catch his breath. At first he hears nothing over his panting. Then a sound comes from behind him. It's close—too close. He has to decide in that moment—continue on the path or plunge into the dense trees, where he might find someplace to hide until morning?

Kris concentrates on the storyteller's low, even voice, conjuring the scene in his mind. He's so mesmerized he's barely aware of the other people in the dorm room.

Illuminated only by a flickering candle on the windowsill beside him, Mark pauses. "They found his body the next morning. Fifteen feet up a tree." He picks up the candle and holds it in front of his face as he looks at each of the four members of his audience in turn. "He was dangling like a scarecrow, impaled on a branch by a superhuman force." He retreats a step, straightens up and replaces the candle on the window ledge. "The end."

A gentle breeze wafts through the open window and dances with the flame. It's so quiet in the room Kris can almost hear his heart pounding. Sinister shadows flicker across his friends' faces. No one wants to disturb the mood Mark's creepy story created.

No one except Johnny, that is. He always has questions. "If he was by himself, how does anyone know what he—?"

Taking advantage of the darkness, Kris lifts his hand from his lap, reaches out and grabs Johnny's shoulder.

Johnny leaps from the bed. "Jesus!"

The overhead fluorescent lights sputter to life, revealing Johnny crouched in the middle of the room, poised as if he's ready to bolt. His fists are clenched and he's panting. "Stop doing that. You know how easily I get spooked." He expels a lungful of air and scowls at Kris. "You wouldn't think it was funny if I dropped dead from fright."

Kris pouts and lowers his eyes. "I'm sorry." It's an act, but he knows from experience it will placate Johnny.

While most other students go out partying on Friday nights or huddle in their rooms playing video games, these five gather to tell each other scary stories. This week's session at an end, Ted, Lee and Johnny head back to their rooms. Johnny is first out the door, looking over his shoulder as if expecting someone else to try to scare him. Kris doubts Johnny will be getting to sleep any time soon.

After the others leave, Kris closes Mark's door and rubs his hands together. "Wanna get Johnny good?"

"How?"

"Come up with a story we can reenact after we're done telling it. We'll scare him so much he won't leave his room for a week." Kris laughs. "He's such an easy target."

"Let's do it," Mark says.

Over the next several days, Kris meets in secret with Ted, Lee and Mark to map out their strategy. He gathers the supplies they'll need from the theater department and distributes them to the others. They're so busy scheming they can barely pay attention in class or complete their assignments.

When Friday arrives, Johnny joins the group in the dining hall for supper, part of their weekly routine. Throughout the meal, Kris exchanges knowing glances with Ted, Lee and Mark. His stomach is churning the same way it does just before he goes on stage.

After dropping their trays on the conveyor belt, they dash down the curving marble staircase to Mark's room at the far end of the hall in the basement. Compared to the floors above, their hallway is short because of the laundry room and TV lounge. It has only eight student rooms and a bathroom. Tonight there's a concert at the student union, so the storytellers have the place to themselves.

Kris makes a beeline for the chair at Mark's desk, which leaves the bed for Johnny, Ted and Lee. Once everyone is settled, Mark retires to his easy chair and switches off the light. With the heavy curtains drawn, the room is plunged into darkness.

A sandpapery rasp is followed by the bright flare of a match flaming to life. Kris watches the undulating teardrop of light float away from Mark's position. The match shares some of its life with a wick, then shakes itself out. The new bud of light flickers, almost dies, then takes hold and grows confident, casting shadows around the room as it whispers and winks. For a moment, everyone seems entranced.

Ted breaks the silence with the customary invitation. "Who's got a story to tell?"

"I do," Kris says right away. Johnny doesn't often tell stories, but they don't want to give him the chance to jump in tonight. Kris couldn't bear to wait another week to play their joke. "Mind if I get a beer?" he asks Mark.

"Go ahead."

Kris selects a bottle from the bar fridge under Mark's desk, unscrews the cap and takes a swig, pretending to summon the story from deep within his memory. "There were these five university students who enjoyed terrifying each other. They would sit in a dark room and tell the scariest tales they could imagine." He pauses. "A lot like us, which is why I thought you'd enjoy this story."

Boisterous students walking past Mark's window interrupt him. He waits until the noise dies down before continuing. As an actor, he's used to taking unexpected disruptions in stride. "One night, the stories were so ghastly they were all a little nervous about going back to their lonely, dark rooms. None of them would admit it, though. No one wanted to look like a wuss. A fraidy cat. So, each one checked under his bed and slept with the lights on."

Kris clears his throat. They've all seen lights under Johnny's door on Friday nights after story time. They know he isn't studying or messing around on the Internet.

"One guy—uhm, Jim—was having trouble getting to sleep, so he thought he'd visit Gary, just long enough to shake off the heebie-jeebies. With exams coming up, if he didn't get some sleep he wasn't going to get much studying done the next day. He put on his bathrobe, grabbed his keys and went down the hall, but Gary didn't answer when he knocked. Jim could tell the light was on, and it wasn't all that late—barely midnight—so he tried the knob. It was unlocked."

Candlelight gleams off the dark glass as Kris takes a swig from the beer bottle. He rehearsed the story with his coconspirators earlier in the week to work out where to pause for maximum effect.

"What he saw was horrible enough to drive anyone mad. Gary was pinned to the wall beside his closet. A knife protruded from his throat. A puddle of blood was forming below his feet, which weren't touching the ground. The look of terror on Gary's face would haunt Jim for the rest of his life." Ted had suggested that line, and it was a good one. Kris delivered it in as solemn a tone as possible.

The room is too dark to see how Johnny is reacting. Kris takes another drink before continuing. "Jim screamed at the top of his lungs. He ran out of Gary's room and down to the end of the hall, yelling his friends' names, but no one answered. The entire floor was quiet. Too quiet. Jim could barely breathe. He pounded on Jerry's door—it swung open. Jerry was lying face down on the floor. His arms were outstretched, like he was swimming in the blood surrounding him. Jim didn't stop long enough to find out how he died."

Kris's voice gets progressively softer. He wants Johnny's undivided attention. "Jim headed to Eddie's room next. Eddie was dangling from a hook screwed into the ceiling. His face was purple and his eyes were bulging out of their sockets. Jim had only one hope left—Martin. His stomach was in knots, and his nerves were shot. He pushed Martin's door open slowly. At first, he didn't see anything. He stepped into the room, checking behind him all the while. Then he saw a sneaker sticking out from the cubbyhole. There was a foot in it. Martin's lifeless body had been crammed under his desk. His neck was bent at an impossible angle.

"Utter panic set in. Jim fled into the hall. There was no one else around. His cell phone was in his room, so he ran back there with his keys in his hands, intending to dial 911. When he reached the door, it was open. He couldn't be sure, but he thought he'd locked it. Otherwise, why would he have brought his keys?"

Kris accelerates his delivery and adds a sense of urgency to his tone. "He reached around the corner and turned on the light. A few seconds later, he mustered the courage to go in. He was paranoid that someone would sneak up behind him, so he closed and locked his door and slid a chair under the knob." Though the others can't see him well, Kris, caught up in his story, crouches and pretends to look under something. "His hand trembled as he poked under the bed with his drafting ruler. Nothing. Still, he couldn't shake the feeling someone was in the room with him.

"He looked in his jacket pockets and on his desk, but he couldn't find his cell phone anywhere. By now he was a nervous wreck and nothing could make him go out in the hall again. He thought about yelling out the window for help, but he imagined the killer in the quad, lying in wait for him. His door was locked and his window was closed, his curtains drawn. He would be safe in there until morning. Or so he thought."

Kris takes a long drink. After he finishes the bottle, he wipes his mouth.

Right on cue, Johnny asks, "Well? Don't stop now! What happened?"

"They found him the next morning, curled up on his bed. Stabbed thirty times. His door and his window were both locked and the chair was still propped under the knob. The cops assumed the murderer was hiding in his closet, but they couldn't figure out how he got out of the room. They never found out who did it, or why." Kris shrugs. "I guess the rest of Jim's life wasn't that long after all. The end."

Mark turns on his desk lamp. "Great story, Kris."

"Gave me the creeps," Ted adds. "It was like something that really could have happened."

"Is it true?" There's a flutter in Johnny's voice, and he looks paler than usual, though Kris thought that might be a trick of the light. "S-sounds like an urban legend."

"That's the way I heard it," Kris replies. "Well, I'm all in. Good night, guys."

"Thanks for the story," Lee says.

Kris can't resist a parting shot. "Make sure you check under your bed tonight, Johnny. You never know what might have crawled under there while we were in here." He laughs at Johnny's dark glance and high fives Mark.

When he gets to his room, Kris closes his door but leaves it unlocked. He pulls a plastic bag from under his bed and dumps out the contents. He slashes his shirt with a butcher knife, coats the blade with stage blood and douses his shirt.

A scream rends the air. Then another. Kris checks his watch. Lee is a few minutes ahead of schedule, but the yells sound great, like someone's committing bloody murder. He considers calling the others to make sure they're ready, but ringing phones might spoil the effect. He positions himself on the floor, places the knife where it will be seen by anyone entering the room, and pours more fake blood to create a pool around him. He pushes the plastic bag and empty vials under the bed.

He can't wait to see Johnny's face.

Though the tile floor is uncomfortable, the beer and a cumulative lack of sleep make Kris drowsy. Some time later, he jolts awake and checks his watch. He's been out for over fifteen minutes. He listens for activity in the hallway, but hears nothing. Too much time has passed. Johnny must have stayed in his room, despite Lee's screams. Kris decides to ad lib to try to save their plan. Leaving the knife next to the pool of fake blood, he assumes the role of a mortally wounded man. "Help me. Somebody please help me," he moans as he staggers up the hall.

Through an open door he sees Lee leaning out his window. Stage blood drips down the wall beneath him. Kris doesn't disturb him.

There's a smear of red on Ted's doorknob. Nice touch, Kris thinks. The door is locked, though. Ted must have forgotten to turn the bolt. Dragging one foot behind him to maintain the illusion in case Johnny appears, Kris continues down the hall to Mark's room. The door is ajar, but the room is dark. When he pushes the door open, it strikes something that rolls across the floor and ricochets off Mark's chair. Kris flicks the light switch and peers into the room.

The floor is streaked with blood. Kris focuses on the object he hit. Once he realizes what it is, his legs turn to rubber. He turns away, drops to his knees and vomits in the corridor.

Mark's head is sitting on the floor next to his desk. The rest of his body is nowhere to be seen. The blood on the floor is real.

His mind swimming with confusion and panic, Kris regains his feet and lurches up the hall to Johnny's room. It's empty. The bed is undisturbed, but a drafting ruler lies on the floor next to it. Kris stands panting in the middle of the room, unsure what to do next. He should call someone. Where's Johnny's cell phone?

Behind him, someone bursts out laughing. "Ha! Got you!"

Kris's shoulders slump and he releases the air that is pent up in his lungs. Double-crossed. Those bastards! He takes another deep breath and turns to face his friends, ready to accept their laughter. He's not sure whether to be angry or amused.

Johnny is standing in the doorway. A dark smudge stretches from his left ear to his chin. The bloodstained knife he is holding looks exactly like the one Kris left on his floor.

"Very funny," he says. "You got me good. How'd you do Mark's—?"

"I told you to stop screwing with me." Johnny raises the knife and rushes him.

Kris freezes until the blade descends. Too late, he puts up his hands to ward off the blow. The first stab nicks his jugular. The next slips between his ribs and penetrates his chest. Kris collapses to the floor. Blood pools around him. He can feel his life oozing away. Pain lights up every nerve in his body.

Through a growing pall, he watches Johnny wipe his bloody hands on his pants legs. He feels his energy fading from his body with every beat of his heart. He has no strength to resist when Johnny slides him over to the wall and props him up.

From the closet, Johnny retrieves Mark's headless corpse and places it next to Kris. Two trips out of the room and the entire group is reassembled, including Mark's head, which Johnny perches on the window ledge behind them. He flicks off the overhead light but leaves the door open far enough for a dim glow from the hallway to illuminate the room. He pulls his chair away from his desk and sits facing his mutilated companions. He's grinning.

As his lifeblood drains away, Kris hears the familiar words one last time.

"So. Who's got a story to tell?"

A Special Place: The Heart of a Dark Matter

Peter Straub

Milwaukee, 1958

"You're going to need a special place only you know about," Uncle Till told Keith Hayward. They were seated on a broad tree stump in the back yard of the Hayward family home, where Uncle Till was a temporary guest. Keith was twelve years old. This conversation took place in mid-July, high summer, 1958, when Milwaukee was hot and humid from morning to midnight. Tillman Hayward's thin, sleeveless T-shirt clung to the sides of his chest and exposed his muscular arms and shoulders. The tilted brim of his gray fedora shaded most of his handsome, long-nosed face, though sweat shone on his cheeks and pooled in the dark hollows at the base of his throat. Tucked in at the knee, his blue pin-striped trousers floated their cuffs nearly a foot above his shiny black wingtips. The coolest suspenders Keith had ever seen, of braided leather no thicker than a pencil, held up the unpleated waistband of the trousers. This man, Tillman Hayward, knew how to dress.

"And let's say you get a place like that, because I'm just saying like, what if? *If* you get a special place all your own, you should be able to lock it up, so no one else can get in. What goes on in that room is private. Nobody should know about it but you. See, if let's say you happen to go down this path, you're gonna have all kinds of secrets."

"Like this is secret, what we're talking about," Keith said.

"Bull's eye! Home run! You got it! Let's go through it again. Your daddy or your pretty momma ask what we were talking about after I warned you about those experiments, the answer is...?"

"Baseball." Keith had been thoroughly prepped on this point.

"Baseball," Till agreed. "That's right. Warren Spahn, greatest pitcher in the National League. Del Crandall, greatest catcher in the National League. Eddie Matthews, greatest *guy* in the National League, right?"

"Right."

"Now *you* tell me their names, boy."

"Warren Spahn, Spahnie. Del Crandall, the catcher. Eddie Mathews, third base. They're the greatest."

In truth, Keith cared nothing for baseball. He didn't see the point of all that throwing and hitting and running when nothing was at stake but the outcome of a stupid game. Everyone around him, including the other kids at school, his parents, and even the teachers and the principal, pretty much everybody in the world except Uncle Till, acted like Jesus himself would stand up if one of the Milwaukee Braves walked into the room.

"Attaway. So anyhow, let's say we got this special place, this secret room. You know what you need to keep it secret? I already gave you a big hint."

"A key to lock it up." Hoping he had understood his uncle's point about *what if,* Keith took a big step into the dark. "That's if, you know, I happened to have a place like that."

"Oh, you're something," said Uncle Till. "Yes, you are."

Keith's face blazed with pleasure; satisfaction glowed in his stomach with the warmth of a good meal.

"Again, just supposing here, just saying *what if,* if you should happen to get the key you need, I could give you a great idea about that. This key we're talking about shouldn't have to sit out in the world all naked and exposed, where anyone might come along and ask questions about it. I mean, what kind of secret would that be?"

"No good, that's what it would be," said Keith, feeling a kind of anticipatory shame wavering flame-like inside of him.

"Damn straight, boy. Now, nothing hides a little key better than a bunch of other keys. We're still playing the *what if* game here, so I'd say if a fellow was interested in the kind of stuff we're talking about, for one reason or another, one smart thing he could do would be to pick up every stray key he happens to find and string them on a good key-ring. You come across old keys lyin' around all over the place, once you start looking for them. In drawers. On desks. In any old place, and by the way, some old building nobody goes into any more, oh, an abandoned house, an empty old warehouse, anything like that, would be a good place to find your secret room. And the basement generally works out real good. God bless basements, is my motto."

The boy had a sudden thought, a vision more than a thought, of an abandoned building located six or seven blocks distant on their nearby commercial avenue. Once it had housed a diner, later on a bar, and after that it had been the place of worship for some religious cult so marginal that the neighbors had actually driven them off in a spasm of high-mindedness. "Like that old dump on Sherman Boulevard?"

"Is there an old dump on Sherman Boulevard?" Uncle Till's eyes shone. "Imagine that."

"I *thi-i-i-nk* so," Keith said, really getting into the game.

"Might be worth a closer look, I don't know. To a fellow interested in that kind of thing, anyhow."

Keith nodded, trying to picture the building in more detail. For a while, the neighborhood teenagers had prowled through its empty rooms, leaving behind dirty mattresses, cigarette butts, beer bottles, and limp condoms, but he had the feeling that it had been left alone for a long time now. The building had a basement, of that he was almost certain.

"I could give you a little tip," his uncle said, capturing his attention once again. "Let's say a person puts together a nice big key ring, fifty keys, a hundred, how does he manage to put his hand on the one or two he actually needs? Well, this is how. You take a little bit of string and tie it in a knot right next to the important keys, and then you can find them in a jif."

From what must have been the extraordinarily deep pocket of the elegant trousers he produced a giant ball of keys and rattled it before his nephew's eyes. Here and there, tiny bits of colored string protruded from it.

"When a man carries a ball of keys like this, nobody ever asks him what he's doing. As good as a badge."

The screen door banged. With a slow, uncertain step, Keith's mother emerged onto the back steps. Her anxious gaze took them both in. At the ends of her rigid arms, her hands hung like tight knots.

"Have a good talk?" The contrast between her question and her demeanor struck Keith as humorous. He nodded, trying not to smile.

"Till?"

"It's fine, Mags," said Uncle Till. "There's nothing to worry about. We have here a fine, fine boy. That poor cat was dead when he found it. No reason to bother Bill about all this. The boy and I have had a good talk. Haven't we, kiddo?"

Nodding, Keith said, "We sure have."

In Maggie Hayward's regard could be read the degree to which she wanted to believe everything her brother-in-law had told her, as well as all that he had implied. "But what about the knife? What about the cat's head?"

"Guilty as charged. I think we can put that down to Keith's sense of curiosity."

"I wanted to see how it was connected," Keith said. "You know, the bones and stuff."

"Scientific impulse, pure and simple," said Uncle Till. "I explained that Keith really has to wait for high school biology before he starts to dissect things. Including any dead animals he might come across in that old vacant lot."

At the beginning of the most rewarding conversation of Keith's entire life, Uncle Till had in fact said something very like this.

"I know better now, Mom," Keith said.

Keith's mother began to move down the three concrete steps to ground level. Her elbows struck a slight angle, and her hands were unclenched. When she hit the bottom step, anguish and disgust momentarily contorted her face. "Well, I hope so, because I just hated seeing...It made me feel so *awful...*"

"Of course it did, honey." Uncle Till stood up and slipped the ball of keys back into his capacious pocket. "I'd feel the same way myself."

"Sorry, Mom," Keith said. "I'll never do it again."

"I hope *not.*" She gave them both a tentative smile. "I'm glad you were here to talk to Keith, Till. And you're right, I don't want to bother Bill with all this stuff. It's over and done with, right?"

"Right," Keith said.

"It looked like you were showing him your keys," she said.

"That I was, Mags, that I was. Here's my thinking. My nephew needs a hobby, that's pretty clear. So I was recommending he go around collecting keys, the way I do. You can get a lot of pleasure out of an old key, imagining all the people that used it and what kind of door it opened."

"Do you like that idea?" his mother asked. She seemed skeptical, with some reason.

"Yeah," he said. "I really do."

"It'd be good for you to have a hobby. Maybe I can keep my eye out for old keys, help you start your collection."

"That would be great, Mom."

Keith glanced up at his uncle. The shadow of his hat brim made a jutting slab of his nose, as though his were one of the faces on Mount Rushmore.

"This boy is going to do just fine," Till said. "Yep, he's on his way. Now let's put the cherry on top. I wouldn't be surprised if one day, Keith turned out to be a doctor. That's right. An honest-to-God, actual M.D. Rise and shine, pretty lady. Your boy has all the tools he'll ever need. He just has to figure out how to put his hands on 'em."

Beneath everything his uncle said, Keith thought, ran another line of thought altogether, intended only for him.

Although he lived in Columbus, Ohio, Tillman Hayward had been staying in his brother Bill's house for a couple of weeks. This information was a secret to all but the family. He slept on the old family bed in the spare room, and now and again he joined the others for meals. Till sometimes stuck around in the evenings to make cutting remarks about *Gunsmoke,* or *The Rifleman,* or whatever they had gathered to watch on the TV, but usually he snuck out in his snappy clothes around nine or ten at night and did not return until just before dawn. Uncle Till did not have an ordinary job. He did "deals" and made "arrangements," he "put things together." Bill Hayward, Keith's father, was putting in his twelfth year on the spray line at Continental Can, and he envied his brother's freedom. Ever since his foreman's application had been denied, Bill came home grudging and morose, grumbling about his job and reeking of solvent. To his younger brother, Tillman's good luck and handsome face had allowed him to escape the prison of blue-collar life. The man was a kind of magician, and whatever he did to remain afloat could not be judged by the usual systems.

Above them both hovered the example of their oldest and best-looking sibling, Margaret Frances, who had changed her name to Margot, talked her way into a good job at a radio station in Minneapolis, and married a pole axed millionaire named Rudy. Margaret Frances/Margot had never been much for family anyhow, and after the birth of her first child, Mortimer, she stopped even sending out Christmas cards. Margaret Frances/Margot had struck it rich, and who could say that Tillman, almost as attractive, would not do the same?

Uncle Till enjoyed a series called *Peter Gunn*. He thought he looked a lot like Craig Stevens, the dark-haired actor playing a private detective who wore expensive suits and hung out in a jazz club. Keith could see the resemblance, though he thought his uncle often operated on the other side of the law from Peter Gunn. Presumably this trait lay behind the secrecy about his uncle's presence in their house. His parents maintained a steadfast vagueness on the issue. Bill Hayward explained the necessity to inform women that Tilly was elsewhere by referring to the sheer number of dames who wanted to get their mitts on him. Hell, the guy *had* to hide out! This obligation to deny Tillman's presence in their house extended to men as well. Instead of calling, the men tended to come over and ring the bell. You couldn't just wait for them to go away, because these guys had no manners. They pushed the buzzer and pounded the door, sometimes yelling, until someone came out to talk to them. They called themselves friends, but they were bill collectors; they said they wanted to pay back a loan, but they were really pissed-off husbands. Or they were cops looking to close old cases by pinning them on Tillman Hayward, whom they secretly envied.

"They should, too," Keith's father said. "Till's got radar they only dream about. My brother, he knows things. He can tell when a cop is keeping an eye on the house, so he just holes up in his room until they go away. Fact is, he'd of been a better cop than any of those clowns on the city payroll. Only, he never wanted to be just a hardass with a gun."

A couple of days each week, Uncle Till squirreled himself away in the old spare room at the back of the house, curled up in blankets and read the paper, listening to the radio, drinking bourbon, sometimes propping his back against the headboard and wrapping his arms around his knees while he stared at the colorless walls. The man always wore his hat, even in bed. Keith thought that was amazingly cool.

"Keith, get out of there and leave your uncle alone," his mother yelled. "Till doesn't want a little boy hanging onto him every second of the day."

"I don't mind the kid," Uncle Till yelled back. "Fact is, he's good company."

There were days Till's radar told him he could not even walk out through the kitchen door into the back garden. They were watching the house that closely—some days, he had to be careful not to walk past the windows.

"I didn't do any of the stuff they want to pin on me," he said. "I'm not saying I never crossed the line, because that's what the line is for. But the Chief of Police here, Brier, is a showboat. He thinks cops ought to be able to shoot *jaywalkers*. Brier would love to put my ass in jail."

He looked down at his nephew, and his face darkened. "You know what's going to happen? One day some cop is going to jump out of an alley right in front of you. This cop is going to ask you, do you know where we can find your Uncle Till? Is he staying at your house, Keith? We just want to talk to him, can't you give us a hand? And you say..."

"I don't know where he is. But I wish he'd come back, because we used to talk about baseball."

"What a kid this is," he said, and leaned forward to rumple Keith's hair. "You and me, right? You and me."

"You and me," Keith repeated, glowing within.

Another time, Keith peeked around his Uncle's door, found him sitting up in bed with his hat on his head, staring at nothing, looking inside himself, the boy thought. Till came out of his trance, invited him in, and wound up telling him about his favorite movies.

"There's this man, one day you're gonna love him as much as I do. Alfred Hitchcock, the master of suspense, they call him. Could be the greatest movie director of all time. Ever hear of the guy?"

"Maybe," Keith said, hoping that his uncle would just go on and on, and not stop to ask him questions. The long muscles under his skin, the angles of his face, the beauty of the hat brim, the poise of his hands, and the curl of smoke rising from the cigarette tilted between his fingers: all of this, and more, he wanted to take in and memorize.

"For my money, his greatest movie is that new one, *Vertigo.* Came out this year. *Crazy,* crazy movie, kiddo. These blondes, they're all the same woman but you don't know that, they're always falling out of windows and off cliffs, and you *know* the bitches won't survive, hell, pardon my French, you know these *women* are either gonna hit the ground or slam against the water and go under, so if they don't drown they're gonna get squashed like a bug. Tightened my throat, Keith. And this guy, Jimmy Stewart, only the *bad* Jimmy Stewart, like his crazy twin, he follows the blonde into this art museum and he stares at her staring at a painting, and he keeps on staring and she keeps on staring, it's so *weird,* there's no one else in this big old room but them, and finally you have to stare at the painting, too. It's really terrible, it's like a damn cartoon! Hell, you say to yourself, this painting's a fake! You'd never find crap like that in a fancy museum. So then you realize half the backgrounds in the movie are complete fakes, too, and the girl is also a complete fake, and the hero is out of his mind, and besides, he's cruel as shit, you should see the way he treats that girl..."

Uncle Till smiled. For a moment, he looked like a cat with a moth trapped beneath its paws.

"Could be the greatest movie of all time. Damn near made me see double. Soon as I got out, I had to go to a bar. *But.* And this is a big, big but. Hitchcock's *second*-greatest movie could have been even better. Slides along like shit on silk. *Shadow of a Doubt.* Came out in I think 1943. You ever see that movie?"

"I don't think so."

"Nah, you weren't even born then, were you? You have to see *Shadow of a Doubt,* though. The great Joseph Cotton, man, if it weren't for Lawrence Tierney and Richard Widmark, he'd be my favorite actor. Only problem with that movie is, Hitchcock loused up the ending. The creeps that own the studios, man, they must have seen what was going on in this movie and sent him a message, pronto. There was a knock on the door, and when he opened it, a big ol' knee-breaker hands him a piece of paper that says, *Change the ending of your movie, or we're gonna burn down your house and kill your wife.* They had to step in and screw things up."

"Why?"

"They want things to look a certain way, see? Right is right, and wrong is wrong, and that's the whole deal. If what they call 'right' doesn't win every time, the suckers in the balcony are gonna get pissed off.

"So what happens in *Shadow of a Doubt?* Joseph Cotton, Uncle Charlie, arrives in the California town where his sister is married to this dodo. They have a good-looking teenage daughter. The sister and the niece love Joseph Cotton, he's the apple of their eye. The whole first half of the movie is like that. Only, us guys sitting out there stuffing our faces with popcorn gradually get the idea that good old Joseph Cotton has a whopper of a dark side, and it has to do with women.

"I mean, that's okay, isn't it? It *ought* to be, for anybody who lives in the real world. If they made a movie about you and me, would you want me to get killed at the end?"

Keith shook his head.

"That's why I know the creeps at the studio made Alfred Hitchcock kill off Uncle Charlie at the end of the movie instead of doing it right. Because the *real* ending would have had Uncle Charlie and the girl going away together as what you could call partners in crime."

"Crime," Keith said, growing even more interested. A ball made of burning nettles was squeezing upward within his throat, and he swallowed to keep it down. "What kind of crime?"

Uncle Till motioned him forward. His face darkened and glittered as the boy approached. When Keith had come close enough, he extended his elegant left arm, gripped his nephew's shoulder with his powerful fingers, and pulled him down until the boy's ear was close to his mouth. He smelled of musky aftershave, tobacco, and dried sweat.

"In the real world?"

He chuckled, and Keith's giblets thrilled.

"Here's what they'd do. They'd get women to give them their money, and then they'd kill them. I don't know how they'd do it, but for sure, if it was *me,* I'd use a knife."

His uncle relaxed his grip. Face burning, Keith straightened up. If he'd had a year to think about it, he still could not have described the tumult going on within him. Uncle Till, utterly relaxed, smiled back from the deep, hidden center of his being. A godlike amusement seemed to irradiate his features as he raised his chin and leveled his eyes at a point only he could see. "Know what the newspapers in *Shadow of a Doubt* were calling good old Uncle Charlie? The Honeymoon Killer. It's funny, how they can libel you with a handle like that."

"Yeah," Keith said, uncertain of the point.

"It's exactly like some reporter in *The Milwaukee Journal* wrote this story where he called you the Pussycat Killer. The Tabby Killer. That wouldn't seem right, would it?"

The flush on the boy's face turned a deeper red. "No."

"There's so much more *to* it. You know what I'm talking about."

Maggie Hayward's voice floated in from the kitchen, telling Keith to give his uncle some peace. This time, Till waved him away.

He walked down the hallway toward the kitchen. A tangle of thoughts and emotions rolled from his chest to his head and back again. He felt as though Uncle Till had sunk a branding iron into his brain. *You know what I'm talking about.*

Did he?

If it was me, *I'd use a knife.*

Was his uncle talking about actually using a knife? How using a knife made you feel? He could never have described how he had felt when, after a titanic battle, he had at last cornered the spitting, hissing cat in the vacant lot at the end of their block and rammed the carving knife into its belly.

He entered the kitchen hoping to pass unnoticed. His mother turned from her cooking and gave his face the customary inspection. From the big metal pot simmering on the stove came a thick odor of carrots, onions, and softening beef. Whatever Maggie Hayward saw in his face made her lower her eyebrows and peer at him more closely. For an uncomfortable moment, her eyes sought and found his own. The moment of live contact underscored the new recognition that Keith and his mother lately had become almost exactly the same height, a fact that both unsettled and excited him.

A ladle slick with pale brown fluid drooped from her right hand.

"Keith, your face is bright red," she told him. "Do you have a fever?"

"I don't think so."

She came closer and pressed her free hand to his forehead. Keith watched stuff like gravy begin to drip onto the patterned blue linoleum.

"Mom," he said. "Your spoon, um."

"Oh, drat," she said, and in a single movement spun sideways to drop the ladle beside the sink, grab a paper towel, bend down, and wipe away the tiny stain. The paper towel flew into the garbage pail.

"What do you and Till talk about in there, anyhow?"

"Baseball," he said. "And movies."

"You talk about movies? What movies?"

"He likes Alfred Hitchcock. But mainly, we talk about baseball. The Braves. Eddie Mathews."

"That's what you talk about? Eddie Mathews?"

"And Spahnie," he said. "But yeah, he says Eddie Mathews is the greatest guy in the National League."

"I like hearing you talk about our team," she said.

"Yeah, it's great to have a good team." With that, he escaped upstairs to his room.

* * *

The next day Uncle Till's prediction came true exactly as described. A heavy man in a dark gray suit emerged from nowhere as Keith was mooning along as though going nowhere in particular, a posture intended to disguise his progress toward the vacant lot. This weed-choked desolation where overgrown bricks lay scattered around a fire-blackened tree stump, where creeper vines matted the chain-link fence at its far end, and where an agile boy could squeeze into a half a dozen little hideaways, lately had colonized his imagination: when he was not celebrating the miracle of Uncle Till, he daydreamed about sliding on his belly through the Queen Ann's Lace outside his little portals, scanning the undergrowth for prey.

Keith was so intent on getting to the destination he was pretending not to have that when the cop stepped in front of him, he acted as though the unknown man was an impediment like a garbage can and tried to dodge around him.

A huge hand clamped his shoulder. A deep voice said, "Hold on a second there, son."

Startled, the boy looked up into a wide, heavily seamed face with an almost lipless mouth and eyes like blue marbles set deep in dark, cobwebby sockets. "Uh," he said, and tried to scramble out of the man's grip.

The big hand tightened on his shoulder and pulled him back into place.

"You're Keith Hayward, aren't you?"

"Yeah?"

"I'm not keeping you from anything, am I? No important appointments, no girlfriend waiting to be taken out on a date?"

Keith shook his head.

"We're gonna get along real good. Because I'm pretty sure that's true, I'm gonna take my hand off your shoulder, Keith, and you're going to stay right there and talk to me, aren't you?"

"Okay," Keith said, and the hand released him.

The man's rusty-looking smile contradicted all the rest of his face.

"My name is Detective Cooper. Cops like me, we're the good guys, Keith. We keep people like yourself and your family safe from the scum of society that might hurt them if we weren't around. Do you have any idea what I want to talk about with you?"

A vivid image flooded his mind. He thought, *I kicked that cat into the fence and then I grabbed it by the neck and shoved the carving knife into its belly.*

"I don't think so."

"It's important you tell me the truth, Keith. Policemen always know when a person is lying. Especially detectives. Maybe I wasn't clear enough. So let me ask you this, Keith. Is anybody staying in your house? Someone not in your immediate family?"

Keith said nothing.

"I mean, someone not your mother or your father? Maybe related to you, though?"

"No," Keith said.

"I don't think you're telling me the truth, Keith. You *know* you're lying to me. Let me tell you something. This is for your own good, and I want you to think about it. Lying to a policeman is a serious crime. If you do it, you can get in big trouble. *Big* trouble. So let's give it another try, all right? You do the right thing, I'll forget all about how you lied to me. Okay?"

"Okay." Detective Cooper fascinated Keith. He was carrying on as though kindness and patience were characteristic of him, but it was all an act, a performance, and not a very convincing one.

"The whole reason I'm here is that I want to talk to your Uncle Tillman. People call him Till, which wouldn't make me too happy, but I guess it's fine with him. Till lives in Columbus, Ohio, but nobody's seen him around there for about a week and a half. I bet Till's camping out in your house. He's there right now, isn't he? If you tell me the truth this time, Keith, I'll make sure you won't have any trouble with the law."

"I didn't do anything!" Keith burst out. "Nobody said I was in trouble until now!"

Cooper's transparent duality, the thin folksy surface over the merciless granite of his actual self, frightened Keith more than what he was saying. The detective's inner self seemed to be swelling up, growing larger and larger, threatening to engulf the outer man. In seconds, his head would be two feet wide, and he would cover the entire sidewalk, still uttering these meaningless reassurances.

A hand closed around his arm and dragged him into the shade of a dying elm. Once they got out of the light, Cooper let go of his bicep and began patting his back. "Everything's going to be fine, kid. Nobody's saying you're in trouble. You can stop worrying."

Slowly, the moment of surreal panic faded, leaving Cooper an ordinary man, not a hideous inflating flesh-balloon. Keith's duties and ambitions came back to him.

"Are you all right, Keith? Take a minute. Settle down."

"I'm all right," the boy said. "I always was all right. Why are you talking to me that way?"

"You looked like you were going to cry on me, Keith. I'm on your side, son, you have to understand that. And I think I know why you wanted to cry."

"I didn't want to cry." *You're not like this, you're a fake,* he thought. Then, *Maybe I do want to cry.*

"Well, I think you did. And do you know what I think is the reason?"

You already told me why, Keith thought, and Detective Cooper filled the silence that followed with precisely the words the boy expected to hear.

"You don't like lying to me, I know that about you, Keith. You want to tell me the truth, but you're afraid I'll hurt your uncle. But I just want to talk to him. That's all, son. And if I talk to him, maybe I can even help him."

Even in the midst of his fear, all that one would expect in a twelve-year-old boy abruptly confronted with a massive policeman, the absurdity that a man whose face suggested nothing so much as a dull knife thought he could help Tillman Hayward made him want to laugh.

"Let's do it one more time, Keith. Way down inside you, you want to tell me the truth. Uncle Till's hiding out in your house, isn't he?"

"No," Keith said. "He isn't staying with us. I wish he was, though, because then we could talk about baseball. Uncle Till loves Eddie Mathews, and so do I."

"Eddie Mathews," Cooper said.

"If you're so sure he's there, why don't you come into my house and look around for him? Check the closets, go down into the basement, look in back of the furnace?"

"Keith, I wish I could, I really do. But the law won't let me. Your uncle doesn't want anyone to see him, does he?"

"My uncle likes all the Braves," Keith said. "We used to talk about Warren Spahn, because he thinks Warren Spahn is really neat."

Detective Cooper thrust his face down into Keith's. The rusty smile was gone, and his eyes had turned the color of dry ice. A sharp, flame-like wave of terror seared the boy's lungs and throat.

"Thank you for your cooperation, Keith. And on a personal note. Just let me say this. I think you have the right to know that you are undoubtedly the ugliest kid it has ever been my privilege to meet. That *is* the truth, Keith. You are one ugly-lookin' boy. Puke on the sidewalk is handsomer than you. If they gave out trophies for terrible faces, you'd win every time. No girl is ever going to go out with you, Keith, you're never gonna get married, you're never even gonna pick a girl up, because every time you try, she'll run away screaming."

Detective Cooper straightened up, spun out of the shade, and disappeared into the downpouring sunlight that bounced off the hoods of cars, windshields, and glittery flecks of mica in the sidewalk.

Keith was not sure he could still walk. He felt as though the massive, grey-faced old policeman had cut off his legs at the knees. The streaks on his face had turned cool before he realized he was crying. Only after he had dragged his sleeve across his face did he think he could continue on his way down the block. When he came to the vacant lot, he kept on walking until he came to Sherman Boulevard, where he aimed himself like a guided missile at the abandoned building Uncle Till had summoned into his mind.

1962-1963

Miller had a first name, Tomek, but no one ever used it. Most people did not even know what it was. Even in grade school, where he had been a friendless victim, he had been just "Miller," as in, "Miller, get down and lick my spit off the playground," or "Miller, what makes you think I'm going to let you live through this here day?" Against all the odds, his life improved in high school, at least temporarily, because in December of his freshman year, he acquired a friend. Unfortunately, that friend was Keith Hayward.

Until the day when he rescued his comrade-to-be from a typical degradation, Keith himself had been basically friendless himself, though not so spectacularly as Miller. The unattractiveness remarked upon by Detective Cooper had if anything deepened during the four years since their encounter, and at the time in question was enhanced by a virulent breakout of acne that sprouted pustules, many of them visibly oozing, from every pore available upon his narrow forehead and flat cheeks. Unless they possess a blazing wit, great social skills, or an unusual degree of self-awareness, the truly ugly tend to have a difficult time in high school. Keith of course possessed none of these, yet he had never been a victim. He owned the secret weapon of his real self, which he hoarded and sheltered and allowed out of its private enclosure only for the purposes of pleasure and self-protection. Pleasure could be sought in the private room he had created beneath the abandoned diner on Sherman Avenue; self-protection occurred at those moments when some bully decided to turn him into a victim like Miller. At those moments, Keith did neither of the two things that born victims fall back upon. He did not look down and fall into silence, and he did not shrink away, hoping for mercy. Instead, he marched squarely up before his would-be tormentor, stared into his eyes, and said something like, "If I were you, I'd back away right now." The actual words were not important. What affected the bullies, who one and all actually did back away from him, was the expression they saw in his eyes. They could not have defined or described it, but it let them know that the smaller and seemingly pitiable boy before them knew more than they about the administration of pain. He enjoyed it more than they, and in a different way. In that area, he had no limitations, none.

By the beginning of his sophomore year, what lay behind Hayward's resolution had earned him a growing reputation for potential danger among his fellow students, although the faculty and staff at Lawrence B. Freeman High School never became aware that slinking down their hallways and unobtrusively carving on their desks was a true wild card. Most of Keith's teachers felt pity for him; the administration knew only that Hayward had maintained both a 2.75 grade point average and an absolute indifference to clubs.

And Hayward, who had barely noticed Miller's existence, did not so much as know his name on the day in early December when he walked into the boy's restroom and saw what the principal called "an unhappy situation" in the arena between the urinals and the sinks. Five or six seniors were clustered around a younger boy kneeling on the floor tiles. One of the juniors had been speaking to the boy, but at the moment he became aware of Hayward he shut his mouth and turned his head to glare at the intruder.

The boy next to him, Larry Babb, whom Keith knew slightly, said, "Get out, Hayward."

"No," Keith said, and in a moment of astonished silence walked past the boys to get to the stalls.

"What did you say?" disbelieving Babb finally asked.

"I don't give a shit what you guys do. Just go ahead and do it."

"Aw, fuck you," Babb said, watching him home in on the second stall.

Instead of going in and locking the door behind him, Hayward turned around, leaned against the jamb, and crossed his arms over his chest, evidently settling in to enjoy the spectacle. "What are you going to do, kick him around?"

The boy who had fallen silent when Hayward came in revolved his head to regard Babb. "You *know* this pimply asshole?"

"His name is Hayward," Babb said, as if that were enough.

"Hayward? Who's *Hayward?"*

"He's a year behind us."

"I know, you were gonna piss on him," Hayward said.

"Get rid of him, Babb," said the evident leader, whose name later turned out to be Tolbert "Rocky" Glinka.

Larry Babb cast him a “why me?” glance. When this had no effect, he swiveled toward Hayward and let his face drop into an expression of weary authority. “You heard Rocky,” he said. “Get out of here while you can still do it yourself.”

“You were. You were actually going to piss on this kid.” Hayward grinned at Babb, then, over his shoulder, at Rocky Glinka. “Real bunch of hot rods here, hey?”

“Whatever that’s supposed to mean,” said Glinka. “Larry?”

Babb moved toward Hayward, trying to look so menacing that the smaller, pimple-infested boy would take off before he had to touch him.

Smiling, Hayward stepped up directly in front of him. He put his hands in his pockets. Babb noticed that he smelled a little off, like something left too long in the refrigerator.

“You were going to take your dick out in front of this kid and show it to your buddies?”

“Go away,” Babb said.

“I’m gonna stick around and watch. I don’t think *you’re* gonna stop me, are you?” He was staring straight into Babb’s increasingly uncertain eyes.

The other boy glanced away and stepped back. “I don’t care what you say, you fucking freak.”

“What?” yelled Glinka.

“You can do what you want, but I’m getting out of here,” said Babb. “The bell’s going to ring in about five seconds.”

“So what?”

“Go on, give ’em the big show,” Hayward said.

The boy huddled on the floor began to weep.

“Miller, you got lucky, but it ain’t gonna last for either one of you.” Glinka parade-marched out of the bathroom, and his entourage followed.

Over the hubbub in the hallway, Glinka could be heard saying, “Will you assholes stop *chuckling?*”

The sound of boys' voices drifted down the hallway and was replaced by the usual between-bells din of pounding feet, shrieking laughter, and locker doors slamming shut.

The boy kneeling on the bathroom floor was not at all part of the usual picture. His head touched the floor, and he was weeping. The position of his head made his tears run sideways across his temples and slide into his hairline. He also appeared to be repeating some simple phrase over and over, although his voice might have been emanating from a jack o'lantern left outside in the weather since Halloween.

"You'll have to do better than that," Keith said, and moved around the boy to step up to the cracked porcelain wall, unzip, fish himself out, and, with a groan of pleasure, let loose. Hayward always enjoyed urinating, the touching, the unaccustomed exposure, the release of accumulated pressure. He thought his penis probably enjoyed the attention he gave it at such times, and sometimes, as now, when the stream had dribbled out, it seemed intent on proving him right. This time, he understood, his arousal came not from the usual sources but from the now comprehensible, though still mushy, words uttered by the freshman boy whose backward-pointing feet and lowered butt he could see by turning his head and looking sideways. The kid was bent over like a Muslim on a prayer rug. In a voice ragged and soft with exhaustion, he was saying, "Oh thank you, oh thank you, oh thank you...I *hate* it when they piss on me...thank you, oh thank you, oh thank you." To that he added what sounded like the word "Sir."

"My name is Keith, okay?" Keith shoved himself back into his pants. The groveling freshman continued to mutter behind him.

"Stop doing that," he said. "And get up, will you? If someone walks in, we'll both be in trouble." He kept facing the urinal to hide the bulge in his trousers.

"Okay," the boy muttered. "I just wanted you to know that I'm really grateful. Getting pissed on is terrible. You have to go home and change your clothes, and everybody knows what happened. Um, my name is Miller."

At last he heard the sounds of Miller scrambling to his feet. "How many times has that happened to you?"

"Just once before. Well, twice. Only the first time it was just Rocky and I was in a ditch."

"So I guess that hardly counts."

"He pushed me, and I fell down. Rocky hates me. But just about everybody hates me." There was a pause. "Why are you looking away?"

Unable to prolong the moment any longer, Keith turned around. His erection, which had lost some of its urgency, still raised a lump alongside his fly.

The small, weedy, milk-white boy before him had hunched shoulders, big hands that dwarfed his wrists, and limp black hair that looked dead. His eyes and his nose were too large for his face, and his whole being looked cringing and elfin. The protuberant eyes skittered off Keith's pustular face, moved to the bulge at his crotch, then slid panicked into the middle distance.

"They were afraid of you," Miller said. "Rocky and them." Dangling from their spindly wrists, his swollen-looking hands were trembling.

"Doesn't mean you have to be."

"Okay," Miller said. "You won't piss on me, will you? I don't think you will."

"Definitely not today." The forlorn expression on Miller's face made him laugh. "That was a joke. Hey, I'd like to hear you thank me for saving you from Rocky and his buddies."

"But you told me to stop."

"That's when you were all bent over on the floor, and you couldn't even talk right. I want you to thank me now, when you're standing up."

"Thank—"

"Hold on, Miller. *And.* I want you to thank me by doing something for me."

The boy's adam's apple jerked up and down. "The bell shoulda rung already."

"Be my friend," Keith said.

"Sure," said Miller, amazed. "I don't have any friends."

"Me, too. So we can be friends, you and me. Right? Only, I rescued you from those guys, so you owe me."

"How long has your face been like that?"

He was trying to change the subject, but both boys knew what was involved, and in a sense they had already agreed upon the terms of their contract.

"Because you were two years ahead of me at Townsend School, and back then you didn't look like that."

"The dear old days of Townsend. How did I ever miss you?"

"You want to know what? In about a year, maybe less, you're gonna look different. The same thing happened to my brother. His whole face was one big zit. When they went away, he just had these little scars."

"You have a big brother? How old is he?" Hayward thought for a second. "Is he in this school?"

Miller gulped air. "He isn't in any school. My brother's dead. My dad got him drunk, and he died. His name was Vatek. Now my dad's in prison, and my mom won't let me see him."

"Where do you live?"

"3355 Auer."

It was only a few blocks from his own house. "On the way home, I want to show you a certain room," he said, and from his pocket produced a giant ball of keys.

It was in this fashion that Keith Hayward acquired the boy known as Miller.

⁂

After an initial period of fearfulness, then a week or so of despair, the hunched, spavined little creature with outsized eyes and hands that looked liked protuberances had learned at least in some fashion to enjoy Keith's private room. There were weekends when he puttered around with the animal heads and tails, the resilient paws and the scabby, shriveling skins, like a child set loose amongst his toys. When busy with his various "projects," Hayward occasionally glanced over at the other boy and smiled like a fond parent at the intricate movements through which the clumsy hands guided his trophies. Of course Hayward was not Miller's parent, but his Master.

Miller learned to resign himself to the sexual duties his role imposed upon him, but in the process he learned also that his Master was sexually excited by the craven and the cringing, by abjection and piteousness, precisely the tactics to which he attributed his survival into his freshmen year of high school. To save himself from tedious stretches laboring over his Master's "tool," which was in any case much smaller than his own, Miller attempted to change some of his behaviors and appear more confident. These efforts had some limited success. By May, during the long hours the boys spent in Keith's secret chamber, he was spending less time as a sex toy and more as a kind of assistant curator who helped arrange the trophies and exhibits.

They had begun to work with the numerous notices for lost cats and dogs that appeared so frequently in the neighborhood. In the beginning, Keith had ordered Miller to rip these posters off the walls and lampposts where they had been put up and throw them away, but near the end of winter, he realized that they could display the posters beside the remains of the pets they described. Matching the dead animals to their owners' drawings and word-portraits proved remarkably easy, although at times the fuzziness of the distinction between "marmalade" and "tabby" drove Keith half-mad with fury. If they had properly matched the posters with the cat and dog remains, there *were* some tabbies with fur the color of orange marmalade, almost a reddish tinge to the hair, but in most cases the animals might have been twins, and the owners just called them what they liked. In any case, the notices and cat skins that covered the walls of Keith's room made it look a bit like a grotesque museum. The hides and heads of small animals and the mimeographed pieces of paper with boldfaced names hung in three long, straight lines down the walls at the sides of the room. Keith found this arrangement beautiful.

It pleased Keith that Miller had instantly understood the necessity to maintain the sacred chamber in an orderly fashion, and he was grateful to his creature for having solved a problem that had grown more serious with each fresh acquisition and might have led, over time, to unwelcome intrusions upon his territory. This was the question of disposal. Keith's work involved the accumulation of a growing pile of what he called "gizzards," the internal organs, lungs and hearts and livers and bowels as well as several other small, wet body parts that he had never identified. Before Miller had been introduced to his room, Keith was in the habit of dumping whatever he had left over—sometimes nearly an entire cat or dog—into a big tin bucket left behind by the banished cult. After every two or three procedures, he poured the messy leftovers into grocery bags pilfered from a kitchen drawer, then carried the stained (often dripping!) bags through the streets to the vacant lot at the end of his block. There he pushed the bags into the corner by the wall and did his best to cover them with dirt. Rodents and vermin made a swift job of eliminating most of the evidence.

The first time Miller had observed this process, he ventured, all but trembling with the awareness of his terrible audacity, that perhaps he might suggest a neater and on the whole less risky way of managing the problem of disposal. What was that? his Master demanded. Miller had a *suggestion?* By all means, let us hear it.

Quivering, Miller mentioned a stack of old newspapers in a broom closet and reminded his Master that *Joe's Home Cooking,* the restaurant two buildings down Sherman Avenue, kept a row of metal garbage cans lined up in the alley. If they maybe wrapped the gizzards in newspaper and stuffed the parcels into the garbage cans, wouldn't that provide a neat, efficient solution to their problem?

Keith liked the way Miller talked. He never said anything the way you expected him to. He talked like a grown-up, but he was never vague or confusing. Miller spoke with tremendous clarity. The best part was the way he kept surprising Keith with the stuff he came up with. Once Keith asked him if he liked what they did with the cats and dogs, and Miller said that he had a few reservations, but it was a lot better than being beat up and pissed on over and over.

"Didn't your parents ever call the school and complain?"

"We don't complain," Miller said. "My parents have very strong foreign accents, and any kind of authority frightens them. They think they have to be submissive when dealing with real Americans."

About half of the other kids Hayward knew might be capable of offering such an analysis, but none of them would be able to articulate it so clearly. You had to be smart to use language that way. The more time that Keith spent with Miller, the more he realized that with only a little bit of work, his creature, his only friend, could easily do very well at school. Yet Miller puttered along on B minuses, Cs and Ds, exactly the grades he desired, neither so glittering nor so shameful as to attract attention. He never did homework, and Keith suspected that at times he deliberately gave wrong answers on tests. His principal goal in life appeared to be to slip beneath the radar and escape or avoid notice. For different reasons Keith felt much the same way.

Over the course of his freshman year, Miller grew more and more to value the circle of protection and safety that Keith Hayward created for him. The price of that magic circle, always distasteful, became less onerous and more merely habitual, over the winter and spring.

At school, and during his walks to and from Lawrence B. Freeman High School, Miller almost daily experienced the benefits his efforts earned for him. Rocky Glinka had threatened to punish both Keith and Miller for his humiliation in the boys' bathroom, and for a month Miller trembled in fear whenever he caught the crude, stupid bully sneering at him in the hallways, but nothing ever came of the threat. With Babb at his side, Glinka once spotted Hayward rummaging in his open locker, swept down on him, spun him around, and tried to ram him into the small, unusually crowded space. Something about the atmosphere within Hayward's locker made him feel threatened. He wanted to back away and get out of there, fast. At the same time, he also wished to pound Hayward senseless and close him up in his locker. Still holding his enemy by the biceps, Glinka moved a half-inch away and shook his head. What was it? A kind of smell?

"Take your hands off me and move away," Hayward said.

Glinka raised his head and looked into Hayward's eyes, hoping to renew his energy and purpose. It was like looking into a cave. Glinka dropped his arms and stepped back. "What's in there, anyhow? Is your locker full of hair?" This was pure bravado.

"No," Keith said, and slammed his locker shut.

"Something *looked* at me," Glinka said, getting closer to his actual state.

Keith turned to Larry Babb, who had been hovering at his friend's shoulder. "Take him away, Larry. Get him out of here."

"You're a freak," Babb said, and did what he was told. No one at that school ever again bothered Keith Hayward or his friend, the boy called Miller.

Keith's life improved in one other significant way, too. By May of his junior year, Keith's face had almost entirely cleared up, so if he were not (nor ever could be) good-looking, he had anyhow ceased to be the kind of a walking suppuration in those days called a "pizza face." Many of the little knife-like scatter of scars that his acne had bequeathed him bent sideways and folded themselves into the long vertical furrows that already divided his cheeks. A little while later, his uncle told him that if he ever went bald, he might wind up looking like the guy in that painting, "American Gothic."

DECEMBER—JANUARY 1964—1965

Christmas was three weeks away, and while with part of his mind Keith pondered what to give his uncle, Miller labored over his naked body. As sometimes happened, in the course of their exertions Miller had himself become excited, and due to the position he had taken over his master's body, for the first time in their relationship the evidence of Miller's arousal hung near his master's face. Keith could not admire his own erection without looking past the daunting organ swaying before his eyes.

A clear drop of viscous liquid drooled out of Miller and swung down on a silver thread. Keith balled his right hand and punched the back of Miller's thigh hard enough to leave a bruise.

"Get off!"

Miller turned his head and started to scramble off the cot at the same time. His eyes were round with shock.

"Are you a fag?" Keith bellowed. "Because I'm not."

"A fag?" Miller slid off the side of the cot and landed on one hip. "I thought you wanted me to..."

"You're not supposed to get a big fruity *kick* out of it!" Keith pointed, and Miller looked down. "I don't want some faggot sucking on my dick, Miller. I'm supposed to be enjoying it, but you're not."

"It's funny," Miller said. "By and large, I don't, actually. I can't really tell you why I got hard this time. It *is* sex, though."

"It's supposed to be sex for me, Miller, not for you. I don't *want* to have sex with you, because I'm not a pansy. And what do you mean, you don't *actually* enjoy sucking my dick? Maybe it doesn't satisfy you, is that it?"

"I'm not supposed to be satisfied," Miller wailed. "You don't want me to be satisfied!"

"You got too fucking close!" Keith yelled at him.

Miller folded himself into a ball, shielding his head with his arms and his chest with his crossed legs. The offensive organ tried to contract into his body.

Keith slid off the table and batted the back of Miller's head. His slave began to groan, "Please please please don't hurt me I didn't know anything was wrong *please* Keith *please*..."

Keith's body responded to abjection in its typical manner. Hitting Miller again only made him feel even closer to orgasm. He placed his hand on his erection and gave himself the few rough up-and-down strokes that were all he needed.

"For God's sake, clean yourself up," Keith said.

His slave crawled away toward the heap of filthy towels, and a wonderful idea came to Keith Hayward. "I want you to meet someone."

Miller quivered.

"Don't worry," Keith told him. "My uncle Till is a very, very cool guy."

⁂

Before he entered high school, Keith had never bothered to wonder about the crimes Detective Cooper thought Tillman Hayward had committed. The air of genial lawlessness that surrounded his uncle seemed a sufficient explanation for police interest in his case. No doubt he had been responsible for hundreds of crimes, maybe more. Indifference to legal technicalities was part of his character. The way the man sauntered down the street, the way he slouched against his pillow with his hat on his head and his hand wrapped around three fingers of bourbon, the way he did practically everything would probably be seen as a violation of the proper order by someone like Detective Cooper. Some people, a lucky few, were born that way, and some of *them,* like his aunt Margaret Francis/Margot, managed to wriggle their way right up to the top of the world, where there was always enough money and you could have all the cars and clothes and good food you wanted. Wasn't that what everyone wanted?

When Keith speculated about specific crimes Uncle Till might have committed, he dared go no further than the assumption that his uncle had a "private" room wherein he, much like Keith in the last few years of grade school, dissected other people's pets. Beyond that, he could not think; beyond that lay an abyss.

All this time, the conversations in the back yard and the extra bedroom, which had been the best conversations of his life, coiled through his mind like smoke, now and then shining with meanings that in seconds melted away. He felt as though he stood trembling before a great dark door, too terrified even to reach out his hand. Keith had never seen the Alfred Hitchcock movie his uncle loved, for *Shadow of a Doubt* was too old for the cinemas and too disturbing to be shown during the family hours on network television.

During his grade-school years, Keith's self-absorption kept him from much noticing the newspaper and radio stories about the Ladykiller. Perhaps for his sake, his parents avoided conversations about the murders and switched channels and radio stations when the subject came up. Keith knew that someone was killing women, three or four of them a year, over intervals wide enough for him to forget about the murders. Although at times he wondered what sort of man the killer might be, these speculations soon darkened to opacity, as if unwelcome in his mind.

Uncle Till slid into town at long intervals, never twice by the same mechanism. If one time he drove up in an unfamiliar car, the next he would arrive by train, or at the bus station. Another time, he claimed to be short of cash and to have traveled the entire distance on his thumb. He arrived in new cars, borrowed cars, cars temporarily left to him by traveling friends.

Not until he was seventeen and a high school junior did Keith realize that the Ladykiller had chosen to murder two Milwaukee women during a period when his uncle had returned to the old spare room alongside the kitchen. This recognition might never have come to him had he not strayed into a shop on his way home from school at the same time a delivery van dropped off tied-up bales of *The Milwaukee Journal,* the evening newspaper. On his way in, Keith glanced at the most prominent headline atop a stack that had just finished rolling across the sidewalk. *LADYKILLER CLAIMS DOWNTOWN VICTIM,* it read. Beneath the headline, Detective Cooper's weary, ironbound face angled down in lamplight at a cobbled alley and a rumpled gray-white sheet from which protruded a pale, upturned hand. The story began:

Police have identified the Ladykiller's probable ninth victim as Lurleen Monaghan, 29, of 4250 N. Highland Avenue, a secretary in the trust department at the 1st Wisconsin Bank. Miss Monaghan's body was discovered by pedestrians in the alley behind the Sepia Panorama, a N. 3rd Street nightclub, at 2:20 this morning. According to Homicide Detective George Cooper, the body had been moved to the alley after death.

"The Ladykiller murdered the victim in a private location and dumped her here, in back of a busy nightclub, where she was quickly discovered," said Detective Cooper. "Wednesday of last week, he followed the same procedure with the body of Laurie Terry. This monster is rubbing our faces in his crimes. Let me put this guy on notice. We are pursuing a number of active leads which will soon lead to his capture."

Keith continued on into the store, thinking only that it was strange that he had managed to stay essentially unaware of this villain's existence. The discovery of Laurie Terry's body had missed him altogether—and so would have this new outrage, had it not bounced up right before him. Now that the phrase had been placed in front of his eyes, he understood that he had after all heard of the Ladykiller. The phrase had entered his consciousness, but only barely. What struck him as strange was that this was precisely the sort of thing he thought he could find...*irresistible,* however greatly his parents would object to his interest.

On the other hand, Detective Cooper, that meaty piece of shit, had not neglected to leave a wide, greasy trail across his memory.

A pad of thumbtacks slipped into his coat pocket. Without breaking stride, Keith moved up the aisle, extended an arm, snapped up a pot of glue, and dropped it into the other coat pocket. He had entered the five and dime on Sherman, in the same block but across the street from his sacred place, his church, his theater, to acquire, ideally without payment, some items useful to him. Recently he had become aware that he could make good use of a hammer, also of a metal file, also of any kerosene-like solvent akin to that employed by his father in the spray room at the can factory, and after he had pocketed a roll of tape he headed toward the back corner where he thought he remembered seeing a little hardware section. The solvent or kerosene or whatever it was would probably be difficult to find, but you never knew. It might turn up right in front of him, like Miller. Or like the bundled newspapers that had greeted him outside the little store.

And from that wandering thought came....

Without even faintly trying, Hayward recognized the meshing of two separate calendars, his uncle's and the murderer's. Laurie Terry had met her death late the previous Wednesday, the day Tillman Hayward had surprised his Milwaukee family by calling from the bus station to tell his brother's wife, *hello, my dear one, here I am, no worries, I'll get to the house on my own.* Twenty minutes later, she had gone to the front window to see, on the far side of a great snow bank, her brother-in-law getting out of a strange woman's car just in time to twirl his suitcase from the back seat and into the arms of his devoted nephew, who was arriving home from another deadly day at Lawrence B. Freeman. Together, Tillman and Keith came up the path through the snow, already deep in conversation.

They had talked long and often since that moment, but never, Keith now saw, of actual murders—murders of human beings. Here was the great dark door before which he had quailed; here was the true, the real abyss. And as he stood before it, the door swung open, and the abyss yawned wide. Lit with bright, wandering fires, his entire body seemed to tremble from within. A great confirmation rang through him and seemed to lift him off the ground. His head reverberated. For a moment he was conscious of nothing but his blood coursing through his brain and body in a continuous, racing stream. Then his knees went rubbery, and he began to slip toward the floor.

A female voice called, "Sir! Are you all right?"

It was like being pulled back to shore. His eyes cleared, and he found he could halt his descent. A woman with piled-up hair and cat's-eye glasses stood perhaps ten feet down the aisle, extending one hand and one foot as though poised between flight and approach. She had big freaky eyes, and her mouth was a beak. He could not permit this woman to place her hand on his coat.

"I'm fine," he managed to croak.

"It looked like you almost fainted."

"Well, *something* happened," he admitted. "But it's over." He straightened his spine, rolled his head back, and inhaled. Uncle Till, seated cross-legged on the spare bed with his hat on his head, a playing card in one hand, dark smiling eyes taking him in…

Oh, tonight I think I'll just wander around, see if anything interesting turns up.

Who was the dame with the car? Just another dame with a car, nephew.

"Can I get anything for you?" She still held the posture of a bird coming in for a water landing.

"No, I was just looking for…" Keith tried to think of something small and affordable. "A notepad?"

"Aisle two." The woman slowly pulled herself upright. She lowered her arms, gave him an uncertain smile. "I ought to get back to the register."

…wander around, see if anything interesting turns up.

Keith smiled back at her.

"Why, you're just a boy," the woman said. "I don't know how I could have thought…"

"I'll get that notebook," Keith said, and turned around slowly, wondering why he had not asked about files or hammers. Wondering, too, what age she had thought him. He had to go home, he had to talk to Uncle Till.

Could you have a conversation like that? One that acknowledged the great open door and the shimmering license that lay beyond it? Or were such conversations conducted in the silences between ordinary words and phrases? With the sense of standing on the lip of a great precipice, Keith rushed down the last aisle past displays of ribbons, pins, elastic bands, and buttons on long cards, seeing nothing.

His Uncle Till was the Ladykiller. Like a general or a great monarch, he had led his forces out into a dark, unknown territory, and seized control of all that lived there. His bed was a throne, his hat a crown. And his scepter...

...I don't know how they'd do it, but for sure, if it was me, *I'd use a knife.*

Just before he sped through the shop door, he glanced sideways at the woman with the weird hair and could not refrain from twisting his mouth into something like a smile. He did not know if it was meant for a taunt or reassurance, and it felt like neither. Instead, it felt like the ghost of emotion—a gesture to an unknown force. The hesitant face under the tortured hair displayed sympathy and curiosity. Then the woman's face hardened with suspicion, and she began to rise from her stool. Keith Hayward and his ghost of a smile had already fled into the cold and snowy street.

When he got back home, he raced through the business of dragging his boots off his feet and shedding his heavy coat and unwinding his scarf and pulling off his cap and transferring his stolen goods to his pants pockets and hanging up everything else. Then, finally, he could pass through the door to the kitchen, where his mother, engaged in an unruly shelf paper project, turned from the cabinets and a rank of plates of various sizes to look him over, make sure his shoes were civilized, and ask him about school. His response, as always noncommittal and vague, should have satisfied her, but instead of turning back to the shelf and the long curl of paper, she said, "What's going on with you, Keith?"

"What? Nothing. Why."

"You seem excited. You're all wound up inside. Tight as a watch-spring."

"I guess I'm a *little* excited, Mom," he said. "Mr. Palfrey gave me a B+ on my *Grapes of Wrath* paper."

She cocked her head and smiled, mechanically. The smile vanished. "You didn't have anything to do with the Rodenko's cat, I hope. Mrs. Rodenko was talking to me about it for half an hour the other day. It's been a week, and she's worried sick. "

Keith put on an affronted, wounded look. "The Rodenko's *cat?* Mom, are you still worrying about that time you saw me doing something dumb? I was twelve years old, Mom. I was a kid. You *know* Uncle Till talked to me all about that. Jeez."

The hide of the Rodenko's cat, an odorous, hissing monstrous creature either marmalade or tabby, hung on the wall of the secret room beside the pathetic poster the Rodenkos had taped to lamp posts and billboards.

"Sometimes I wonder about you and my husband's brother," she said.

"What?"

"Just lately, I don't know...Does he tell you what he does when he goes out at night?"

"Mom, he sees people. He has dates. You know."

"Oh, I know. Yes. I do." She looked down at her hands, then cast a glance behind her at the stripped shelves and the curl of paper. "At least that policeman stopped hanging around here, making me feel like something was wrong. *Bad* wrong."

"All that was a long time ago, Mom."

"That man was very sure of himself. I *saw* him once, out in the alley. He was trying to look through our windows."

"He doesn't come around any more."

"That doesn't mean something won't bring him back."

Now Keith understood: his mother had been reading the newspapers.

"You shouldn't worry about him, Mom. Don't let yourself get carried away."

She smiled. "That's what your father says."

Keith forced himself to smile back.

His mother said, "You look more relaxed than you did when you came in."

"You do, too," he said. "Uncle Till's here, isn't he? Is it all right if I go see him?"

"Don't make a nuisance of yourself."

She waved him off and turned back to her work. Keith went out of the kitchen and stood before his uncle's door. For a second he shocked himself by wondering if he should knock, if he should speak, if he should go ahead. Uncertain, he stood before the immensity of the choice that faced him. Stay or go? Speak or leave in silence? For one thing, he had just realized for the first time that his mother might be able to hear whatever passed between his uncle and himself: but the choice went far beyond questions of privacy. Breathless, he raised his hand, and yet he hesitated, unable either to knock or walk away.

"Keith, is that you?" came his uncle's soft and rasping voice. "Come on in."

He lowered his hand, and was surprised that sparks did not leap from the knob. Turning it slowly, he heard the bolt slide into the plate.

"Good boy," the voice whispered.

Keith pulled the door fully open to reveal his uncle seated on his green blankets, his hat on his handsome head. Till had been reading a magazine, but had turned to face the doorway, that he might regard whatever spectacle was unfolding there. He was smiling, and his eyes were alight. "You can do it," he whispered.

In full recognition of what he was doing, the boy came forward. Let this be said for Keith Hayward: when he came to the door, he entered his ruinous estate without hesitation. Once inside the room, he whispered back, "You *do* it, Uncle Till."

"Oh?" Till's look of amusement deepened.

For the first time, Keith understood what sentimental authors meant when they spoke of falling into someone's eyes. Long and narrow to begin with, his uncle's eyes seemed to widen and enlarge with anarchic mirth. Tillman Hayward was irresistible: a satyr, a faun, a devil.

"Meaning what?" he said, softly.

In silence, Keith closed the door behind him. For a moment, he stood there with his hands folded behind his back. Here was another great threshold, and with only a second's pause, he crossed it to stand within two feet of his hero.

In a voice just above a whisper, Keith said, "Lurleen Monaghan." He searched his memory, and as a bear dips into a stream and snatches up a glittering fish, speared the second name. "Laurie Terry."

"Well, now." Till's amusement spilled over into soft, chuckling laughter. "Laurie Terry, eh? Lurleen Monaghan, is that right?"

"I guess so." In fact, Uncle Till's response left no doubt as to his accuracy.

"How did you happen to learn those names, Keith?"

"The front page of the Journal."

Never taking his eyes off his nephew's, Uncle Till nodded, slowly, like a judge coming to a conclusion about a complicated legal point. "Our secret just got bigger, didn't it?"

"I guess *so.*"

Till drew his head back a couple of inches. His eyes got narrower. Evidently he reached a conclusion about that complex matter. "Could be time I showed you my little place. What do you think?"

"I'd like that," Keith said.

After dinner, Till asked Keith's parents if it would be all right for him to take their son to a theater on the east side, the Oriental, to catch a screening of a movie they both wanted to see. It was *Charade,* with Cary Grant and Audrey Hepburn, which one reviewer had called "the best Hitchcock movie Hitchcock never made."

"Leave me out," said Keith's father. "Cary Grant's a homo, and Audrey Hepburn looks like a praying mantis."

Keith's mother looked wistful, but asked only if Keith had any unfinished homework.

"I did it in study hall, Mom," he said, which was not entirely a lie. Shortly after dinner, uncle and nephew set off through a cold night glittering with stars.

Till led him past the vacant lot and around the corner, then down another long two blocks and around another corner before walking into the street and pulling out the keys to a long black Studebaker Keith had never seen before. Freezing inside his heavy coat, the boy waited for his uncle to get in and open the passenger door for him. The white clouds of his breath seemed to hang before him for an unusually long time, as if preserved by the cold. Although Uncle Till was wearing merely his hat, a sweater, and an unzipped leather jacket, he seemed to be unaffected by the temperature, even while blowing on his key to warm it.

"Aren't you cold?" Keith asked.

"Fact is, I like cold weather," his uncle replied. "Sharpens you up. In the heat, things get sloppy."

Till wound through the city until he got to Capital Drive, then drove straight west. Keith gazed out at neighborhoods and businesses he had never seen before, a ball bearing factory, an enormous shopping center, Roy Rogers and Arthur Treacher restaurants, a Howard Johnson's, a used car lot with pennants like colored icicles and huge spotlights sending yellow-white beams into the black sky.

Finally they passed 100th Street, a straight, narrow line rolling past small, comfortable-looking houses down a low grade, then up another, steeper grade. 100th Street! Keith had no idea the numbers went up so high.

"Where is this place, anyhow?" he asked.

"You'll see."

"Is it far?"

"You'll see."

In a suburb called Brookfield, Till veered off Capital Drive and cut through streets lined with big houses on wide, snowy lawns to Burleigh, where he turned west yet again. Ten minutes later, a metal sign advised them that they had entered the town of Marcy, population 83. A wilderness of white fields lay behind a narrow town hall, a frame house without windows, and an abandoned bar. Across the street was a one-story grade school. The town looked as though it had been stolen by aliens and set down in a desolation. Uncle Till pulled in and parked the car between the windowless house and the shell of the old tavern. Keith got out and watched his uncle tug his huge ball of keys out of his pocket and, smiling, start flipping through them.

"I wanted to have a place out of town, see? Far away from Detective Cooper."

Till held up a long, blunt key. "So I drove around until I found this place." He nodded at the bar and started walking toward it. "Nobody ever comes to this side of the street, and the kids and faculty are all gone after five o'clock."

"What about Columbus?" Keith asked. "You have a place there, too, right?"

"No—no—no—no. In Columbus, everything's completely different. *I'm* different. In Columbus, I have a wife and two daughters. They don't know anything about this, and they never will."

"Come on." Too astonished to move, Keith watched his uncle walk around the hood of the car. "You don't. You can't."

"Oh, but I can, I do. I recommend that you think about doing the same. We all have to make some sacrifices, after all."

Mouth open, Keith crunched across the gleaming snow to join his uncle at the door.

"But what do they think you do?"

"I own a bunch of apartment buildings. Well, my wife inherited them from her father, so actually we own them jointly."

"You're rich." This was astonishing.

"I'm comfortable. I never told your dad and mom because I wanted to be able to keep coming back here as a bachelor."

Silent, Keith watched his uncle slip the key into a round metal lock newer than the door it protected.

"How can you keep coming to Milwaukee?"

"I'm looking for investment properties in my old home town. Let's get inside."

After relocking the door behind them, Till produced a small flashlight from an inner pocket of the leather jacket and played its beam over a dusty wooden floor, a long dark bar, and rickety-looking barstools. With

Keith behind him, he set off past a rank of glum booths and ancient coat hooks. The air was frigid. When he came to a second, narrower door, he opened it, flipped a switch, and flooded the basement with bright fluorescent light. He started moving quickly down the stairs, and Keith followed, filled with wonder.

"Peace and quiet, comfort and security," said his uncle. At the bottom of the stairs, he looked up over his shoulder and smiled. "Behold."

While the ever-amazing Tillman Hayward wandered around turning on space heaters, Keith did as commanded and *beheld*. As clean as an operating theater, the long, wide basement contained two sparkling metal tables with drip trays, a shiny tile floor dotted at intervals with drains, metal wall panels hung with knives, saws, and hatchets, and on the other side of the cement circle where the furnace had stood, a back wall lined with green lockers, each with a padlock. The rectangular windows set high in the walls had been bricked over.

"Did it all myself, " said Uncle Till, answering an actual though unasked question. "If I'd hired workmen, I would have had to kill 'em, and that was an unacceptable level of risk. Took me over a year, but now this place is pretty much the way I want it. The heaters will take the chill off in a minute—they get it up to about sixty degrees, which is warm enough. In summer, it gets too damn hot down here, but all I can do is plug in some fans."

"Amazing," Keith said.

"I have to admit, I'm kinda proud of what I was able to accomplish here."

Keith walked up to a shiny metal table and touched its leather wrist and ankle restraints.

"So you...?" He let the crucial question hang.

"I put a little something in their drinks to cool 'em out. Bring 'em out here, got plenty of duct tape over in the cabinet, but nobody can hear 'em anyways. Lift 'em up on the tables and go to work. Before I start in, I strip off, hang up my clothes—plumbed in a little shower over there next to the lockers."

Keith's face and hands felt hot, and his heart was booming. "Do you screw them?"

Uncle Till grinned and laid a hand on his nephew's shoulder. In the shadow of the hat brim, his eyes looked molten. "You want to know if I fuck 'em, son? Hell, yeah. Most of the time, anyhow. And not just once, and not just in the one hole. Tell you the truth, nephew, sometimes I think I'd fuck a woodpile if I knew a body was in there. Wouldn't matter what kind, neither."

Not long after, they were driving back home through a world that looked both exactly the same and utterly transformed.

⁂

Two years later and three weeks before Christmas, under the same wintry skies Keith Hayward at last realized that for the first time in his life he had it in his power to offer his uncle a gift that would actually be worthy of him. Because Tillman always returned to Ohio by the 17th or 18th of December, he knew he had about a week and a half to set things up. Keith's parents explained Till's pre-Christmas departure from their house as the result of his natural desire to spend the holiday with friends and intimates in Columbus, thought to be of a more sophisticated circle than any available to him in Milwaukee. To include Till in their modest family celebration, they exchanged gifts the day before his departure. Bill and Maggie always gave him things like socks or handkerchiefs, and he replied with gifts of a slightly more lavish nature, a bottle of expensive bourbon or a robe for his brother, a pretty scarf or blouse for his sister-in-law.

In the past, Keith's parents had always solved the problem of his gifts to his uncle by going to a shop called Notes & Notions, buying a cheap picture book about New England lighthouses or fancy cars or something similar, and wrapping it up with an attached card upon which he had scrawled his name. Uncle Till, ever cool, always thanked him for these gifts and acted as though they interested him, but everyone understood that the photographs of Concord Point Light and Edgartown Light, of Bugattis and Dusenbergs, amounted to mere place-holders that would serve until Keith grew old enough to select gifts by himself. In December of 1962, that date was assumed still to lie in the future, and the place-holder, forty-eight pages of handsome yachts, had already been purchased.

Keith's real present could not be wrapped in Christmas paper and settled beneath the tree. On the afternoon of Friday the 14th of December, he ordered Miller to meet him in the secret room at seven o'clock the following evening; after a dinner during which the host's brother offered a hilarious, never-before heard account of his brief experience as a soldier in the United States Army, Keith followed his uncle back to the spare room and said he hoped Till would be free the next evening, because he had a surprise he wanted to give him.

"A surprise? That sounds interesting." Uncle Till was leaning toward a mirror, watching his hands wind a polka-dot necktie into a handsome half-Windsor knot.

"It's my Christmas present to you. The real one."

"Well, well." From the mirror, his eyes flashed an electric shock into his nephew's. "I gather this involves our private concerns."

"Yes."

"Let's be careful, then."

Till turned away from the mirror and slid his beautiful hands into his pockets. His head bent forward.

For a moment, he regarded the scuffed-up sisal rug that covered the floor.

"You tell your parents that you're going to hang out with the famous Miller, and I'll just say I have to meet a friend. We leave separately, we come back separately. Does that work for you?"

"It's good."

"Where do you want to meet up?"

"At my place."

"Easy as pie. What time?"

"Seven."

"Seven it is. I'll say this for you, kid: you got me interested."

"What are you going to do tonight?"

"Gotta check my traps, boy, gotta check my traps." Till's sudden grin caused him, if only for a second, to resemble a large, untrustworthy dog.

After a long séance before *The Alfred Hitchcock Hour* and *The Fugitive* on the TV, during which his mind could barely comprehend the action or dialog, Keith assented to his mother's suggestion that he looked tired. It was only ten-thirty, half an hour before his usual bedtime. Sticking effortlessly to his own schedule, his father lay stretched out and lightly snoring in his lounge chair. In half an hour, Channel Twelve was going to show *The Indestructible Man,* but his mother was right, he did feel oddly exhausted. However, when he put on his pajamas and slipped into bed, he discovered that he could not sleep.

Late in the night, he heard his uncle come in through the back door. Soft, light footsteps crossed the kitchen and passed into the spare room. A few minutes later, Till emerged to let himself into the downstairs bathroom and release a long, thunderous cascade of urine. He flushed the toilet and returned to his quarters. When silence returned to the ground floor, Keith switched on his bedside lamp and looked at his clock. It was three-thirty. He fell asleep soon after.

Four hours later, he came downstairs in jeans and a warm flannel shirt, wandered into the kitchen to get something to eat, and found his mother seated at the table, exhaling cigarette smoke over both a bowl of Cap'n Crunch and an open copy of the morning paper, *The Milwaukee Sentinel.*

"Good morning, Mom," he said.

"Morning." She looked up from the paper and squinted at him. "You never get up this early on a Saturday. And you look as tired as an old dog. Why aren't you still in bed?"

He saw no reason not to tell her the truth. "I couldn't sleep any more."

"There's something wrong. What is it? You tell me right now, Keith."

"Mom," he said. "I just couldn't sleep." He turned from the table and began to rummage through the boxes in the cereal bin.

"That's not healthy."

Keith could feel her eyes on his back. He waited for whatever it would be.

"Is something going on with that Miller?"

A tingle of alarm passed through his nervous system. "No, Mom, nothing's going on. Not with Miller or anyone else."

"You want me to make you something for breakfast? It's no use waiting for your father, he won't be up for another two hours. And I don't blame him, don't think I do. He works long, hard hours, that man. If you ask me, his brother should be more like him."

"Dad wishes he was more like Uncle Till."

"Well, he shouldn't. Till is never going to marry a rich woman, he's just going to chase girls and stay up late in bars and pick up money whichever way he can. And I don't think you should be spending so much time with a man like that. Come away from that cereal and tell me what you'd like for breakfast."

He turned around and saw his mother taking him in as thoroughly as she could. She stubbed out her cigarette. "Well?"

"Scrambled eggs?"

"If your uncle didn't clean us out when he came in last night." She stood up and went to the refrigerator. "Good. Plenty of eggs, plus some bacon. He even left us some orange juice." She took a half-gallon container of milk from the refrigerator and reached for a glass. "Sit down."

He sat. "I never saw you reading the paper before, Mom."

"If something terrible happens, I want to know."

"Oh."

"Things are going on you shouldn't even know about." She placed before him a glass of milk and a smaller glass of orange juice.

"In this paper?" Genuinely curious, he slid the paper a quarter-turn toward him and looked over the headers. Most of them concerned local politics.

"No, thank goodness. Now give that paper back to me."

When she set his breakfast before him, the odors arising from the plate almost made him groan with hunger. Until that moment, he'd had no idea that he was ravenous.

"I don't think you should spend so much time with your uncle."

He shoveled a forkful of eggs into his mouth and added a two-inch bite of bacon.

"You're not going out with him again, are you?"

Around his food, he said, "Mom, it was just a movie."

"I don't care what it was, I don't want you doing it again."

He swallowed, struggling to keep his alarm under control. "Mom, what's wrong? Don't you like Uncle Till any more?"

"Everybody likes him, that's the trouble. But I'm not saying I trust him, mind. And you shouldn't be tagging along behind him any more. The world isn't as safe as you think it is, sonny."

Unable to reply to this absurdity, Keith forced himself to eat slowly. His mother joined him at the table, turned a page of the open newspaper and ran her eyes across the columns, then jumped up again to refill her coffee cup from the percolator. When she again took her chair, she lit another Kent.

"Tell you the truth, I'll be glad when he leaves in another few days. Your father worships that man so much, neither one of us ever stopped to think about what kind of influence he might be on you. Decent people don't live that way."

"There isn't just one way to be decent," he said.

There this conversation ended.

For the rest of the day, Keith did little but watch a parade of cartoons on television and meander around the house, waiting for Uncle Till to come out of the spare room. He flipped through the latest *Life,* which, no surprise, had a picture of the late President Kennedy on the cover. As Keith roamed through the magazine, he wondered how, in an entire extra-long issue devoted to the Kennedy assassination, a magazine thought to be so great could include only one lousy single article about Lee Harvey Oswald. He turned page after page about the dead President, many pages about Jackie Kennedy (whom Keith privately considered probably the most boring woman on earth), and a surprising number of pages dedicated to Lyndon Baines Johnson. There should have been much, much more about Kennedy's mortal antagonist, his opposite number. To make matters even worse, *Life* ran only a few pictures of the assassin, and he was the man who had made everything happen. Keith had lived long enough to understand that very few people even came close to sharing his point of view, but wasn't it obvious that this guy, Oswald, had more or less changed the rules? You could come up out of nowhere, you could appear to have led a misguided and wasted life, and yet all it took was a gun to place you on the same level as the President of the United States—if *he* was the most powerful man in the world, then you were *right beside him.* After a while, the refusal of influential Americans to recognize the amazing transformation Lee Harvey Oswald had created in their national life, to comprehend the actual revolution this former loser had brought about, made him feel so frustrated he could no longer bear to look at the magazine.

His uncle emerged only long enough to take a shower and walk, bathrobe flapping, into the kitchen to make a peanut butter and jelly sandwich. He took it back into his room and dined alone. While Keith numbed himself with *Rocky and Bullwinkle,* Maggie Hayward cornered her husband, Bill, at the breakfast table, and in whispers and quiet words conducted what her son knew to be a tireless military campaign. Bill Hayward shook his head, he remonstrated, he protested, but as all the while he was also consuming the fried eggs, crisp bacon, warm buttered toast, and hot coffee his wife had prepared for him, it could be said that he had already capitulated and all his apparent counter-campaigning amounted to mere smokescreen and misdirection. Maggie Hayward had changed her mind about her brother-in-law. She saw him in a new, unflattering light, and his days under her roof were numbered.

"Look, kid," Till said to him that evening, "it's crummy, but I understand it. Your mother saw the same newspaper you did, and it scared her a little. Maggie didn't want to think what came into *your* mind right away, and she doesn't, that's for certain, but something flickered in her noggin, and all of a sudden she thinks I'm a bum and a bad influence on you."

"I don't get it," Keith said. They were parked at a meter on Sherman Boulevard. It was a few minutes before seven.

"Unlike you and me, most people hide their real motives from themselves. They have no idea why they do the things they do. Oh, they talk all day long about what made them do this and that, but what they tell you isn't even close to the truth. Because they don't *know* the truth. And why is that? They can't let themselves know it. The truth is unacceptable. Every human being on earth tells millions of lies in the course of his life, but most of those lies are to himself about himself. Your mother is a perfect example. Well, well. Could this be your buddy?"

Keith had already seen Miller's huddled form, hands in the pockets of his hooded coat and watch cap on his head, trudging toward them. His head was bent, his eyes fixed on the sidewalk.

"That's him," Keith said.

Miller plodded right up to the hood of the Studebaker. Without looking in, he swung sideways and darted into the shadowy space between the empty building and a long display window filled with television sets and washing machines. Soon he had disappeared into the darkness. According to the dashboard clock, it was exactly seven o'clock.

"He'll wait by the back door," Keith said. "Merry Christmas, Uncle Till."

"That kid is my present?" Till burst into soft laughter. "God damn. You're something else, you are. Keith, I am truly impressed."

The boy took this in with the warmth of a benediction: it was a blessing more paternal than any his father could have given him.

"Let me tell you one thing, sonny boy. You're going to do amazing things. Maybe no one will ever know about them. Doesn't matter."

Uncle Till patted Keith's left knee with his shapely and ungloved right hand, and the chill of his touch burned through to the skin.

"Fact is, it'd be better that way—if all your accomplishments are as secret as the room in there. But I'll know, somehow or other." Till's frozen grip tightened on Keith's knee and burned snow and ice straight into the bone. "I'll always know."

Keith could not imagine how his uncle was able to tolerate such coldness. Any moment, he would be forced to cry out. Then his uncle released him.

"Let's meet Miller," Keith said.

Uncle Till smiled at him. "In a second. Miller will wait. I'm happy to say that I have a present for you, too."

"You do?" Keith was stunned with pleasure.

"Open the glove compartment. Let me know what you find in there."

Keith pushed the button on the glove compartment and folded down its door. The inside light had burned out long ago, but visible atop the usual heap of maps and manuals lay a long, narrow white box bound with a red ribbon.

"A box," he said.

"A box? Well, get it out of the glove compartment and see what's inside."

With something like reverence, Keith removed the box, set it on his thighs and removed the ribbon. Then he raised the top of the box and lifted out a white bag. He already knew what his present was, and that it would be better of its kind than anything he had ever known.

"Oh boy," he said. "What's that word? Sabat—Sabateer."

"Sabatier," Till said. "You can't do better, I don't care what anybody says."

Keith drew the long knife from the bag and rested it across the palms of his hands. "Boy. Thanks."

"That's a chef's knife. You can use them for damn near anything, chopping, slicing, even deboning. Keep it clean and sharp, and it'll give you good service for years. For decades."

"Is this like the one you use?"

"Sure, I have a knife just like it," Till said. "In time, you'll have a whole collection. But your chef's knife, that's the centerpiece, that's your show pony. Do I have to tell you that you can't let your mother find it?"

"I won't even bring it home. I'll hide it in here."

Uncle Till cracked open his door. "What say we let poor Miller get in out of the cold?"

In seconds, they had slipped into the narrow passageway between the buildings. The sleeping washing machines in the enormous window gave way to grubby brick. Underfoot, empty beer bottles and crumpled cigarette packets lay upon a track of frozen earth a foot and a half wide. Inside the passage, the walls seemed five or six stories high. The chef's knife rode inside his belt at the small of his back, and it felt as though he had been carrying it there for months. Coming along steadily behind him, Uncle Till perfectly matched his pace. Then at last Keith burst out into the alley and saw Miller hunkered down in front of the back door, hugging his knees for warmth.

"I wondered if you were ever going to show up," Miller said. "It's too cold to make me wait out here."

Then he saw Till moving out of the shadows and, more quickly than Keith had ever seen him do anything before, jumped to his feet. When Till moved up beside Keith and gave him a look of frank inspection, Miller folded his coat around him and tried to disappear into the bricks and mortar behind him.

"Whoa," he said. "What is this?"

"Didn't I tell you I had a surprise for you?" Keith asked.

"No," Miller said. He sounded resentful.

"Sorry. I thought I did. Well, it's a *wonderful* surprise, Miller. This man is my uncle. Uncle Till is the best teacher I ever had. I thought he deserved a really special Christmas present. So I'm giving you to him. You know what I think, Miller? I think you're in for a wild old time."

"This is going to work out just fine," said Uncle Till. "What are we waiting for?"

"I don't think this is a good idea," said Miller.

"Too bad."

"You can't give people as presents to other people."

"Not usually."

Keith pulled his ball of keys from his pocket and quickly located the one that unlocked the back door.

Still leaning against the brickwork, Miller was only a foot and a half to his left, both staring down and flinching away. His pores seemed to exhale an odd, metallic smell. Bronzy and unpleasant, it also floated from his open mouth. Beneath the hem of his winter coat, Miller's knees were jigging in his blue jeans. The smell was fear, Keith realized: fear was a physical property, and it stank.

"I wish you'da let Rocky Glinka piss on me," Miller whispered.

"At the time, you sang a different tune," Keith said, passing through the door. It was nearly as cold inside the building.

"You want me to piss on you, Miller?" Uncle Till sounded amused.

"Not really," Miller said. He followed Keith inside.

Till came in last and closed and locked the door behind them. "Because if you have any special requests, I could always fit them into my schedule."

In the darkness, Keith took a small Maglite from his coat pocket and played its beam across the floor until the circle of light centered on a new-looking Medeco lock about three inches across. "Hold this, will you?" he said, and passed the flashlight to Till, who kept it shining on the lock.

"Good work," Till said. "Yours is in the basement, too?"

"Just like yours."

Keith unlocked the Medeco, reached in, and flipped two switches that illuminated the basement and the rickety-looking wooden stairs leading to it. The treads creaked as he went down into the light.

Miller moved onto the first step and looked up over his shoulder.

"You can rest easy, kid," Till said. "I've never killed anyone with a dick, and I never will. Unless, you know, one day, I don't have any choice."

Downstairs on the cement floor, surrounded by the familiar animal hides and the posters for lost pets, Miller seemed less terrified. His knees no longer vibrated, but he kept shifting his eyes sidelong to glance at Till. His pallid face was stiff with fear. He asked the floor, "What are we going to do, exactly?"

"We're going to enjoy ourselves and experience life to the fullest."

"I see," Miller said, looking extremely unhappy.

"And for me to enjoy myself in the deepest possible way, nephew, I'm afraid that I really will have to be left alone with my Christmas present."

Miller's eyes flared at Keith.

"Are you sure about that?"

"Oh, yes, Keith, I am absolutely sure about that. That won't be a problem, I trust."

"It might be a problem for Miller."

"If Miller has a vote, it *is* a problem," said Miller. "A big one."

"Boy, I'd like to see you take your clothes off, so why don't you indulge me by doing that little thing?"

"It's cold down here," Miller said, but he shed his coat and began to unbutton his shirt.

"Pretty soon you won't notice that any more," said Uncle Till. "Are you hung pretty good, kid?"

"I don't know," Miller mumbled.

"We'll find out soon enough. There's a lot of things we're about to find out, Miller." Till turned his face to Keith and raised his eyebrows.

"Oh!" Keith said. "Okay. Ah, there's a diner down the street, I'll get a coffee and some fries, or something."

"Try their cherry pie," said his uncle. "Fit for a king, that is."

Uncle Till looked like a king—*regal,* Keith thought, with his head back and his perfect hands folded in front of his chest. He looked like a famous hunter Keith had once seen in a photo, posed with one foot on a dead lion in Africa.

"When should I come back?" he asked.

"An hour is all I'll need."

Keith nodded and turned toward the stairs. His last impression of Miller was of his comrade and slave shirtless and fish-white, shrinking into himself, his eyes dull and hopeless.

Upstairs, he left the basement unlocked and followed the beam of the Maglite to the rear door. Before he had let himself out, Keith heard Miller emit a sharp, high-pitched outcry, as if scalded. Before leaving for the diner, he revolved the key in the back door's lock and heard the bolt snick safely home.

He set off a little bell when he went into the coffee shop, but nobody, not even the waitresses or counter staff, looked up. At the end of the counter, a fat man in a cloth cap and a dirty brown overcoat sat over a ham sandwich and a cup of coffee, reading the same issue of *Life* Keith had seen at home. Worn-out couples ignored each other in two of the booths. The air smelled of cigarette smoke, and the floor was filthy with tracked-in snow. Keith took a seat at the end of the counter. An overweight waitress with dyed blond hair placed her cigarette on the lip of an ashtray, pushed herself into motion, and came toward him.

When she had covered half the distance between them, the indifference of her regard sharpened into curiosity. By the time Keith could smell the smoke on her clothes and her hair, the expression on her face said that her curiosity had passed into confusion, and she resented it.

"Why, you're just a kid," she said. "I coulda sworn... Anybody ever tell you that your face sometimes gives a person the wrong impression?"

"No," he said, which was at least technically the truth.

"No offense. I just thought you were older."

"You got any cherry pie?"

"Oh, all business now, are we? Yes, sir, I believe we still have one fine piece of our cherry pie left in the kitchen. Would that be your pleasure for tonight, sir?"

He didn't get why the waitress was acting all huffy and sarcastic. What had he done to her?

"Yeah, that would be my pleasure," he said.

"And what would you like to drink, young sir?"

"Gimme a coffee."

She frowned. "Are you old enough to drink coffee? Might stunt your growth."

He was going to tell her it was cigarettes, not coffee, that was supposed to stunt your growth, but it was too much trouble, and the world was seedy and poisoned all about him, just look at those mopes in the booths, dead already though they still drew breath. Keith slumped on the stool and said, "Okay, gimme a coke."

"Sure, honey," she said, which surprised him. Then she gave him a greater surprise by bending over the counter and saying, "It can't be that bad, you know. Whatever it is. You're blowing it all out of proportion. I know, I really do."

"What are you talking about?"

"Whatever made you look so worried the minute you came in here. Honey, it put years on your face. You want to talk about it with me?"

"I'm not worried about anything," he said. "You're wrong."

She backed away. "Just trying to see if I could help you in any way I could."

"Help somebody else," Keith said, too loudly. It seemed to him that everyone in the diner had turned to stare at him, the old fart in the cap, the stiffs in the booths, the other waitress, the cashier, even the cook.

"One cherry pie, one coke, comin' up," she said, and scribbled on her pad. By the time she slapped his order slip on the service counter, she was already taking a long drag, shaking her head, and blowing smoke all over the cash register.

The cook moved out of view, but the others, stiff as wax figures, were still looking at him with flat, two-dimensional eyes.

Keith Hayward bent his head and stared at the smeary patterns left on the counter by a wet rag.

In minutes, the waitress slid his slice of cherry pie and his soft drink toward him and vanished sideways without a word. He could feel the curvature of his spine and wondered if his new knife made a tent under his coat. He didn't care if it did. On the whole, he would be happier if the dreary people in the diner knew he was carrying a weapon.

When he bit into his cherry pie, he remembered to look at his watch. He wanted to give Uncle Till the full hour. That was his present, all sixty minutes, every one of its three thousand, six hundred seconds. That was a lot of seconds, and in each one of them, something only barely imaginable was happening. Though his pie was juicy, it tasted like dust. He could barely force himself to swallow the pulp in his mouth. When he tried to wash the cud down with Coca-Cola, the liquid in his glass felt oily and dead. It had no taste at all. The seconds had only barely begun to tick. Somewhere, a boy screamed and a man smiled. Inside his head, the screaming sank and flared like a candle flame on a terrace at night.

Maybe there was no screaming. Miller was not a screamer. He absorbed the pain and kept on going. Maybe he talked like an English teacher, but Miller, it turned out, was a goddamned soldier. For a second, Keith had a vision of Miller playing amongst the skulls and pelts, talking to himself, doing the voices of the dead animals. He had been like a child at those moments, and Keith had been surprised by the pleasure he took in this spectacle.

Out loud, he said, "I have feelings, too." The sound of his voice startled him.

The waitress, who had been talking with the cook through the service hatch, said, "Of course you do, honey."

Keith's head snapped back into position, bent to within only a few inches from his food.

"How's that pie working out for you?"

"I can't really taste it," Keith said. "I can't taste anything right now."

She planted her hands on her hips and came toward him. He heard her feet scuffing the floor, and the reek of tobacco smoke intensified.

"Would you like me to call someone for you, son?"

"What? No. I have to sit here an hour. A little less now." He forced himself to pull down his sleeve and examine his watch.

She leaned on the counter directly in front of him, but he did not lift his head. "Somebody told you to wait here for an hour?"

"I *gave* somebody an hour. The hour was my present. That's why I'm here."

Keith slid a small crescent of pie, less than a bite, into his mouth. It tasted like a dead animal.

She tried again. "An hour's a funny present."

"Maybe to you," he said around the bit of pie.

"But I suppose we could all use more time."

Without looking up, he swallowed the raw, oozing meat he had been chewing. The waitress watched him section off another tiny sliver of pie and slip it into his mouth. "Well," she said, "I'll let you wait out your hour in peace and quiet."

He nodded. The waitress scuffed her way back to the wall between the serving hatch and the cash register. The fat man in the greasy cap turned a page of *Life* magazine with the crack of a brisk wind snapping out a canvas sail.

Sometimes the pie in his mouth had the texture of raw flesh, at others it felt like cardboard. At intervals he glanced at his watch, always with dismay at how little time had passed. One of the silent couples left the diner, and ten minutes later a man rolled in on a tide of cold air, dropped onto a stool fifteen feet from Keith's, and announced to the waitress that he was fed up with Milwaukee and was looking forward to living in Madison, where he had just landed a good job at a mental hospital.

"J-job's a p-piece of cake," he said. "You j-just hang around this Common Room, m-make sure the d-ding-d-dongs d-don't fall down and swallow their t-tongues."

Keith tilted his head and peeked down the counter. The man who had taken the job in the hospital was about thirty, with a high, tight crew cut riding above his squashed-in profile. He was instantly identifiable as a bully, a grown-up Rocky Glinka. Keith snapped his head forward and gazed down at the little that remained on his plate.

"I'm strong, see? They l-like that. If the l-loony t-tunes act up, we p-put 'em in restraints. Or p-punch 'em out. You gotta be s-strong, or at Lamont, they wouldn't look at you t-twice."

The Lamont Hospital sounded like every school Keith had ever attended.

"You're g-gonna miss me, ain't you, Avis?"

"We'll all miss you, Antonio." Her tone of voice, at once muffled and sharp, made it clear, at least to Keith, that everybody in the diner detested the man.

"Now, d-don't you go feelin' s-sorry for me up there," said Antonio. "What's M-Madison, huh? Tell me. What's M-Madison?"

"State capitol."

"That d-doesn't count. Come on. Come *onnn.* What else is it? That kid down there, he knows. Hey, kid! You! Kid!"

With dread and horror, Keith realized that the kid in question was himself. He raised his head perhaps a quarter-inch and risked a narrow glance at the horrid person now addressing him.

"Come on. Kid, t-tell her. What's the b-big thing about Madison, what's the b-big attraction they got up there?"

A single possibility appeared in Keith's mind. "The college?"

"The University, that's right! The big U! And what makes a b-big university like that so g-great?" He extended his arm and made an encouraging, keep-'em-coming gesture with his cupped hand.

"Umm," Keith said.

"You can say it, go on." He paused, and when Keith said nothing, generously answered his own question. "Girls! Girls from all over the s-state, from a-all over the country, thousands of 'em. *Thousands!* G-girls up and d-down both sides of every street, girls in every building, girls walking along those campus paths... hell, kid, I *know* you wanna go there and meet college chicks, right?"

"Uh huh," said Keith, who until this moment had never considered the possibility that he might go to college. It had not occurred to him that girls, thousands of them, might line both sides of a college town's every street. It certainly sounded more interesting than high school.

"Damn right you d-do. And you know what else? Soon as you c-can, get your ass into a f-fraternity. F-fraternity boys, they get hot and c-cold running dames."

"Sounds pretty good," Keith said, realizing that this was the closest thing to a normal conversation he'd had with anyone, including Miller, in months.

Evidently concluding that the boy had served his purpose, Antonio returned his attention once again to Avis. He wanted a burger, and he wanted it big, cooked all the way through but still with plenty of that good grease, and he wanted his fries so crisp you could snap 'em like twigs. And on toppa that...

Keith stopped listening. He desired no more conversation. The one he'd just had called for certain internal adjustments, at present obscure in nature. Experimentally, he inserted into his mouth a section of cherry pie no larger than a dime and found on his tongue the chemical, metallic flavor of cherries long dormant in a can and congealed into a thick paste. For the rest of the hour Keith divided the remainder of the pie into ever-smaller sections, separated the pulp from the crust, which still had the taste and texture of cardboard, sucked the red mash off his fork, and wished it tasted more like actual cherries. Whenever he thought of Miller, he pushed cherry-goop around his plate until it melted into red gruel.

The check erased most of the dollar bill folded into his pocket. After he got off his stool and shoved his arms down the sleeves of his coat, Keith remembered Uncle Till's mention of tossing a five-dollar tip onto a bar and pushed a dime toward the waitress. She smiled, and Antonio, his mouth full of well-done burger, nodded farewell.

The walk back through the cold and darkness seemed to take twice as long as he knew it should: chunks of time fell into a black abyss, and Keith came back to himself to find that he had gone no further than where he had been before he lost consciousness. He was taking the same step at the same place on the sidewalk, and he knew there had been a period when his body had walked on without him. Yet he had advanced not an inch, how could that be? The anomaly grew worse when he reached the appliance store with the long picture window. Between every other step, time vanished, suspending him in a void where he both moved and, apparently, did not. Minutes passed while he toiled past a hulking Maytag washer that through its huge circular eye mocked him for his inability to move beyond its reach. Silly boy, always dropping away, always remaining in the same place.

Silly boy, who...

Keith wrenched himself out of the Maytag's sphere and heard the hateful sentence die away and become nothing. This display of will power kept him intact all the way to the narrow alleyway. He ducked in, and a wandering thought diverted him: *What kind of guy would actually like the idea of working in a mental hospital?*

Across the floor he went, guided by flashlight. He had left the door with the Medeco lock unlatched, and after he had opened it, Keith looked down the stairs to an empty, illuminated floor. To his relief, no sounds came from that realm. He realized something he had not previously understood, that he had been braced for screams, whimpers, quiet groans, the noises of Miller's distress. Down there, nothing seemed to be moving. Then he saw a shadow moving left-right across the gray concrete, and felt a quick, frigid blast of fear.

The shadow wore the shape of a human head. It occurred to him that on the whole he wished to hear at least some kind of noise from Miller. Absolute silence struck him as ominous.

"Uncle Till?" he called down.

"I thought I heard you," came Till's voice. "Enjoy your pie?"

"Sort of." He stepped onto the first tread.

"Did you order cherry?"

"Got the last slice." Keith came down onto the next step. "Wasn't all that great."

"You stayed there a long time, so I thought you were enjoying yourself. I certainly was. Best Christmas present I ever had. Weren't you, Miller?"

Miller neither assented nor demurred. Miller maintained a stoic silence.

"I guess he doesn't feel like talking. He's been working hard, old Miller." His uncle's voice came nearer as he spoke, and soon he emerged into view, wiping his hands on one of the old blankets. His jacket was off, and his shirtsleeves were rolled up just below his elbows. Beneath his hat brim, Uncle Tilly looked both weary and refreshed, and utterly at peace with himself. He smiled up at Keith. "Are you coming down, nephew? And what was wrong with your cherry pie?"

What was wrong was your Christmas present, he thought. "A guy told me I should go to college."

"Uh huh. I see." Uncle Till nodded his head. "And that affected your appetite."

"I guess." Keith began to move down the stairs in the usual way, without pausing at each step.

"Sounds good to me, though. Get away from home for a while, spread your wings."

Keith took his eyes off his uncle and looked past him. Blood spots and spatters lay strewn like red lace across the concrete at the rear of the long basement. At the convergence of the delicate, brush-like spatters stood an empty wooden chair, its back and seat dripping with blood. Keith moved off the last step. His eyes followed a long, distinct smear of blood that ran from the side of the chair to a rucked-up blanket placed eight or nine feet away. A huddled white form covered half of the blanket, and that white form was Miller. Animal skins and torn posters hung on the wall beside him.

"Go check on your friend over there, will you?" Uncle Till stepped back and swept his arm toward the chair and the blanket. "I doubt he has much to say."

As he crossed the hard basement floor, Keith's legs felt like stilts. When he got to the blanket, he knelt beside poor Miller. Over much of his body, especially the arms, shoulders, back and legs, the whiteness of his skin had a blue tinge that spoke of the formation of deep bruises. Bright streaks and splashes of red covered his chest and obscured his face. Long straight gashes down the ribcage and inside of Miller's arms continued to leak blood. A big section of his hair had been ripped from his scalp, leaving a stippled pink-and-red bald patch that oozed red. Beneath eyebrows like thin dark pencil marks, his puffed-out eyes had swollen shut. Keith could see that a lot of the bones had been broken in the hands held cupped beneath his chin. His lips were purple. Till had also sliced into Miller's topmost cheek, and every breath opened a flap of skin, exposing his clenched teeth. His entire body was shivering.

Keith at last dared to bring the palm of his hand into contact with Miller's upper shoulder. The skin felt hot.

He whispered Miller's name.

"He's not going to say a lot, you know."

Keith jumped: he had not known that his uncle had come up behind him.

"It's up to you now, Keith."

The boy turned his head to take in his uncle's handsome, smiling face. "It's his time, son."

Keith blinked.

"Use your present on mine."

"Now?"

"He's half-gone already. Hell, the cold would get him if we just left him here. We can hardly take him to a hospital, can we?"

Keith looked back down at Miller's battered, shivering husk.

"Didn't you know that it was always going to turn out this way? Sure you did. You'll do me proud, kiddo. This is your graduation. Welcome to the world, son—I mean that."

"Tell me how," Keith said.

The phrase that had just trickled from his throat hung visible in the air before him, like frozen steam. He could not look at his uncle: he wanted to see nothing, nothing at all. The animals had turned their faces to the wall, happy to be dead and blind.

"I'll tell you everything you need to know, son," came his uncle's soft, caressing voice. "You'll do all the right things in all the right ways." A cold, cold hand patted his shoulder. "Reach around under your coat and fetch out that good-lookin' knife."

Keith groped around the small of his back, grasped the knife's handle, and brought it out into the light. It looked long, blunt, and businesslike.

"There you are, my boy, your instrument in your hand. Now scoot around a little higher on his body, so you're right behind the back of his head."

He managed a crab-like shuffle that moved him about a foot up Miller's body.

The soft voice came again, folding itself toward his interior. "This part's real important, son, so get it right.

Take your left hand and get it right around under that boy's chin. That's right. You're doing good now, Keith, real good. Pull that chin up away from his neck."

Keith raised the other boy's chin, awkwardly. The back of Miller's head dug into his thigh, and he inched backward to give himself more room to do what had to be done. He thought he could feel Miller's head turning feebly from side to side, but he could not be sure. Miller's whole defeated body was trembling.

"Now take your knife, Keith, and place it all around on the other side of his neck. No, farther, boy, farther. You want to do this right."

Keith settled the blade of the knife against the skin of Miller's thin neck, just beneath his chin.

"That's a sharp knife, so you don't have to do a lot of heavy pushing. Use your arm muscles and sink it in as deep as you can go. It'll just slice right in there, you'll see. Then give the knife a good hard pull all across the neck and jump backwards, mighty sharp, because that blood's gonna leap out, and you want to get out of its way."

Keith braced himself to draw upon his muscles and sink the blade. Uncle Till tapped his shoulder and bent down to send even softer words into his ear.

"When this part's done, Keith, we're gonna burn down this building, and you're gonna retire from this business for a couple of years. I'll be gone—all my stuff is in the car. You go to college, you set yourself up in Madison, or wherever. You find another private room, and do your business there. You can do girls, but only one a year. Two at the most. Don't be in any goddamned hurry, son. Bide your time. Understand me?"

He nodded.

"Then go to it, Red Ryder."

Under Keith's grip, Miller twitched and uttered what might have been a word of protest that was instantly engulfed by the gout of blood that flew from his body. In the next instant, Hayward flexed his legs and propelled himself backward onto the concrete.

Till snatched the knife from his grip and swiped it against a blanket. He extended a hand to his nephew, who let himself be lifted to his feet. On the floor, Miller shuddered once, then sank into bodily quietude.

The next morning, Tillman Hayward had once again gone his mysterious way, and the *Sentinel* reported that a fire of unknown origins on Sherman Boulevard had destroyed an abandoned building and a neighboring appliance shop.

Author Biographies / Story Notes

"Serial" by Blake Crouch & Jack Kilborn

According to the authors: "Since we first met at Left Coast Crime in El Paso, Texas in 2005, we'd always talked about writing something together. Of course, talking is easier than writing, so we talked and talked and talked and talked but never wrote anything. Then, last year, Joe sent Blake an email:

"Now, let's consider hitchhiking. You aren't supposed to go hitchhiking, because the driver who picks you up could be crazy. You aren't supposed to pick up hitchhikers, because they could be crazy. Now if we were to collaborate, I write a scene where a driver kills someone he picked up. You write a scene where a hitchhiker kills the guy who gave him a ride. Then we get these two together..."

Blake responded:

"Oooooh, I love that idea...let's do it.....should we write our initial pieces in isolation? And then bring our characters together? I'll write 2 pages, you write 2, back and forth, and let the ending just emerge naturally from the story. This is gonna be fun."

And it was. We never could have imagined the response this story would get. From staying #1 on the Amazon Kindle bestseller list for six weeks, to a quarter-million downloads, to a film deal, to the expanded Serial Uncut edition we just released, this story has turned out to be the most loved, most hated, and unquestionably most-read thing either of us has written.

And if we've saved one potential hitchhiker from sticking out their thumb and being brutally murdered, or one driver from picking up a hitchhiker and being brutally murdered, then it's all been worth it."

"The Crate" a novella by Stephen King

Stephen King has written more than forty novels and two hundred short stories. He is the recipient of the 2003 National Book Foundation Medal for Distinguished Contribution to American Letters and he also received the O. Henry Award for his story "The Man in the Black Suit." Among his most recent worldwide bestsellers are *Under the Dome, Cell, Lisey's Story,* and *Duma Key.* His books from Cemetery Dance Publications include two volumes of *The Secretary of Dreams,* the deluxe Limited Edition of *From a Buick 8,* and the World's First Edition of *Blockade Billy.* King lives in Bangor, Maine, with his wife, novelist Tabitha King.

"The Last Beautiful Day" by Brian James Freeman

Brian James Freeman's short stories, essays, novellas, and novels have been published by Warner Books, Leisure, Cemetery Dance, Borderlands Press, Book-of-the-Month Club, and many other publishers. He is the managing editor of *Cemetery Dance* magazine and the publisher of Lonely Road Books. You can reach him on the web at www.BrianJamesFreeman.com.

"Cobwebs" by Kealan Patrick Burke

Kealan Patrick Burke is the Bram Stoker Award-winning author of *The Turtle Boy, The Hides, Vessels, Midlisters, Currency of Souls, Master of the Moors, The Living, Seldom Seen in August,* and the collections *Ravenous Ghosts* and *The Number 121 to Pennsylvania and Others.* He is also the editor of the anthologies *Taverns of the Dead, Tales from the Gorezone, Quietly Now, Brimstone Turnpike,* and *Night Visions 12.* Visit him on the web at www.kealanpatrickburke.com

"The Old Ways" by Norman Prentiss

Norman Prentiss recently won the Bram Stoker Award for Superior Achievement in Short Fiction. His first book, *Invisible Fences*, was published as part of the Cemetery Dance Novella Series. Other fiction has appeared in *Best Horror of the Year*, *The Year's Best Dark Fantasy and Horror*, *Tales from the Gorezone*, *Damned Nation*, *Postscripts*, and the *Shivers* anthology series, and at the *Horror Drive-In* website. His poetry has appeared in *A Sea of Alone: Poems for Alfred Hitchcock*, *Writer Online*, *Southern Poetry Review*, and *Baltimore's City Paper*, with essays on gothic and sensation literature in *Victorian Poetry*, *Colby Quarterly*, and *The Thomas Hardy Review*.

"Waiting for Darkness" by Brian Keene

Brian Keene is the author of over twenty books, including *Darkness on the Edge of Town, Kill Whitey, Urban Gothic, Castaways, Dead Sea, Ghoul, Unhappy Endings* and many more. He also writes comic books such as *The Last Zombie* and *Dead of Night: Devil Slayer.* His work has been translated into German, Spanish, Polish, French and Taiwanese.

Several of his novels and stories have been optioned for film, one of which, *The Ties That Bind,* premiered on DVD in 2009 as a critically-acclaimed independent short. Keene's work has been praised in such diverse places as *The New York Times,* The History Channel, The Howard Stern Show, CNN.com, *Publishers Weekly, Fangoria,* and *Rue Morgue.*

"Like Lick 'Em Sticks, Like Tina Fey" by Glen Hirshberg

Glen Hirshberg (www.glenhirshberg.com) won the 2008 Shirley Jackson Award for his novella, "The Janus Tree." Each of his story collections, *American Morons* (Earthling, 2006) and *The Two Sams* (Carroll & Graf, 2003) received the International Horror Guild

Award and were selected by *Locus* as a best book of the year. *The Two Sams* was also named a Best Book of 2003 by *Publishers Weekly*. He is also the author of an acclaimed novel, *The Snowman's Children* (Carroll & Graf, 2002). His next novel, *The Book of Bunk: A Fairy Tale of the Federal Writers' Project,* will be published by Earthling in late 2010. With Dennis Etchison and Peter Atkins, he co-founded the Rolling Darkness Revue, a traveling ghost story performance troupe that tours the west coast of the United States each October. His fiction has appeared in numerous magazines and anthologies. He teaches writing and the teaching of writing at Cal State San Bernardino.

"Ghost Writer In My Eye" by Wayne Allen Sallee

Now over half a century old, Wayne Allen Sallee will have a poetry collection, *I Can't Come Clean,* published in late 2010, with a trade anniversary edition of his first novel *The Holy Terror,* in 2011, both by Annihilation Press. *The Holy Terror* is available as an audio book by CrossRoads Press, and is available on Kindle. As he hates technology, Sallee takes time away from writing by staring into the bathroom mirror and sighing. For those of you who enjoy writing to prisoners on Death Row or celebrities like Lady Gaga or Glenn Beck, you might want to check out Sallee's website, www.frankenstein1959.blogspot.com.

"Palisado" by Alan Peter Ryan

Alan Peter Ryan began appearing in print (as Alan Ryan) in 1978. His early stories in *Twilight Zone, Shadows, Whispers, F&SF, Amazing,* and many anthologies earned him a nomination for the John W. Campbell Award. He was nominated three times for the World Fantasy Award and won a WFA for "The Bones Wizard." His fourth novel, *Cast a Cold Eye,* has been called "one of the best ghost stories ever written." He also edited five anthologies: *Halloween Horrors,*

Haunting Women, Night Visions 1, Perpetual Light, and *The Penguin Book of Vampire Stories.*

For many years, he wrote about books, music, travel, and culture for the *New York Times*, the *Los Angeles Times, USA Today*, the *Washington Post,* the *Chicago Tribune, Smithsonian, The American Scholar, Travel & Leisure, Islands, Playgirl,* and many other newspapers and magazines, and also edited five anthologies of travel literature, for which he won a Lowell Thomas Travel Journalism Award.

He returned to writing fiction in 2009 and quickly began selling stories to *Cemetery Dance, Shivers, Postscripts,* and various anthologies. In late 2010, Cemetery Dance will publish *The Back of Beyond: New Stories* and a novella called *Amazonas.*

He has traveled widely and now lives near the famous Copacabana beach in Rio de Janeiro.

"Stillness" by Richard Thomas

Richard Thomas is the author of *Transubstantiate* (Otherworld Publications) a neo-noir, speculative thriller. He was the winner of the ChiZine Publications 2009 "Enter the World of *Filaria*" contest. His work is forthcoming or published in *Murky Depths, Eternal Night: A Vampire Anthology, 3:AM Magazine, Word Riot, Dogmatika, Opium* and *Vain.* He is also pursuing an MFA at Murray State University. He has guest edited for *Colored Chalk* and is Co-Editor of *Sideshow Fables.* Visit www.whatdoesnotkillme.com for more information.

"In the Raw" by Brian Hodge

Brian Hodge is the author of ten novels, close to 100 short stories, and four full-length collections. Recent books include his second crime novel, *Mad Dogs*, and the new collection, *Picking the Bones*, both from Cemetery Dance Publications. He lives in Colorado, where he's at work on a sprawling new novel that doesn't seem to want to end, and ricochets between indulgences in music and sound design, photography, Krav Maga, and mountain air.

"In the Raw" was originally commissioned for an anthology of stories based on songs by a popular singer-songwriter-activist-man-of-the-people, but was ironically forced out when the singer had his lawyers set last-minute content conditions to retain his continued blessings on the book.

Connect with Brian Hodge through his web site (www.brianhodge.net), on Facebook (www.facebook.com/brianhodgewriter), or follow his blog, Warrior Poet (www.warriorpoetblog.com).

"I Found a Little Hole" by Nate Southard

Nate Southard's books include *Red Sky, Just Like Hell, Broken Skin, He Stepped Through, This Little Light of Mine,* and *Focus,* which was co-written with Lee Thomas. His short fiction has appeared in such venues as *Cemetery Dance, Thuglit,* and the Bruce Springsteen-inspired anthology *Darkness on the Edge.* Nate lives in Austin, Texas with his girlfriend and numerous pets. He loves food, comic books, and muttering under his breath. Look him up at www.natesouthard.com. He's friendly enough.

"Fallow" by Scott Nicholson

Scott Nicholson is author of 10 novels, including *Drummer Boy, The Skull Ring,* and *Speed Dating with the Dead,* as well as more than 60 short stories. He also created the comics series *Dirt, Grave Conditions, Little Shivers,* and *Dreamboat.* A freelance editor and journalist in the Blue Ridge Mountains of North Carolina, he runs the blogs *Write Good or Die* and *Indie Books Blog.* His virtual home is www.hauntedcomputer.com.

“Last” by Al Sarrantonio

Al Sarrantonio is the author of more than forty books, including novels, short story collections and anthologies in the horror, science fiction, fantasy, mystery and western fields. He is a winner of the Bram Stoker Award and has been a finalist for the World Fantasy Award, the British Fantasy Award, the International Horror Guild Award, the Locus Award and the Private Eye Writers of America Shamus Award. His website is www.alsarrantonio.com.

“Mole” by Jay Bonansinga

The author of twelve internationally renowned books, including the ITW-nominated *Shattered,* Jay Bonansinga is also a busy screenwriter whose film work has been honored at numerous festivals, including the Queens International, Houston Worldfest, Iowa City and Chicago International. He has been called “one of the most imaginative writers of thrillers” by *The Chicago Tribune,* and has collaborated with horror film legend George Romero. Jay’s 2004 non-fiction debut, *The Sinking of the Eastland,* won the Certificate of Merit from the Illinois State Historical Society; and his feature film debut, *Stash* (based on a *Cemetery Dance* short), premiered in fifty million households in 2009 on On-Demand. Jay lives in the Chicago area with his wife, Jeanne, and sons Joey and Bill. You can find Jay on the web at www.jaybonansinga.com.

“The Shoes” by Melanie Tem

Melanie Tem’s work has received the Bram Stoker, International Horror Guild, British Fantasy, and World Fantasy Awards and a nomination for the Shirley Jackson Award. She has published numerous short stories, eleven solo novels, two collaborative novels with Nancy Holder, and two with her husband Steve Rasnic Tem. She is also a published poet, an oral storyteller, and a playwright. *In Concert,* a collaborative short story collection with Steve Rasnic Tem, was published in August by Centipede Press. The Tems live in Denver. They have four children and four granddaughters. www.m-s-tem.com

"Bits and Pieces" by Lisa Tuttle

Lisa Tuttle was born in the United States, but has been resident in Britain for almost thirty years. She began writing while still at school, sold her first stories at university, and won the John W. Campbell Award for Best New Science Fiction Writer of the year in 1974. She is the author of eight novels (most recently the contemporary fantasy *The Silver Bough)* and many short stories, in addition to several books for children, and editor of *Skin of the Soul,* an anthology of horror stories by women. Her short story "Closet Dreams" won the International Horror Guild Award in 2007. Ash-Tree Press is to publish a multi-volume collection of her short fiction, beginning with *Stranger in the House: Collected Ghost and Horror Stories, Volume 1* scheduled for September 2010.

"Trouble Follows" by David B. Silva

David B. Silva's short fiction has appeared in *The Year's Best Horror, The Year's Best Fantasy & Horror,* and *The Best American Mystery Stories.* In 1991, he won a Bram Stoker Award for his short story, "The Calling." His first collection, *Through Shattered Glass,* was published by Gauntlet Press in 2001. In 2009, Dark Regions published *In The Shadows of Kingston Mills,* a collection of eleven new stories and one reprint.

In addition to his short stories, Silva served as the editor of *The Horror Show* from 1982 to 1991. This small-press horror magazine won a World Fantasy Award in 1988 and went on to publish the early works of influential horror authors such as Bentley Little, Brian Hodge, and Poppy Z. Brite.

Currently, he's working on a variety of new fiction, as well as editing the free horror blog, Hellnotes (http://hellnotes.com). You can keep up with his work on his personal website at: http://davidbsilva.com

"Keeping It in the Family" by Robert Morrish

Robert Morrish is the former editor of *Cemetery Dance* magazine and *The Scream Factory* magazine, and has edited or co-edited anthologies such as *October Dreams* and *Thrillers II.* His blog covering the small press horror scene can be found at www.twilightridge.net. His short fiction has appeared in past anthologies such as *The UFO Files, Subterranean Gallery, At Ease with the Dead, The Texas Rangers,* and the *Shivers* series, and is slated for forthcoming anthologies such as *In Laymon's Terms, Holy Horrors,* and *Shocklines.* Morrish's "The Outsider," which appeared in *The Texas Rangers* and was his first Western short story, was selected as one of three finalists for the Western Writers of America Spur Award for best short fiction.

"It Is the Tale" by Bev Vincent

Bev Vincent is the author of *The Road to the Dark Tower,* the Bram Stoker Award nominated companion to Stephen King's Dark Tower series, and *The Stephen King Illustrated Companion,* which was nominated for a 2010 Edgar Award and a 2009 Bram Stoker Award. His short fiction has appeared in places like *Ellery Queen's Mystery Magazine, From the Borderlands, When the Night Comes Down, Evolve,* and every even number in the *Shivers* series. He is a contributing editor with *Cemetery Dance* magazine and a member of the Storytellers Unplugged blogging community. He also writes book reviews for *Onyx Reviews.*

"A Special Place: The Heart of a Dark Matter"
a novella by Peter Straub

Peter Straub is the author of seventeen novels, which have been translated into more than twenty languages. They include *Ghost Story, Koko, Mr. X, In the Night Room,* and two collaborations with Stephen King, *The Talisman* and *Black House.* He has written two volumes of poetry and two collections of short fiction, and he edited the Library of America's edition of *H. P. Lovecraft's Tales.* He has won the British Fantasy Award, seven Bram Stoker Awards, two International Horror Guild Awards, and two World Fantasy Awards. In 1998, he was named Grand Master at the World Horror Convention. In 2006, he was given the HWA's Life Achievement Award.